KILLER

"May I see your identification again, please?"
Khalil asked. Without waiting for an answer, he
drove his right fist hard into the solar plexus of
the slender man. The blow was soundless, except
for the sharp "Ooof!" as breath was driven out.
"Thank you," he said, for the benefit of the
microphone. He put one hand over the mouth,
gripped the back of the head, and twisted
sharply. "Goodnight then, my friend," he said
clearly, as he lowered the body to the floor on
the thick carpet.

THE LAST RAMADAN

NORMAN LANG

HarperPaperbacks

A Division of HarperCollinsPublishers

HarperPaperbacks *A Division of* HarperCollins*Publishers*
10 East 53rd Street, New York, N.Y. 10022

Cover photography by Norman Lang/Woodfin Camp & Associates

First printing: October 1991

Printed in the United States of America

HarperPaperbacks and colophon are trademarks of HarperCollins*Publishers*

10 9 8 7 6 5 4 3 2 1

To Molly and Louis,
and Cheryl and Andrew

Chapter 1

WHEN THE United Arab Airlines Comet landed at Cairo airport, one of the passengers in first class rose promptly. A tall, smiling man, but the type who is a little clumsy physically, he laughed when the plane lurched and made him bump against a stewardess. She smiled as a firm hand rested on her shoulder for a moment.

The first-class passenger was not held up by customs. After passing a pound note to an official, he was taken immediately to a booth, ahead of passengers from another aircraft. There his travel bag and briefcase were searched carefully. Unobtrusively, the official made photocopies of his passport, which was routine with a non-Egyptian, and other papers in his possession were checked closely. The passport was well used. It showed extensive travel in the Middle East and Europe—not in Israel, the official noted. The passenger was from Syria. His reason for being in Egypt was an extended business trip, which he was asked to specify. The name opposite the photograph was Ali Hamsa, a businessman from Damascus.

Mr. Hamsa took a taxi into central Cairo. It was late afternoon and the streets were full of people, who moved among the cafés and bazaars, talking, gesticulating, shouting. The galabiya was still the dominant form of dress. Some of the men wore pants and shirt, with a smattering of bright red fez or tarbush. There were women too, in the outdoor markets, wearing a variety of long dresses. Head scarves were popular, but not too many veils these days, the visitor noted. The ramshackle traffic looked the same. Old men on bicycles, their galabiyas hitched above their knees, carrying bakers' trays of bread on their heads, wobbling among the cars and buses. The visitor winced as he watched an ancient Mercedes bus career around a corner. The driver had probably had his first pipe of the day already.

Hamsa had booked a room at the Nile Hilton. This was in the center of the city, off Midan el Tahrir, "Freedom Square." The room was on the fifth floor, and had a balcony that overlooked the river. He saw some children down there, swimming in the brown water, and smiled nostalgically, wondering how they survived. The room was a capsule of American efficiency—with Egyptian overtones. Within minutes, he had found the listening bug in one of the bedside lamps, well away from the television set. As he moved around, unpacking his bag, Mr. Hamsa hummed a melody. Even in the foreign hotel, with its air of transience, he had a feeling of homecoming, of being back in his city.

For the first few days, he did some typical tourist things. He visited the Egyptian Museum and the pyramids of Giza, and spent an afternoon among the bazaars of Khan Khalili. He did a good deal of walking; sometimes taking a taxi here or there, then walking again. In the course of his wandering, he passed by a number of addresses that he remembered. Each time, a brief inspection told him that the people he had known no longer lived there. There was one piece of business. After examining a certain building, which was up for sale in an older part of Cairo, he visited a real-estate broker and began negotiations for the purchase of the property. The building was in a narrow street opposite the entrance to a mosque. On Friday morning, Mr. Hamsa worshiped in the mosque, and examined his potential property, measuring distances and angles from the entrance to the mosque.

On the evening of his fourth day in Cairo, after taking dinner in the hotel restaurant, Mr. Hamsa had a glass of Perrier water at the bar. Wearing horn-rimmed spectacles and an American-cut suit, he could have passed for a foreigner of many nationalities, though he communicated with the barman in classic Arabic. On being asked directly, he admitted that he was in the travel business. He represented a company in Syria that was thinking of opening an agency in Cairo. The barman, of course, reported to the police. He was only doing what was expected of him, and which might bring him a reward if detectives turned out to be interested in the foreigner. This done, he went on to suggest how the visitor might spend his time in Cairo.

"Very close to here," the barman said, "there is a club, called Maxim's Bar, on Solimon Pasha Street, now Kasr el Nil, where there is a snake dancer who is English. She is blond and very beautiful—and a very friendly lady, if introduced by the right person, my sister, for example."

A woman at the bar looked up and nodded. She was young, with a pretty painted face. Mr. Hamsa looked at her and smiled. Then he finished his drink and politely took his leave. The barman shrugged. So far as he was concerned, a middle-aged traveler on his own was likely to be interested in one of two things, girls or boys. If he had cared to wait a little longer, he would have heard where he could find both.

On his way to the elevators that evening, Mr. Hamsa found himself intercepted once again. A young man, who introduced himself as the night manager of the hotel, stopped him and asked if he were enjoying his stay, if there were anything he needed in his room. Mr. Hamsa said that everything was fine, that the service in the hotel was excellent. He noted that the boy seemed more refined than most. As he walked on he reflected that the "City Eye," the surveillance of foreigners by civilians, was as ubiquitous as always.

It was eight P.M. when Hamsa left the hotel that evening. As though embarking on an evening stroll, he walked up Kasr el Nil, past Maxim's Bar, where a doorman who must have been all of twelve years old invited him to enter. Shortly after that Hamsa hailed a taxi. He gave no address, but specified an intersection in the northern part of the city.

The taxi headed for the river before driving north. Soon it was in busy streets again, in an area not frequented by tourists. Through the open windows of the cab, Mr. Hamsa heard the night sounds of the city, and smelled souvlakia from a Greek café.

The cab stopped in a main street in the Bulak area near the docks. The crowds had thinned, but there was still activity around the small bazaars, where men talked loudly and boys leaned coquettishly against the walls. Mr. Hamsa paid the driver and climbed out. Half a block away, he could see the wooden doors of the *hammam*, the baths. If ever questioned, the driver would probably guess that this was his foreign passenger's destination. Mr. Hamsa walked that way until the cab was out of sight, then turned off.

As he walked away from the main street, Hamsa's manner underwent a subtle change. In an area where passive surveillance would be minimal, his back straightened and his feet seemed to take the ground in a more convincing way. He was now in a place where the streets were of earth, and sleeping bodies lay against the walls. There was no glass in the windows of these houses, and everything was stiller here, with harsh voices in the darkness. But the tall visitor walked easily, no sign of trepidation in his manner, as eyes watched him from the dimly lit cafés.

He came to a café near the river. Inside it, men drank coffee and talked loudly, playing chess or backgammon by the light of hurricane lamps. In the street outside, a few assorted tables stood unoccupied against the walls. He selected one, sat down, and lit an American cigarette.

Opposite the café, there was a large old building set back from the road. The downstairs part was a commercial frontage, with a sign saying, "Hassan Badaway, Tailor" in Arabic script. The upstairs part looked like the residence of a single family, quite grand for the neighborhood. Wooden shutters slatted the light that came from upstairs windows. The visitor's pulses quickened as he settled into the shadows and looked across.

A small boy in a galabiya came out of the café and approached the table. He looked at the visitor with the eyes of a calf. "You are of what nationality?" he asked, as though ready to respond in any language. Hamsa smiled. He sat forward and spoke in Arabic, close to the boy's ear.

"Listen closely, my son. I am an old friend of Hassan the tailor. I haven't seen him for many years, and I want to surprise him. First bring me a glass of water and a pipe. Then go knock on Hassan's door and tell him a customer is here. Tell him there is a gentleman from France, who has heard that he is the best tailor in Cairo, and who wishes to be measured for a suit." He gave the boy a twenty-five-piastre piece.

The boy scampered back inside. When he returned, he put a glass of water on the table, and a holder with a large wooden pipe on the earth at Hamsa's feet. Hamsa felt the moist, brown tobacco in the pipe, and glanced up inquiringly. The boy grinned and went back inside.

A moment later he was back, swinging something that glowed in the darkness. Coals, in a wire holder. He passed something to the man for his inspection.

Hamsa rolled the small brown pellet in his fingers, and sniffed it. "Camel dung," he said.

"Good," the boy said, grinning. "It is a gift from my father—only five pounds."

"Ah!" Hamsa gestured his apology. "If it is a gift from your father, then I know it is the best." He agreed to pay two pounds, which was twice the value of the hashish. He arranged the soft tobacco, and the boy applied the coals.

For the next few minutes, he puffed the thick, smooth smoke, pulling it deep into his lungs. The pellet of hashish was in his pocket. He had only pretended to push it into the tobacco. Sitting back against the wall, he watched the boy cross the way and knock on the door of the tailor's shop. A moment later a portly figure appeared.

It was Hassan Badaway. The watcher saw him peer this way, trying to penetrate the shadows, and his tension rose another notch.

When the boy came to retrieve the pipe, he smiled to see the glassy eyes of his customer. His grin broadened when he received another twenty-five-piastre piece. He willingly helped the man across the way, and the big stranger seemed to lean on his shoulder as they crossed the flagstones of the courtyard.

At first glance, he thought Badaway hadn't changed a bit. The same jowly face and hooked nose beneath the bald dome. Even the black, three-piece suit seemed familiar, with a watch chain hanging from the waistcoat pocket, and the well-worn collar of a white shirt around the neck. Then he saw the changes. The looser skin around the eyes, and the stiffness of the rounded body. The eyes were still bright, though.

Hassan the tailor assessed his visitor. He saw a tall, stooped man, with sympathetic eyes. Speaking in French, the visitor admired the shop, and asked if it were too late to be measured for a suit. The tailor said that it was not too late, and pulled out his samples. The visitor knew cloth. He picked an English worsted and readily agreed to pay a deposit on the suit. As they chatted, the tailor began to revise his first assessment of the man. There was a hint of humor in the eyes, and in the lips, which curved slightly as he glanced around. Nor was he as physically clumsy as he had seemed at first. Even before the measuring began, Badaway sensed the presence of athletic musculature. Old training stirred, and the tailor began to work on automatic pilot, as his brain went to full alert.

"Vous portez à gauche, ou à droite, monsieur?"

"Comment?"

"Vous portez à gauche?"—with emphasis—*"ou à droite?"*

"Oh! *À gauche.*"

Suddenly the visitor burst out laughing. Badaway rose sharply, from measuring the inside leg. The visitor took off his spectacles and removed a wig. Then he dug out padding from his cheeks and ruffled his true hair, which was black. In a part of the shop where they were concealed from the uncurtained windows, he grinned broadly at the astonished tailor.

Badaway stared at the dark, handsome face. Even the texture of the skin appeared to change, as the face turned leaner, the black hair curling on the brow. A row of fine teeth dressed the grin, and he looked ten years younger.

"Ibrahim! Ibrahim Khalil!"

"Who did you think, you old goat?" The visitor now spoke in Arabic. He saw the tailor staring at his eyes. "Contacts," he said. "I'd better leave them in." The contacts made his eyes look brown, like those of most Arabs. His own eyes, as Badaway well remembered, were an anomalous blue-gray in color.

Badaway took the hand of the younger man in both of his. It was a warm greeting, though his eyes were thoughtful. "How long has it been, Ibrahim? Five years?"

Khalil nodded. "I was here in '67, but we didn't meet."

Badaway studied him. So why were they meeting now, he asked himself.

Badaway opened a door and called upstairs to the residential part of the house. A minute later one of his five children came down with a pitcher of fruit juice and two glasses. While the little girl was there, Ibrahim Khalil kept his back to the door. Then the two men walked into the tailor's office and closed that door behind them.

"To the future of Egypt," said the man who had entered the country as Ali Hamsa.

Badaway drank to that. "And to . . . your success in being here?" That was a question, but scarcely asked. Badaway didn't want to know. He loosened his collar, as though feeling the heat in the room.

Khalil sipped the orange juice. Like Badaway, he
was a devout Muslim and shunned alcohol. He seemed
thoughtful as he gazed at his old friend. "I am out
of touch, Hassan," he said. "It's really amazing, but
Egypt is no longer the hub of the universe when you
move out of it. Tell me how things are these days?"

Badaway scratched the gray hair above his ear.
Khalil would not be so out of touch, he thought. But
he answered seriously.

"Things have gone from bad to worse, Ibrahim. You
remember they were catching spies in '65?" Khalil nodded. "Well, since then, everyone in the country has
been paranoid. The civil service grows daily. There
must be over a million of them now, not counting the
army. All handpicked for loyalty and lack of political
ambition. Internal Security has doubled. I have given
up, Ibrahim. I'll tell you frankly, I have given up.
What were you doing here in '67?"

Khalil gestured. "Oh, visiting my family."

"We shall never recover from that debacle," Badaway said, referring to the brief war with Israel. He
went on to speak of the increased repression in Egypt,
and the growth of the secret police, against whose
vigilance it had become impossible, he claimed, for
any antigovernment group to work effectively. The
whole pattern of espionage had changed. With strict
passport control and the surveillance of foreigners,
the traditional spy networks had all but dried up and
atrophied. Khalil listened closely to all this. None of
it was news to him, and some of it he knew to be not
quite true, but the tailor spoke without interruption
all the same.

When Badaway had finished, Khalil sat thoughtfully
for a while. He looked relaxed, his long legs crossed,

a cigarette between his fingers. "Well, it's good to be back," he said, smiling. "I swear to you, Hassan, there is no country in the world to be born in but Egypt." He smoked contentedly. There was still no mention of what he was doing here. "It's a hot summer though," he observed. "I used to curse the summer in Cairo— do you remember?" He smiled. "When does Ramadan start this year?" he asked casually.

Badaway went still. He had been expecting this, but all the same, like the final confirmation of bad news, he heard it with dismay. "Ramadan? Isn't it early in September?"

Khalil counted on his fingers, smiling. The Islamic festival of Ramadan came eleven days earlier each year, though this had nothing to do with the previous exchange. Khalil had now finally identified himself, and Badaway's face had drained of color. After a moment, the tailor broke down completely.

"I can't do it, Ibrahim! Whatever the cost to myself I cannot do it—even if they kill me! I explained all this when they contacted me. I think my name is probably on file—though I'm not being watched," he added quickly. "My contacts are all extinct, and in any case—I just can't do it." His eyes moved up to the ceiling, above which his family went about their business. "My heart is still with you. You know that. But I had to tell them that I just can't do it anymore."

"Who approached you?" Khalil asked quietly.

Badaway's eyes dropped. "It was carefully done."

Khalil hoped for his sake that it had been. It was Khalil who had chosen Badaway to be his main contact in Egypt. While he was in transit, others, already in the country, had been detailed to approach Badaway and prepare him for participation in a highly secret operation. This was done without knowledge of any details of the operation, or Khalil's identity. He had relied on Badaway. It was an error of judgment. How bad an error would be assessed.

None of this showed in Khalil's face as he smiled at his old associate. "Come, Hassan, my old friend. No one wants to force you into anything. You are a family man. You have your priorities." His eyes narrowed. "Is there a message?"

Badaway rose from behind the desk where he had been sitting. He paced to the window, glanced outside, and paced back again. There was no purpose to this. It was sheer tension that had lifted him. He sat down again and his fingers shook as he raised his drink, while Khalil watched impassively.

"There is an Englishman, called John Baldwin. He is one of the few foreigners still living in Cairo. He has been here since the time of Suez, and is well established. He is a businessman, an entrepreneur. To put it bluntly, he fleeces foreigners for the benefit of government officials. He has some high-up friends. His wife is the mistress of at least one of them. And he is not a fool. He is a clever man, but greedy."

Khalil mulled this over. Inwardly, he was seething with anger, and by no means happy with the situation. "An Englishman? Is it possible that he is not under surveillance?"

"I don't think so," Badaway said. "He has friends on the Supreme Committee. He goes to their homes and drinks with them in their gardens. He was once a member of British Intelligence. It is said that he advised Nasser at the time of Suez. I think they like him."

"Or they like his wife."

"I met her once," Badaway said. "She combines two things that I once thought impossible. She is both empty-headed and miserably unhappy."

"Is she an American?"

Badaway put back his head and laughed. For a moment his visitor saw the man of old, the fiery Dr. Hassan Badaway, of Cairo University, forced to resign for his criticism of the revolutionary regime.

Before he left the tailor's shop, Khalil replaced his wig and the dark-framed spectacles. As he resumed the role of Ali Hamsa, one shoulder dropped, his feet turned outward, and his whole demeanor seemed to change. He had always been a master of disguise. The tailor came with him to the door, and they shook hands warmly, if distractedly.

"God be with us," Khalil said. "And don't worry, Hassan, you will not hear from me again . . . Not until a new day has dawned," he added quietly. As he shook the hand of the older man, he gripped the elbow and squeezed it, in a gesture that Badaway remembered from the past.

Khalil walked out of the area and back to the vicinity of the *hammam* before hailing a taxi. As he drove back to the hotel, the busy, aimless nightlife of the city still went on in the crowded streets. Khalil gazed out pensively. He could not believe that things had started off so badly. That Badaway, of all people, had let him down. He stopped the taxi in Kasr el Nil and walked the last few blocks to Midan el Tahrir. He was preoccupied, and maybe that was his mistake, as he strolled into the hotel.

When he reached his room he saw immediately that it had been searched. This was no surprise, being routine police procedure, but it put him on edge as he moved around, humming to himself. He had been back for only a few minutes when there was a knock on the door. He had just removed his jacket and thrown it over a chair when he heard the quiet tap, and froze. He had a presentiment of what this was. Downstairs, when crossing to the elevators, he had met the eyes of the young manager who had spoken to him earlier, and it had seemed to him that the fellow took a second look. Only then had it occurred to him that maybe he wasn't fully in the role of Ali Hamsa at the time, and he had smoothly corrected that as he walked on. But what now? Instinctively he looked around the room. Was there any detail here that could have caused suspicion? He was sure that there was not. Glancing to the east, he touched his head and waist and muttered the words "*There is no god but God, and Mohammed is His prophet,*" before going to the door and speaking in the voice of Ali Hamsa.

"Who is it?"

"It is Abdel Sa'id. Your night manager."

"Oh!" After a moment to compose himself, Khalil opened the door. "Hello again, Mr. Sa'id. What can I do for you?"

The young man bowed in greeting. But he turned one hand and showed identification that Khalil recognized immediately.

"Detective Sergeant Sa'id," said the "night manager." "Internal Security. But please don't be alarmed. This is just routine. May I come in, please?"

Khalil's training stood him in good stead. He showed a moment of surprise, and some alarm, which was natural, before rallying, like a man whose mind was clear. "Internal Security? What in heaven's name have I done now?" He stood aside and invited the man in.

The young policeman was in his mid-twenties. He was as light-skinned as Khalil, who could pass for

European, with a trace of a mustache on his upper lip. Just about old enough to have done a couple of years in the Police Academy, Khalil thought. Thin face, intelligent brown eyes. He seemed apologetic for the intrusion, making no attempt to intimidate or bully.

"I'm sorry to disturb you, Mr. Hamsa. But it is part of my job to be concerned about foreigners staying in the hotel. It's just routine." He glanced at the television set, which Khalil had left playing. There was an endless love scene going on, with a boy and girl sitting under a tree. "Do you mind?" He waited for permission, then switched off the set, smiling. "I'm still not really used to it," he said as he cleared the way for the hidden microphone.

The young policeman was in no hurry. He went to the window and gazed out at the view over the river. To the left, there was the Tahrir Bridge, leading across to Roda Island. A little to the north, the lights of the exclusive suburbs of Gezirah and Zamalek. "Beautiful . . . Don't you think so, Mr. Hamsa?"

"Indeed."

There were a couple of felucca on the river: small boats with a single sail. They were loaded, with cargoes of cotton, or pottery, from Upper Egypt. "Did you know that you can charter these, Mr. Hamsa? One can have an evening picnic on the Nile? It is romantic." He gazed again at the lights of the rich suburbs of Gezira. "It is a dream of mine to have an apartment over there someday. A far-off dream on my salary, but one never knows." He looked over his shoulder. "My wife is expecting our first child. Already I feel that having a son will make me ambitious. Is that wrong, do you think?"

Khalil came closer to the window. It occurred to him that the boy might be offering his favors. "The prophet

encourages diligence and study. Diligence should be
rewarded."

"How true." The young man looked at him with
interest. "You are a student of Islam?"

Khalil shrugged. He held the policeman's eye, and
said nothing.

The young man studied him. "I don't want you to
misunderstand this, Mr. Hamsa. I can see that you are
a gentleman, and I want to make it clear that you are
under no suspicion. It's just that I want you to enjoy
your time in Cairo, and it concerns me that you seem
to do a lot of walking in what I might call the back
alleys of our city. Not that there's anything wrong
with that," he emphasized. "It's just that I'd hate any
misfortune to befall you. You should make use of our
taxis. Whatever you might want, they can take you to
a safe place." He smiled pleasantly. "Where did you
go tonight, for example?"

The sudden question took Khalil by surprise. He covered this by smiling in return. "Oh, I walked around. I
took a taxi, then walked around some more. I passed
Maxim's Bar."

"Did you go into Maxim's Bar?"

"No, I didn't."

Khalil didn't have a reading on him yet. He still
wasn't sure if he had attracted suspicion, or some
other kind of interest. He made an observation that
had been forming in his mind. "You speak well," he
said. "May I ask where you were educated?"

The boy looked out again, across the river. Khalil saw
his head in silhouette against the window. "I studied at
El Azhar," he said.

Khalil was astonished. He had named the most
famous center of Islamic study in the Middle East.
"Then you are a scholar."

"I was going to be."

"But you changed your mind?"

"That's right. And became a policeman."

The young man turned again. When he did so, he found the other looking at him with a kindly, rumpled smile. Beneath it, Khalil was worried. When would he learn the purpose of this visit? The young man's smile had a trace of bitterness.

"And so it becomes my duty to work in a hotel at night. To keep watch on the foreign guests, and sometimes to watch over them." The smile remained as he switched smoothly back to business. "When you returned tonight, you didn't take the taxi all the way to the hotel. Why not, Mr. Hamsa?"

Khalil's eyebrows rose. "I felt like walking."

"Again? It's almost as though you like to make my job difficult." The boy grinned suddenly. Then: "You still haven't told me where you went."

Khalil felt a distant tug of fear. The man's persistence worried him. "I went to the Bulak."

"The Bulak!" The boy pursed his lips. "Now that is certainly not safe, especially at night. Were you alone?"

Khalil touched the spectacles against his nose. After thinking for a moment, he came to a decision, reached into the pocket of his jacket and withdrew the pellet of hashish. The young policeman took it, rolled it in his fingers, and sniffed it.

"Illegal."

"Then you have caught me."

"How much did you pay for this?"

"Too much."

"And for what purpose do you bring it back here? As a souvenir?"

Khalil smiled. "I smoke cigarettes. It helps me to

relax." But it shook him, that little piece of irony. "A souvenir?" There was something about this boy. He might just be the kind to notice something different in the way a man had walked. He cursed that moment of inattention.

"And of course, you'd rather not say where you bought it?"

"Some small café. I might be able to find it again."

The young man moved away from the window. As he did so, his face came into the light, and Khalil saw that it looked clear of suspicion. Happy for a sign of hope at last, he was ready to breathe a sigh of relief when the policeman asked: "May I see your passport, please?"

Khalil looked up inquiringly. Outwardly, he was a middle-aged, mild-mannered man, brow rumpled as he peered over his spectacles. Inwardly, he went cold.

"Is this still routine?"

"Oh, yes. I just have to check a couple of things."

Khalil took the passport from an inside pocket of his jacket. The young policeman opened it and carried it to the hallway by the door, where he pressed a light switch. Khalil's eyes narrowed in the sudden brightness, as the boy glanced at his face and compared it with the photograph in the passport. The document was genuine. It belonged to a real Syrian, who worked for a travel agency in Damascus, and would withstand scrutiny. All the same, sweat poured from his armpits as instinct continued to warn him that something was amiss. He saw the boy's eyes harden, glancing from the passport to his face, and suddenly he realized.

The cheek pads! He had forgotten to replace the cheek pads! Now he knew. He knew the reason for this visit, and for the feeling of threat that he had sensed from the beginning. Something like a little spring came loose inside him.

"Have you lost weight, Mr. Hamsa?"

"Oh . . . Yes, I have. That was taken a few years ago."

"You look better for it." The young man closed the passport, and tapped it thoughtfully against his thumb. His eyes were grave, not hostile.

God is great: there is no god but God: Mohammed is His prophet.

"I have to take this with me, Mr. Hamsa. Just to check that everything's in order. I'm sure you understand. I'll return it to reception before morning."

Khalil smiled, and his training ensured that it reached the muscles around his eyes. He shook his head, as though amused at the suspicions of the younger man, while his brain worked quickly. He was almost sure that the young policeman had followed him up here without making a report. He had scarcely had time to go through channels, convincing a superior, possibly being redirected, almost certainly being robbed of any credit if his hunch turned out to be correct. Before coming here, he could hardly have felt that he had much to report in any case. But now he knew that Khalil was in disguise. Not only that, he had the passport, without which Khalil could go nowhere. At this point, there was no room in Khalil's mind for anger or disappointment. That would come later. "I understand," he said. "May I see your identification again, please?" Without waiting for an answer, he drove his right fist hard into the solar plexus of the slender man. The blow was soundless, except for the sharp "Ooof!" as breath was driven out. "Thank you," he said, for the benefit of the microphone. He put one hand over the mouth, gripped the back of the head, and twisted sharply. There was a grating sound as the head cricked round till it faced backward on the shoulders. "Good night then, my friend," he said clearly as he lowered the body to the floor on the thick carpet. After opening the door, and looking out into the corridor, which was empty, he closed the door, went directly to his jacket, found the pads, and replaced them in his cheeks. Then he sat down, ignoring the body on the floor, and silently gave way to rage and disappointment.

Chapter 2

LIEUTENANT COLONEL Mohammed Mahrous woke at six forty-five A.M. His first act was to switch on the radio for news. Then he rose and opened the curtains of his bedroom, which was on the eighth floor of a modern high-rise building. The building was on the edge of Garden City. The rent was high, but the view over the river was magnificent. After gazing out for a moment, he pulled off his nightshirt and headed for the shower.

While he dressed, he heard a couple of news items that did nothing to improve his mood. He had wakened with a touch of melancholy this morning. He heard that the United States was reacting positively to Nasser's May Day speech earlier in the summer, when the President of the United Arab Republic had astonished everyone by openly appealing to the President of the United States for help in the Middle East. The other

item was that the rest of the Arab world was reacting extremely negatively. Seeing his expression in the
mirror, Mahrous warned himself against his thoughts.
Thoughts became words, which might be why he had
recently been passed over for promotion once again.
He knotted his tie and adjusted it with one hand. The
empty left sleeve of his shirt was folded to his side. Or
maybe he was just no good at his job. It was only after
losing an arm in the Yemen, in 1962, that he'd been
transferred to Intelligence.

It was one of those mornings when he noticed that
he was on his own. As he breakfasted on instant coffee,
he thought of other sunny mornings, not so many years
ago, felt the senseless tug, resisted it, then glanced in
spite of himself at one of the doorways to the kitchen.
No more the bobbing walk, and mischievous morning
face of his young son, never tiring of getting up and
asking if he would eat at home this morning. Young
Mohammed had been born late to his wife, Amirah.
He had been born after the loss of Mahrous's arm,
which had done great things for the marriage for a
while, before destroying it. He fought the memories.
The memory of years of closeness, after years of active
duty, living in Cairo with their child, and agreeing on
absolutely nothing. He finished his coffee, and rinsed
the cup, the old habit of a married man. Then he
took the elevator down and began the short walk to
his office . . . And yet, in love, he remembered.

Mahrous's office was in a building that had once
belonged to British Staff Headquarters. To the south
of central Cairo, close to the main tourist hotels, it
was one of a group of buildings that housed a branch
of Internal Security. There was a report on his desk
that had just come in by telex. It had the red stamp of

top priority, which didn't impress him much till he read the first few lines. Then all preoccupation vanished as he sat down and read quickly.

There had been a murder in the Nile Hilton. The victim was a young officer called Abdel Sa'id, and Mahrous's stomach turned when he read the name. He knew that boy. The body had been found by a chambermaid, who had entered a room that had been vacated the day before. She had entered early this morning, to wash her personal underwear she said, and something had made her open the slatted doors of the clothes cupboard. Looking for forgotten items, probably, Mahrous thought. She had found the body lying on its side, its back to the room, but with the blanched face staring straight at her.

Mahrous was momentarily stunned. Instantly, there was something about this that triggered revulsion and fear. Then he looked at his watch. It was seven forty-five. The body had been found only half an hour ago, and had probably not been moved. He thought of grabbing an official car and rushing over to the Hilton. Instead he grabbed the telephone.

A team was already there at the hotel. He was connected to the room where the body had been found, and spoke to the police surgeon, a good man called Boziegan. The experienced surgeon sounded shaken. Death was due to a broken neck, and he affirmed that the head had been twisted almost completely from the body. There was no sign of a struggle, no obvious motive. Just the momentary work of someone with maniacal strength. The victim had been dead for several hours. The estimated time of death was eleven P.M. the night before, give or take an hour.

The line was passed to a major from headquarters who was in charge of the investigation. He spoke tensely, sounding breathless, but was willing to go over what he knew with Mahrous. The last occupant of the room had been an airline stewardess who was a frequent visitor to the hotel. Whether or not she might have helped Sa'id to pass the lonely nights was being investigated, but seemed unlikely to be relevant. She had checked out of the hotel the previous morning. Since then, the room had been cleaned routinely, and nothing untoward reported. It seemed that Sa'id had entered the empty room, met someone there, and been killed. Had it not been for the chambermaid looking for a place to wash her underwear, the body would not yet have been discovered. While saying this, the police officer broke off and there was an exchange in the crowded room at the other end. Mahrous strained his ears till the man came back, sounding a mite more confident. They had found the motive, he announced. Drugs. There was a pellet of hashish in the young policeman's pocket. Undoubtedly he had met someone, probably to traffic in the stuff, and they had quarreled.

Mahrous didn't like that theory. It seemed to him that there was more to this than petty dope dealing. He asked if the occupants of nearby rooms had been checked. Had any of them gone missing, or checked out unexpectedly since late last night? The policeman turned defensive. He said that he had only just got there, that his men were still arriving, and Mahrous slowed down. Speaking more calmly, he suggested that no time be wasted before checking on all guests, especially foreigners, starting with those on that floor of the hotel.

Mahrous sat back and stared at the wall. He remembered that Sa'id's wife was expecting their first child, and his face screwed up for a moment. He lifted the receiver again.

He called the Data Lab. After some delay, he got onto the right operator and asked that last night's tapes from the Nile Hilton be checked immediately. He wanted to know of any contacts between Abdel Sa'id and guests of the hotel. Then he called the airport.

The number that he dialed was answered directly by the manager of Cairo airport. A Farouk-like figure in dark glasses, sitting in his shaded office, he recognized the voice at the other end and was immediately attentive. Mahrous asked that passenger lists be checked carefully on all international flights out of Egypt. He wanted to hear of any passenger leaving from the Hilton Hotel this morning, or any passenger seeking to purchase a ticket at the last minute. Inwardly, he agonized. With no strong rationale for rejecting the drugs theory, which in a foreign-money marketplace like the Hilton was always a possibility, he wanted to order all international flights delayed, but hesitated to do this on his own authority. He was wrestling with this one when his boss walked in.

Egyptian Internal Security was run by a director with the rank of general, who reported to the Minister of the Interior. Beneath him were a number of departments headed up by career officers, all with army ranks, roughly divided into Operations and Intelligence. Surveillance of Foreigners came under Intelligence. Its basic business was the collecting and processing of data. This came from automated sources, like the hidden microphones in restaurants, bars, hotels, and other public places, as well as the routine collecting of information from waiters, barmen, taxi drivers, telephone operators, gas station attendants, doormen, prostitutes, and beggars in the streets. The department was headed by a Brigadier Touhami. Charged with coordinating this large effort, he was the author of many lengthy documents on procedure, whose study was the life's work of a nest of underlings. Passport Control was Mahrous's responsibility. He spent his days supervising the checking of passports, making sure that those of significant foreigners were photocopied, and tracking the movements of certain people around the world. Sometimes there was a spark of interest in this work. Every so often their vigilance was tested by someone trying to come in under a false identity. These usually turned out to be common criminals, but there had been terrorists and other agents. The spy business was not dead. Once an intruder was detected, there were decisions like whether or not to let him run for a while, which brought interaction with other departments, but when a case got interesting, Mahrous usually lost it to his boss. The nickname for their department was the "Eye of the City," referring to the use of ordinary people to maintain surveillance on foreigners.

Touhami walked past Mahrous's office without greeting him. A tall, thin man with a gray face tinged with brown, he wore sunglasses at all times and was obsessed with his health. He looked up, brow wrinkled, when Mahrous appeared in his doorway.

"There's a telex from Police Headquarters, sir." Mahrous indicated the copy on Touhami's desk. "A murder in the Hilton last night—one of ours, I'm afraid. Young Sa'id. They found the body forty-five minutes ago, and I think we should act quickly on this one. The killer could be running at this moment—out of the country, I would guess."

Touhami glanced up from the report, which he had now lifted. "Do you mind if I read this?" he asked.

Mahrous chafed while his chief read and reread the report. Still standing, he itched to get to the telephone again. He wondered if he should have contacted car-hire companies.

Touhami finished reading, and sat back. He was about to deliver one of his lengthy appraisals, complete with a set of cut-and-dried decisions, when Mahrous interrupted. He broke in and added what he'd learned from the police surgeon and the major in charge. He was trying to get to a statement of his own gut feeling that there was something different about this killing, but when he came to the pellet of hashish, he was interrupted in turn.

"Oh, well, that's it." Touhami sighed, and threw the piece of paper on his desk. "Why didn't you tell me that straight off? This is local stuff. No foreigner would kill for a few piastres or a pellet of hashish, but a local trader would. Our man probably had a business going."

"Excuse me, sir, but did you know Sa'id? Because I did, and I can't believe that very easily. And look at the manner of death. Someone broke that boy's neck like breaking a doll."

Touhami's brow was wrinkled in thin lines. He disliked being asked if he knew one of his own men. "So it's a horrifying crime. Which is hardly a penetrating observation. Do you have some point, Mahrous?" He looked at his watch.

Mahrous turned to go. Then, once again, he broke his own rule never to argue with Touhami, because it was a self-defeating process, never profitable, and took years from your life. He'd made that rule a hundred times, and broken it as often.

"I agree that the evidence points to drugs. But suppose that's a blind. Suppose Sa'id noticed something, and tackled someone in his room."

"It was an empty room."

"Maybe that's not where it happened. Maybe he went to question somebody—"

"Without reporting in?"

Mahrous took a breath. "I know it's against procedure, sir. But sometimes—"

"So then what? Someone kills him, and starts to carry him around the corridors? I'm getting tired of this, Mahrous."

Mahrous was waiting for the telephone to ring. He had no urgent calls to make, just to receive. "Suppose Sa'id blew someone's cover," he said. "Someone serious, here for God-knows-what. The killer now wants to leave. Suppose he wants to leave the country. But he doesn't want to spend the night sitting at the airport with a dead body in the room behind him. If he leaves in the night, the taxi driver will probably report him. They'll check to see if he has skipped from his hotel. He probably knows his room was bugged. But he could guess that the tapes would not be processed till today. There's something about this killing, sir. I think we're dealing with someone very cool and very dangerous. He might have decided to sit it out, hide the body in an empty room, and leave in the morning."

Touhami's face had no expression beneath the shaded eyes. His instinct was to differ, but he had no desire to be proved wrong. He was a married man with four children. Mahrous had often wondered what the atmosphere was like in the Touhami home. Probably his wife gave him hell. Finally, Touhami shook his head.

"No, I don't think so. Sitting in his room with a body on the floor? They don't come as cool as that." He threw the report into a basket on his desk. "No, whoever did this ran for his life. I don't think it's one for us." As he finished saying this, a ring came from the telephone in Mahrous's office.

"Excuse me, sir, that's mine."

Mahrous strode back to his desk. It could have been worse, he thought, he could have been ordered off the case. He still had jurisdiction at the airport.

It was the Data Lab and the analyst sounded breathless. They'd struck gold, he said. Sa'id had visited a Syrian businessman late the night before, and had appeared to take his passport. But the passport was not on the body, and had not been found. After that, the businessman had sat up late in his room. The analyst spoke of the persistent humming of classical music, a detail that chilled Mahrous. There had been no suspicious sounds. But the Syrian, who was supposed to have been here for an extended stay, had checked out early this morning and taken a taxi to the airport.

The telephone rang as soon as he set it down. This was due to an internal system that took calls when an officer's line was engaged, then got to him as soon as he hung up. It was a message from the airport manager. A Mr. Ali Hamsa, who had checked out of the Hilton Hotel this morning, had booked a last-minute seat on a UAA flight to Athens. This was scheduled to leave in fifteen minutes time. The passengers were already in the departure lounge, waiting for the call to board. Mahrous didn't hesitate. With a glance in the direction of his chief's office, he gave instructions that the plane be boarded as scheduled, but not given clearance to take off. A team of men would be there directly to arrest Mr. Ali Hamsa. After that, he rang Abu Zaabal, the location of a military prison to the north of Cairo, and requested that a team be sent immediately to the airport to arrest the Syrian. He stressed the need for extreme caution, entering the aircraft from a door behind the target if possible, taking him by surprise, and assuming that he was armed and dangerous. He

should then be blindfolded and taken to Cairo Central
Prison, where Mahrous would now head to explain all
this. He should be there by the time the team returned.
If his boss didn't take this from him, he thought, as he
hung up.

Touhami was matter-of-fact when he heard the news.
Even knowing the man as he did, Mahrous marveled
at the smoothness with which he shifted his position
slightly, but continued to play safe. Mahrous arranged
for a car to take him to Central Prison. As he looked out
at the morning traffic, he prepared himself to meet this
Ali Hamsa, the killer of Abdel Sa'id. He looked forward
to placing the man like a bug between the jaws of a steel
pliers.

After killing Abdel Sa'id, Khalil fell into deep despair. He had come to Egypt as Ali Hamsa on a mission
to be performed under that identity. Months of planning
were now void, and the mission in ruins. The problem
with Badaway was not serious. He had needed Badaway
as a link with people who had no need to meet him
personally: he could have worked around that. But
now he had no identity, no communications, nothing.
Now there was only one priority—escape.

After checking in at the airport, Khalil did not go
directly to the departure lounge. He had a coffee in the
coffee shop, and kept his eye on the group of passengers
from a distance. He had not checked in any luggage.
His traveling bag was small and he preferred to carry
it. He bought a book for the journey.

The call to board came at eight forty-five. He watched
the passengers line up, and start to head across the open
ground to the aircraft. There was nothing to alert him.
No ripple in the routine that he detected. All the same
his heart was pumping, and the adrenaline flowed. His

palms sweated at the thought of entering the confines of the aircraft. There would be no relaxation till he reached Athens and walked out free.

They had given the last call for boarding, and he had picked up his bag and briefcase, when he saw the portly figure in sunglasses, and hesitated. The man was hurrying, sweating, nervous. He looked like a senior official, and this was confirmed when he spoke to the captain and copilot of the Athens flight—who had not yet boarded. Khalil drew back. Joining a group around the Oriental Bazaar, he watched the distant figures and saw them examine something. There was clearly no danger of the plane taking off meantime. What were they looking at down there? Then he saw two late passengers arrive. But instead of hurrying out with their boarding passes, they spoke briefly to the official, glanced at something, and stared out at the plane. Khalil faded back into the crowd. Eyes blazing, he scanned the vicinity of the departure gate and saw other figures— talking, lighting cigarettes, asking information. Police! They must have a copy of his passport photograph and seat number. Any minute now they'd learn that he was not aboard.

Walking casually, he headed down to the arrivals area, looking for a men's room. Entering the first he came to, he found an unoccupied cubicle and locked himself in. Speed was of the essence now. He took off the wig, the glasses, and spat out the cheek pads. These and the contact lenses he flushed away, pressing twice. He tore off his jacket and his tie, stuffing the tie in the pocket of the jacket, which he folded over his arm. There was one other occupant of the men's room, who had been there since he came in. This was an airport worker who had urinated, washed his hands, and was now endlessly combing his hair. Khalil fumed and felt the agitation in his chest. It was like an inner force, pushing him to action . . . Finish, damn you! He could pull the man in here and kill him quickly. But if others should choose that moment to walk in? The feet went to the door. Khalil strained his ears and fought for calmness while the man dallied again, for a last look in a mirror, before finally going out. Khalil followed quickly, stuffing the wig and spectacles into a trash bin. Some of these decisions might not be the best possible, but he had death on his heels.

The man who walked away from the men's room was a different figure altogether from the one who had entered it. Tall and lithe, with black hair curling on his brow, he had a strong, lean face and a relaxed expression, with his coat over his arm against the heat that rose already from the desert. He stepped outside, hailed a taxi, and had a badly needed piece of good luck. The taxi swerved in his direction, and the driver asked where he was headed. Khalil sank into the back seat. "Opera Square," he said, knowing that he could change that if he chose. As they pulled away, he saw two men appear at a jog from a nearby doorway and come outside, looking around. Just in time, he thought. Just in time.

Khalil closed his eyes and rested his brain for several seconds. He was sure that he had not been seen. But they might not be far behind, once they realized that he had left the airport. How had they done it? How had they put so many things together, and acted in unison for once, almost closing in on him?

As they drove into Cairo, he watched the traffic behind them and wondered what had gone wrong. With average luck, he should have made it onto the plane and across to Athens before there was any organized search for him. He had hoped that the body wouldn't be found till morning. Even then, what had made them seal the airport? Not only that, they had targeted his flight, and seemed to be looking for him specifically. Khalil's eyes narrowed in the back seat of the cab. He could not believe that he had been betrayed. But it was too quick, too efficient. Had things changed so much?

The driver was chatty. He was a jaunty man with his sleeves rolled up and a flat cap on his head. he asked where Khalil had traveled from. Rome, Khalil said. He had noted an incoming flight from Rome. They barreled along, shaving cyclists and pedestrians on the busy highway.

"I would like to travel someday," the driver called over his shoulder. He blared his horn and cursed a slower vehicle as he wheeled around it. "Is it so very different overseas?"

"It is a different world," Khalil said distractedly. He saw that they were not being followed, and relaxed slightly. Surely there was no way that they could catch him now.

They drove through Heliopolis, which was familiar territory to Khalil. His old school was situated here, and he entertained brief memories. El Madrasa el Nasr was originally a British school, which had been taken over in the fifties. It was now one of the most exclusive schools in the country, for wealthy families from all over the Middle East. Khalil had not been raised in Cairo. He had been sent here as a boarder to the school. Relaxing further, he remembered the old Englishman who had been housemaster to the younger boarders. A man called Cunningham, whose family had died tragically during the wartime blitz in London, so the story went; Khalil had always doubted it—he had lusted after the bodies of some boys and had lived his life in a kind of poignant terror . . . How strange. Khalil dwelt on the variety of worthless things that people allow to dominate their lives.

Still checking behind, he felt that they were in the clear. The trap at the airport had most likely been a fluke. All the same, he decided to take precautions.

"Why don't you turn off here? Let's take the back streets."

The driver wheeled off the main drag. "The back streets, eh? To Place de l'Opera? Are you an actor, or a singer?" He looked around, grinning, as Khalil shook his head. "I suppose not. All the big stars are from overseas—or is that not true? I can tell that you're not from overseas. You're from here." Ahead of them, a boy in a galabiya was crossing the road. He was taking his time, signaling mockingly for the cab to slow down, but his expression changed and he jumped for his life when the driver drove straight at him. "My girlfriend always wants me to take her to the opera. She is very modern, very cultured. But when she spends her own money, it is on Beatles records for her stereo. Are the Beatles still famous in their own country?"

"Oh, yes." Khalil wished that the man would stop looking around at him. He was not concerned about danger on the road, but disliked being scrutinized. He was becoming edgy again.

"Have you done a lot of traveling?"

"A good deal."

"To the United States?" Khalil nodded. "Is it really the Big Satan?"

Khalil answered after a moment. "It is decadent and false. They are ready to burst like a ripe pod."

The driver was interested. He would have liked to draw out his reserved passenger, who struck him as a man of consequence. But there was something inaccessible about the man. Khalil was thinking of the problems of being in Egypt without papers. That was even more immediate than what had happened to his mission.

He was sufficiently preoccupied that he almost made another grave mistake. When the cab's radio crackled into life, and the driver answered it, Khalil thought nothing of it at first. It was only when the driver seemed to have trouble hearing and leaned closer to his speaker, dropping his voice, that Khalil sensed something in his manner. "Er-ayewa," he heard softly. "Ayewa . . ." Yes. "I am now passing the YMCA. Heading for Opera Square." Khalil strained his ears. But from the back seat, he could make out no words till the driver spoke again. "Ayewa . . . I understand." After that, there was no more cheerful chatter from the man. He drove looking straight ahead. Khalil sighed, and his eyes closed slowly, like those of a lizard, before opening suddenly.

"I have changed my mind," Khalil said. "I would like to go to the Victoria Hotel."

"The Victoria?"

"Yes, we have just passed it. Why don't you turn here, and loop back? Turn here!" he said urgently, seeing a quiet street. The driver obeyed. Khalil sat forward, looking out the windows to both sides, while his mind reconstructed what he'd heard.

Listen carefully, the radio would have said. *Do you have a single passenger just picked up from the airport?* Er-Ayewa. *A male, six feet two or three, dark hair, with a small bag and briefcase?* Ayewa. *Where are you now, and where are you going?* I am now passing the YMCA. Heading for Opera Square. *Then listen carefully. Take him to where he wants to go. If he changes his mind, take note of his appearance*

*and call in as soon as he leaves you. But do nothing to
alarm him. Do not try to stop him. Do you understand?*
Ayewa. *We'll be right there. You will be rewarded.* I
understand . . . Khalil pulled his briefcase toward him
and opened it. Sitting forward, eyes bright, he studied
the surroundings as they turned another corner.

"Pull in right here." The driver's eyes went to the
mirror. "Right here," Khalil insisted calmly, "by this
tree."

It was a quiet street. On one side, there was the
wall of what might have been a mosque, on the other,
a broken-down apartment building. No bazaars, no
figures near the taxi. "How much do I owe you?"
As the driver turned, Khalil closed his fist around
a wooden pencil that he'd taken from the briefcase.
With the eraser end against his palm, the shaft coming
out between his fingers, he drove the point hard into
the driver's eye. There was no blood. The other eye
flew open for an instant, as did the mouth, as the shaft
went deep into the brain. As he stepped out of the
cab, Khalil wiped his knuckles on the fabric of the
seat. Some stuff had squirted from the eye. He went
unnoticed. The driver lay on the front seat of the cab
as Khalil walked away.

His plan now was to head for the main road and
catch a bus.

Chapter 3

YVETTE MONTAGNE noticed the foreign-looking girl just before the lights were dimmed, and the overture started for the performance of Verdi's *Rigoletto*. She was seated in the stalls, and Yvette used her opera glasses to focus on her from the balcony, where she was in a box near the stage . . . Blond hair. That proved nothing, of course, but it looked genuine, and her features lacked the curviness of most Arab women. On her own? Why would a girl like that be attending the opera on her own? From her vantage point above, Yvette focused on her breasts, in a dress that was immodest only by Egyptian standards. Slim-line tits. Good hands, reading a program—with no eyeglasses, in the poor light. Yvette sighed. At the age of thirty, she could hardly read a damn menu these days without her spectacles. There was something about the girl that kept her looking, trying to see her face, until the lights went down.

During the first act, there was a young girl in the chorus. Wearing an Egyptian headdress, with no sign of hair under it, she had a peeping face, with the hugest eyes and a mouth that seemed to go all the way across. What natural grace! With the long hands and fingers that you saw sometimes, and equally long feet, she swirled the cotton dress, with a waistline level with her crotch, her slim legs suggested nicely. She looked about fourteen years old.

Yvette paid little attention to the fat soprano, or the little bantam cock of a bellowing tenor.

During the intermission, she surprised her escort, the Japanese cultural attaché, whose name was Tachikawa, by suggesting that they go for coffee instead of to the bar. This was because she had seen the blond girl head that way. The girl had come out of the auditorium, smiling to herself—one of those who lived in her own world?—and turned on her heel toward the coffee shop in a way that swung her dress to one side. The firmness of the movement, on long legs that went to racehorse ankles, confirmed the guesswork of Yvette's previous inspection. "Let's have coffee, Tatch," she said. "I don't care for a drink, do you?"

"Ahhh, no," said Yutaka Tachikawa, who was dying for one, and disappointed that he wouldn't have the chance to ply her with alcohol. His wife was at home in their elegant apartment.

The coffee corner was popular. Arabs drinking Turkish coffee and calling it Greek. The blond girl had found a table by a potted plant. She was one of those people who looked lost to the world, but at peace with it, and far too beautiful to be adrift like this, on her lonely cloud. Yvette simply walked that way, heading for the vacant seat beside the girl, who looked up and smiled.

"Please feel free." She indicated the other seat of the table for two.

"Why thank you. How kind!"

Yvette sat down. Tachikawa touched his spectacles. English, Yvette thought. Cultivated English. A rare specimen of another dying breed.

"My name's Yvette Montagne. I'm sure we haven't met."

The girl smiled. She might have heard the slight emphasis on the word "sure." "I'm Mary Miles." She glanced at the hovering Tachikawa.

"For God's sake, Tatch, pull up a chair," Yvette said.

They discussed the performance. Not Tachikawa, who occupied himself with getting them served, but the two women. Mary spoke as though she had just been waiting for someone with whom to talk opera. Sitting forward, elbows on the table, her enthusiasm bubbled quietly as she discussed the music, the production, and the beauty of the building. Yvette smiled inwardly. An innocent. Sitting back, relaxed, she mentioned the fact that this was almost an anniversary performance. The Opera House had opened just over a hundred years ago, with a performance of *Rigoletto*. Mary knew this. She also knew that *Aida* had been commissioned for the occasion, but was not ready quite in time. Yvette was charmed. An English girl who knew some local history, spoke to strangers, and was not ugly. She was, in fact, quite a lively talker. Bare forearms rising from the flared sleeves of the dress she wore, she made little gestures that garnished what she said—but all on the subject of the music. When Yvette's deep voice came in, asking if she had noticed the young girl in the chorus, Mary thought for a moment, shook her head, and went on with what she had been saying. A true addict. If you told her that she had the most beautiful blue eyes that you had ever seen, she would come back with something about the performance.

Mary Miles-Tudor was a shade embarrassed. She was embarrassed for the Japanese escort, so totally ignored,

and she found it hard to ignore the penetrating black
eyes of the woman opposite. Yvette Montagne had a
straight nose and brow. Huge eyes, full lips, and clean
lines to the jaw and neck. A Latin beauty. Her hair
was black and long, with gentle waves. As soon as
she'd walked in, Mary had noted her physique. It was
the physique of a woman who stood out. Even from a
distance, your eye went back there. Mary would have
liked to bring the conversation to a more personal turn,
but the Japanese escort disconcerted her.

When the time came, it was Yvette who handled
this with typical directness. "You're on your own,"
she said as they rose from the table. "Let's meet at
the end and we'll drive you home." Mary said that was
very kind, and they went their separate ways back into
the auditorium.

As one of the perks of his assignment in Egypt,
Tachikawa had a Mercedes automobile, with blinds
on the windows, and a chauffeur who waited patiently wherever he went. When the car rolled up to the
pillared gateways of the Opera House, Yvette climbed
into the back, invited Mary to sit with her, and left her
escort to sit with the chauffeur. "It's so nice to meet
a European," she said. "We don't see many of them
these days. Would you like to join us for a drink?"

Mary had anticipated this. But she couldn't bring
herself to intrude any further on the evening of the
long-suffering Tachikawa. "I'd love to," she said. "But
I think I'd better not tonight. I have work in the
morning."

"Work?" Yvette looked at her blankly.

"I'm teaching summer school. At the Madrasa el
Nasr."

"Oh, really?"

"Do you know it?"

"I know of it. I thought they'd got rid of all the Brits."

Mary smiled. "They almost have. But I've signed a contract for next year."

Yvette looked steadily at the English girl. She might have seen a hint of a smile, as one eyebrow rose minutely.

Mary's apartment was in Midan el Tahrir. On the way there, she divulged a little of her history. Raised in the south of England, she had gone to Oxford and studied mathematics. She had a First. Then she'd spent a year in Paris, as *assistant d'anglais* at the Lycée Condorcet, Jean Paul Sartre's old school, before deciding to spend a year in Cairo. After that she would go back to university, try for her Ph.D., and probably end up in an academic career. Music and mathematics were her two great loves.

"Mathematics . . ." Yvette shook her head. "How can anyone have a Ph.D. in mathematics?"

When they reached Mary's apartment, which was in an old building on the side of Midan el Tahrir opposite the Hilton Hotel, they exchanged telephone numbers and promised that they would be in touch. Tachikawa, after jumping out and opening the door for Mary, then climbed into the back and smiled at Yvette, whose eyes followed the statuesque English girl.

The Cairo dwelling of Yvette's family, where she now lived alone, was to the south of Garden City, toward old Cairo. From the outside, it showed little to the world except high walls of white stone, two stories high, with metal grills and shaded windows on the upper level. Surrounded by sidewalks lined with palm trees, the house stood apart from other dwellings, a rare thing in Cairo.

The house was entered through a vaulted tunnel just wide enough to take the car. A heavy gate of ornate ironwork was opened by a servant. The tunnel led to a massive inner courtyard paved with marble. There was a pond, surrounded by orange and pomegranate trees, and other plants that filled the air with fragrance. The beautifully decorated living areas lay around this courtyard, with upstairs galleries leading from the bedrooms.

Yvette did not move when the car stopped in the courtyard, under a weeping willow tree. She had been silent during the drive from Tahrir, with a growing itch, as her mind dwelt on the English girl. Tachikawa touched his spectacles and smiled weakly. He did not assume that he would be invited inside. He was in awe of this woman. He had been astonished when she accepted his invitation for this evening, and had no idea what to expect. His heart almost stopped when she now seemed to notice him for the first time, regarded him with her great, dark eyes, and raised a hand to his cheek.

The Japanese surprised Yvette. He had obviously never made love in a car before, and had no aptitude for the engineering problems involved. But he had a long, smooth penis, and his eager grunting, as he maneuvered it into her, masked her own quick gasp. She went down on her back, her body arched toward him, as he thrust once, twice, thrice . . . Tachikawa's spectacles fell off his nose, and Yvette's thin cry rose briefly, as he exploded into her.

The Arab chauffeur sat rigidly in front, his eyes staring straight ahead.

The main room of the house was two stories high. In one section, there was an octagonal fountain of ornate marble, surrounded by tiled floor. A long couch ran around the walls, embroidered with silver and gold.

Low tables, inlaid with jade and mother-of-pearl, occupied another section, and Chinese porcelain, silverwork, hookahs, and incense burners stood in alcoves around the walls. Light came from the courtyard and stained-glass windows high in the walls. It was nighttime now, but even in daytime, the scented air was cool and silent, save for the ripple of water in the fountain. In less traditional Islamic style, there was also a music room, with a grand piano, and a library. There were Persian rugs and high shelves of books between the inlaid marble and ceramic tiles.

Yvette's bedroom was on the upper level. Leading onto a balcony that joined with others around the courtyard, it had a floor of enameled brick and a high ceiling of carved wood. There was matting and carpet on the floor, a huge, modern bed—instead of the traditional couch—which somehow did not clash with the painted wooden chests and cupboards in which she kept her clothes and jewelry. As she approached the room, from the stairway of wood and marble, she smelled the cigarette smoke almost before she entered.

"Oh, God!" said Yvette. "Must you smoke in my bedroom?"

The man seated by the open window did not turn to face her. He drew on his cigarette and inhaled deeply. "Is it worse than what normally goes on in here? Or down there?" He stared down. "Whoring with the Japanese in your own courtyard."

She began to smile, studying the back of his head. Then: "How did you know he was Japanese?"

"Did you enjoy the pretty English girl? Did she whet your appetite?" He turned now with a mocking smile.

"You bastard! Have you been following me?"

He smoked again and studied her. "I took the MG. Your infidel head servant didn't like it, so I gave him his one warning of my trip. I think everyone is due one warning, don't you? How are you, sister? Not changed much, I see, except a little more mature, physically."

Yvette walked into the room. She threw her bag onto the bed and started to remove her outer clothing. He watched as she unpinned her hair and threw it around her head.

"Three years," she said. "You seem a little heavier."

"That's deliberate," he said.

"Working out?" She looked at him with amusement. His eyes were like the eyes of an animal in this light. "Weren't you strong enough?" She saw that there was nothing casual in his manner. He was serious, staring at her intently. Yvette felt a moment of weakness and sat down. "All right, Ibrahim," she asked softly. "What brings you here this time?"

Khalil finished his cigarette and flipped it across the balcony. Then he rose, walked over, looked down at her for a moment, and kissed her briefly.

"I didn't plan to be here," he said. "That's why I didn't let you know in advance. But I've run into some trouble." He seemed to stare through her for a moment. "I'm stuck here without papers. Worse than that . . . there are things I still have to do." His eyes focused on her. "I'm going to need help."

Yvette rose and walked across the room. She went to an ornate mirror on a dressing table and began to comb her hair. "Who sent you this time?" she asked. "The Americans? The Russians? The Israelis?"

His laugh was short, with no humor in it. "You know I wouldn't work for the Americans. Or the Israelis— unless it suited us." He grinned wryly. "The Russians are out of things. Same with the Americans—except for an idiot who wants to bring them back."

"Put it this way," she persisted. "Who stands to gain?—or think they do?"

He lit another cigarette. "You never understood these things, did you? It isn't always win or lose, like a game of poker, where a win is always another's loss. Sometimes it's like a business deal, where all parties hope to gain."

"At the expense of someone else?"

"Oh, yes." He began to smile, but that changed. For a moment, she expected an outburst of temper, but he controlled it. "Oh, yes," he repeated.

Yvette combed her hair. "Well? Are you going to tell me what you're here for?" In the mirror, she saw his head come up, and again tensed involuntarily.

"I am here to avenge the death of our father."

"How?"

"And the death of Egypt!"

"Ibrahim!" She spoke sharply to him in the mirror. "Please don't start." She was backing off now, regretting her persistence. She wanted to know, but didn't want to get him started on a tirade: she feared his fanaticism.

He went to the door of the bedroom and closed it. It was a heavy door of teak. Then he closed the walk-out windows to the balcony. The walls of the house were several feet thick and totally soundproof. "That *kaffrien* servant," he explained. "He creeps around like a cat. Maybe I'll cut his tongue out. And his fingers." Yvette closed her eyes. She pictured her head servant, who was a Coptic Christian, with nothing but a thumb on each hand and the root of a tongue in his throat.

"I'm going to need papers," he said. "I have friends who can arrange this, but I have to make contact with them first. I'm going to need a radio."

"A radio!"

"Yes. Tell me. Have you met an Englishman called John Baldwin?"

"Baldwin . . ." She thought for a moment. "Yes, I have. He's a member of the Sporting Club."

"Have you slept with him?" he asked bluntly.

She compressed her lips. "He weighs four hundred pounds." Khalil went on looking at her. "No!" she said furiously. "I have not slept with him."

"I'm going to need a radio transmitter. Modern, good quality, and some other things. I hope the stores have improved."

"They haven't. But the police are very organized these days, and you can't use a radio. I happen to know that. They have new equipment and can zero in on a radio transmission almost instantly."

"Not instantly. It takes them thirty seconds or more."

"What's the difference? What message can you send in thirty seconds?"

"That's my problem." He looked around. "Don't worry, I won't set up here. I'll use different apartments around the city."

"But you'll stay here?"

"Certainly." He glanced at her. "My bags are in my room. I'll need money for a while. You'll get it back when I have papers. Apart from that . . ." He paused, thinking. She saw with relief that he seemed calmer now, his brain working coolly. "I don't know what else I'll have to ask of you. Yvette. Not more than I can help. There will be danger," he said quietly.

Before retiring to his room, he kissed her again, and his old smile flickered. That taunting smile that had always struck strange chords in her. It was possibly the only thing he didn't know about her. That his image had once haunted her, in the shivering fantasies of adolescence.

*   *   *

Yvette Laila Fatima Khalil—Montagne was her mother's maiden name—had little sleep that night. In the quiet of her room, she drifted half awake from one scene to another, till the birds in the trees outside began to chirp, and she heard the morning call to prayers from a distant mosque in old Cairo. It was a freak of acoustics that they sometimes heard that call, especially in the summer, when the wind was from the south . . . *God is great: there is no other god but God: Mohammed is his prophet: come and pray*, repeated over and over by the muezzin in his distant tower. Yvette was not religious, but she rose and faced Mecca, as she knew her brother would be doing in his room. It was frightening, yes, it was always frightening, but she tingled with excitement to have him home.

Chapter 4

MAHROUS PUT water to his face and hands at the fountain in the courtyard of the ancient mosque. Then he joined the group facing the sanctuary, where the simple casket stood. It was mostly family. Women dressed in black to their ankles, heads covered, wearing veils, and men in dark suits. He thought he identified the father, a proud man with a stricken face. The young wife, or the one he took to be the wife, was a huddled figure shaking with sobs. The father stood beside her, ready to help her if necessary, but where was the usual comforting shell of women, ready to exhaust her with their wailing? There was a small group from the department. One or two sergeants, and the lieutenant who had been Sa'id's immediate boss. Touhami was not present. The family seemed to be all Sa'id's, not the wife's.

The service was brief. One of the imams climbed the steps to the pulpit. This was in a niche off the courtyard facing Mecca, with lamps hanging from wooden beams across the ceiling. Everyone knelt, and touched his face to the matting on the floor, while prayers were read. The women wailed around the grieving parents, and the young wife shook with silent tears, as everybody rose again. The father took her arm, and she covered her face as they passed by the casket. It seemed to Mahrous that the girl was on her own. Where was her family?

The grieving family remained in the mosque. Mahrous walked out with the small group of other guests, but he noticed that an official car in addition to his own remained. Mahrous was not here officially, but the others were. Sure enough. As he had suspected, the huddled figure of the wife came out, walking head down beside the father, while the police driver opened a car door for her. She climbed in, put her face in her hands, and was driven off alone. Mahrous put his car in gear and followed.

The Sa'ids had lived in a small, tumbledown apartment building close to the Cairo railway station. The rooms they had were accessed by a narrow staircase outside the building. Mahrous watched the police car leave, gave the girl time to get inside, then climbed the stairs himself. There was something so bleak about it all. He knew nothing of this girl, but he knew that it

was a terrible time to be alone. Besides, there were
some things he had to say to her. With a feeling of
nervousness, having no idea how to handle this, he
knocked on her door.

She had removed the veil, to reveal a delicate, light
brown face, with no special feature to it, but pleasing
enough. Under the robe, it was hard to tell how pregnant she was, but he guessed that her time was close.
An older woman would be spreading more, and more
encumbered. She was young. God, she was young.
Large, grief-stricken eyes stared blankly at her visitor.

"Mrs. Sa'id. My name is Mohammed Mahrous. I
knew your husband. I wanted to pay my respects . . .
and to tell you something about how your husband
died."

She let him in. They had two small rooms with hardwood floors, a couch, a table, and some chairs. There
was a crib ready for the baby. Also some clothes and
a few things she had collected, rattles and toys. Apart
from that, the only furnishings were homemade shelves
lined with books. Yet it was homey. Pretty curtains
and a bright cushion here and there. She bade him sit
and offered him tea. He refused, she insisted, and he
changed his mind. During this exchange, she threw back
the cowl and he was surprised to see long, light brown
hair, almost blond. She saw him blink, and a minute
smile appeared, together with a flicker of something
like defiance in her eyes.

"Mrs. Sa'id. I just wanted to say how sorry we all
are about what happened. I knew Abdel a little bit.
I liked him, and I admired him. You don't often get
to say that about our young recruits these days, but I
respected him." Again, he saw the faintest movement
of her lips. She was stunned with grief, and staring at

the future, but his words were going in. She was still
alive, he thought, and felt a little better.

"It's kind of you to come," she said. "And I recognize
your name, Lieutenant Colonel. He used to speak of
you." Mahrous looked at her in surprise.

They discussed the simple ceremony and burial
arrangements. Sa'id's family would take the body
to Luxor, where he was from. They'd had the little
ceremony here for her sake, for she had no family in
Luxor. Nor in Cairo, she added. He waited, but she
did not elaborate. Still no hint of why she appeared
to be alone in the world. He wanted to ask. But she
was intelligent enough to know that he was wondering,
and if she chose not to explain, that was her business.
The baby was due in six weeks time, she told him. She
would have a small check from the government till she
could work again. She had worked in a bookstore. That
was how she'd met Abdel. She almost broke down at this
point, but recovered, dabbing quickly at her eyes.

Mahrous cleared his throat. It was time to come to
the point. "Mrs. Sa'id," he began again.

"Julia," she said.

He paused. He'd been about to tell her some facts
that Touhami had not authorized to be made public
but now he paused, hearing her name, with its ethnic
connotations. Suddenly he thought he understood. It
all began to fit—even the attitude of Touhami, back in
the department.

Mahrous rose and examined a bookshelf. He saw
an ancient volume of the Five Books of Moses, the
comprehensive Torah, or Talmud and the Bible, as
well as the Koran. "Your husband was a scholar," he
said. She nodded, watching him. "Why did he give it
up?" Her eyebrows rose a fraction, and her lips made
that little movement that wasn't quite a smile. "Did he

have problems with his faith?"

"Not with his faith," she said calmly. "With mine. I am Jewish."

It was getting dark by the time he left. She had lit a small lamp by then, for the building had no electricity. There had been nothing overt at El Azhar, she'd said, when Abdel married her. It was just that he'd gradually found that he was no longer as popular as he had been. He'd found the same thing with the police. Almost qualified to be an officer, he'd been made a sergeant, and was still studying. But the worst blow was to his family. To them, his children would be Jewish, through the mother's line, and would always carry that stigma. Spiritually, the two faiths were close, and tolerant of one another. But politically, it was a very different matter. Julia's family had all gone to Israel. Every last brother and sister, and her parents. That was why she was alone, and would remain so, unless she too went to Israel. That was her plan. She would have the baby, then make her arrangements. That was why Mahrous stayed as long as he did. Because now there was something he could do, something crisp and definite to help her. Passports were his domain. He could have one for her anytime she wanted it—and more, he thought, thinking she'd need money. His heart went out to the girl. And yet in a strange way, he almost envied her. She was young. With a little help, she would make it in her life, and she still had her child. He left the small apartment with a definite feeling that something had gone well, that his instinct to come here had been right. That was enough to blow away some of the cobwebs for a while.

When Mahrous left, Julia Sa'id watched him from her window. She felt the baby move and put her hand

on her stomach as she gazed down. She wondered
what his secret was, this policeman with his kind,
black eyes and the empty sleeve pinned to his side.
Why had he gone out of his way to come here and
comfort her? With his dark hair brushed thickly to
one side, the heavy eyebrows, and the mustache that
didn't really suit him, he had the appearance of a man
of rank. He looked like a man who should be more
highly placed than she knew him to be. He had spoken
kindly of Abdel. In strict confidence, he had told her
that her husband's death was honorable, and that she
was not to believe any stories she might hear about
shady drug dealing. This was espionage. Dangerous
espionage he believed. And they would get this man.
Lieutenant Colonel Mahrous had promised her that.
He was detailed to the investigation, and he would not
rest until they had found this killer.

Even Touhami was affected by the murders. After his
initial reaction of questioning the wisdom of putting out
a call to taxi drivers while a dangerous killer might be in
the cab, he had fallen silent, looking a little gray around
the gills. This may have been due to the implications
that he now saw.

Mahrous had put together a description of what was
known about the killer. This was for circulation to
all personnel of the regular police force, as well as
Internal Security, and was to be seen by as many
as possible of the thousands of "City Eye" inform-
ants in Cairo. His work was examined critically by
Touhami.

"Six feet two or three," he read aloud. "Dark hair?"

"I guess that from his wig, sir. I don't think he'd
have changed the coloring too much."

"Hmm. There are such things as dye, you know?"

Mahrous kept silent. He did not mention that there were also such things as body hair and stubble.

"But you don't guess about his eye color?"

"No, sir."

"That seems rather cautious . . . Speaks perfect Arabic," he read on, "but has European features. Thirty to fifty years old. That seems broad enough. Athletic build?" He looked up inquiringly.

"That's a bit of a guess, sir. In his disguise, he was kind of shambling."

"Well, that might be very clever . . . An educated man . . . That comes from the tapes, I suppose, if it's not obvious. They wouldn't use a dunce . . . Probably does not possess papers . . . I suppose you checked out this Ali Hamsa person?"

"Yes, sir. And he exists, or did exist, as a junior employee in a travel firm in Damascus. But he has disappeared. Without trace so far. That's what convinces me that this is professional."

"Hmmm . . . And his room was searched without finding any sign of duplicate papers. Not that a professional would leave them lying around."

"They would also be dangerous to carry," Mahrous said. "Or enter the country with. I tend to think he had only one set of papers, and planned to leave with them."

"That's how we'll get him," Touhami stated. He studied the passport photograph. "Why haven't you circulated this?"

Mahrous cleared his throat. "I didn't see much point, sir, if it doesn't look like him. We've no idea what his real hair is like. Those spectacles do a lot to conceal the eyes. The face in the photograph is rubicund. His own may not be. I thought it better just to stick with what we know." It was then that Touhami made the kind of observation for which he was famous, especially in his prickly contacts with Mahrous.

"Pity you didn't think to ask the taxi driver some of those questions, when you had him on the radio. Hamsa wasn't in disguise then, was he?"

Mahrous gave orders that the city be flooded with leaflets. He wanted the staffs and proprietors of all hotels, rooming houses, and public places to be on the lookout for this man. He ordered an extra tightening of passport security, which was already very strict. Anyone who looked halfway suspicious was to be searched to ensure that he or she was not carrying extra papers. He thought about money. The man might be in difficulties there. This led to other precautions.

There were a number of men and women still living in Cairo who had been under suspicion since the early sixties, when foreign spies had started turning up all over Cairo. Mahrous requested the files of all such individuals to be pulled, and selected a number of them for renewed surveillance. His reasoning was that whatever his purpose, the killer was now in an emergency situation and might need contacts. He then started on the files of all individuals, Egyptian or otherwise, suspected of any kind of antigovernment activity, and pulled all "City Eye" reports on Ali Hamsa during his few days in Cairo.

During this work, Mahrous stopped from time to time and examined the passport photograph. There was something about the face that haunted him, though he had no recollection of ever having seen anyone who resembled it. The case was getting to him. Especially as the days went by, and the trail got colder, he found himself becoming nervous and irritable. There was a report that nagged at him. It concerned a building in old Cairo that Hamsa had apparently been interested in

purchasing. Mahrous interviewed the broker. But the
man knew nothing of Hamsa beyond his profession and
seemed above suspicion. The trail on the Hamsa identity
likewise petered out. What was the man's business here?
Why had he wanted to buy an old building and where
was he now? Mahrous had promised Julia Sa'id that
he would catch the killer of her husband. If he failed,
it would not be because he had left a stone unturned.

Chapter 5

KHALIL CAUGHT a taxi on Kasr el Eini and told the
driver to head north. Following a similar route to the one
he had used when visiting Badaway, he stopped the cab
near the Bulak baths and walked the rest of the way.
He did not go directly to the dimly lit doorway of the
hammam. First he walked past on one side of the street,
and then on the other. There was no surveillance.

Inside the doorway, there was a hallway and a pair
of swing doors. Affected by the strangeness of it, he
went through them, into a very different world from
the street outside. It was a large room about the size of
a tennis court. Dimly lit, with green enamel walls and
floor, and a fountain in the center. In the waters of the
fountain, a group of naked men were washing languidly.
Some of them glanced up when Khalil appeared, seeing
the western-clad figure. It was not unknown for foreign
celebrities to visit the humble place. In the background

shadows, there were openings to other rooms, from which came the sound of voices and running water. The air was hot and steamy.

Along one wall, there were the doors to half a dozen rooms. These were private cubicles where wealthier customers could undress and leave their clothes. Khalil was still getting his bearings when a voice spoke behind him.

"You would like a private room?"

The Arab was short, fat, wearing a galabiya and a fez. His grin was wide and happy, showing missing teeth. Behind him, through the open door of a small office, Khalil saw two other men, who looked like Musselman warriors. Baggy pants, broad, naked torsos, one with a shaven head. They looked at Khalil impassively.

Khalil chose to speak in French. "*Monsieur le Patron?*" The grin bowed. "Yes, I would like a room."

"Five pounds, please."

The grin faltered slightly when Khalil didn't haggle over price. The proprietor was thinking he should have asked for ten pounds, or maybe twenty. Khalil was given towels and a basket for his clothes.

It was good to be back in Cairo. Although he had never frequented the baths, he felt at home again as he stepped out naked. He was not relaxed, however. He hated being naked. Not because of shyness, but because of vulnerability. He thought about the virtual impossibility of fleeing like this, and prayed that nothing would go wrong tonight.

The first room he entered was a shower room. In semidarkness, relieved by night-lights here and there in some of the rooms, he heard the harsh voices of his fellow bathers, as they discussed the body of what they took to be a European. Khalil smiled inwardly as they discussed his development. In a totally nonsexual

way, surrounded by these scrawny youths and older
men, he found a slight tumescence in his penis, which
didn't bother him at all—except for one thing. He was
becoming too relaxed. Recent experience had taught
him the danger of relaxing. He was here on business.
He walked out of the shower and into another room.

In this room there was a sulfur bath, surrounded
by mats. Some of the mats, in the deeper shadows
around the walls, were occupied by prostrate figures,
and from at least one, there was the rustle of skin on
skin. As Khalil eyed the foaming water, a boy of about
fourteen, who sat nearby, started slowly masturbating
his smooth penis, eyes fixed glassily on Khalil . . .
Drugged. Otherwise, he would never put his manhood
on the line like that, in front of other men. Animal
sounds rose suddenly from one of the mats. Deep,
grunting gasps of pleasure. Other things being different, Khalil thought, he might be tempted to take this
boy, penetrate his body, and discard him like a used
condom, but not now. As he rose to go, the boy spoke
angrily in Arabic, comparing his ancestors to the filth
of dogs.

There was one other major room in the *hammam*.
This was the biggest of all, apart from the main room
with the fountain, but was the least populated, being
fully lit. It contained a swimming pool, with tiers of
benches stacked around it, as though for spectators to
witness a sporting event, which seemed unlikely. On
the upper levels of these benches sat a dozen or more
naked little boys. These were probably neighborhood
urchins, allowed in out of the night air—not sexual
fodder surely. In the pool, there was one man. Khalil
saw a great blob of a head, enormous shoulders, and
a shimmering belly underneath as the lone bather wal-
lowed and gazed around him. The man's eyes came his

way, settled for a moment on the figure in the doorway, and passed on again. It was John Baldwin.

Khalil dived, hitting the water with a smack. After powering for a stroke or two, he dipped beneath the surface, swam to the end, turned like a torpedo, and came up in a fast crawl. As a teenager, he had been selected to train for the Egyptian Olympic swimming team. Tiring of that, he had concentrated on what had been his second sport, judo, and had gone to the top in that while living in France. He swam half a dozen lengths, churning the water, before stopping in the middle of the pool beside Baldwin.

Apart from the great, fat-covered shoulders—which had pumped a lot of iron in their time, Khalil observed—the only visible part of Baldwin was his head. It was an outsize head that came to a point on top, with a little patch of hair. Below this, an enormous double chin, a mouth that struggled to smile amid the fat, and a pair of hazel-colored eyes, bright with intelligence.

"Mr. K, I dare to say. How are you, sir?" Baldwin spoke in English. His tone was loud and merry, as a great white fin rose from the water and offered itself to Khalil. The hand was huge and oddly shaped, as the fat fingers poised themselves and brushed against Khalil's.

Khalil looked around. There was nothing but the gallery of children, but he was ill at ease. "Where can we talk?" he asked.

Baldwin seemed amused at this refusal to indulge in small talk. "We can go to my room . . . if that won't embarrass you."

Khalil's blue-gray eyes had no expression as they met Baldwin's and he nodded.

Yvette had not exaggerated about the man's size. As he climbed from the water, hitching a kind of loincloth around his waist, Khalil saw a frame that must have weighed at least three hundred fifty pounds. It was hard to determine the purpose of the loincloth. It certainly did little to improve his decency, as his huge legs swung in circular motions beneath it. He was not young either, but there was a certain bounce in the elephantine stride as they walked across the room with the fountain. Baldwin nodded and smiled at anyone who looked his way, his huge arms hanging down around the outsize chest.

Baldwin's room was a mirror image of Khalil's. There was a couch with a colored cloth spread on it, and a wicker chair. Baldwin took the couch. On a small table sat a bottle of vodka, a pitcher of orange juice, and two glasses. Khalil shook his head when the fat man offered vodka. Baldwin half filled a glass with liquor and splashed in some juice. "First of the day," he said cheerfully, in his booming British voice, and swallowed most of it. Khalil put a towel around his waist and sat in the chair, his impressions gathering. Baldwin was fat and self-indulgent, but was not to be underestimated.

John Baldwin had a second in Classics from Cambridge University. He'd missed his "first" because of cards—too much bridge in his final year—and had joined M15 instead. Nor had he found his niche in the "Firm," as Baldwin called it. Too outspoken and too bright, he said cheerfully, giving Khalil a brief history. Khalil smiled. He had heard of Baldwin as a man with an unusual brain, who'd seen a lot and forgotten nothing.

Baldwin drained his glass and filled another. Only then did he seem to focus on Khalil, as though wondering for the first time who he was. "This place is safe by the way," he said. "Abdul is an old friend of mine. There are no devices, and they don't report to the police." He studied Khalil with his crushed-up smile. "So what can I do for you, sir?"

Khalil nodded, accepting Baldwin's assurances. All the same, he disliked it here, and was anxious to get out. "I need two things urgently," he said. "One is a radio transmitter, and the other is a set of papers. The papers will have to be brought in from overseas. On an ongoing basis, I need communications with certain people in Cairo, as well as with the outside. The problem is that I do not wish to contact the local people personally, which is why I need a go-between. You are well known, but not in the public eye. You also have certain experience. And you have been recommended by a man I trust." Khalil assumed that he had been well screened, as he was mentioned by Badaway.

After thinking for a moment, Baldwin nodded. "We might be able to do business. You also come highly recommended. But the radio is out of the question. Hard to obtain, and you couldn't use it anyway, old chap. That's not the way things are done, these days. Why don't you get yourself a messenger?"

Khalil saw a buzzer by the couch and touched it. "That would be cumbersome and slow. Also insecure. As for the papers, I do need someone—you, I hope— to go overseas and get them. I am assured that you can manage that. As for the radio, all I need is that you tell me where to find one." There was a knock on the door in response to the buzzer. Khalil asked for his clothing to be brought from the next room. They sat in silence while a frozen-faced guard brought the basket.

When they could speak again, Baldwin shook his head. "I don't think you understand, old chap. I said I can't help you with the radio."

Khalil took a check book from his coat pocket and put it on his knee. He opened a pen and held it poised. "I

don't think you understand, Mr. Baldwin. How much?"
Baldwin blinked. For a moment, there was a blank
expression on his face before his mouth came unstuck
as though to speak. "How much?" Khalil repeated.

"Fifty thousand," Baldwin said. "Sterling."

Khalil wrote the check, making it payable to John
Baldwin, and signed it with his own name. "If you
present this in Geneva, you will find that my signature
is good. They will either pay you in cash, or transfer
the money to whatever account you choose to specify.
While you are out of Egypt, I want you to contact
some people. You will explain to them what I need,
and they will supply you with a package. I understand
that you travel frequently. How often do you find your
hand-held baggage searched by customs?"

Baldwin sipped his drink and lit a Belmont cigarette.
He glanced at Khalil, his eyes bright. "Almost never.
I have friends." At this point there was a knock on
the door.

Khalil froze, the pen still in his hand. Baldwin too, his
eyes fixed on the door. Without waiting for an answer,
the proprietor opened the door, slipped in with an air
of urgency, and spoke quietly. "The police are here,"
he said in Arabic. "There is a colonel from Internal
Security in my office asking questions." Khalil rose
immediately. His first instinct was to get dressed, but
he saw Baldwin's chalk-white face and checked himself.
"I am not alarmed," said the proprietor with amazing
calm. "But in case the gentlemen were about to leave,
I thought you might prefer to wait here meantime. I
must go." He bowed, a tense smile flickered, and he
slipped out again.

Khalil tore the check in half and gave part of it to
Baldwin. He shredded the other half, prior to putting
it in his mouth. "I can write another of those," he said

as he sat down again. "Pour me a glass of juice, will
you?"

*God is great. Every day of my life I will mourn the
murders of the sons of Ali.*

Naked, and in possession of no identification papers
in Egypt, Khalil sat down, watched Baldwin masticate
the paper, and began to ask the fat man about his life
in Cairo.

Mahrous had known that Hassan Badaway was lying.
He'd seen the tension and the desolation in the eyes,
made allowance for natural fear and acting, and ended
up with a kind of sadness, knowing that the man had
guilty secrets.

Badaway's name had come to his attention as one
of many who had been investigated in the past, but
never arrested. This was part of the routine screening
Mahrous had ordered, but there was another reason
why he had picked out the ex-professor for a personal
visit. On the night of Abdel Sa'id's death, the killer
had visited this part of Cairo. In seeking a reason,
Mahrous had kept returning to the file on Badaway,
who now lived in the poverty-stricken Bulak area.

Hassan Badaway, born in Cairo, was a devout
Moslem, but not a fanatic. All the same, his opinions
as a younger man had brought him into conflict with
many of his countrymen in a variety of ways. During
World War II, when he was a historian at Cairo University, Badaway had vocally despised the view, held
by many, that a win for Germany would free Egypt
from the British yolk, and be a welcome change for the
country. Mistakenly, he was taken for an anglophile,
just as later, when heard criticizing the military rule
imposed after the revolution in 1952, he was taken
as a supporter of the deposed King Farouk. In later

years, Badaway realized that he should have known
better than to trust in the rationality of other men. It
might not have changed anything he did or said, but he
should have known better than to expect reason, even
from men like his colleagues in the university. "Under
the British, we could at least complain," he had said,
speaking, as he thought, to friends. "Nothing was done,
but at least we could vent our feelings. Who dares to
complain now?" In retrospect, he was lucky not to have
been thrown in jail. What happened was that his teaching load had been increased, made bottom-heavy with
junior classes, he had been given miserable schedules,
and had found himself excluded from meetings held in
the department, as well as any chance of advancement.
A proud man, he had resigned his position, taken up
the profession of his father, who had been a tailor, and
become active in the Muslim Brotherhood. After the
attempt on Nasser's life in 1954, Badaway had found
himself an outlaw. During the ensuing crackdown on
the Brotherhood, his opinion of the military regime had
not improved, and he had been young enough in those
days to be willing to risk his life and family by actively
opposing what he hated. It was during those years that
he had come to know, and fear, a man called Ibrahim
Khalil.

If Badaway seemed a broken man these days, it was
because of what he had seen in 1967. What he had seen
then was the total humiliation of his enemy—Nasser—
though it was also the humiliation of his country. Nasser
should have been destroyed in 1967. Yet he was still
there, stronger than ever, endorsed by mass demonstrations in the streets. Disgusted, disheartened, and
ashamed deep down, Badaway had withdrawn to just
living with his family—until now. Now he was involved
again, though it was the last thing he wanted. After

visits from the past, from men who had struck the fear
of death in him, not just Khalil, he was now being questioned by this one-armed Lieutenant Colonel, who was
polite, even sympathetic, but who missed nothing.

Badaway was clinging to the letter of the truth. The
name Ali Hamsa meant nothing to him. The face in
the photograph that he was shown was not the face of
anyone he knew. It was not the true face of Ibrahim
Khalil. Mahrous pinpointed the very night when Khalil
had visited. Had Badaway been visited by anyone that
night? The tailor began to fumble as he prevaricated.
Customers sometimes came at night, to collect suits or
be measured for them. Sometimes foreigners, who left
deposits if the tailor didn't know them. But there had
been no one that night, he said, not that he recalled
for sure—and Mahrous knew that he was lying.

Mahrous had no wish to persecute the tailor. He
did not believe that the man was involved in current
activity against the government, and the chances that he
knew anything relevant to this investigation were really
very small. The chances were that he'd been talking
to some old associate whom he didn't want to name.
Mahrous had come here as a long shot, working late.
Did he really want to drag this man across the coals?
That's what he was trying to judge when there was an
unplanned interruption. A little boy had peeped into
the workshop and asked when his daddy would come
up to supper. Mummy was upset because the food was
getting cold. In retrospect, Mahrous would see it as
another proof that he would never be a policeman.
He should have been ready to tear the facts from
the man's throat if necessary. Instead, he had seen
the look of desperation in the tailor's eyes, and had
stood up, shaken hands, and let the poor bastard off
the hook.

In the alleyway outside, he met the detective who had been questioning the owner of the café opposite. He reported that no one remembered seeing any foreigner that night, or any tall, well-dressed man. This was not surprising. In this area, the people were not police informers.

By the same token, Mahrous had wondered if it was worth visiting the *hammam*. A taxi driver, who believed that he might have carried Ali Hamsa that night, assumed that his passenger had visited the baths, though the proprietor, who had already been routinely questioned, denied this totally. Tired and dispirited, expecting no success, Mahrous had taken a last-minute decision to stop the driver and question the proprietor himself.

The man was as smooth as a drop of olive oil. With his eyes fixed on Mahrous's, chest, his grin in place, he repeated silkily that many foreign gentlemen visited the baths—many *famous* foreign gentlemen, with faces that one recognized from movies. Some night ten days ago? He shrugged with great elaboration. Maybe none, maybe several. He held the photograph at arm's length and studied it. Mahrous wondered how a man who lived in an atmosphere of soap and steam could have black fingernails. At this point, he thought he noticed something. A minute narrowing of the eyes, as the man stared at the photograph. Thoughtfully, Mahrous pushed open the swing doors to the baths. He saw that two of the private rooms were occupied. "Do you have anyone here tonight that I would recognize?" he asked. The black eyes blinked, and the grin faltered for a moment, but the man said nothing.

Mahrous allowed the door to close. He saw no point in terrorizing the homosexuals. He regarded the killer's movements pointing to the baths that night to be most probably a blind. The chances that he was here again tonight were infinitesimal. Mahrous thanked the proprietor and asked the driver to take him home.

When the proprietor came to the door again and told them that the police had left, Baldwin and Khalil unfroze. They learned that the policeman's name was Mahrous, that he was a lieutenant colonel with an arm missing. Baldwin shook his head, unfamiliar with the name, while Khalil's eyes narrowed for a moment. So this was the man who was hunting him. What strange mischance had brought him here tonight—only to stick his head in and then leave? He wrote another check for Baldwin, whose fat face looked tense and crafty, as he sat smoking like a breathing mountain.

Chapter 6

KHALIL HAD lived to curse the moment of inattention that had led to his being stranded in Cairo without papers. There were inconveniences, and work he could not do, but worst of all was the nerve-wracking fact of not being legal. He had no driving license. All it took was a fender-bending accident, or a policeman deciding to stop him for some reason while he was driving his sister's car, and he would be in an emergency situation. On two occasions he drove past the mosque that he had visited as Hamsa. Each time, instinct told him that the house opposite was tainted by Hamsa's inquiries. Even now, his feeling was that every policeman in Cairo was on the lookout for him. If he hadn't had a place to stay, for example, he would probably be a dead man by now.

Life at his sister's house had fallen into a routine. Yvette was preoccupied with the English girl she'd met. They were forever having lengthy conversations on the telephone, meeting in Gropi's in the afternoons for tea and cakes, or going to the symphony orchestra at night. Khalil was familiar with these long seductions of his sister's. Eventually, but not before she was ready, she would bring the girl here, seduce her, and then most probably cast her aside. Yvette was not a true lesbian. Certainly not the type to want to live with any of her victims. She was too much of a nymphomaniac for that. She had shown no further interest in his doings, and he had certainly told her nothing as he sat around the house, studying newspapers and thinking. Yet it was she who inadvertently gave him the clue to what would turn out to be his destiny.

She was in the kitchen one morning around noon, glancing at the *Al Ahram*, having her first cup of coffee of the day. He had been playing the piano, after spending the morning in the library, and walked into the kitchen just as she gave a sharp cry of triumph. "Hah! We're in the news," she said sardonically. "They've chosen to make a big thing out of our land appropriation." She threw the copy of the newspaper across the table. On an inside page there was an article about the continued land reform of the "people's, government," and mention of a ceremony to be held in Cairo later in the summer. "They do this every so often," she said. "Sadat'll probably be there, surrounded by cameras while they give away our land. It is our land too. Look at the list of villages." Her eyes brooded for a moment, thinking of their mother, who still lived in Egypt for a part of every year, while Khalil read the article with keen interest.

Khalil took the paper to his room and reread the article. Since early in the revolution, the government had formed the practice of taking land from those who owned it, and distributing it among the peasant farmers. This served two functions. On the one hand, it was a convenient way to persecute the wealthy families, who were not noted for their revolutionary zeal, and on the other, it was a pleasing form of socialism, to go alongside better mass education and the like. The function described in this article was to be held in the Semiramis Hotel, and was scheduled for September. There was going to be a fair, at the official opening of which there would be a ceremony, where the title deeds would be handed out to farmers. Khalil's interest grew as he studied this. It was only a germ of a plan as yet, but he saw possibilities. At the same time, his morale received a boost. This was what he was here to do, and by God, in spite of everything, he was going to do it. The idea of giving up had never seriously occurred to him.

The need for a communications link was now paramount. It was essential to initiate planning from without. This could not be done through Baldwin. It was Khalil's decision not to discuss details with Baldwin. He chose the day that Baldwin left for Europe to go in search of the transmitter.

Baldwin had come up with the name of a man called Hartmud Schmidt. He was a German Jew who had been active a few years ago, a very competent spy for the Israelis, who went under the code name Cupid. Cupid had been lying fallow for a while, but had not left Cairo, because he was dedicated. According to

Baldwin, he lived for the chance to serve Israel again, and if they played their cards correctly, that's what he would think he was doing. "At least he'll know he isn't serving Nasser," the fat man had remarked, with his probing smile. He was always trying to pry information from Khalil. As for acquiring the radio, the risk was high. But Schmidt was described as a cool and clever operative, not currently under surveillance. He worked as a technician in the television tower in Cairo, was known to have a high-quality radio in his possession, and after careful contact from Baldwin, he was expecting a visit from Khalil.

Schmidt lived in an apartment building on the banks of the Nile, close to the television building. Khalil drove there in his sister's MG and cruised slowly by, studying the buildings opposite. He took nothing for granted. The manhunt that had been mounted by the authorities was not over, and its thoroughness indicated that they suspected more than drug dealing or a random killing. For all that, Khalil preferred to visit Schmidt himself.

He spotted the surveillance when the German left the building at midday. By this time Khalil had parked the car and was having a lemonade in a nearby café. Schmidt worked nights. Khalil had been waiting to see if he would come down for lunch, hoping for a look at the man before visiting him, when the German walked out of the building, triggering an absurd sequence of events. First a doorman rushed out, signaling to a window of the building opposite. This evoked an angry signal in return, from a man who came out onto a balcony, telling the doorman to be still. The panic seemed to be that the German was heading for his car, which was apparently unusual at this time of day. Khalil paid for his drink, bought a newspaper, and walked to the MG.

It was clear that the surveillance was nonspecific. It was part of a net that had been thrown widely, and police resources were spread thin. A Ford sedan picked up the German's car. The single driver didn't even look in his mirror as he concentrated on not losing the car in front of him. Khalil followed well behind. Driving with one hand, in the open car, he tuned into the Second Program on the radio and found some violin music.

They went to Cairo airport. At a level below the rational, Khalil's heart began to beat nervously in the all-too-familiar setting. The police driver used his identification rather than pay for parking. Definitely not the first team. Khalil wished that his sister had a less conspicuous car, but felt in no danger of being noticed.

The German was here to meet a girl. Black-haired and Caucasian, wearing a green dress that showed her thighs, she seemed excited to be here, as they embraced publicly, before throwing her bags into the car and heading back for Cairo. On the main road from Heliopolis, Khalil actually had to accelerate past the police car as the driver got himself caught behind a changing light. The driver's response to this was simply to drive through the red light with his horn blaring.

The couple went to the Nile Hilton. Again the setting made Khalil's heart tighten as he followed them inside, hearing the girl's laughter. He sincerely hoped that the German knew that he was being followed, and was not up to some folly.

He was sitting in an armchair in the lobby when he suddenly became aware of danger to himself. The German had waited while the girl checked in. Their conversation made it clear, however, that he was now on his way to work and wouldn't see her again till late that night. She was an American. Long, pretty legs and a

youthful figure. Glancing up over his newspaper, Khalil
had just noticed the backs of her thighs, beneath the
green dress, and experienced a surge of desire, when he
saw that he too had been noticed. Two men in dark suits
were looking his way. Khalil's eyes deepened furiously
as once again he cursed the unparalleled thoroughness
of this manhunt.

He rose immediately. An unsure policeman was like
a thief, or a mugger, or a shark. The worst thing one
could do once noticed was to dally in front of him. Nor
did Khalil wish to leave the hotel and find himself being
followed. As the girl gave her suitcase to a porter and
headed for the elevators, Khalil went that way too.
Seeing the approach of his tall figure, she dropped her
eyes, instantly attracted, and he made his decision.
"Hi, there," he said in English. He took the suitcase
from the porter, who glared at him in resentment. "Go
masturbate yourself," he muttered in Arabic, handing
the man a pound note. After a moment of astonishment,
the man grinned. "Let me take this for you," he said
to the girl. "I don't hear a voice from home too often
these days. Which floor?" he asked, smiling at her.

Her face was beginning to light up. "Eight," she said,
studying him. "Where are you from?" As the doors
closed, he saw that the policemen hadn't moved.

"I was going to ask you that," he said. "Mississippi?"

"Hey!" She couldn't believe it. She didn't have a
strong country accent, and most Americans would not
have pinpointed her home state. "I'm from the Gulf
Coast. Biloxi."

He nodded. "Long Beach."

"No kidding? Hey, that's too much!" She was very
young. Very happy to meet a boy from home. A student
probably. "Which high school did you go to?" she asked
incredulously.

"St. Stanilaus," he said, mentioning a private school in the area. Khalil had spent three years in the United States. He had loose backgrounds, which he used for meeting people, in California, the Northeast, and in the South. His accents were perfect. He had a perfect ear, and had practiced long with tape recordings. He had similar vignettes of background from England, France, Germany, and other parts of Europe, as well as the Middle East. When he wished, he could be almost anybody's brother.

"Too much!" she said excitedly. "My brother went there!"

Khalil was made. By the time they reached her room, she was talking animatedly. He spoke in her ear. "I've got a couple of joints. Want to relax after your trip?"

Her face turned serious. Khalil saw the decision being made now, in her young, pretty face—not a decision about drugs. "That sounds good," she said slowly.

After the first joint, he showed her the bug in the room. She couldn't believe it, and was inclined to giggle. He did not inform her that in the neighboring country of Iraq, drug users were executed, and that even in Egypt it was a serious offense. He certainly did not inform her that those listening, who might even be doing so manually at this very moment, were interested in something much more serious. He was badly shaken at being noticed downstairs. He could only guess that this was because of his general description, and the proximity to Schmidt—and the zeal of the man who led this incredible witch-hunt. He could only pray that his tactics would divert them.

The girl was getting glassy-eyed. Breathing deeply, stretching, stroking her limbs. He saw that even her underwear was green. Her skirt had gradually moved up her thighs, and now he saw the bull's-eye when her knees opened briefly. She was a student at Mississippi State, spending the summer in Paris, where she had met a friend of Schmidt's. There was nothing between herself and Schmidt, she thought it relevant to tell him as he pulled down her underwear, then allowed his strangled penis to pop out.

As he moved over the girl, Khalil had the absurd thought that he didn't want the police to burst in now. If this had to be the end, he wanted it to come, not now, but after he had possessed this paper doll. Her thighs were smooth, and had been developed by workouts. She was as pretty and unreal to him as a Barbie doll, or something in a television cartoon.

After the cartoon girl had been exploded, she lay facedown on the bed. Khalil glanced at the bug, wondering how they would react to what they'd heard. There could surely be no doubt about the authenticity of the lovemaking. Khalil retreated to a small table, where he found a pen and note pad. After waiting for a while, watching the door, he came to a decision and began to write. He wrote in Hebrew, in a fast scribble. No one who wasn't fluent in the language would have a chance of deciphering the note. He was prepared to take the chance that the girl was not fluent in Hebrew.

"Dear Cupid," he wrote. "I hope you know that you are under surveillance. Your apartment must be monitored and all your telephone calls. I believe this to be aimed elsewhere, not at you. You are probably on file, and are being watched as part of a fine-tooth comb search for someone else. But we must have the transmitter. We must have it," he repeated, underlining the words. "Get it to your apartment. I know it's not there now, or they'd have found it. Get it there, and I promise that I shall collect it within minutes. I don't think they'll stop you in the street. Their instructions are to watch closely, not to arrest every foreigner in Cairo. Shalom. God be with you."

It wasn't easy to waken the girl. When he did, she seemed unsure of where she was. He carried her into the bathroom, sat her down, and spoke seriously.

"Debbie, I want you to listen carefully. I don't want to have to say this but once," he said, still speaking in the accent of the southern United States. "Your friend Hartmud is being watched by the police. This is not because he's done anything wrong, but just because he's a Jew and these people are paranoid. I want you to warn him. I want you to warn him that he's in danger. That's all." He opened the front of her panties and pushed down the note. "Give him this. Keep it safe and give it to him when you see him tonight. And give my love to yourself." He kissed her on the lips. She clung to him, bewildered and wondering. He told her truthfully that she would probably never see him again.

Khalil walked out of the hotel with a deliberate, pleased smile planted on his lips. With peripheral vision, he watched one of the policemen who had begun to notice him earlier, and saw his own smile echoed as the man glanced at him with envy. So far so good. He walked away, leaving Yvette's car in the parking lot. With any luck, the police would make no report. At least nothing of sufficient moment to reach anyone who mattered. Now he would find out what the Jew was made of.

Once clear of the hotel, and sure that he was not being followed, he sat down in a café and waited for the feeling of nausea to pass. It was always the same, as the unused poison of adrenaline drained from his veins. He would collect the car later in the afternoon.

                    *   *   *

Hartmud Schmidt wasted no time in responding to the note. When he left for work the next evening, he was carrying a briefcase. When he had returned the night before, on his way to meet the girl, there had been no briefcase. By now, he must have seen the note, and the briefcase was a good sign. Khalil saw that the German was not followed during the short walk to the television building. They probably relied on doormen and other such people to keep an eye on him, in the loose surveillance.

The German worked a shift from four till midnight. It was Khalil's hope, which might be optimistic, that he kept the radio somewhere in his workplace, being an electrical engineer. Thinking ahead, Khalil bought himself a similar briefcase that afternoon, and a book and a newspaper to go into it. The tension of all this made him snarl at Yvette as he took her car again that evening. She wanted it herself. Khalil cursed this zealot of a one-armed colonel, who was hunting him so remorselessly. Someday he would find out what his problem was, and hack off his other arm.

When Khalil entered the German's apartment building that night, he wore a red and white striped galabiya, black plastic shoes, white socks, and a red fez on his head. Unshaven, with stubble on his chin, he wore sunglasses and carried a briefcase. His black hair, greased with Vaseline, stuck out in curls underneath the fez. No one gave him a second glance as he strolled along the street and into the building. The building was of the older type, with no security or even an elevator. It had a dozen or so apartments, on three levels.

The German's apartment was on the second level. Khalil climbed up and saw three doors. To one side, there was the sound of children fighting behind the door. To the other, the sound of American pop music. Thinking that Schmidt could afford better than this, he tried a couple of skeleton keys and easily opened the door.

It was eight P.M. He reasoned that if a routine search of the apartment were planned for tonight, it would probably have been done already. There had been no sign of activity in the building opposite, and the superintendent of this building had gone off somewhere. The German was safely at work. Khalil had entered at what he hoped would be a dead time in the surveillance. He soon found the bug. It was in a light fitting in the ceiling. He sat down in the shadows and composed himself to wait.

The woman in the next apartment screamed at her children. Every so often, the father's harsh voice cut across, threatening mayhem if they didn't all shut up. The American music went on incessantly behind the other wall. People arrived. Girls' voices rose above the music, and after a while, there was the rhythmic movement of a couch against the wall. Things had changed in Egypt. Women going out and getting rutted as part of their evening entertainment. Earlier in the day, he had seen the young wife from next door. She was quite a pretty woman in a cotton dress. He wondered if she'd ever visited the lair next door, while her husband was at work. Khalil sat very still, straining for every sound in the corridor outside. Not relaxed enough to think constructively, he occupied his mind with trivia.

At fifteen minutes after midnight there was a new step in the corridor outside. Khalil had heard it on the staircase, light and quick, and was sure it was the German. As a key fitted in the lock, he rose and moved quietly to the bathroom.

The man entered the apartment cautiously. In his thirties, looking younger, a blond Adonis, he soon noticed the briefcase, which Khalil had deliberately left lying on the bed. There was a silence while he stood and sensed around. Then he closed the curtains of the room, and put on a small light and a radio, before coming to the door of the bathroom.

The German pushed the door open all the way. In the small room, he saw Khalil as a tall shadow by the shower curtain. They looked at each other. Then the German stepped in and closed the door behind him. "They're used to that," he said in Hebrew. "I always close the door, even when I'm on my own. Do you mind if I put on the light?"

"Please."

He switched on the light, but didn't even glance at Khalil's face. A professional. Khalil rejoiced to have had a stroke of luck at last. The German was nervous as he opened the briefcase on the toilet seat, but that was understandable.

The radio was compact, of American manufacture. Khalil saw immediately that it was good for his purposes. Whispering quietly, Schmidt showed him the features and assured him that the batteries were fresh. It would easily reach Tel Aviv, he said. Khalil did not say that he would not be transmitting to Tel Aviv. Then came the urgent warning.

"They have tracking stations around Cairo," Schmidt said.

"Three," said Khalil.

The German stopped short. His eyes came up for a second to the impassive, shadowed face, still concealed behind sunglasses. "I see you are aware. Do you know their capabilities?" Khalil nodded. "Then I won't waste your time." Intelligent. He should be out in the field, not rotting here in Cairo, but then if he were, he would be working for the Mossad.

Khalil made a last-minute decision not to kill the German. The man had seen him. He was also in jeopardy, and might be arrested at any time. But if Khalil killed him now, the American girl would be questioned. If he killed both of them, there were still two policemen who had seen him at the hotel, who might put two and two together. It was a close decision. In the end, it was the man's competence that saved him. He might be useful again, someday.

The German already had a second briefcase, identical to the one that carried the radio. All the same, it did no harm to have another, the one that Khalil had brought along just in case. He lifted it and fingered it, guessing that Khalil had wiped it clean. A professional. They shook hands briefly, and Khalil left.

As he drove back through the streets of Cairo, Khalil laughed aloud in the open car. He looked at some people in the streets, pitied them their miserable lives, and laughed again, thinking of the briefcase in the trunk. He was ecstatic. Pride welled up in him as he thought of how he had triumphed against difficult odds, and he was transported on a wave of happiness.

He was a man who was moving toward his destiny.

It was close to dawn the next morning when Mahrous finally got home. He had been working late a lot these days, as he had done during his marriage, when he was new in the job and still hoping to make something of it. He remembered the trouble this had caused at home with his wife and child. He had always told himself that he would make it up to them someday, but now that would never happen. Why was this so much on his mind these days? During the biggest, and, as it was turning out, the most frustrating investigation of his life? He kept thinking of Julia Sa'id and her baby.

Touhami had been unbearable today. Sarcastic, critical, and obstructive. One out of the scores of reports that Mahrous had read that day had excited him immediately. An American girl, visiting a suspected Jewish operative in Cairo, had in turn been visited, and very thoroughly seduced in her hotel room, by a man who had seemed to be previously unknown to her. The man, according to a verbal report—which Mahrous obtained only by hunting down the policemen on duty and digging it out of them—answered the general description of the killer whose trail was getting colder every day. There was something about this that fitted in Mahrous's mind. Nothing he could put his finger on, but he had taken action immediately—or tried to. Unfortunately, such action had to be cleared through Touhami, who had summoned Mahrous, and the junior man had seen right away that he had problems.

Touhami was seated at the desk that he worked at keeping clear, to show that he was on top of his job. He had in front of him requests, signed by Mahrous, that two foreigners be arrested and pulled in for simultaneous questioning. His manner was close to being insulting.

"I expected more of you," he said. "I suppose you know that that tape has been listened to by every analyst and computer operator in the department. If you bring that girl in for questioning, there will probably be a crowd at the gates waiting to see her. You may not find this embarrassing, but I do. And why do you want to question her? Are you also curious?"

Mahrous told himself to take it calmly. "There's something about it, sir. A hawk like this ready to pounce on the girl the moment she arrives. If you heard the tape, you know that his American accent is convincing—it convinced the girl. Yet I have no record of such a foreigner in Cairo."

"Who says that he's a foreigner? From what I see here, he speaks colloquial Arabic."

"Precisely. I just think it's all a bit unusual. And you see the description."

Touhami took a long, patient breath. "I see the description. It's a description that fits every second gigolo in Cairo. But you think it's unusual. You think perhaps the girl is an international spy?"

"Not the girl," Mahrous said patiently. "The man who met her at the airport. He is under loose surveillance that I ordered recently. Admittedly, I ordered the same kind of surveillance on a lot of other people. This 'gigolo' as you call him might have noticed that. Maybe it's Schmidt that he wants to contact. I think we should pull them in."

"I disagree." Touhami's chin rose. "Our mandate is to keep an eye on foreigners, not harass them." Mahrous threw up his eyes. Touhami saw the gesture and was angered. "If the police arrest this girl, they will be obliged to charge her with smoking marijuana. Is that what you want, Lieutenant Colonel? For the sake of your light entertainment?"

Mahrous rubbed his brow for several seconds before saying, "There is a killer out there. I happen to believe that this girl's life could be in danger. I want it put on record that I requested these arrests." He rose and walked out of his chief's office, knowing that this could be the end of his career.

The day had not improved with time. Fretting that he couldn't be in two places at once, Mahrous had chosen to follow the girl, keeping what contact he could with those watching Schmidt. They had reported nothing unusual in the vicinity of the apartment building. Then the German and the girl had met for a late supper. After that, when they returned to the German's apartment their conversation was quite innocent. More discouraging still, Mahrous had sensed a lightness in the German's manner that left him feeling thoroughly depressed. He was either wrong, or he was too late. He had left the stakeout when they started making love.

There was one last thing that made the day about the worst in recent memory. Deciding not to try to make it to his desk before noon, he opened a bottle of Scotch that had been in the house for years. Sitting at a small table in the kitchen, he drank the fiery liquor, hoping to drug his mind and catch a few hours sleep. He switched on the radio for morning news.

The report had been going on for some minutes before it registered. Something about a freak tornado that had struck a small town in the United States the day before. Many of those killed were at a school ceremony in the town hall. The children were singing, and their parents and teachers hadn't heard the rising wind outside—except for one woman, who went to the door, looked out, and saw a terrifying black cloud. They had a tape of her voice, speaking of her anger and her guilt. Her anger was at God, she said, for letting it happen. Her guilt was because she had rushed inside and told the people to stay where they were, for it had seemed the safest place—only to have that building picked out by the tornado, killing dozens of children and adults. "The children were singing,"

she said. "They didn't hear the storm." Gripped with
a susceptibility that took him completely by surprise,
Mahrous clenched his fist, struck the table, and continued smashing down until the piece of furniture was
at his feet.

At that moment, he felt that there was one thing left
for him in life, just one. He wanted to catch the killer
of Abdel Sa'id.

Chapter 7

JOHN BALDWIN was impressed by the smoothness of it
all. When he arrived in Switzerland, he made a call from
the airport to a number that Khalil had given him. Then
he went directly to his hotel, which overlooked the lake.
He checked in, freshened up, and had just settled on the
terrace, having his first martini before dinner, when he
was joined by a man who introduced himself as Laszlo,
a friend of Ibrahim Khalil's. Baldwin concealed his surprise. They had evidently checked on him already, and
ascertained that he was not being followed, all without
Baldwin being aware of their existence. Smooth. No
fuss, no nerves. They were getting good these days—
or he was getting old. Whoever Khalil was tied up with,
they were professionals.

Laszlo was a middle-aged man of medium height,
wearing a gray suit and spectacles. He brought a well-
used passport made out to Khalil, already stamped for

entry into Egypt a few days ago. The ticket stubs and boarding passes were in the passport, as though they had been carried that way and left there—a nice touch, Baldwin thought—and Laszlo added that there was a complete official record of Khalil's supposed journey. Baldwin had no idea how all this had been managed. Laszlo then confirmed that he represented certain people who had contacted Baldwin even before Khalil had done so in Cairo. Khalil was the man for whom certain preparations were being made, and Laszlo emphasized that his identity must never be divulged to anyone. Baldwin was impressed anew. It was clear that whatever was brewing here, it was brewing in high circles. There was one small detail that he noticed. Laszlo was not Hungarian, as his name implied. He was a Russian. Baldwin detected the small difference in accent, though they spoke in English.

Laszlo then took another package from his pocket, this one sealed. It contained information, he said, regarding a radio link that had been set up and was waiting for contact from Khalil. He did not hand over this package. It would be delivered to Baldwin last thing in the morning just before he caught his plane. Laszlo then had only one more question. He asked Baldwin how sure he was of not being searched when he returned to Cairo. Baldwin repeated what he had told Khalil, that he was well known at the airport and that his briefcase had not been searched for years. It was the kind of risk that one could take—and it was his risk too, he pointed out, since he was the highest point if lightning struck. Laszlo smiled, not at the truth of this but at Baldwin's eagerness. Baldwin learned a little lesson in containment. It was true that he was eager to work for these men, because he could see that they were playing for high stakes, but he should keep his cards a little closer to his chest.

After that, Laszlo shook hands, promised that the package would be delivered in the morning, and left Baldwin to enjoy his dinner.

Sitting on the terrace, in the pleasantly cool evening, Baldwin wondered who was behind Khalil. It was easy to guess, but he was slow to jump to conclusions, for these were subtle men. One could guess nothing from morality or methods. Baldwin had been with M15 long enough to have no delusions about that. Even purpose was a hard thing to judge by where the Middle East was concerned. The major powers had common ground in the Middle East. They wanted stability, they wanted an end to the war of attrition between Israel and Egypt, and above all each wanted to preserve its foothold in Egypt and Israel respectively. For a decade now, Egypt had been under the control of Russia. It was dependent on Russia economically, for protection of its airspace against Israel, and the Kremlin had become Cairo's spokesman in international affairs. But even that relationship was under strain. Nasser was finding out what it meant to have no ally but Russia.

In the early fifties, Baldwin had been involved with an American intelligence tool known as "the Game." This had consisted of an ongoing war game played in Washington, D.C., in which the numerous players—intelligence experts, military men, politicians, university professors, businessmen, and others—were assigned the roles of national leaders around the world, supplied with culled intelligence reports containing information considered available to their respective roles, as determined by an army of analysts, and then brought together in interacting groups with a view to gaining insight and predicting key decisions. Imaginative though it was, for a product of bureaucracy, "the Game" had success in a lot of cases. Baldwin himself, included as an expert in Egyptian affairs and playing the part of President Nasser, had nationalized the Suez Canal several months before Nasser actually did so. Seeing that this went by without major reprisal in the war game, Baldwin had then, in real life, committed his first act of serious espionage. He had conveyed the information to a member of the Revolutionary Command Council, who was Nasser's representative in the United States at the time, that the canal could probably be nationalized without catastrophic result.

Since then, sometimes with Baldwin's continued help as a secret adviser whose stock was growing in Egyptian circles, the new player on the board—Nasser—had scored many points in the real "Game of Nations." This was a term invented by Zakariah Mohieddin, when he was vice president of Egypt. In a lecture given to the Egyptian War College, which Baldwin had attended, Mohieddin had defined this game, and described it as differing from other games in several important ways. First, each player in the game had his own aims, different from those of the other players, which constituted "winning" in his eyes. Second, every player was forced by his own domestic circumstances to make moves in the game that had nothing to do with winning, and that might, indeed, impair his chances of winning. Third, in the Game of Nations there were no real winners, only losers. Losing, of course, was to be avoided. But of even greater importance was the common aim of every player to keep the game going. When the game ended, or became hopeless for some players, the result was what most players sought to avoid, war.

This was what had happened in 1967. Things had broken down, there had been war in the Middle East,

but the war had not served its usual purpose of elimi-
nating players. The "loser" was still there, Abdel Gamal
Nasser, even stronger than before—or was he? Baldwin
didn't know if "the Game" still went on in Washington,
D.C. But he knew that there was one factor that did
not distinguish the players, and that was morality. In
his day, they had always taken account of the public moralities of different governments and political
leaders. They had also taken account of their private
moralities, which were, of course, entirely different.
But there were no "good guys," or "bad guys": no Good,
no Bad. There were only good moves, bad moves, and
sometimes . . . necessary moves.

Baldwin was convinced that what he had just seen,
and was now involved in, was the beginning of a tense
new combination of moves in the real-life Game of
Nations.

Chapter 8

AFTER DISMISSING her last class of the day, Mary Miles-
Tudor went to the open window for a breath of air. The
hardwood floors of the classroom were littered with the
shells of roasted pumpkin seeds, which her students
liked to eat by the handful, spitting the shells out one
by one. It wasn't having to walk on these, like a sea
of cockroaches, that bothered her. It was the smell

of them in the hot air. She had thought of outlawing eating or drinking in the classroom, but she was new, an outsider, and it seemed to be a bit of a tradition.

It was one of those days when she wondered if she was doing the right thing, seeing a bit of the world before settling into a profession. Teaching quadratic equations to young students didn't seem to be her forte, though she liked the children. Her colleagues were pleasant enough. A bit blah—like herself, she suspected—but she didn't see much scope for social contact. There was one other Brit: a cheerful Scotsman with the British Council—married, loads of kids—quite good company, but totally dedicated to getting her into bed. Apart from that, not much that she could see in school circles.

During the ride back to central Cairo, on one of the ramshackle buses that plied the route, Mary wondered about Yvette Montagne. In particular, she wondered what it was that she found in common with the woman, that made her anticipate her phone calls as the highlight of the day. Yvette was a Cairene, sophisticated and dangerous. Mary was from Wiltshire, raised among horses and green fields. Yvette scorned education, but seemed to know everything. Mary was highly educated, but naive. Yet when they swapped stories, they both laughed like blazes. Mary had never had a serious conversation with Yvette. Nor had she ever been bored in her company. There were other differences between them. Yvette was gay, or at least bisexual, and Mary, so far as she knew, was straight.

Mary's apartment in Midan el Tahrir was direct-ly opposite the Nile Hilton. The rent that she paid was higher than the monthly salary of her Egyptian colleagues at the school, but that was how it went in Cairo. They knew what it cost foreigners to live. It was the unexpected things that were amazingly cheap. Mary had a servant who came each day, who kept the place straight and did some cooking. All that for a few pounds per week. Mary didn't mind if the woman gave tea parties, grand-hosting it to other servants in the building. The apartment had tall windows. The sun poured in on wooden floors, with alcoves and archways, and the furniture was adequate. Compared with what she'd been able to afford in Paris, it was a palace. As she stood in the shower, Mary thought that life was not so bad in Cairo: not on a Thursday night, the day before Sabbath, when you were invited out to dinner.

When she arrived at Yvette's house, Mary was wearing a gray skirt and a white blouse, her blond hair up. She paid the taxi driver, who could not stop staring at her feet, encased in a pair of red high-heeled shoes. A servant opened the gate for her.

Mary was prepared for elegance, and even luxury in Yvette's home, but not for the sheer opulence. Once inside the outer walls, she gazed at the rooms and galleries around the courtyard, and the exotic trees and the cool waters of the fountain. A servant in a galabiya came out and spoke to her with great politeness. In broken English, he told her that Miss Yvette was in her bath. Miss Mary could wait in the garden, or in the living room, or proceed to the bar. She could have a refreshment if she wished, but Mr. Ibrahim, who was visiting at the present time, preferred that alcohol be served only in the bar. The servant told this with a certain stiffness. Seeing the entrance to a splendid main room, Mary asked if she could wait there.

Beautiful silverware and objets d'art, figurines, coffee cups on delicate filigree saucers—there was antique beauty everywhere. A marble staircase seemed to rise into the air, which was fresh and cool from the waters of a fountain. After prowling for a while, she crossed a hallway to another room, where she saw a grand piano behind a stretch of Persian rug. There was music on the stand. It was the solo piece from Beethoven's First Piano Concerto. Mary smiled and wondered if she dared. She hit a few notes standing up, loved the tone, and sat down.

As she played the haunting little melody, which was one of her favorites, Mary felt almost intoxicated. The beauty of the sound, and the other man-made things around her, induced a mixture of euphoria and excitement. She played the piece through, then picked it up again, timing the revival of the first solitary notes to start just as the climax died away. Totally engrossed, she played the piece again and was about to quit when she was startled by the appearance of another hand on the keyboard. It was a strong hand, matted with black hair. As the last chords died away, it came from behind her, went to the high notes, and once again the beginning of the piece was brought to life. Startled though she was, Mary smiled and followed. She tried to twist her head around to see the man who stood behind her, but couldn't manage this as well as play. The music rose to a crescendo. She gave it everything she had, laughing excitedly, and was about to spin around and meet her unexpected partner at the end . . . when the persistent little melody began again. This time, she almost didn't follow. She was exhausted. But the plaintive notes had a demanding ring—he was a true pianist—and her fingers took them up again before she knew it. This time it was riveting. Her breath came faster as the music filled the room, and her mind flew off on a strange tangent. The memory that came was of finishing the mile race at school. Back on the track, alone in the world, running all out, with a sensation like a vacuum on fire inside her, but bursting with triumph, she drove on to the elusive tape. It was a memory that had come to her more than once during orgasm.

As she had routinely done after running the mile, she all but collapsed when the music finished. There was certainly a moment of faintness as the last chords died away. Then she turned and saw him. He had thrown himself into an armchair by then. Dark and strong, he looked at her with a feral grin.

"We must put that to music sometime," he said.

Yvette was standing in the doorway. She wore a flowing dress of light silk that did nothing to conceal her striking body. Her black eyes were as cool as marble.

"It's so nice to hear music in the house again." She came into the room, her eyes on Mary. "Especially such clean, celestial music—like the lovemaking of the gods, don't you think?" She smiled at her brother. "How are you, Ibrahim? On your way out, I trust?"

He laughed. "Don't worry. I've got things to do."

"Elsewhere?"

"Lighten up, sister. I wouldn't spoil your fun." He rose smoothly and turned to Mary. "Miss Miles-Tudor, I am Ibrahim Khalil. I am the black sheep of the family, who shows up occasionally. Yvette is our skeleton in the cupboard."

"It's a very beautiful cupboard," Mary said.

He glanced at her. Then, seeing the direction of her gaze, he realized that she was speaking of the house, and laughed. "That's cute," he said. "And you play the piano very well."

"I wish you wouldn't talk like an American," Yvette said, frowning.

"So do you," Mary said, still looking at Ibrahim.

"Perhaps we'll meet again sometime."

"I hope so," she said.

Yvette took Mary by the arm. "Let's go and have a drink. Ibrahim doesn't, by the way. I hope you like lamb," she said as she steered Mary to the door.

"Oh, I love it."

Left alone, Khalil laughed softly. But his eyes were thoughtful as he watched their retreating backs.

Khalil went upstairs to his room. He sat at the open window, facing east, and lit a cigarette. The English girl was certainly beautiful. Her waist was so narrow you could easily put your hands around it. Undressing her mentally, he imagined the long legs and concave belly, and found himself priapic. He might have to take the time to get to know this girl.

Spread out on a table in the room, which was a room that he kept locked, was the radio and other equipment. Included were two tape recorders, one of adjustable speed, that could be hooked into the transmitter unit. Using equipment that was mostly already in the house, Khalil had built himself what was basically a primitive telemetry unit, of the type used on satellites and other remote sensing apparatus. Using two frequencies, he could digitize a coded message, compress it, and store it for transmission. When it came to operation, he would first transmit a brief signal for identification purposes, which would alert operators at the other end, then mount the tape and transmit the body of the message in a burst that would last for only a few seconds. Computer equipment at the other end would unpack the message, decode it, and print it in readable form within microseconds. Incoming signals were no problem. If the Cairo-based tracking stations tried to locate them, they would come up with essentially parallel lines. The stations were too close together to pinpoint the distant city. Khalil was expert at the rapid use of abbreviated

Morse. All the same he would not use the equipment manually for more than a few words at a time. Trained in electronics, he knew the strengths and shortcomings of the tracking system installed in Cairo, and the details of the Russian-made equipment.

Khalil was satisfied with the radio. Even with the modules he'd added, it could still be packed into the briefcase. He turned his attention to the package he'd received from Baldwin.

The passport was in order. It was genuine, as it had to be for the operation he was now seriously planning, identifying him as an Egyptian national under his own identity. His occupation was given as that of businessman, associated with an import-export company in Greece. He had used this cover for years, in Europe and the Middle East. In the early sixties, when German scientists were trying to build rockets for Egypt in the Sahara Desert, it was a suggestion of Khalil's that Israel should use German nationals to spy for them, and he had helped train some of these men. This was in spite of the fact that one of his goals in life was to see the eventual destruction of Israel. The liberation of Egypt came first.

The package contained instructions on what transmission frequencies to use at prearranged times of day. There were also frequencies that would be monitored around the clock for emergency messages. Khalil was pleased to see that he had been given all the facilities he'd asked for. There were twenty sheets of code. These were one-time pads, each specifying a random association between letters of the alphabet and binary numbers, the association changing randomly as the letters were used. There was no way to decipher such codes, which were numbered for use in successive transmissions, to be rotated if he needed more than twenty. Khalil studied them, approving the design. He did not attempt to commit the densely packed numbers on each sheet to memory—not yet. The time might come for that. He could not wait to transmit. He was anxious to hear the reaction to the plan he had in mind, but which he could not begin to carry out unaided. There would be reservations. He had no doubt of that. It was going to be a tense and difficult operation.

He was brooding in this way when he heard the distant call to prayers from the mosque in old town. Rising immediately, he faced the open window, knelt on a prayer mat, and touched his face to the floor. Khalil was a devout Moslem. But he was neither a fanatic, nor an enemy of the related religions of Christianity and Judaism. The Book of Moses predicted two prophets. Christ, who had entered Jerusalem on an ass, to fulfill the prophecy of John the Baptist, and Mohammed, who had entered on a camel. The Koran, in Khalil's eyes, was a continuation of the Bible and the Jewish Torah, revealed to Mohammed through the archangel Gabriel. Khalil had a scar on his head from attending a ceremony in Lebanon to mourn the murders of Hassan and Hussein, the sons of Ali, Mohammed's son-in-law, whom the fanatical Shiah contended to be the true successor to Mohammed. With all the others in the crowd, he had allowed his head to be cracked open, on a small shaven patch on top, and had wailed and spent the day tapping on his wound, to maintain the flow of blood during that emotional ceremony. He remembered the stench of human gore, and had wept at the sight of men and children dropping from the loss of blood. But Khalil was not a Shiite, any more than he abhorred the Shiites. He was an Egyptian, and a Sunni Moslem. In the course of his career, he had used others to further his objectives. More precisely, he had used

political enemies of Egypt to attack an even greater
enemy at home. He was at peace with this, and could
proudly say that his own gain, even his own life, was
never a consideration. He believed that Mohammed
was the true prophet of the one great God, and that
those who followed him sincerely, giving their lives if
necessary, would be rewarded in the Moslem paradise.
He was not afraid to die. And he had killed. Not only
men of Satan, but others, sometimes, to preserve his
functionality. They would understand. They were now
in paradise before him, and when they met again, they
would shake his hand and thank him.

It was close to midnight when Khalil finally roused
himself in the darkened room. Realizing that he must
have dozed for a while, he packed away his equipment
and stepped out onto the gallery that ran around the
courtyard. Yvette's room was softly lit, the curtains
open. He could see that they were not there—was it
all over already? He lit a cigarette and strolled around
the connecting balconies. He walked past the room his
mother used when she was in Cairo, and the room that
had been his father's, the black curtains permanently
closed. Smiling with curiosity, he reached a point that
overlooked the dining area.

They were still downstairs, at a low table, with the
debris of the meal between them. Yvette looked groggy.
She was the one who had been smoking hashish. Mary,
he could tell, had stuck to wine. Yvette's robe was
around her thighs. Her magnificent legs were on display—no underwear, probably. Mary sat on a leather
pouf. Her golden knees stuck up, calves tapering to
firm ankles, still wearing her red shoes. Her hair was
down and a glass of wine was in her hand, as she
spoke and gestured with some animation, but she was

in control. Khalil grinned wickedly in the darkness. It looked as though Yvette had met her match at last. While he watched, his sister fell back on the couch, laughing throatily, her knees in the air. He'd been right. No underwear.

Back in his room, he was disinclined to sleep. He opened again the painted chest that had kept his secrets since childhood, now with a modern combination lock on it, took out a numbered pad, and began to plan his first transmission.

Chapter 9

DR. GIRGIS Green, in spite of his last name, was a full-blooded Egyptian, though he didn't look it. He had light brown hair, a head of an unusual shape, and freckles. The head-shaping might have occurred at birth. The result was an appearance that is often associated with mental deformity, though this, too, was a false impression. Green was smart. Not only at what he did—he was a scientist—he was well read and articulate beyond the province of most technical men. The truth was that he had studied psychology before switching to computer science while serving with the Egyptian air force, but he seldom advertised that fact. He was also more of a mathematician than most computer scientists—which wasn't saying much, as he often remarked in the company of colleagues. Green wasn't quite the material to be a top researcher in a university, and he knew it. It was one of his idiosyncracies that he accepted certain limitations, and was happy in what he did. He could certainly have gone to the top in industry, had things been different. The combination of technical skill and verbal competence would finally have risen above the defensive elements that are often found—had it not been for his abrasive personality. This was something Green did not admit. He reckoned it was the fact that he had been born a Christian that made people refuse to get along with him. That and the fact that a majority of them, very justifiably, he thought, felt threatened by anyone above the intelligence level of a primate. For whatever reason, Green worked for Military Intelligence. His specialty was putting together computer systems for distributing and analyzing data. An oddly built man, in his early thirties but looking older, he was one of the technical czars in the day of the computer, and didn't care who knew it. For all this, he was a basically contented man. He had a good wit, a lively sense of humor, and enjoyed every day of his life.

One thing that Green did not enjoy was meetings with the brass. Meetings where the brigadiers and colonels would occupy the head of the table, and exercise their divine right to pontificate, whether they knew anything or not. Green did not object to rubbing shoulders with senior men. It was just that sometimes he felt ready to explode while they droned on among themselves, confidently speaking up and interrupting, often missing the point completely. This was the kind of thing he had expected when summoned on a sunny morning to attend a technical "briefing and discussion" on the subject of the tracking systems. Lieutenant Colonel Mohammed Mahrous? Green had never heard of him. My God, it's the one-armed bandit, he thought, seeing the big mustache and large, dark eyes, when he walked in.

The Lieutenant Colonel started by asking for a rundown on how the tracking systems worked. This didn't surprise Green. They often started off this way, before butting in to show the five cents of knowledge they'd picked up from reading a couple of reports. But this one listened. When he had a question, he would raise one finger, wait politely, and after a time, it came home to Green that the questions weren't stupid.

Green explained the workings of a directional antenna. Turning constantly, about once every fifteen seconds, it would sweep the frequency bands likely to be used for long-range transmission until it locked onto something "interesting." This was done automatically, using software Green had written. He was not asked for details of that, or of the manual control that could override it. The system then recorded the precise angle at which the signal strength was maximal. This occurred when the antenna was pointing directly at the source. At the same time, other antennae would lock in, record the message being transmitted, and alert operators with a beeping message on a screen. All this took place at three tracking stations in the Cairo area. At one of these, the master station, a highly trained operator was always on duty, ready to alert the others when a suspicious transmission was detected, telling them to concentrate on that frequency. If two out of the three stations were on the money, the direction lines would intersect at one place, the source of the transmission. Green gave details of range and accuracy, while Mahrous stroked his jaw, thinking as he listened.

"Thank you, Dr. Green, that was very clear." Green smiled thinly. The little pat on the head from Big Brother. "But I'm wondering about this manual control. Isn't there a quicker way to coordinate these stations, when something really interesting comes up?"

Green shrugged. "There's nothing much quicker than the speed of light, Lieutenant Colonel."

"But a man has to tap things on a keyboard," Mahrous persisted. He raised his hand. Green noticed the uncommon width of that right shoulder, compared to the other, the one with the empty sleeve beneath it. "Let me emphasize that this is not my field, so you'll forgive me if I say something stupid. But couldn't a signal be sent automatically, from computer to computer? I know that you rely on a man's judgment in critical cases. But couldn't programs be written to do a lot of this and coordinate the stations automatically? I don't know if I'm expressing this too well," he said. "Do you get what I mean?"

Green thought for a moment, his head tilted. "I do," he said. "And it might even be practical—if there were a need for it."

"You talk about slave stations," Mahrous went on. "Is there any reason why one has to be the master? Couldn't any of the three be allowed to take the initiative and to do it automatically?"

Green glanced up with respect. The man had a grasp of what was feasible. "I suppose they could. I think all this could be done—but to what purpose?" he repeated. "As it is, we can guarantee a fix on a continuous signal within fifteen seconds of it first being noticed. Is there a reason to improve on that?"

Mahrous nodded. "I'm afraid there is, Doctor. Two reasons. One, there's a chap out there sending short signals. Two, they're not continuous. He knows how we operate."

Green stared in astonishment. "You mean, someone's getting out?"

"Someone's getting out," Mahrous confirmed. "We can't read his messages, and we can't locate him. There's a lot of argument about who he is, or might be. I personally think he might be connected with another investigation, of which I happen to be in charge. Others don't agree with this, but we all want to find out who he is and what he's sending out. Now you understand our concern." Green did. This sort of thing hadn't happened for years.

"Here's how he works," Mahrous went on. "First there is a brief transmission, which we're sure is an identification signal. That tells the other end to sit up and take notice. We have never tracked it. Even if one of the directional antennae goes through a peak, that just gives us a line, unless one of the others happens to be lined up, and we haven't been that lucky. Then he's off the air long enough for the systems to start sweeping frequencies again. Then he comes back with another extremely short burst of totally indecipherable data. We believe that is the body of the message, compressed in some way. We've never tracked it. From the stray lines we've got, we can tell that he's moving around Cairo. The lines intersect in different places, but none of them is meaningful. What we need is the ability to lock on fast with a coordinated system—and now I have another question. Instead of turning randomly, can we have these antennae turning in phase? That way, if we got lucky, we would have a fix."

By the end of the history-making meeting, Dr. Girgis Green had learned a couple of things. One, there was a bureaucrat who knew what he wanted and could ask the right questions. And two, there was a spy out there who was causing high-level panic. Involved in another project at the time, Green had not been informed of these extremely worrying transmissions. This might also

be a measure of the secrecy attached to them. When he
left the meeting, he had been assigned full time to the
project of coordinating and sharpening the tracking
system. The only time that Mahrous had cut him off
was when Green wanted to explain that the only reason
these improvements had never been considered before
was because there had been no reason to consider them.
Mahrous wasn't interested in that, or who took blame
or credit. He just wanted it done now, and he wanted
it badly.

There was something else that Dr. Green had learned.
He mulled it over as he walked away through the midday sun. Whoever was out there, transmitting messages
from Cairo, had an implacable enemy in Lieutenant
Colonel Mahrous.

Chapter 10

KHALIL LEFT the house at seven P.M. Driving Yvette's
car, he headed north to Midan el Tahrir, exited on
Kasr el Nil, drove for about a mile, and then took a
side street. The Mentakis restaurant had a terrace with
some outside tables. These were about half-filled with
people having drinks in the early dusk. He drove past
slowly. A couple of people glanced up at the white sports
car, but none that he recognized. He had the top up, so
no one could see much of his face, peering out through
the plastic window. He drove around the block, saw

nothing that disturbed him, and finally pulled into the parking lot of a nearby apartment building. He locked the car and walked back to the restaurant.

After sitting on the terrace for a while, with a glass of Scotch that he hardly touched, Khalil rose and went to the men's room. Then he left the restaurant, leaving his unfinished drink on the table, and walked back to the parking lot. Making sure that he was not observed, he took the briefcase from the trunk of the car and walked back by another route. Wearing a dark shirt and slacks, he came to the block that contained the restaurant, but did not turn into it. Instead, he entered an apartment building on the corner.

It was a typical older building. In daytime, there was usually a doorman who sat outside, bare feet sticking out of his galabiya, soaking up the sun. But at night, as Khalil knew from observation, this person was seldom at his post, and there was little coming and going in the run-down building. There was an elevator that clanked up and down, as slowly as any in Cairo. Khalil took this, and was lucky enough to reach the top floor unobserved.

At this point, he had to take a small risk. Of the three apartments on the top level, one was rented by a waiter who worked in the Mentakis restaurant. The others were rented by a taxi driver, and a couple of girls who worked in Maxim's Club. These occupants should all be working at this time. The waiter certainly was, because Khalil had seen him downstairs. But who could tell what other male or female layabouts might be in one of the apartments? Khalil put his ear to the waiter's door, hearing nothing. Then he tapped gently, not wishing to rouse anyone who might be next door, in the thin-walled building. To his surprise, there was a muffled sound inside. Khalil's lips moved as he cursed

silently. He had planned this carefully, and hated to
have his plans upset. But no one came to the door.
He listened again, eyes narrowed, and tapped a second
time. Again a quiet grunt and a snuffle from within,
nothing more. He took his decision and fitted a key.
After a few tries, he found one to which the door yielded.
He did not hesitate. Face impassive, ready to kill if
necessary, he opened the door and stepped in. The
German shepherd pup blinked at him uncertainly.

Khalil had not expected this. The dog was not a
common pet in Egypt. But the waiter, being Greek, had
apparently acquired one. The place stank of excrement.
There was a newspaper on the floor, which the pup had
pretty well ignored. Stepping with distaste among the
litter, Khalil cleared a space on a table by the window.
Wearing plastic gloves, he removed the remains of several meals and dumped them unceremoniously in the
sink. The window overlooked the restaurant. Careful
not to be observed, he opened the window a crack and
set up his aerial. The pup came forward, wagging its
tail, but retreated when he hissed at it warningly.

With the tension that he always felt when doing this,
he tapped out the identification signal. This was not
strictly necessary. They should be set up to receive
him around the clock. But it would alert the operator.
Khalil lit a cigarette and smoked nervously. He knew
that his transmissions had been noted and were causing
high-level concern. The radio responded to a distant
signal, and he knew he'd been received. All he had
to do then was press a button on the small cassette,
which whirred for a few seconds as his message was
transmitted.

While he waited, he looked down at the restaurant.
He saw the waiter whose apartment he was borrowing
serve a meal of fish to some people at an outside table.

The little dog whinnied. Khalil spoke sharply beneath his breath, and it ran to another room.

Khalil's message was received in the communications room of a house in Damascus that belonged to a foreign embassy. After pressing a buzzer to alert the occupant of a nearby office, the operator did his routine work, seeing nothing of the text that came out on a line printer in the next room. The man who came quickly in response to the buzzer was a senior official in the same organization as the operator. A heavy-wristed man, with hands still scarred from manual work that had been done in his yard at home, in his own country, he looked as though he might still live and earn his bread on the farm on which he had been raised in Eastern Europe. In fact he had graduated first in his class with a degree in philosophy and politics from Moscow University, and was the author of a series of papers that had become pivotal in determining Soviet policy in the Middle East. After glancing at the text of the incoming message, he spoke to the operator, telling him to signal the Cairo operative to stand by for a reply. The pulses beat a little faster in his oxlike body as he reread the message, feeling the pressure of the words.

FURTHER CONTACT NERO NOT ENCOURAGING   INVES-TIGATION SHOWS THAT SERVING STAFF AND GROUND STAFF ARE CLOSELY SCREENED   SECURITY STAFF EVEN MORE SO   TIME IS PASSING AND I SEE NO ALTERNATIVE TO THE PLAN I HAVE PROPOSED   QUESTION   WHAT IS THE STATUS OF THIS   QUESTION   CAN THE PRESENCE OF NECESSARY PEOPLE BE ARRANGED   QUESTION   CAN I COUNT ON FULL SUPPORT UNDER THE CONDITIONS OF OMEGA   ONE LAST THING   THE HUNT FOR ME IN THIS LOCALE IS UNUSUALLY COORDINATED AND INTENSIVE COULD IT BE THAT SOMEONE HAS CONNECTED THESE

TRANSMISSIONS WITH OTHER ACTIVITIES AND PERHAPS
EVEN GUESSED AT THE UNIFIED OBJECTIVE IF SO CAN
THIS BE NEUTRALIZED OVER

The man in Damascus pressed thick fingers to his
forehead. He knew that every second he delayed added
to the risk for the Cairo operative. But the man had
a way of packing thoughts and questions into his con-
densed transmissions, and was pressing hard for things
that were difficult to guarantee. He turned to a terminal
and typed rapidly.

THE PLAN YOU FAVOR IS UNDER SERIOUS CONSIDERA-
TION RISK FACTORS ARE HIGH BUT WE DON'T HAVE AN
ALTERNATIVE AS YET THOUGH ONE IS BEING SOUGHT
PROBLEM NECESSARY PEOPLE OUT OF EGYPT AT THE
MOMENT RETURN SCHEDULE UNKNOWN BUT IN THE
INTERESTS OF BEING PREPARED SHOULD OMEGA BE
APPROVED I AM AUTHORIZED TO SAY THAT WE SHALL
ATTEMPT TO PROVIDE YOU WITH A CONTACT IN AN
APPROPRIATE GOVERNMENT AGENCY DETAILS OF THIS
AND YOUR LAST POINT WILL BE ADDRESSED IN THE NEXT
TRANSMISSION COURAGE COMRADE OVER

This text was written to a secure file that would be
used as input to a program that would code the message
for transmission. The computer code for this program
had been written by a technical specialist, and was on
a top security disk to which only the senior official had
access. Within microseconds, the coded message was on
a screen in front of the operator, who began to transmit
manually in rapid Morse. The senior official then waited
tensely. The Cairo operative would have to decode the
message by hand before he could reply.

In a paper written fourteen years ago, in 1956, Andrei
Varsanyi had predicted three things that were not obvious to all observers at the time. He had predicted 1)

that Soviet-style communism would be economically disastrous for Egypt, 2) that Russian influence would be sought and then sloughed off as had British and American influence before it, and 3) that the cycle would turn back to the United States unless the present leadership in Egypt were changed. The latter point had been elaborated to the effect that a change of leadership in Egypt might be very difficult once the incumbent regime had set up a repressive base at home. These views had not been popular with Eastern bloc leaders at the time, who were already committed to certain lines of action. Varsanyi accordingly was directed to other things, and his career had been in limbo for a while. As time went on, the official position had not changed visibly, but President Nasser of Egypt had changed. Especially after the humiliation of 1967, and the mind-blowing response of his people that had followed, Nasser had become precisely the kind of manic-depressive demagogue that Varsanyi had predicted, a fact that Varsanyi had noted with private satisfaction. Then, when he least expected it, Varsanyi had found himself summoned by none other than the Director General of the organization for which he worked. He had been asked for advice, for his solution to a problem that was now admitted to exist, and was then assigned to an operation that was a bit mind-blowing to Varsanyi himself. In support of a group that Varsanyi would never have guessed he might be asked to work with, but which undeniably was extremely powerful in the Middle East, it had brought him to Syria on what was ostensibly a routine assignment, but which in fact was a covert operation. From being an obscure analyst in his hometown, Varsanyi found himself handling communications that were classified most secret, and reporting to the Director General with no one in between. It was an opportunity to soar to stardom at one stroke.

The Cairo operative's reply was brief. It had to be against the threat of detection for a manual transmission.

ROGER I AWAIT APPROVAL AND THE DETAILS OF A CONTACT OVER AND OUT

After closing up, Varsanyi returned to his office, but did not think of going home. That was how it was on this assignment: his wife would have three lovers by now. Instead, he called a private number in the city and spoke in Arabic to a man with an Egyptian accent. They arranged to meet. Before leaving, he read the communications one more time. "Nero" was John Baldwin. The Cairo operative did not seem too taken with Baldwin. "Omega" was the code name, not so much for the specific plan proposed but for a type of operation. It was a type of operation that was not the first choice of Varsanyi or his superiors. Varsanyi did not know the identity of the Cairo operative. But the man had courage, there was no question of that. "Necessary people" meant President Nasser of Egypt.

The tracking station in old Cairo was the first to pick up the start of Khalil's transmission. Because of the position of its antennae at the time, it picked up a strong signal, from a nearby location, that triggered its electronic brain. In response to new software, the system locked onto that frequency, instructed the other two stations to do the same, and registered the angle where the signal had peaked. Neither of the other stations found a peak during the short, digitized transmission. But using new algorithms designed by Dr. Girgis Green, they specified a point in Cairo and an area of uncertainty, estimating the source of the transmission. This was transmitted, together with an alert to mobilize that went to command posts around the city, and the directional antennae went on turning.

Mahrous was visiting Julia Sa'id when he heard his driver calling frantically from below. He had visited her unannounced, for the girl had no telephone. Her face had lit up spontaneously when he appeared, but this had turned to embarrassment when she saw the gifts he'd brought—the vitamins, the tins of meat, and—greatest prize of all—an American chicken from a Care package. Only the other day there had been a horrifying story about a woman waiting in a long line for an American chicken. After standing all day in the heat outside the government store, she'd seen the last chickens being dispensed before she would reach the counter, and had inadvisedly tried to push forward. She had been strangled and trampled by the crowd.

When he walked into Julia's apartment, Mahrous had noticed the small signs of preparation, for the coming event: the bits and pieces of baby clothing, and the used plastic toys she was collecting. She looked well, though. Clean and groomed, and it was hard to believe that the baby would be dropping any week now. He accepted the offer of a cup of tea and had just sat down when he heard the driver's voice. In his urgency, the man simply bellowed from the street. Mahrous leapt for the door. Julia was left standing in the kitchen, a saucepan in her hand, as his voice came up the staircase saying that he had to go, that he'd explain later.

Khalil wrote down the text of the return message. He tapped out his brief sign-off then immediately packed up, not waiting to decode it. His purpose had not been to start a dialogue tonight. He just wanted them to know that the time had come when he needed decisions and support, and that there was no limit to his own commitment. On his way to the door, he stepped on a piece of excrement and cursed as he skittered to regain his balance.

As he stepped out of the building, planning to take the briefcase to his car before returning to the restaurant, a car pulled up at the far end of the block. It was a black Peugeot, not a taxi, and he stopped instinctively. Almost simultaneously, there was a squeal of brakes, and another car pulled up at the corner where he had been about to emerge. He saw four men in dark suits as the doors began to open.

As a reflex, he turned and ran back through the building. Light-footed and fast, but not thinking yet, he reached the backyard, ducked, and ran, the briefcase under his arm. As often happened in these tenements, the backyards were connected, not divided by walls. He saw the shapes of communal garbage bins and other obstacles in the darkness. It was as well that he had ducked instinctively. Otherwise he might have been decapitated by clothes lines stretched across the yards. He crouched against a wall and took stock.

First, he had to calm down and stop panicking. Then he had to get rid of the briefcase and out into the open. He was anxious not to lose the briefcase. But freedom was the first priority. Cursing the turn of events, he took his bearings. He determined the direction of the parking lot where he had left the car and realized that he was heading that way. Good luck, or good instinct. He began to move more cautiously, eyes trying to penetrate the darkness, ears alert.

It was almost like being in the water at night. Khalil had dived at night in dangerous conditions. Groping underwater, hearing his own heartbeat, he knew the sensation of suddenly sensing something and being struck by a shark, coming in to bump. There was nothing to compare with that, but when something large reared up and struck him in the darkness, for a moment he had images of severed bones and blood. He cried out, and an arm came up defensively before he pivoted, ready to kill. His attacker gave another loud bray, and hooves clattered on the hard ground.

It was a donkey. Someone had tied up a donkey in the backyard. His night vision improving by the moment, Khalil saw a small cart nearby. There were some bits and pieces in the cart, and a pile of hay—the donkey's breakfast, presumably, sadistically left just out of reach while it slept on its feet. Khalil made a quick decision. Seeing no lights come on in nearby windows, he shoved the briefcase under the hay. Then he shoved it farther back into the cart, under a box of some kind.

The parking lot of the modern building where he'd left his car was surrounded by a brick wall, about twelve feet high. After looking in vain for something to climb onto, he leapt up, caught the top, and looked over. A couple were on their way out of the building. He held himself in place, teeth gritted, till they seemed safely distant, getting into their car. Then he slung a foot on top of the wall, and waited again while the young man took his time, as people do when you want them to get moving, kissing the girl and getting his stereo going before pulling out. Khalil dropped lightly on the other side. Moving behind the cars toward the MG, in confirmation of his worst fears, he heard voices in the street outside and saw more cars. The young couple were stopped and told not to drive out. Khalil opened and closed the door of the MG and straightened. My God, they were everywhere! The dark-suited figures were like black snowflakes on the ground.

"All right, who are you?"

Khalil turned, eyebrows raised. "My name is Ibrahim Khalil."

"ID." A meaty hand scraped fingers and thumb impatiently as the policeman looked him up and down.

"I suppose this is official?"

"Don't get smart. This is Internal Security."

Khalil took out his driver's license and other papers. Still without identifying himself, the officer looked at these closely. These men weren't just going through the motions. They were serious.

"You don't live here. What are you doing in this parking lot?"

"Parking." Khalil's smile vanished. "I was planning to eat in the restaurant," he explained quickly. "I just walked back to get my cigarettes."

The policeman scraped his jaw. "Which is your car?"

Khalil opened up the MG. As the policeman searched, he explained that this was his sister's car. He lived abroad most of the time, and was home on vacation—mostly. Maybe he would do a bit of business. He worked for an import-export firm in Greece. The policeman searched carefully. Finding a galabiya in the trunk, he lifted it and passed it through his hands. Khalil took out his cigarettes. It was a thorough search. He was glad that there was nothing in the car to incriminate him.

"What's that you're smoking?"

"Have one."

The policeman took the American cigarette, and passed it under his nose. "Toasted?"

"I developed a taste for them. They're probably more harmful to your health than good old Belmont."

The policeman inhaled deeply. "I should worry about harmful to my health. I should worry about a couple of cigarettes"—he cast his eyes—"in this business."

"I know what you mean." After a moment, Khalil asked quietly, "You said Internal Security?"

"That's right. We're looking for a spy. Some of these bastards play for keeps."

"I'm sure they do," Khalil said sympathetically.

He was allowed to return to the restaurant, but not to leave the vicinity. An area three blocks square was cordoned off. There was a car at every intersection, and plainclothes policemen everywhere. Khalil was staggered. He could not get over the speed with which they'd pounced, flooding the area before he could possibly have left it. He thanked God that he had chosen this night to stay in the vicinity, to have a valid reason for being here, and prayed that they wouldn't find the briefcase.

By the time Mahrous came on the scene, the police had checked everyone who was in the streets. From the timing of the last transmission, he felt sure that the spy was still in the area. Scanning windows, he thought the odds were that the man was up there somewhere, watching what was going on below, becoming desperate maybe. He had warned his men to be extremely careful, to work in twos and threes, and not to relax for a moment.

The intersection of the tracking lines was in the block containing the Mentakis restaurant. After a quick look around, Mahrous pointed to the tall building on the corner. "Let's start with that one," he said. "We'll take it from the top."

All three of the top apartments in the building were empty, except for the one with the dog in it. Mahrous considered it sinful to acquire an animal that needed exercise and then confine it to an apartment, but there wasn't much room in his head for thoughts like that.

The apartment with the dog faced east, the general
direction of the return transmission. He noted the
cleared table, and the half-open window. "This could
be it," he muttered, feeling the excitement. "Get the
owner up here to make sure. This could be it!" He
saw the slide mark on the floor. "Don't walk on that.
Check it for treadmarks. Something tells me he left in
a hurry . . . Don't give the owner a hard time," he
added. "I think his place was borrowed."

So the spy was on the streets. Interesting. Yet he
hadn't been caught. Mahrous thought it through as he
went down in the elevator. There was no way the man
could have left the area. Cling to that, he told himself,
believe that, and you've got the bastard! Work out how
it could have happened.

He walked to the mouth of the close that ran through
the apartment building, saw the police car on the corner, and stopped. Snapping his fingers, he turned and
retraced his steps, past the elevator shaft, to the stretch
of communal ground behind the buildings. Standing
there, he let his eyes become accustomed to the darkness. Seeing a garbage can, he walked quickly to it,
lifted the lid, and was disappointed not to find the
radio. He tried others nearby. No luck. Still . . . he
stared up at the sky. Even if the spy lived nearby,
after almost being caught, he might choose to hide the
radio outside. Otherwise, he might be crouching in a
back court, or indoors, or in a public place, like the
restaurant. Mahrous turned on his heel. In the street
outside, he called his lieutenants together. "We have
him trapped," he said confidently. "All we have to do
is find him. I want you to search everywhere. The
backyards, the apartments, and the public places."
He divided them into teams. "Look in the garbage
bins," he specified. "You're looking for a radio, or

a man. If you flush out a man, we'd like to have him alive. But keep your gun in your hand at all times and don't hesitate to use it if you have to. Work in threes. I want a team of three to knock on every door—every door, bar none!" he emphasized, seeing the expressions on some faces. "I want every room of every apartment searched carefully. Don't bully people. Just be polite— and for God's sake, be careful. Same in the restaurant. Check customers and staff. The streets are vital," he said to the leader of that team. "He cannot leave this area without crossing a street. He's trapped. Now let me give you a couple of tips on how to know him when you find him."

I've got him, he told himself again. This time I've got the bastard!

Khalil had returned to mental stability. The worst was over, he told himself: all he had to do now was keep his head, and hope they didn't find the radio. Not that there was anything in the briefcase to point to him, not even a fingerprint, but he still needed that equipment.

He was staggered by the size of the operation. There had to be a hundred men out there, who had arrived in unison, sealing off an area within minutes. That took planning. That took clear instructions on the move, which was not easy. Back on the terrace of the restaurant, he sipped the alcoholic drink, which was still where he had left it, as his eye scanned the street outside for the leader of the group.

He noticed the one-armed figure as soon as he appeared. Dark hair beneath the peaked cap, stocky build. Sitting in the shadows, he studied the face as the man strode into the center of things, wasting little time before the one arm swung upward and pointed to the top of the very building where Khalil had been. Khalil's eyes narrowed. So this was he. The dedicated hunter. Suddenly, Khalil's face changed. The half smile vanished from his lips as he stared in astonishment . . . Mohammed Mahrous! Good God! The last name had not triggered his memory. Nor the one-armed description, even when he saw the figure at first glance. But the face. Khalil knew that face, and his head moved back instinctively, closer to the shadows by the wall.

Mahrous! Now Lieutenant Colonel Mahrous. Khalil stared at his memories, going back to childhood, and wondered how the idiot had lost his arm.

A group of people arrived at the restaurant. From their conversation, it was clear that they'd been stopped and questioned. Tense again, Khalil had to give credit to his hunter. It was shrewd to round up the visitors, instead of sending them away. He saw the face he was looking for and rose to greet her.

Mary seemed unworried by all the fuss. Like most people raised in a democracy, where the individual had rights, she assumed that having done no wrong, she would have no problem. The Egyptians present had no such confidence. She looked good enough to eat. Hair pulled back, with that touch of primness that made you want her all the more, and those marvelous blue eyes. Distracted as he was, Khalil felt a tightening in his loins.

Mary was happy to sit on the terrace and observe the activity outside. She ordered a martini, and Khalil added water to his Scotch. The only light out here was from the windows of the restaurant, and small candles on the tables.

"Are you hungry?" he asked.

"Starving."

"Why don't we order?"

They ordered jumbo prawns, sautéed in butter. Khalil asked for a bottle of wine to be sent immediately with the bread. "These prawns are the best you have ever tasted," he said confidently. "They are brought fresh from Alexandria each day."

She was studying him. He cursed the situation that left him so distracted. "Thanks for the invitation," she said. "I'm glad you called." He held her eye for a moment. It seemed to him that she knew exactly what she was doing tonight, that she had been alone in Cairo, and that she had come out to get done.

Mary was wondering if she would end up in bed with Yvette's brother. He was not the man for her, she could tell that. But there was a feral attraction that might win out, just for a night, if he put his mind to it. In spite of the warm air, she felt a quiver in her pectoral muscles as she smiled calmly at him.

They talked about what was going on outside. Khalil told her that he had been questioned by a policeman who had hinted at espionage. The political situation in Egypt was getting tense, he told her. Cairo had always been a hotbed of spies, and they were probably swarming around again, trying to get wind of when the next confrontation with Israel would be. He spoke lightly, so he thought, but there was an assessing smile that seemed to grow on her lips as she watched his eye. She noticed something. He realized that she was no fool.

"Are you so worried about peace with Israel?" she asked.

Khalil shook his head. "Not for their sake," he admitted. "Not for their sake." He sipped his wine and changed the subject.

He told her of the village on his father's land, where he had been raised, in northern Egypt. From early days

he had seen how people can be kept, like contented
cattle, though life hadn't been so bad for them on
his father's farms. His mother, who was French, had
hated it. Not because of the poverty of the peasants,
but because it was so different from what she was
accustomed to in Paris. His father had married out
of his faith. Devout Moslem though he was, he had
married a Roman Catholic. Khalil had been educated
in Cairo, in the school where Mary now taught. She
acknowledged that with an interested nod. Then he
had been sent to France, after the revolution, in 1952.
Mary, who had lived in France herself, still chose not
to be drawn. He followed her eyes as she gazed outside,
as though she guessed that that was where his mind was,
really. The police were in a huddle down there. He saw
a couple of them look his way, and realized that they
would soon be in the restaurant.

"Do you see the policeman with the one arm?" he
asked.

She nodded immediately. "Yes, he seems to be in
charge. I wonder who they're hunting for."

The police huddle broke up and a party of them headed for the restaurant. It was clear to Khalil that they had
been briefed for a systematic check on everyone. While
he spoke, a part of his mind went on working, checking
and rechecking the story he wound tell, looking for any
detail that might give him away.

"I happen to know him," he continued, and now
Mary looked interested. "He was brought up in that
very village I just described. He lived in an area with
a bunch of Jews and Christians, all poor as dirt. But
he made good. He was an athlete—he had two arms
then—and became head boy of the school. I remember him well. He was ten years older than me, but
we noticed each other all the same." Khalil laughed

suddenly. "When I was fourteen, I seduced the girl he was about to marry. She was eighteen at the time. Do you think he'll remember me?"

Mary had been nibbling bread and sipping wine. Now she stopped and looked at him. "I should think he might," she said, and looked outside again.

"Don't look that way!" Khalil said quickly. "I don't want him to notice us." That was true. He had no wish to be recognized. Yet he went on talking. It was nerves.

"We had a chess match once." Khalil chewed a piece of bread that became so dry in his mouth he couldn't swallow it. He sipped his almost untouched wine. "He was the local champion, and I was the rich brat from Cairo. All his friends bet their piastres, and I covered them. He was so nervous when we started that he couldn't think. He was a positional player. The dogged type, who tries to get to the end game with a small advantage. I turned up late for the game, and his friends had set the clock ticking. He was already upset about that. Then I made a few fast moves, reading my newspaper while he thought, and he blundered. After thinking for ten minutes, he made the wrong move, and I pounced. There was an air of gloom, as though the king had died."

Mary listened to this, her eyes going to his face from time to time. She wanted to ask if this had happened before or after he seduced the fiancée, but was unwilling to reveal her curiosity. From a distance, she liked the face of the one-armed policeman. He looked very confident and controlled. Khalil, on the other hand, was off key tonight. He seemed nervous, as though a part of his veneer were missing. Or maybe that was just resentment, because her own desire for him had slipped away. She couldn't make him out. With the candle shining upward on his face, showing the hollows of his cheeks and temples, he looked different, skeletal, his lips moist with wine, but distracted.

If Khalil had been himself, he would have been more responsive to the English girl. He'd have seen her negative reaction to what he said, and would have buttered her with kinder thoughts. In his mind, he was still worrying over something that gnawed at him. Something that he sensed, or thought he sensed about these policemen, as though they had something up their metaphoric sleeve. He wondered if the restaurant staff had noted his absence from the terrace. Experience told him that people were very bad at estimating time in such circumstances. He wanted to underplay the time he'd been away. Thank God he'd had the instinct to pack up quickly after the transmission. A few more seconds up there and it might have been too late. Suddenly he thought of something.

"What's wrong?" Mary paused, her glass raised. "You look as though you've seen a ghost."

He rose quickly. "It's all right." He wiped his lips on the serviette. "I just have to excuse myself for a moment."

Under strict control, Khalil walked casually to the rest room. On the way, he signaled to the waiter for another bottle of wine on their table, winking and raising a thumb. The waiter grinned broadly. Khalil knew that every man in the restaurant had noticed his companion, and that waiters would be questioned about the demeanor of their customers.

In the rest room, there was some old fellow trying to get started in the urinal. He glanced at Khalil with the unintended resentment sometimes seen in such circumstances. Khalil went into the single cubicle, which was empty.

He removed his right shoe and examined the sole. It wasn't much, but the traces of dog shit were discernible. He took a pile of toilet tissue, dampened it, and scrubbed the sole. Then he used fresh tissue to carefully dry the shoe. For safety, he gave the same treatment to the other shoe, wiping off traces of dry earth. He flushed the tissue, stepped outside, and carefully washed his hands. He was ready. There was nothing for it now but to keep cool, pray to God, and brazen it out.

Chapter 11

DETECTIVE SERGEANT Ali Goma was sure of one thing: he had never seen such a beautiful girl. Girl, woman— they were all girls to him, at his age. But he was not so old that they were all as beautiful as this one.

"I hope the lady will excuse me, but I know that you are English," he said to her. "I hope it does not offend you if I assume that you'll be more comfortable if we speak in English?"

Mary smiled. "It doesn't offend me at all. I wouldn't understand you if you spoke in Arabic. I'm Mary Miles-Tudor." She astonished him by offering her hand. He took it, bowing, before writing down her name and returning to the man.

The restaurant was packed with people. Other policemen were interviewing customers at other tables, and members of the Mentakis family were out in force, apologizing, throwing their eyes to heaven, sending complimentary drinks. Serving was disrupted, but not totally prevented, while staff as well as diners were being questioned.

"What I'm going to have to do is ask you a few questions, Mr. Khalil. I know you've been questioned already, and I'll try not to repeat too much, but I have my orders. So let's kick off. What time did you get here tonight?"

"Seven? Seven-thirty?"

"You were to meet Miss Miles-Tudor at what time?"

"Eight."

"But you wanted to get here well in advance—I understand. So you ordered a drink on the terrace. But after a time, you went to your car to get some cigarettes?"

"That's right."

"At what time was that?"

Khalil sighed. "Seven-thirty? I could be wrong by fifteen minutes either way."

"Not either way?" the policeman said gently, and something in his tone made Mary glance at him. "Unless you spent a long time walking to your car, I think it must have been later, rather than earlier." Khalil shrugged. The truth was that he had left the terrace at seven-fifteen. "You went directly to your car?"

"I did."

"Did you see anyone on the way? Anyone who might remember seeing you?"

Khalil shook his head. "There was a young couple in the parking lot. I sat in my car and watched them pulling out."

"Why did you do that?"

"No reason . . . I was in no hurry. I just lit a cigarette and sat for a while."

Sergeant Goma wrote in his notebook. "Then you spoke to one of our detective sergeants. He noted the time as seven-fifty, by the way. But he didn't see you enter the parking lot." Goma looked up inquiringly.

"I didn't see him either."

"And the young couple didn't see you. Even after being asked specifically, they both deny it."

"But I saw them. They were kissing."

"I see." Goma said that as though it explained everything. He caught up with his note-taking, and verified a couple of points. "I see you have been overseas?"

"Yes."

"I don't suppose you have your passport with you?"

"It happens that I do."

Khalil took out his passport. Goma opened it, glanced at the photograph, and checked the entry date. It was clear to Khalil that he had been instructed to do this in the case of foreigners. The entry date was after the time of what the newspapers had described as the "Taxi Driver Killing."

"Let's see, where were we? Ah, yes, you were walking back from the parking lot. Did you enter the apartment building on the corner?"

Khalil blinked. "You mean—?" He looked along the road outside as though puzzled.

"The tall building on the corner," Goma repeated.

"No, I didn't."

"You're quite sure of that, Mr. Khalil?"

"Of course, I'm sure. What is this?"

"Let's get this clear, sir. You did not enter that apartment building, take the elevator to the top floor, and enter one of the apartments?"

"I've told you, no. What are you driving at, Sergeant?" He met Mary's blue eyes, narrowed on him for a moment. Khalil felt cornered, as though they both knew that he was lying.

"I am just trying to establish, Mr. Khalil, where you were and where you were not at a certain time this evening. It is now noted that you were not in the apartment building on the corner. What about the back courts behind that building? Were you in any of the back courts?"

Khalil came subtly forward in his chair. It was hard to move quickly from a relaxed position. "You can note that I was not in the back courts."

The sergeant did so, smiling. "Good. Well, I don't think I have to keep you much longer, sir. May I see your shoes, please?"

Khalil sat still for a long moment. Outwardly, he continued to look puzzled; inwardly, he assessed things quickly one last time. Did they have specific information? Or was this just a smarter than average policeman, well briefed on how to question anyone who answered a certain general description? Finally he smiled, took off both shoes, and handed them to Sergeant Goma.

It was all he could do not to bray aloud in triumph. He saw the policeman's beginnings of a smile as he glanced at the sole of the right shoe, then at the other, the smile widening as he sniffed self-consciously. This was obviously a part of his detailed instructions, as was the little war of nerves that had gone before.

"I am sorry for your trouble, sir. Pardon the inconvenience. Now if I may ask a few questions of the lady?"

Khalil calmed slowly. It wasn't over yet, he thought, thinking of the radio, but for the moment the important thing was . . . freedom!

                    *   *   *

In a back court behind the tenements, a police officer nearly died of fright when he walked into the donkey. After that, he unleashed a stream of abuse on the subject of the animal's antecedents. A couple of other men joined him in the darkness.

"He said to search through garbage bins, not donkey shit."

"Right!" The first man kicked the donkey in the rear.

"Ah, there's nothing here . . ." The Lieutenant moved things in the cart. As an afterthought, he stuck his hand into the hay and felt around. "No radio transmitters. Let's go."

The policemen continued to search the back courts with a fine-tooth comb.

"As you might have guessed, we were never close friends," Khalil said. "But when you see someone from the past like that—someone from your childhood—it makes you think of how you've spent your life. Maybe that's why I didn't want to speak to him. I don't want to think of how I've spent my life. Besides, I could see he was busy."

"He certainly looked intent," she agreed.

They were walking down Kasr el Nil. He'd suggested walking her to her apartment, instead of driving. It was a pleasant night. The police were releasing people from the area. They were still thick back there, but getting discouraged—and a bit fed-up with their persistent boss, it seemed to Khalil. They had drawn a blank, he thought elatedly. It was obvious that they had not found the briefcase. But Mahrous might notice his name, even in the mountain of reports that had been generated. That thought troubled him.

Mary was still enigmatic. From a woman he had intended to demolish sexually, she had evolved into something problematical, almost like his sister. He wondered for the first time if she might be gay.

"I understand you went to Oxford?" She nodded. "Did anyone notice you there, while they were discussing their theories?" She smiled. "Is there really such rivalry between Oxford and Cambridge?"

She shrugged and walked a few paces. "We have rugby matches. And the boat race."

"Doesn't Cambridge usually win?"

"Maybe." Then, totally deadpan: "They tend to try a little harder, the people from these newer universities."

After a moment, Khalil roared with laughter. It was a veritable bellow, which echoed from the walls. Mary grinned, drawn in for a moment, and wondered why she had lost interest in him. She spoke unprompted for almost the first time that evening.

"I used to play chess. I played against a computer once, in Paris."

"Really? What was that like?"

"It was an American program, designed for the big Cray. The Sorbonne didn't have anything like that, but they had the program on some other mainframe. It's quite funny, actually. The computer likes to grab material. It thinks about it first, and if it sees a trap it will refuse it. But it has to go through all this each time, and if you can leave the trap there for a number of moves, there's a chance that it'll grab the piece eventually. It's as though it just can't resist it any longer." She laughed. Contrary to her general demeanor, she had a soft, ringing laugh that he found seductive. "Then it gets into time trouble and can't figure out its move in time. The program I played would print up the word

'Rushed! Rushed!' like a person making excuses. But if you slip up and get mated, it sets off a bell that clangs in triumph."

"Did you ever beat it?" Khalil was smiling, relaxing at last. She nodded matter-of-factly. "You must be a strong player."

"Not all that strong. It wasn't hooked up to its book of openings at the time. When I played pawn to king four, it used Alekhine's defense—pawn to king's bishop three?—which I suppose seemed very logical to it, attacking the pawn and developing a piece." Seeing that he understood, she described the game in detail.

There was hesitation when they reached her apartment building. His mood was strange, with a kind of flatness to it. He was still on edge about the briefcase, and having his name on file. He wanted to be alone to think, but his brain was tired, he needed rest. He might even be too tired for sex. Maybe she sensed that, and maybe that was why her eyes softened slightly as she smiled at him. The mother instinct. Maybe that would be her ruin.

"I was hoping you'd invite me for a cup of coffee," he said plaintively. Her brow wrinkled. "Do you have a chess board? You could get Mahrous's revenge for him," he said with an odd piece of insight.

Her lips curved together, before grinning suddenly. It was an open grin that reached her eyes. "One game," she said. "No rematch if you lose."

We'll see about that, he thought.

Standing at the bottom of Kasr el Nil, where it joined Midan el Tahrir, the police watcher lit a cigarette and checked the time as the couple he had followed went into the building.

Mary moved pawn to king four, and smiled when he played knight to king's bishop three. She attacked the knight, and he began to move it around the board, in the strange defense attributed to the great Russian World Champion Alekhine. "He probably never played it except for fun," she said. Khalil knew what he was doing. Before long, her pawn center was under attack. But Mary played at close to Master strength, and knew her way through the position very well.

"Did you have many lovers at Oxford?"

She frowned. "Speak during your own thinking time."

"Did you have many lovers at Oxford?" he asked after she had moved.

"One or two. When you're playing chess, you're supposed to keep your mind on the game."

He moved a piece. "I can't concentrate when I'm losing."

"Oh, I see. You fall apart when things get rough?"

He smiled at her and sipped his coffee.

A few moves later, Khalil turned over his king in resignation. "I've never done that before," he said. "I've lost games, but never turned my king over. It's against my nature." He rose and walked to the window. The police watcher was no longer at his post. As Khalil had guessed, it had been a routine follow-up, and was now over. Even Mahrous had to quit sometime. As he looked out, keeping his back to her, he heard Mary packing up the board.

She was completely at his mercy and she knew it. She probably wouldn't even scream if he simply started to remove her clothes. He could sense her nervousness. It was almost palpable. She had allowed him up here. Her safe upbringing, and the sense of security it fostered, had gotten her into this, but it couldn't get her out.

Khalil might have given way to an impulse to unleash himself. But he had been severely scared this evening.

Even now, he saw black clouds on the skyline. Mahrous! The hell with it, he thought. Take the girl, a voice said. She is there to be taken—do it and do your worrying afterward. Then he thought of something else. He was gazing out across the roofs of Cairo, feeling the almost irresistible pressure in his loins, when a geometrical fact suddenly came home to him. Khalil had an almost photographic memory. Using it, he studied a map of Cairo in his mind, looking at the locations of the tracking stations, and this apartment, and saw a possible solution to one of the problems that now faced him . . . The demon died. It was a strong demon, but he quelled it. He could not destroy this girl—not yet—because he needed her.

Her eyes came up when he looked round at her. Her face was pale: but she saw the expression in his eyes, and hope flashed.

"I'm going to ask you a favor," he said mildly. "Do you mind if I sleep here for a while? Don't worry." He raised a hand, smiling. "I mean *sleep*. I mean right here, on this couch. I'll be gone by morning."

"Do I have a choice?"

"Not really." He flopped on the couch and put an arm over his eyes. But before she closed her bedroom door, he said seriously, "By the way, Mary . . . You have the best lines of any woman I have ever seen."

As Khalil closed his eyes in the big, darkened room, his thoughts were of the briefcase. Something told him that they hadn't found it. It was still there in the workman's cart and he wondered how he could retrieve it. He thought of a café on Kasr el Nil that opened early. A couple of hours from now he could be sitting there, outside of the area occupied by the police, but with a view along the street past the restaurant. They would have to call the hounds off sometime. Even Mahrous . . .

That was the next problem. One of those unexpected things. He would have to deal with Mahrous.

Finally, he half slept.

Mustapha Abdel Ali Bose was fifty-five years old, and looked seventy. Shrunken from his youthful stature, which had not been tall, he was thin and wizened, with gray wisps of beard, a couple of teeth in the side of his head, and nothing in the world except his galabiya and his donkey. The donkey's cart did not belong to him. It belonged to the Jew who owned the furniture business for which he worked. The place he slept in did not belong to him. It belonged to the dried-up woman who let him stay there for the few piastres he brought her every week. It was very clear that the food he ate did not belong to him, since it went its way, leaving him no fatter than before and scarcely less hungry. He lived on the pita bread and fava beans that the Jew gave him every day for carrying bits and pieces of used furniture from place to place. Mustapha had once had his own cart, for the donkey to pull. But as Allah had willed, it fell apart one day, and that was that. Mustapha didn't mind being poor. He had always been poor, his brothers were poor, and his father had been poor before him. He didn't even own the water that he used once a week, to wash his hands and face when he went to the mosque on Friday nights, and he surely didn't own the scraps of hay that the Jew gave him for the donkey. Mustapha never wondered which of them would die first, himself or the donkey.

It was still before dawn when Mustapha came down to the back court and spoke to the donkey. It was standing there, ears up, knowing that its night of waiting was over. Mustapha believed that the donkey was glad to see him in the mornings, not only for the scraps of hay. It liked to hear his voice. He dropped some hay at its feet, patted its muzzle, rubbed his hands around his face to waken himself up, and hitched the cart.

The policemen with the car outside looked tired and pale. Parked so that no one could pass, they stirred themselves and moved the car, grumbling to each other that this could not go on much longer. Mustapha had heard them in the night, knocking on doors and going around, wakening the sleepy people in the building. He'd heard that murderers were on the prowl, and gone to sleep again. Sitting on the seat atop the cart, still yawning and scrubbing his hands around his face, he did not notice the white sports car that crossed an intersection far to his right, and appeared within sight of him another couple of times as the donkey found its way to the furniture shop.

Mustapha did not pull up at the front of the store, which was not yet open for business. He went to the back, opened a gate, and went inside, calling to the night watchman who slept under the corrugated tin roof of the yard. He was unaware of the figure in a galabiya that came into the alleyway, took something from his cart, and walked away again, unseen.

Khalil thanked God that the police had not troubled to follow him this morning. He thanked God that the old donkey driver had risen early, and not rummaged around in his cart. He put the briefcase behind the driver's seat, accelerated out of the area, and immediately began to think about his next problem—information. Without the radio meantime, he would need some other means of getting what he needed. Cursing the necessity, he stopped at a public telephone, called John Baldwin, and arranged to meet him later in the day.

Chapter 12

IT WAS getting light and there was traffic in the streets when Mahrous finally called off his men. By that time they had searched every inch of the area, including the rooftops, and entered each one of the incredible number of apartments to be found in a small area of Cairo. There was no one there. As they had been telling him since midnight, there was no one there whose presence had not been noted: no tall male who had not been questioned, and no radio, no spy. Maybe if they'd cordoned off a bigger area? Mahrous was sure that he would soon be hearing about all the things he might have done differently. As he walked away dejectedly, he found himself peering at a beggar who lay in the street with twisted limbs, then at a peanut vendor with one of those small, portable machines that roast the nuts on street corners. Thinking of John Buchan's tale, *The Thirty-Nine Steps*, where a man evades his hunters in the Highlands of Scotland by disguising himself as a roadworker, quickly attending to details like broken fingernails and scuffed shoes, he dismissed absurd thoughts about a master of disguise.

The Deputy Director of Military Intelligence called a meeting for ten o'clock that morning. This gave Mahrous time to dash together a preliminary report. It was a Friday, and the cafeteria was closed, but he

cadged a cup of coffee from the Operations Room,
where they worked around the clock.

The Deputy Director was a grim-faced brigadier general who made the right decision about fifty percent of
the time. That was a good average for a man who didn't
suffer from his own mistakes. The division chiefs were
also present, including Touhami, like a cadaver from
some ghostly beach, in his dark sunglasses. Mahrous
felt the atmosphere as soon as he walked in. No jokes,
no bonhomie, all the signs of a "roast the Lieutenant
Colonel" session. They were meeting in a conference
room adjacent to the Deputy Director's office.

Things started briskly. As though under pressure
from his own superiors, the Deputy Director asked
Mahrous to justify again his view that the man who was
sending radio transmissions out of Cairo was the same
man who was responsible for what the newspapers
called the "taxi driver killing." Mahrous repeated his
view that this killing was the work of a professional
whose cover was blown in the Hilton Hotel. In terms
of timing, like the fact that the transmissions started a
few weeks later, he thought there was some supporting
evidence. There had also been some activity involving
a tall, dark-haired man that he thought might be relevant, but that was probably too vague to mention, he
said, receiving a hard glance from Touhami. He could
not guess who "Ali Hamsa" represented, or what his
mission was in Cairo.

To his surprise, this was greeted without too much
skepticism. The Deputy Director indicated that there
was some credence to the view that Hamsa was a spy.
If so, he had come here armed with knowledge of their
technology, and how to get around it, and had shown
terrifying resourcefulness in evading capture. This had
been seen the night before, when he seemed to have

slipped out of their net again. Mahrous was asked to
tell them about that.

Mahrous started by pointing out that the investigation was not yet over. It had only just begun. Then he
tried to give them the events in order.

Last night's transmission had been in two parts, a
rapid burst of the type to which they had become
accustomed, and then a brief manual transmission.
It seemed safe to conjecture that the spy could not
prepare a digitized message in the field, but had to
do so in advance. The digitized part had not been
long enough to allow perfect localization of the source.
But in response to new software, a ballpark estimate
had been given and police units mobilized, while the
tracking stations went on full alert. Then had come
the short manual transmission, they had nailed him,
and information went to units on the move. The raid
had gone according to plan. Within minutes of the
transmission ending, a nine-block area of the city had
been cordoned off, including the block from which the
transmission was now known to have originated. They
had surrounded the very building, and a two-block
area on all sides of it. Whoever had used that radio
was there! Mahrous said, his fist clenched. But did
anyone know how many people lived in a nine-block
area of Cairo? He estimated about ten thousand. Most
of these were low-probability suspects, but every one
had been documented. So far, they had seen only
the top of this enormous pile, the most likely males.
Disappointingly, this had yielded nothing so far. But
they would work down. The man was there—he had to
be—or the woman, damn it! Neither man nor woman
could simply vanish in thin air. As he repeated this,
Mahrous's exhaustion and frustration began to show.
Whoever had used that radio was now on file. He had

to be! As though triggered by the signs of weakness, there was now open skepticism.

"And the radio?" The question came from Touhami. His shaded eyes were like black holes as he looked across at Mahrous. "Do you have the radio on file? Subtly disguised, perhaps?"

Mahrous cringed at the sarcasm. "I can't explain that," he admitted. "God only knows what he did with the radio."

"So you haven't found it?"

"No, sir."

"But you still say that an arrest is imminent?"

Mahrous closed his eyes and took a long moment before answering. "I can only say we're going to get him." His eyes opened. "If I don't get him this time, he will try again, and the next time, I will catch him."

This impressed no one. For the next few minutes they talked around him, as though he weren't there. Mahrous had just launched one of the biggest raids in the history of Internal Security. He had organized a hundred men, and it had all worked like clockwork—pity it had come to nothing. Maybe he had enclosed too large an area. There were too many people. In the future maybe they should try to pin things down a bit. What did they know about this man anyway? Except that he was tall and dark?—or had even that gone by the board? What about an accomplice? Mahrous looked up with interest at this point. It had occurred to him that there might well be an accomplice. The absence of the radio was a killer, though. If the radio had gone, the chances were that the spy had gone with it, never mind how "impossible" that was.

It was Touhami who brought things back to the level of personal criticism. Suddenly addressing Mahrous, he asked him where he had been when the alarm went up.

Was it true that he had been holed up in some back street without even a telephone? Mahrous took a deep breath.

"I was with a friend."

"A friend?"

"The widow of Abdel Sa'id . . . That was the policeman killed," he reminded the Deputy Director.

For once in his life, Touhami almost smiled. "Mahrous tends to get personally involved," he said.

"With young widows?"

"She is eight months pregnant," Mahrous put in.

"Oh . . ." The Deputy Director's brow cleared somewhat. "Nonetheless, it seems a bit inadvisable," he said. Unpredictably, the discussion turned more serious after that.

They discussed the nature of the transmissions. As well as using new technology, each of these was coded in a way that could not be deciphered. This was ominous. There was nothing haphazard or dilettante about this operation. It was a major operation, run by professionals, and the Deputy Director contributed the fact that people were worried at high levels. The information going out—was it military, scientific, or political? And what was the purpose? Some kind of terrorism? The atmosphere was grim around the table. The possibility of terrorism was being taken seriously, the Deputy Director said. He had already given orders for a tightening of security around national leaders, including the President. Someone asked if there was any doubt that the transmissions were going to Tel Aviv, and they all turned to Mahrous. He could say only that the replies seemed to come from a location to the north and east of Cairo.

The Deputy Director brought things to a close. This unsolved case was causing concern at the highest level, he said. There was pressure to catch this spy and find out what his mission was in Egypt. They would not be taken off guard, he said. Major public places would be watched closely, and official buildings had been made all but impenetrable. Foreigners would be screened with double care, and even the passports of infants would be scrutinized at the borders. This matter was now top priority. They wanted this man caught. Here it comes, Mahrous thought. The investigation was going to be moved to a higher level. But the Deputy Director looked at him instead. "You were quick to see the importance of this case, Lieutenant Colonel. There is also some approval of the way you've handled things so far. You will remain in charge. Working through your division chief, of course, and with every cooperation. Let's get that clear," he said, glancing around the table. "I don't want to hear of any unanswered telephone calls on this one." Mahrous blinked in surprise. Aware of a stony silence around the table, he glanced at Touhami, who looked as though he had bitten into a lemon, and wondered if his career had just received a boost or the last nail in its coffin.

When he returned to his office, he tried to force himself to work. Spurred by the unexpected vote of confidence, he selected the reports from the Mentakis restaurant, which he still thought was a likely place for the spy to try to hide, and sat down to read. As he would recall in days to come, there was one report that caught his eye that afternoon. It was a report on a girl who had been in the restaurant. He noticed it because she was English, with an Egyptian companion, and also because there was something about the report, something in the way it was worded, that made him wonder if the Detective Sergeant had noticed things that he did not quite express. Rereading this, he frowned exhaustedly.

Probably just a pretty girl. But—as he would always
remember afterward—there was something in the name
of her companion—Ibrahim Khalil—that rang a distant
bell. It was around then that he closed his eyes, and
seconds later was asleep.

Chapter 13

THE APARTMENT building was on Rhoda Island. It
overlooked the divided river, and had a fine view of
the city on the one side and the desert on the other.
Khalil rode the elevator to the fifth floor. It was an
older building, with only two apartments on each level.
Elegant living at low cost, for established residents.

When he rang the bell, the door was opened by a
youngish woman wearing very short shorts. She had
dark hair that fell around a pretty face. Khalil had
expected a maid, and was about to speak to her that
way, but checked himself.

"Er—Mrs. Baldwin?"

"Yes?" With the merest smile at his surprise.

"My name is Ibrahim Khalil. I think your husband
is expecting me."

"Ummm . . . he didn't say." As she glanced behind
her, Khalil recovered from his second surprise. Mrs.
Baldwin spoke with a broad cockney accent. She looked
him in the eye again. "He's having supper at the
moment. I suppose you can come in." Thinking that

there seemed to be a certain lack of communication between this man and wife, Khalil followed her into the large, shadowy apartment.

Baldwin was at a table in the formal dining room, surrounded by food and bottles of wine. Khalil saw roasted chicken, a dish of vine leaves cooked with meat and rice, fried okra, olives, salad, bread, and cheeses. As he entered, a maid came in with a tray of other foods.

"I am disturbing you," he said coolly. They had arranged to meet at this time. Baldwin waved this down, his mouth full. Unlike his wife, he was dressed for the city, in pin-striped pants and a white shirt. Khalil noted that the wife was not eating, and his impression grew of a rather strange household.

"Nonsense, old chap. Sit down. Have a drink."

"No, thank you."

"What? No sun-downer?" Baldwin boomed merrily, dabbing at his lips. "Marina!" he bellowed, though his wife was right behind him. "A drink for Mr. Khalil."

She went to a cabinet stocked with liquor. After looking at him in the mirror for a moment, she selected a bottle of Scotch and brought it to the table. She stood with the bottle raised inquiringly, over a glass that she placed on the corner of the table, inches from her crotch. He nodded, and she filled the glass, still with that cryptic smile. Baldwin made no effort to introduce her and she walked quietly away, her incongruous slim legs retreating from the paneled room.

Baldwin ate a piece of quiche lorraine. While still chewing, he popped an olive in his mouth and pulled a plate of cheese toward him. He cut off a quarter of a pound of Brie, poured red wine, and Khalil watched the huge fingers working daintily as he touched the cheese, testing it with satisfaction. He noticed Khalil's silence.

"Relax, old chap. It's safe to talk."

"The hell it is."

Baldwin glanced up with a stranded smile. Then he shrugged and drained the glass of wine, dribbling some of it. Since moving his head would be too much effort, a good deal of food had also landed on the bib across his chest. Leaning on the table, which groaned mightily, he heaved himself upright. "Don't clear up!" he bellowed over his shoulder as he stuffed bread and cheese into his mouth. "This way, old chap." Khalil followed him across the parquet floors.

Baldwin's study faced south. From the open window to the balcony, dry air blew in from the desert. On a clear day, one would be able to see the pyramids of Giza from here, behind the sharp dividing line where verdure turned to sand. Baldwin ignored the desk, which was in front of the doors leading to the balcony. He went to a fireplace of wood and marble, with a flag of Egypt mounted above it. "You see why I like it here—couldn't live like this in England." He dropped into an armchair. Khalil also sat, and looked around. When he came back to Baldwin, he found himself being studied.

"When did you last check this room?"

"Relax. There hasn't been a bug in this place in ten years."

"When did you last check it?"

"An hour ago."

Baldwin's smile struggled as he opened the door of a drinks cupboard that was conveniently at hand. He selected a bottle of Benedictine liqueur and filled a glass. "Desert." He raised the glass and savored the sweet, spicy alcohol, still watching Khalil.

Khalil lit a cigarette. He wondered how any man could be so self-indulgent. After his narrow escape the night before, he had spent a tense day at home. Now he wanted news.

"So, I'm back to square one," Khalil said. "For a while. Meantime, I am expecting some important information that may have to come through you. How are your lines of communication working?"

"Smoothly." Baldwin savored his drink. "My contact is a man I've known for years. I see him at the Sporting Club, where we often pass the time of day. I can also go to his office, if need be." He shrugged. "Wouldn't want to overdo that, but if it's an emergency . . ."

"Suppose you have to exchange written material? You wouldn't want to do that too often at the club, would you?"

"Maybe not." Baldwin thought for a moment. "The chap in question is a friend of my wife's. He sees her from time to time."

"Would that be safe?"

"She is totally reliable."

Baldwin lit a cigarette and cleared his throat. Khalil sensed a certain sensitivity as regards his wife, and was inwardly amused. He reflected that the arrangement might not be a bad one. He knew that the man in question was a Cabinet minister. He was conspicuous, but could see the wife routinely, without raising eyebrows. All the same, it meant another person, another risk.

"I leave that up to you," Khalil said. "Just be aware that there might be something extra, and that it is important. Now, let's talk about the tracking stations. Did you get the information I asked for?"

Baldwin nodded with a twisted smile. Khalil could see that he relished being used, but resented the fact that it was only in an emergency. "Your assumption is correct that the system has recently been improved. This was instigated by Lieutenant Colonel Mahrous, whom I'm

sure you remember we almost met one night." His eyes
rose and fell. "Mahrous is a late starter in the Intelligence business. That means he doesn't have much
clout, and I hear he's unpopular with his bosses. But
they have just confirmed his command of this case.
He seems to be unusually dedicated." Khalil nodded,
indicating nothing one way or the other. The problem of
Mahrous would have to be solved, but for the moment
there were other matters.

Baldwin held the glass to his lips and drank from it
in three short sips. This was his way of getting to the
contents without moving any major muscle mass, only
his fingers. "As for details on the stations, the man you
have to get to is a Dr. Girgis Green. He's the scientist
who set up the system in the first place, using Russian
equipment, and he's the one who modified it recently.
Unless you know how these things go, it might surprise
you to hear that he is actually the only one. The only
one who knows the details of the system, I mean. So
he's the one you have to get to."

"How do I do that?"

Baldwin tilted back his head and a smile flitted. Say
one extra word, he thought, and the man would prod
you back on track. "Well, I don't think bribery's
the answer. Green's not the type to go for money—
though he's very tight with it, I'm told. Nor is he an
idealist. Not the type to pee himself with pleasure
when his own kind are losing out. He has a weakness,
though. You'll be charmed by the originality." Baldwin
grinned. "He likes women. With a taste for the exotic—
a spice that probably eludes him in his life. They say
you'll often find him on a Thursday night, sipping
beer in the fancy bars along the Nile, ogling the young
lovelies."

"Only on Thursdays?"

"He is a man of moderation and habit. After dinnertime too—he doesn't want to meet anyone before dinner—too expensive. My guess is that he probably snags the occasional middle-aged tourist." Baldwin gazed at Khalil, who was deep in thought. "So there you have it, old chap. Find yourself the right girl."

Khalil looked up. "What about your wife?"

Baldwin's leer vanished. "What about her?"

"She's foreign—doesn't that mean exotic? And experienced."

Baldwin's eyes were flat. For a moment there was no humor in the mercurial, fat face, and in that static posture, Khalil noticed for the first time that Baldwin's nose had been broken in the past. Seen like this, the fat face was no longer jolly. It looked tough. Khalil knew that Baldwin had been trained. Even today— even with a bottle or two of wine aboard, and half a bottle of brandy after lunch—he was still a hard man to beat on the judo mat, as many a young bull had discovered in the Gezira Sporting Club. Baldwin had great strength. He was a great deal faster than one expected, and his foot sweep was deadly. But Khalil looked back at him with equanimity. He knew how to deal with an elephant like Baldwin, on the judo mat or off it.

"She would be compensated," he said.

All of a sudden, Baldwin laughed. It was a resonant whoop that filled the room, but the merriment didn't reach his eyes. "I like your style, old chap, I really do. You don't give a monkey's, do you?" he said in his polished drawl. "But let's leave Marina out of this, shall we?"

Khalil shrugged. He had been only half serious, intrigued by the passing thought of shoving his own penis into Baldwin's wife. "As you wish," he said. "Speaking of women, there's another matter."

For the next few minutes, Khalil did the talking. He told Baldwin what he knew about Mary Miles-Tudor, describing her background, her character, and explaining what he wanted. Khalil was not overly happy about all this involvement of John Baldwin. But in the circumstances there didn't seem much choice. The fat man listened closely, trying to read between the lines, as always. At the end, he had an almost grudging smile.

"Ingenious . . . Very bold . . ." His small eyes met Khalil's. "I can understand your interest in this particular apartment. But how do you plan to gain access to it—or is that a foolish question?"

"She is a friend of my sister's."

"I see." Baldwin pursed his lips. "Is she your candidate for Girgis Green?"

Khalil's nonanswer to that one was: "I hadn't thought of that," which was a lie.

Before Khalil left, they discussed current affairs for a while. Baldwin confirmed that Nasser was in Russia at the time on an unpublicized visit. Whatever he wanted there, he wouldn't get it, they agreed. Nor was Brezhnev likely to get whatever he wanted. Nasser's plea to the United States had shocked the Arab world as well as Russia. It was seen as an act of desperation that threatened to upset the delicate balance in the Middle East. And yet, it was not totally unpredicted. Nasser had painted himself into a corner politically, and the question now was: Would Russia let him walk across the floor? If so, it would certainly be out of character. During this discussion, Khalil's inner tension rose. Aware that Baldwin was probing for information, he kept his observations brief and neutral—until suddenly the fat man hit a nerve. They were discussing the 1967 war with Israel, when Egypt was humiliated while her powerful supposed ally, Russia, stood by. Baldwin was interested in this, and in the political motivation. Could the real reason for this "war" have been a plan—a common, or even universal plan?—to get rid of Nasser? If so, it was interesting to speculate on just who might have been involved. Strange things happened behind the scenes, not only in bedrooms. Much more unique was the way it had all come to naught. When the most ignored and insignificant of players—the people—the Egyptian people at that—had risen up and demonstrated in the streets, refusing to accept the resignation of their bloodied and humiliated leader. That must have put some major noses out of joint, Baldwin was saying, when Khalil suddenly exploded.

"Demonstrated in the streets! You think they demonstrated in the streets?" Khalil's eyes blazed. "That was orchestrated! Mass psychology! You know of the instructions that went out that day, to the army, and the civil service, and all the teachers, and professionals, and practically the entire work force of the country? You know what they were told? They were told that when Nasser spoke on television that day, they would be at their place of work. Not at home with their wives, but in front of their bosses and coworkers. That was how they made sure of unanimous support—clever, isn't it? I was in Alexandria that day. I saw the bus loads of 'spontaneous demonstrators' being shipped to Cairo, as they were shipped from all over the country. Then Nasser came on, supposedly resigning. But it was all the glory of Egypt. Then Mohieddin came on, pleading with him to remain—oh, how spontaneous! By this time, they were shouting in the streets. And of course the crowds came flocking out. What else do you expect in Cairo? Don't talk to me about demonstrations in the streets.

Talk about intimidation and deceit, and the most successful piece of mass manipulation in history!"

Khalil didn't stay long after that. Grim-faced and silent, after his outburst, he rose while Baldwin was still talking smoothly, and announced that he must go. When he left, there were ten 100-pound notes lying on the coffee table, and a very pensive Baldwin, staring at his thoughts.

Baldwin's participation in this operation had not begun when he was approached by Khalil. It had begun before that, when he was summoned to a house in Heliopolis and given a proposition that he basically could not refuse. Not that he had learned much, either then or since. Only that he was helping in something "of vital importance to Egypt," and would be well rewarded in the future. There were men of rank involved. But Baldwin's guess was that even they were not privy to the details of the operation. This explained Khalil's obsessive need for radio communication. It was Baldwin's guess that the main reason for this was security. Whatever was said in these transmissions, it was something he could not discuss with anyone subject to arrest in Egypt.

It was not that Baldwin didn't guess the broad purpose of Khalil's mission. He did guess. That was why he could hardly sleep these nights and was living on his nerves.

Mahrous was talking more than he had done for years. It was the quiet atmosphere, her gentleness, and a sudden need he felt to unburden himself. He had wakened in his office feeling more dead than alive. With a sense of failure that was especially strong, he had risen from his chair feeling that he could not go home to an empty apartment. He had been reprimanded for visiting Julia. A reprimand of that sort was like an ultimatum, and if they hadn't made it an order, it was only because they were confident they didn't have to. He would obey. Mahrous thought about this as he signed out a car, bought some supplies in a delicatessen, and drove to her apartment.

She didn't want to eat in front of him, but when she saw that he was ready to eat too, she promptly set the table for both of them. He saw that there was nothing left of what he had brought on previous visits, and was pleased. It was like the pleasure you get when a child eats well—which might have been what set him off a little later. "You need a telephone," he said, and promised to arrange that. It was absurd to be alone and pregnant without a telephone. She was unpacking the bag. Smoked oysters! She had never eaten such things. He was happy at her pleasure. So young, so shaken in life, and with nothing in the world except the life within her, yet with remarkable strength. She might never recover from her husband's death, but she was facing the future and her responsibilities better than he was at the moment.

"I admire you," he said, after they had eaten. "I almost envy you—do you believe that?"

That gave her the clue. She looked at him, her brown hair bundled around her head, in the shadowy light by the window. "Have you ever been married?" she asked, and that set him off.

"I married late in life," he told her. "Is thirty-four late these days? I was a career soldier. My wife was a lecturer at Cairo University, eight years younger than myself. She had her career. I was away from home a lot, and things worked pretty well—while I was away." He smiled. "I don't know if she was faithful. I know I wasn't—till the child was born. She was a statuesque woman. Very light-skinned, straight blond hair. A lot of people must have done their damnedest to get into bed with her. Randy students and free-thinking academics—but we were always glad to see each other when I came home. Until one day I came home without an arm." At this point, he suggested that they move to the couch, thinking it might be more comfortable for Julia. In the near darkness—they had chosen not to light a lamp—it was almost hard to tell that she was pregnant, unless you saw her from the side. He realized what a slim, fit girl she must have been.

"Not that she was put off by the amputation," he went on. "We loved each other, in our way, and there was nothing small-minded about Amirah. But it made me an invalid for a long time, and I'd never been an invalid before. I hated it. Then she got pregnant. I don't know if she intended it or not, but it happened, and after a bit of crying on her part, we both got to like the idea. Little Mohammed was born in 1963. By that time, I was no longer on active duty. Even as a policeman.

"Ah, yes, living in Cairo." Mahrous stared out at the night sky. "With a little boy, and no family nearby. Amirah was from Alexandria. I came from a village in the delta. It's tough on a woman, being trapped with a child, no family to help. She gave up her job. I did what I could when I got home. It was tough, but we loved every minute of it.

"Well, that's how it seems in retrospect. It's hard to remember how we both felt at the time. I didn't like my job. It wasn't 'me,' dealing with self-interested bosses, and things got me down sometimes. Amirah looked like a saint. But she was the kind who fought back. Maybe it was only a matter of time before we'd both be on a short fuse, and just blow up together. Mohammed was in his fourth year when it happened. He was learning so fast, and asked questions that really astonished us sometimes. Then one night I came home. I'd just been passed over for promotion for the second time—the time when you really get the message. Mohammed had been driving his mother crazy. She was telling me all about it—unloading—giving the baby hell for my benefit— you know the sort of thing—or maybe you don't," he said, remembering her youth, "when I suddenly went off the deep end. It was my fault. I don't know what got into me. I remember the baby crying and staring at me, then running away to his room. I hope you're too young to have had experiences like that, Julia, when things just get to you, and you say a hundred things you don't mean. I stormed out and went to a café. I sat drinking Stella beer and cried like an idiot. I'm going to cut this short," he said, his voice thickening. "When I got home, I found an empty apartment. She had packed some things and left in her car—our car. She took our son. She took the road to Alexandria, where her parents lived. It wasn't going to be the end of the world. She was just going back to her mother for a while, and my parents would be close by too. She always got on well with my parents. And we loved each other, damn it!"

He paused for control. Julia didn't move, gazing at him in the darkness. "But some old bedouin came off the desert in his truck. I suppose he misjudged her speed, and he probably didn't have good lights. At least it was quick. From what I heard, neither of them could have suffered. When I heard the news, I fainted right out. I thought I would die, and may- be I did. When you lose a child, and the other per- son closest to you, I think you die." The tears did not come. Something stemmed the tide. But Julia's face was wet down both sides as she reached a hand toward him. He turned to her, and she kissed him on the lips.

It was after sunset, the nighttime hour of prayer, when Khalil returned to Yvette's house. The cries from the minarets were in the air as he drove up to the iron gate, which was opened immediately. Once inside, he hurried to the fountain in the downstairs room, removed his socks and shoes, and began the purification ceremony. He washed his hands and face, neck, head behind the ears, rinsed his mouth and nose, washed his arms to the elbows, and his feet. Facing Mecca, he recited the opening passage of the Koran, then prostrated himself, touching his nose and forehead to the floor, repeating other prayers. He ended the ritual by wishing the mercy of God on the guardian angels who watched over him. When he rose, he noted that the cooks and maids were likewise praying in the courtyard. The head servant was a Christian, who did not join the Moslem prayers.

After the ritual, he went up to his room. Feeling cleansed, he threw off his shirt and lit a cigarette. He checked that the wooden chest containing the transmitter had not been opened, and paced the floor, thinking. Hard muscle packed his shoulders, and his body tapered to a hard, strong waist, as he paced silently, staring into the shadows of the room.

Yvette was in her bath. Khalil realized this when he walked into her bedroom, saw clothing strewn around, and heard the gentle splashing from next door. He went into her bathroom, perched on a stool, and remained deep in thought, while she looked at him inquiringly. She had a glass of wine within reach, and he knew that she could be settled for the night.

"I've got a job for you," he said finally. She reached for the wine. Her glance might have said, Oh, you have, have you? "It is of vital importance to me, therefore to you, and to all of us. Are you sober?"

She sighed. Her hair was wet and black as pitch, showing the perfect oval of her face. She said nothing, but waited to hear what was coming.

"I want you to get to know a man. He is a scientist who possesses some knowledge I must have. I can tell you how to meet him. It should be easy. Then we'll figure out what to do from there." She looked at him with a kind of wonder. His eyes were narrowed, thinking, calculating, almost oblivious of her. "The problem is time. I can't afford to wait around for dribs and drabs of pillow talk. You're going to have to blow his mind."

She sat upright in the bath. Her skin glistened against the background of tiny inlaid tiles, mostly white, but patterned with yellow and green. Seeing that her robe was out of reach, she compressed her lips for a moment, then rose abruptly, showering water. His glance slid down to her belly, to the black bush beneath, and he smiled faintly.

"You'll do," he said.

He rose, towering over her. Her eyes came up as he stepped closer, and he saw that look that made her face like the face of a child again. He had never touched her sexually. But he sensed the haunted mixture of desire and fear that his physical closeness aroused in her, and which never failed to intimidate her.

"Yvette . . ." He put both hands on her shoulders. "I am not asking this for myself. You know that I ask nothing for myself. I am asking this for Egypt, and for the memory of our father. And for God," he added. "The Koran says, 'If you see an injustice, correct it with your hand. If you cannot correct it with your hand, correct it with your mouth; and if you cannot correct it with your mouth, correct it in your heart.' Too long have we suffered in our hearts and spoken with our mouths. Too many of us have done this for too long. I am here to correct an injustice, sister, and you will help me."

She moved away. It always made her stronger when he spoke righteously. He smiled inwardly, wondering what it would be like if he ever decided to possess her sexually.

Yvette walked into her bedroom and went to the window, arms folded. "Give me a cigarette," she said, and he knew that he had won again.

Chapter 14

IT WAS Thursday, the last day of the week. Mary had come home tired from the school, and was thinking of a quiet meal, when the telephone rang and she pounced on it. As always, Mary was pleased to hear Yvette's voice on the telephone. Before she knew it, she was grinning at some story about the inefficiency of salesgirls in expensive stores. A pub crawl? Could one do that in Cairo? It was a good way to meet foreigners, Yvette said, making Mary wonder what she was up to.

They started by meeting in the Hilton. Yvette was already there when Mary arrived, after walking across from her apartment. The bar was quiet. Without

Yvette, it would have seemed quite empty, a little capsule of middle-class America. With Yvette, seated on a bar stool, one shapely leg draped across the other in a tight skirt, it was like a tableau in a fashion magazine, advertising the latest chic drink or cigarette. She was drinking Pernod. To Mary's horror, she was drinking it straight, no water. Mary had never known anyone to drink Pernod without water, but then she had never known anyone like Yvette.

Mary tried to order beer, but Yvette vetoed that. Saying that they were not in England now, she prescribed a straight-up martini, and further exceeded her mandate by making it a double. Mary tried to change the order, but the barman didn't seem interested in her instructions.

"Are you well known here?" she asked.

"Darling, this is my town. Of course they know me."

"So what's the occasion? For getting drunk, I mean?"

"Do you feel like getting drunk?" Yvette looked at her delightedly. "Let's do it!" she said. "Let's get drunk! Let's get laid!" She looked around. "Not here, though. This is Dullsville," she said, ignoring other customers at the bar. "Let's go."

"Just give me time to drink this." Mary couldn't bring herself to waste the martini.

They chatted for a while, swapping news. Mary told Yvette about something out of the ordinary that had happened that day. One of her colleagues at the school had asked her to do him a favor. He was a little Greek man, whose mother was ill in Athens. He had decided to go home for what remained of the summer, but had no wish to keep his apartment in Cairo. What it came down to was—he had asked Mary if she would keep some things for him in her apartment. No furniture,

just some things that he would like to have back if
he ever returned. Mary was kind of sorry for him.
He seemed to have no friends in Cairo. Anyway, she
had said that she would do it. He was going to bring
his bits and pieces by the next day on his way to the
airport.

As Mary had expected, somehow, Yvette had her
doubts.

Mary smiled. "I can't see the harm. He seems such
a worried little man."

"What does he look like?"

"Short. Dark. Huge, heavy eyebrows."

"Cute?"

"Not to my taste."

"Then I think you're crazy. He'll put you to endless trouble over his junk, and you'll get no thanks
for it."

"Well, it's done now."

Mary's drink went down rather fast. I can do that
once, she told herself. Not more than once.

Although as fit as a fox, Yvette was not a person
who believed in walking. Mary felt the pressure on her
back as Yvette managed to produce wheel spin from
her tiny MG on the way out of the parking lot. They
zoomed along the road by the Nile, and screeched into
the parking lot of Shepheard's.

Mary had never been in the long-established, cosmopolitan hotel. She eyed the modern easy chairs in
a lounge they passed through, and the open, winding
staircase that rose like a magic carpet, nothing seeming
to support it. The bar was busier here, with businessmen and others, and a few colonial characters of the
type that still existed in spite of everything. Yvette's
eyes swept the room. "Come!" she said, and Mary was
almost surprised not to be taken by the hand.

Yvette headed for the bar, where there were some empty places. But she did not take the first available position. She walked on choosily, and Mary was quite surprised at where she came to roost, next to a character whose head spun around to look at them. Mary saw large spectacles on a freckled face, thick lips, and a curiously shaped head with brown hair on it. He was dressed in a green sports jacket with patches on the elbows, and was drinking draft beer. Yvette spoke to the barman in French, then returned to English, speaking to Mary. Right away, Mary sensed that her companion's conversation was now not quite natural. It was for the benefit of whoever happened to be listening.

"One thing I like about the British," Yvette said, "is that they stand around the bar. I can't be bothered with people who separate themselves off at little tables— why come to a bar? Why does one come to a bar, after all?"

When Mary saw that she was waiting for an answer, she said, "To have a drink?"

"Very good. And why does one drink alcohol?"

"To get drunk?"

"You're catching on. And why does one get drunk?"

Mary laughed. "To get laid?" she whispered.

"You *are* learning! And why does one get laid?"

"Oh, dear. I think I'd better give up on that one."

"One gets laid," Yvette said, "so that one can sleep well and start all over again the next day. That is the object of life. To be a good whore, and make it to the next day. Are you interested in philosophy?"

Mary sipped her second pungent drink. She could feel the first one glowing in her belly. "Is that philosophy or politics?"

"That's quite astute," Yvette said. "That's very astute. I can see you've known some politicians." At this point she leaned closer to Mary and whispered quietly, "Is he listening? The weirdo behind me?"

Mary spluttered. "He's agog."

"I think he's kind of cute."

Mary stared at her in astonishment.

Yvette then went off on one of her tangents. Khalil was a true oaf, she said. In spite of being educated at the Sorbonne, he would be quite at home sitting in a galabiya, in a sawdust-floor café in Cairo, talking politics and other higher things with his potbellied friends, while his little wife scrubbed away at home, clearing up the meal that she had prepared for him—and served to him—not eating with him, of course—she ate with the children—while he went out and puffed himself senseless on a hookah. Mary probably didn't know the way of life for most Egyptian women. Married off at an early age by agreement among her relatives—her male relatives, of course—with the right to refuse, oh, yes—like the right to elect a president when only one candidate was offered—and you knew damned well it would cost you your job, or worse, if you didn't vote for him—and the results would be rigged anyway.

Oh, yes. Women were protected, even by the words of the Prophet in the Koran. But just try defying the conventions, and it could cost you your damned life—not only out in the country—right here in Cairo. Yvette had not been raised that way herself, because her mother was civilized. But this was no fault of her father, or her brother. Khalil's habits around the house were particularly loutish. He would say his prayers five times a day—which was all right, if you didn't mind people standing barefoot in your front room, throwing water around—terrorize the servants if they didn't do the same, then walk into Yvette's bathroom while she was bathing, blow cigarette smoke in her face, and tell her what was wrong with the way she ran her house. The youngest servant walked in fear of him. She was just waiting to be summoned, fucked silly, and kicked out of her job if she didn't like it. The poor girl needed her job. She also needed her virginity. He was worse than Farouk. "Do you have brothers?" she asked. Mary nodded. "Do you find them uncouth?" Mary nodded, smiling. She saw the green sports jacket sip his beer, eyes flickering. He had just learned that the woman beside him was not speaking of her husband, or her lover, but of her brother only. Mary could hardly believe it, but she knew that all this was for his benefit.

The two of them got talking while Mary was in the ladies' room. Mary could only assume that Yvette had started it. When she came back, Yvette was turned on her bar stool, totally relaxed, while the green jacket sloped toward her, like the leaning tower of Pisa, hanging on her words.

"Mary. I'd like you to meet George. He's got a Ph.D. in something, and he's not as English as he looks."

Mary took the hand that was offered. It was an oddly shaped hand with prickles of blond hair on it. "Pleased to meet you," he said, and she knew immediately that he was not English. Then he grinned unexpectedly. "Actually, it's Girgis. Sorry about that," he said to Yvette. "You meet a lot of foreigners in here."

Mary ended up walking back to her apartment. It was a beautiful evening and she didn't mind a bit, leaving Yvette with her newfound friend. Yvette really was a puzzle. Obviously bisexual, she seemed to have the strangest taste in men. Mary went home and spent the rest of the evening curled up with a book.

Chapter 15

MICHAEL PAPPAS waited on the roof outside of his now-empty apartment. A truck had come by that morning and taken his furniture and other valuables. The promise was that these would be delivered to the address he'd given in Athens. He had told the English girl that he was renting a furnished place, but this was not true. He still lived in the apartment in which he had been raised, before his parents returned to Athens to live with his brother. God knows why he had stayed on in Egypt. Things were not so good these days for foreigners. The strange events of the last two days were proof of that.

All the same, it was nostalgic. Pappas looked at his collection of potted plants, which he would have to leave behind, and found it hard to believe that he would never see this roof again.

Never again. That had been made very clear. Pappas was leaving Egypt, and he was leaving it for good.

The taxi came promptly at eight A.M. It contained the same two dark-suited men who had approached him a few days ago and told him what he was going to do. One of the men was totally uncommunicative, and said nothing. Pappas believed that he was there in case of trouble. The other did some smiling, as he spoke patiently, but with no taste for small talk. Financially, it was a very good deal for Pappas. No explanation, no by-your-leave, but for doing what they wanted him to do, he would be paid more than he would earn in five years at the school. The men possessed identification that featured the words "Internal Security." Pappas had not been encouraged to scrutinize these documents, nor was it necessary. He was convinced.

The taxi contained two suitcases and a couple of boxes, both well sealed. Pappas put his own suitcases in the trunk and was warned not to confuse them with the others when he got to the girl's place. His passport was returned to him, and he was given the air tickets he'd been promised. He was assured that a small fortune in hard currency had been deposited in his name in Athens. The talker of the two reminded him, as they shook hands and parted, that all this was strictly confidential. His story to his family would be that he had just decided to leave. He was reminded that he could never return to Egypt.

Mary was up and about when he reached her apartment. She was dressed in shorts, and there was the smell of toasting bread in the air. Pappas carried up the boxes and the suitcases, and put them in a cupboard she specified. She was totally unsuspicious. He marveled at her innocence. His interpretation of all this was that the secret police were setting up a British citizen to be arrested as a spy.

When Michael Pappas landed in his new home, the land of his fathers, the first thing he did was check that the money was there. It was. Then he traveled to his brother's house, where he was treated to a mound of calamari and a kilo of retsina wine. The meal was witnessed by observers in a town house opposite. The conversation too was overheard. Local instructions were that Michael Pappas would be watched closely until further notice. He had served his purpose. Nor was he in any danger, if he behaved. At the first sign of any problem, he would be eliminated.

Later that evening, Khalil entered Mary's apartment using one of his own keys. He soon found the cupboard where she had stored the boxes and suitcases, and checked that the briefcase containing the transmitter was there, in one of the locked suitcases. Mary was out at the time, having dinner with Yvette. He reflected that that relationship would have to be preserved, unsullied by sexual advances, for example. He had warned Yvette to that effect, without giving her the reason. His own relationship with the unwitting keeper of his equipment would likewise be kept as it was, distant. The transmitter was not in an east-facing room. It would have to be moved and replaced each time he used it. He chose a room that seemed to be a guest room. It had a small table by a window with a curtain that could be closed. The window opened easily, and he saw how he could rig the aerial. There would be no problem. The problem now was to disable the tracking stations.

Before he left the apartment, Khalil spent a moment in the main bedroom, looking around and smiling. This operation had become extremely delicate. In order to accomplish what he had to do, he was being forced through a series of preliminaries, all more dangerous than he would like. Khalil was optimistic though. Not given to contemplating failure, he was convinced that he could achieve whatever he set his mind to do, momentous though it was, in this case. After that . . .

He smiled again as he looked around. With a sudden reaction in his loins, he thought that Mary Miles-Tudor might still experience love à l'Arab when this was all over.

*   *   *

Mary was in good spirits when she returned to her apartment that night. Yvette had been at her bizarre best, and they had eaten a memorable meal—grilled pigeon, meat and rice wrapped in those delicious vine leaves, spicy lamb kebab, eggplant, and good wine. Yvette had answered vaguely when Mary asked her how things had gone the night before with—what was his name?—the 'Englishman'? She seemed to have forgotten that, and her talk now was of another matter.

Yvette was going to have a party. It was going to be soon—she never planned parties in advance—and it was going to be the party of the season. Mary was invited. Not only that, she was commanded to attend! This was going to be a debauch. There would be food and drink and drugs and nudity. It was going to be a costume party. Everyone must plan a splendid costume. Yvette was working on the guest list. There would be some married couples—why not? Some of the best-looking men were married—women too. But they would be well chosen, and well warned. She was going to put it on the invitation. "This party may be hazardous to your relationship."

When she returned to her apartment, Mary poured herself a nightcap and paced around. There was a full-length mirror in the bedroom, and the image in it caught her eye. She turned to it, chin raised and smiling. Ariadne, she thought inspirationally. Why not? Straight from Mount Olympus to Yvette's party. She had sandals and gold braid, and a white dress that was almost made for it, which she went to look at immediately.

Chapter 16

TRAVELING IN two cars, five of the eight members of the
Supreme Committee of the Arab Socialist Union crossed
the Tahrir Bridge and took the road to Giza. Had it been
daylight, they would have seen the pyramids, including
the Great Pyramid of Cheops, as they bowled along the
tree-lined highway. They pulled into the driveway of a
home set back from the road.

The door was opened by a servant, and the lady of the
house was there to greet them. She addressed each man
by his first name, and passed the time of day, offering
tea or soft drinks, till her husband appeared. Unlike the
visitors, who were dressed in business suits, the man of
the house wore an old pair of pants and slip-on shoes.
After another round of greetings, the men headed for
the study, where blinds were drawn on tall windows.
They selected seats on the chairs and couches of the
room.

The spokesman for the group was a senior minister
in President Nasser's Cabinet. He was a man with a
voice that carried assurance, not much emotion, who
was greatly feared by those who worked for him. "I
hope you don't mind us coming here, Anwar," he said.
"But rumors are flying, and I thought it time we got
together." He gestured shruggingly.

Anwar Sadat noted two things. The mild reproach,

and the assumption of authority—*I* thought it time we got together. "I know," he said understandingly. "We've been so tied up these days, I hardly see my wife. But don't worry about coming here. It's not the first time I've talked politics in this room." He grinned, a gesture that was not reflected in the faces of the other men. "What's on your mind, my friends?"

"I almost don't know where to start," the spokesman said. "Since the May Day fiasco, things have gone from bad to worse. What possessed him, Anwar? Did you have any idea that he was going to"—he gestured again, with an air of anger this time—"practically beg the United States to interfere in our affairs?"

This was the kind of question that Sadat did not answer. He took out his pipe and stuffed it with tobacco. Since his first heart attack, at the age of forty-two, he had switched from cigarettes to the pipe, which he now found to be an excellent stage prop. "Oh, I wouldn't take that too seriously. Gamal is just a bit frustrated, as we all are, aren't we?" When the others looked blank, he gestured with the pipe. "The Israelis have American equipment, and American Intelligence reports. That's why they can hit us deep into our territory, like last January." Sadat was referring to a raid in which dozens of people were killed at Abu-Zabal, on the edge of Cairo. "You all know what our Soviet allies have delivered to us in the last three years in terms of arms. They won't even replace the ammunition when we send a few shells across the canal. In January of this year, they promised us SAM missiles by March. They promised us TU-16 fighter planes by April. March came and went. April came and went. Nothing. So Gamal made his May Day speech."

One of the other men sat forward. Before speaking, he received a nod from the spokesman. "There has been talk of a 'deterrent weapon.' One that Gamal asks for repeatedly. Do you interpret that to be the SAM missiles?"

Sadat looked at him. "Of course."

The man sat back slowly. The denial of his suspicions caused a silence. Sadat vowed one thing inwardly. Anyone who even breathed the thought that Nasser might have asked Russia for nuclear weapons was dead—politically dead—from that point onward.

The spokesman's mouth was set in a hard line. "Going back to the May Day speech, I hope we can assume that he did not mean what he said—that it was all talk to put pressure on our allies?" Sadat smiled and shrugged elaborately, a response that gave the spokesman no satisfaction whatsoever. "I understand that the Americans have responded. That they have come up with some plan for a cease-fire. What do you know of this, Anwar?"

"It's called the Rogers Plan," Sadat explained. "It calls for several things. An Israeli withdrawal from the Sinai, a ninety-day cease-fire, and a United Nations mediator from some Scandinavian country." He grinned suddenly. "Mr. Rogers must be a genius, don't you think, to come up with such a plan? His name will go down to posterity."

"Is there any truth in the rumor that Gamal is considering accepting it?"

Sadat put a match to his pipe, and for several seconds there was silence in the room. "It has been considered. We are considering all courses, naturally."

The spokesman almost showed his anger. He was not interested in what Sadat was considering, and resented the Vice President's way of always trying to imply that he had political power, when in fact he had none. Part of the purpose in coming here was to see which side Sadat would be on if it came to influencing Nasser. "But an

American solution! That would surely be unwise, to say the least."

Sadat smiled. "Don't worry about it," he repeated.

One of the other men cleared his throat. "I spoke to Venogradov the other day," he said, referring to the Soviet Ambassador. "He called me on a separate matter, but it was really this that he wanted to talk about. Apparently Brezhnev is furious. If Gamal is foolish enough to raise this in Moscow, I can't imagine the consequences."

"How did this idea get to Moscow?" Sadat asked quietly. "How do they know what we are considering or not considering?"

The spokesman wondered why he felt defensive. The Rogers Plan was public knowledge. "They do not know what we are considering, but they conjecture," he said. "Maybe they've heard rumors. In any case, Gamal must be warned. If he talks this way in Moscow it could cause a rift with the only ally we have left in the world."

Sadat grunted. "An ally that has done very little for us of late."

"Unless you count the Aswan High Dam. And protecting our airspace."

"Which they think entitles them to dictate our policies to the world. But don't get me wrong," Sadat said, his sharp tone melting away. "I have no more time for the Americans than you have. It's just that we feel we need a little elbow room." He moved his elbows outward, fists clenched, smiling. "We don't want to be boxed in."

The spokesman glanced at the faces of his group and saw that they were totally unsatisfied. As always, Sadat was keeping his options open, and divulging nothing. "There has been so much secrecy of late," the spokesman said. "All of a sudden, he tells us nothing and has become unpredictable." Sadat's face was impassive. They must notice a difference, he thought, from former days, when Nasser's so-called friends had routinely manipulated his attitudes for their own purposes, very often just prior to major public speeches. The same men who now sat opposite had more than once provoked the President into launching tirades against the United States, for example, by timely whispers in his ear. "How sick is he, do you think?" the spokesman asked.

Sadat looked up. "He's as strong as an ox."

"His nerves?"

"He is under pressure."

It was always the same. No position, no disagreement, affability. The man would never be a leader.

One of the men present was a minister close to Nasser, and a fanatical leader in the war against the old families of Egypt. He and his colleagues had been tapping telephones and gathering information for years, and were said to be ready for another great purge, in the name of "counterrevolutionary activity." "It is a nervous time," he said. "We are surrounded by enemies, and literally don't have a friend left—other than the Soviets. We in turn are their friend in the Middle East, and it must remain that way. If we lose the support of Russia, it is not only the Israelis who would be down on us like a pack of hyenas. There are enemies within."

He should know about that, Sadat thought. As the president of the Council for the Abolition of Feudalism, he was one of those who had created enemies within, while gathering power into his own hands.

"I'm sorry." Sadat sat forward. "I think I lost the thrust of that. Enemies within?"

There was silence in the room. Seconds ticked by before the spokesman said, "We are speaking of threat, Anwar. To the revolution. Our economy is in tatters, as is our ability to defend ourselves. We cannot afford to antagonize our friends."

Sadat puffed on his pipe, nodding. He was thinking that they got less subtle every day, these men who thought they were in charge of Egypt. "Well, I think we have no basic disagreement," he said. "Gamal is frustrated, as I've said. He doesn't like to be boxed in—by our Soviet friends or anyone else. But I can give you my personal assurance. We shall not accept the Rogers Plan."

The spokesman nodded. At least that had been achieved. They discussed related matters for a while. Nasser's recent actions had angered the Arab world. The Palestinians in particular had threatened violence and terrorism. There was concern. Security forces were gearing up for the President's return from Moscow.

The meeting broke up finally. The visitors left, swatting at mosquitoes that seemed to fill the sky around the house, and returned to Cairo in their chauffeur-driven vehicles.

The basement under the house in Damascus ran the full length of the building. In the past, it had been used as a wine cellar, but the wooden bins were empty now, standing in rows that rose to the ceiling. The marksman stood at one end of the cellar, looking down a narrow corridor between the bins. The weapon he aimed was small, made of stainless steel, and his target was a hundred twenty feet away, at the far end of the basement. Andrei Varsanyi stood tensely, his back to the marksman. He did not hear the sharp breath of sound when the trigger was squeezed, but he felt the tiny prick between his shoulder blades. The impact was not visible to the naked eye.

Varsanyi removed his jacket, and had to use his

fingers to find the dart that was caught in the material.
Looking closely, he saw the little packet of flared metal
and the needle-sharp point that had pricked his skin.
"Ingenious," he said. "I don't know how a thing of
that shape can fly—or does it open up on contact?"
He looked back along the corridor between the bins.
"I don't know how he gets such range with such a tiny
weapon." He turned and nodded to a man who had
watched impassively. "It looks good to me."

The gray-suited man came forward and took the dart
between his fingers. He saw that a delicate structure
that had made it aerodynamic had been crushed on
impact with the cloth, causing it to be held in the fabric.
"Did you feel the prick?"

"Hardly. A man might notice it, but he would think
nothing of it."

Unless he were a professional, the other man thought.
"Let's suppose he doesn't." He turned and spoke to
the marksman, who was walking toward them. "What
happens next?"

The marksman was a prematurely graying man with
tousled hair. He was also the weapon-maker, and had
the unmistakable look of a scientist rather than a strat-
egist. He spoke deferentially, but with pride in his
work. "After being shot, the victim will walk on and
go about his business. The poison is chemically bound,
and will not act immediately. After three hours, maybe four, he will become aware of some physical dis-
comfort. His limbs will become heavy, he will sweat
and feel nauseous—but not for long. When he finally falls, it will be with the symptoms of a sudden
heart attack. An autopsy would reveal that this is
not the case, but in Egypt"—he shrugged—"autopsies
are not popular with the Muslim faith. If the heart
attack seemed credible—" He shrugged again. He had

never been told for whom his weapon was intended.

The gray-suited man looked doubtful. He turned, walked away for a few paces, then turned back. "This sounds all very well except for one thing—the removal of the dart. For this we need a close friend of the victim. One who can touch his back and deftly remove the thing, or who can be there when he falls. But this is not as simple as it sounds. We speak of skill and ice-cool nerves. We speak of properties that are rare enough in a professional. There are other imponderables. The victim might remove his jacket. He might proceed to his own house and go to bed. Where would this be delivered?"

Varsanyi hesitated. "There is a certain mosque. It was hoped to plan a visit there and to use a building opposite. The building is still vacant."

The other shook his head. "At another time, it might succeed. As things are now, given the security, they will not ignore a vacant building. I like the poison. But I would recommend another method of delivery."

Varsanyi replaced his coat. He looked more grim than surprised. "There is another plan," he said. "It's the one preferred by the man in Cairo, though I don't know if it's less risky." He spoke again to the weapon-maker. "Thank you, Vlastamil. Your work is of the highest quality, as always." After dismissing the weapon-maker, he spoke privately to his other colleague.

The gray-suited man listened to Varsanyi, his eyes fastened on his face. His reaction to what he heard was conveyed by the intensity with which he listened. When Varsanyi finished, his eyes unfocused for a moment.

"Who is this agent? Do I know him?"

Varsanyi shook his head. He did not explain more.

"Can it work?" he asked.

The gray-suited man stared at Varsanyi for a moment. "I'll say this. They'll never reconstruct it if it does."

"But can it be done? What are the probabilities?"

"I don't know. I wouldn't want to be the one to try it."

After shaking hands with his visiting colleague, and seeing him out to his car, Varsanyi went upstairs, his shoulders hunched, and sat in the darkness of his office. So what to recommend, he asked himself. Knowing that the man in Cairo was working on reestablishing the radio link, he settled down to another night of waiting.

Chapter 17

AT TIMES it seemed that every room in the house was ablaze with light. Then one walked through rooms of darkness, or near darkness, where groups collected around a hookah, a small lamp showing their faces, talking quietly, convulsing in laughter now and then, or where couples swayed to the slow music, the men feeling the bodies of the women. The haunting voice of Um Kalthum seemed to permeate the rooms, singing one of her endless love songs, and there were bursts of revelry, as well as calm spots, on the galleries, and in the fragrant air of the courtyard.

Mary had never smoked hashish before, and it was a

habit she had no intention of acquiring. But the atmosphere of Yvette's party was like a living thing, and it was hard to be there and refuse. After a few margaritas from the bar, surrounded by people who were totally unrecognizable in their fantastic costumes, she found herself beginning to dissociate and flow, becoming one with the common personality. Anyway, it happened.

The invitation that she finally accepted came from an Englishman dressed as an Arab. He had curly hair, a harelip, and a quietly insistent voice, and Mary never did find out what he was doing in Cairo. He might have been even younger than herself, or ten years older, as he quietly took charge of her, introducing her to a group of people as he lit the pipe and pushed in a pellet of hashish. Mary sat on a cushion like the rest, the robe of flowing white she wore tucked around her knees, as she took her turn and puffed, first tentatively, then with more confidence.

Surprise! The smoke was as gentle as the fragrant air. She smiled and pulled on it again, down into her lungs, letting it trail out from her nostrils, the way she saw the others doing.

The Englishman told her stories about Cairo. Some of these involved Yvette, and Mary laughed at his descriptions, while Yvette, who was dressed as a wicked queen, or sorceress seemed to be everywhere. In a purple costume of loose folds that could either cover every inch of her, or reveal most of it, according to how she moved her limbs, she could transform in an instant from the regal, hard-faced queen to a statuesque and almost-naked demon. Mary had seen this transformation earlier, while they were both talking to a tall young man, whose costume consisted of paint, a grass skirt, and a fishing pole across his shoulder. Yvette had burst out laughing at something that was said,

raised her arms, and there she was, wearing nothing
but daubs of silver on her breasts and genitals. The
fisher boy's mouth had opened like a cave. Then he
moved the pole, which turned out to have a string
attached, and his enormous penis had snaked up from
the grass skirt, to nudge the silvered pubis of the queen.
Mary had collapsed with laughter as Yvette shrieked,
spun with her arms around her, and disappeared into
her robes again . . . Exotic mystery and magic. That
was the theme. Mary, in her austere white robe and
sandals, was a rapidly deteriorating goddess.

"I don't feel anything. Is this really hash?" she asked,
filling her lungs. The harelipped Englishman smiled
and nodded, gazing at her breasts. Then she tried to
move.

A record player in a corner was playing jazz. The
record ended and Mary volunteered to flip it. Seconds
later—or was it minutes?—she realized what she was
doing. She was still in place, struggling with the cushion
she'd been sitting on as though unable to get free of it.
The demure goddess had a robe that no longer played
around her ankles. Kicking feebly, her long legs were
exposed to her white underwear. Nor was there laughter
from the group. In her box of memories, Mary would
retain a picture of the fixed stares of the men and the
quiet smiles of the girls.

Exotic mystery and magic. The dissociation of the
mind and personality. Like a dream in which you see
yourself from some external vantage point, she moved
through time, watching herself dance with a succession
of partners. She felt very confident and in control, as
she smilingly refused more than one dance to each.

Mary was never sure how the game had started. She
would not remember going to the main room, following
the flow, but she remembered gazing up at Yvette,

who stood on the staircase with her arms raised for
silence. The only light was a candle that cast shadows
on the walls. Effective, Mary thought. Very spooky and
effective. Yvette's deep voice came rolling down as she
addressed them.

"My friends, the time has come. The time has come
for the abandonment of all that inhibits us, and with-
holds us from each other's dreams. We are at the gates
of Castle Bianca. That stately home where all who enter
must submit to the common will. Beware ye timid and
fainthearted. Prepare to shed your modesty and pride.
There is no modesty in Castle Bianca. No secrets and
no shame. Dear friends, it is my trembling pleasure to
introduce to you . . . Mustapha!"

With a flourish that threw aside her robes, Yvette
leapt high, arching backward, seeming to disappear in
the air as she closed her robes and someone snuffed
her candle. Mary knew that Yvette worked out each
day, took hormones, and dieted. All this was seen in
that instant of exposure, before she vanished. Almost
simultaneously, another small lamp came up in a far
corner of the room behind them.

The Arab sat cross-legged on the floor. In striking
contrast to what they had just seen, his oily, black-
stubbled face smiled up at them. Unlike the other
guests, he was not in costume. He wore a red and
white striped galabiya, with black hair curling greasily
around a fez, and gold teeth that glinted as he grinned.
For all that, he was a strangely sensuous figure, neither
young nor old, as his black eyes seemed to find each one
of them, gazing out. He addressed them in polished, but
accented English.

"The game we are about to play, my friends, is an
ancient and subtle game. From the courts of Castle
Bianca, in medieval Europe, it is a game that plays

upon our psyche, and evokes our primitive desires.
So be prepared to be surprised, to have exposed those
inner fantasies that maybe you don't even know you
have."

The Arab snapped his fingers. From another room
two little girls came in, as black as pitch, wearing almost
nothing but huge grins. They struggled with an earthen
pot between them, big enough for either one to hide
in, which they placed on the floor and stood beside,
beaming at their audience. The Arab went on.

"In this pot," he explained, "there is a charm for
each person in the room, with some to spare. The
charms are all of silver, except for one, which is of
gold. When we draw the charms the chances are that
the gold one will be drawn. If not, the keepers of the pot
will quietly take it, and one of us shall join the game."
His smile caressed the little Nubians, whose eyes and
teeth shone in the lamplight. "The person with the gold
charm is the attacker. No one knows who the attacker
is except himself—or herself, as the case may be. But
when the lights go out, we all know that an attacker has
been chosen. We then go about our business, friends,
doing what we will, while the attacker stalks the rooms.
Now listen closely, my dear friends." There was excited
muttering and some nervous laughter in the room.

The Arab went on in his smooth, mesmeric voice.
"The attacker makes his presence known by touching
the victim on the throat. This may be done violently, to
evoke a scream—ladies sometimes do this, for reasons
that you'll see—or very gently, as a soft caress. If the
victim then screams loudly, there has been death, in
Castle Bianca. We reassemble for a time of mourning,
return our charms, and draw again. But if the victim
does not scream"—the Arab paused, and his gold teeth
glinted in the lamplight—"it is the solemn duty of the

attacker to . . . rape him, or her, as the case may
be . . . Rape . . . I wonder how you feel about that
word, my friends. To some, it is the most evocative
word in the English language. Let me define what it
means in the context of our game." There was total
silence as the Arab pulled his robe around him, and
his omnivorous black eyes gazed out.

"If the victim does not scream at the first touch,
the attacker and the victim must proceed as follows.
They must come together, and the attacker must do
whatever is necessary to induce orgasm in the victim.
Whatever is necessary," he repeated. "At the choice
of the attacker. Success will be judged by those who
watch." He grinned suddenly and wickedly. "By those
who watch," he repeated once again. "Because once it
is clear that someone is being 'raped'—which is usually
rather clear, however quiet they may be—the other
players are entitled to light lamps and gather around—
in fact it is their sacred duty. This is the commonality of
Castle Bianca. It is also our way of knowing if the attacker and victim have acquitted themselves honorably. A
word of warning at this point. You must keep your
charm. For if time goes by and nothing happens, a
gong will sound, in Castle Bianca." He gestured, and
one of the small girls struck a gong. "That is a warning.
If time goes by again, there will be a second gong—" The
other little girl banged lustily. "The lights will then go
up. We shall assemble here. And any person who cannot
produce a silver charm will be quickly tried, sentenced,
and . . . punished. Sentence will be passed by me." He
smiled and bowed. "It will be carried out in public, will
always be appropriate, of course, and I've been known
to take part in it myself." His peel of laughter rang
out in the room. "The attacker must attack. Unless, of
course . . ." His slow smile scanned the darkened faces

in the room. "I have known occasions, friends, when a gentleman, or a lady, has failed to attack, and then pretended to be most upset when they cannot produce a charm. There are those who find their minds working in strange ways, in Castle Bianca, usually to their great surprise . . . No one is forced to enter here. Before we start, you will have the opportunity to leave." He pointed to the iron gate to the outside. "Consider well, before the gates are closed."

By now the crowd was seething with excitement. Mary saw the doubt in some faces. This is the time to leave, she told herself. Get out of here, before this madness starts. But she did not leave. Nor did she notice anyone else heading for the door.

The Arab lit a hand-rolled cigarette. Mary realized that there was probably no one present who was not drugged. "There is one more important rule," said the strange master of ceremonies. "The attacker is not allowed to speak, or to announce himself in any way, except by touching the victim on the throat. Violation of this will mean a public trial. That's where the subtlety comes in. If a male victim, for example, is touched caressingly in the darkness, he does not know whether the attacker is the woman of his dreams . . . or me!" he bellowed, with a great leer. "There are many variations. A modest player, for example, can always opt to 'die,' by emitting a blood-curdling scream. True, but the curious and fascinating thing is that it doesn't always work that way. When the time comes, there often is no scream, even when it is most intended. There are strange powers in the psyche. People don't always do what they intend, in Castle Bianca. So be warned, and be prepared."

Leave, Mary told herself again. You've made enough of a fool of yourself for one evening. But as the Arab pointed out, one could always scream if "attacked." The chances of having to be the attacker were quite small. For whatever reason, she still stayed.

The servants closed the iron gate to the outside. It was understood that they would open briefly between rounds of the game. Yvette had chosen her group well. No one left that Mary observed. The master of ceremonies raised his arms.

"Let the game begin. I now declare this house to be . . . Castle Bianca!"

The little Nubians stood beside the pot, grinning tirelessly, as people lined up for the draw. "One charm only, please," they said repeatedly as people thrust their hands into the jar and peered into their cupped hands.

For a while, Mary took her chances in the crowd. Not that there was any risk, she told herself, when all she had to do was scream, but it was nerve-wracking all the same. The whispering darkness seemed alive when the lights went out. The Arab's words: the fear that fingers would somehow take her by surprise, and she would fail to find her voice . . . It did not occur to her that she could challenge the mandates of the game. That was one of the strange things. In the atmosphere of this bizarre party, it became the law that if someone took you by the throat, and you did not scream instantly, you would be publicly raped, and that was that.

There were a couple of early screams, splitting the darkness. Those were the ones that got away, people said. But then the victim was identified—and not accused of wasting everybody's time—but that was the feeling, as they all lined up again. Others did not scream. Mary saw a boy in his teens possess a slim woman in her thirties. He possessed her on the stairs, to a maximum crowd, which cheered wildly when the woman came. As time went by, submission became the norm. Sounds were heard by those around, a crowd gathered, and lamps went up, as a couple writhed in ecstasy or humiliation. The spectator part became equally ingrained. People watched and even clapped politely.

There was another strange thing. After a time, the party seemed to go on pretty much as usual. People danced, and smoked, and whispered in the darkness until an event took place, whereupon they would gather as though for a routine piece of entertainment. Mary stayed with a group who told each other that they found all this to be rather sick as they smoked their marijuana and took only passing interest when the cry went up. But then they all lined up again when it was time to reassign the gold coin. After a time, she began to wander on her own. It could have been the drug, the alcohol, or the strange spell that seemed to be on all of them that induced a period of blankness, or disconnectedness. One of her clear thoughts was that one can grow accustomed to anything.

She had found her way to a room upstairs that was obviously a bedroom. She had entered, not by the door to the inside of the house, but by a French window to the gallery, one door of which was—probably inadvertently—unlocked. By the size and nature of the room, which she could see in outline by the glow from the courtyard, it was a currently occupied main bedroom. It was certainly not a servant's room. That suggested that it must be Yvette's, or her brother Ibrahim's— which set her wondering where Yvette's brother was tonight. In a corner of the room, where the darkness was complete, she sat on something that appeared to be a wooden chest, and kept her eye on the window for a while. She was very tired. It occurred to her that she was trapped here if anyone should come along, but the level of brain activity was low. Eventually she crept onto something—a bed or a large couch—her limbs like lead, pushed some papers and other items to the floor, and passed out.

When her eyes snapped open, the fingers were making circles on her breast. With reconstructive memory, she knew that they'd been higher, on her throat. She began to sit up, but the strong pressure was immediate. "I am the attacker," a voice breathed, and she relaxed. It was a woman's voice. Her numbed brain relaxed because it was a woman's voice.

She felt her knees being gently parted. Raising her head, she saw her own pale legs in the moonlight. "No!" she said as the hands on her became strong again. "No!" She struggled, but against the strength of the other woman, she tired quickly. There was a strange sensation as hands crept over her . . .

Khalil knew that Yvette had the gold coin. As in any authoritarian regime nothing important was being left to chance. He knew where Green was. Dressed as an unimpressive Satan, but unable to do without his horn-rimmed glasses, the scientist could be seen in the courtyard every now and then, afraid to come in and walk the rooms, but too fascinated to retreat, detected by glimmers of reflected light from the large lenses. Khalil sat back and lit a cigarette. He wondered if it might amuse him to watch this. It was overkill, of course. Yvette could have seduced this bumpkin in the middle of Midan el Tahrir. But it was a long time since Khalil had taken time off for a party, and he enjoyed the decadence. When Yvette did not appear in the courtyard, he sat up sharply, his smile vanishing.

Straining his eyes and ears, he stared into the house, trying to sense her. There were points of light where people smoked. But Yvette was the attacker. She would be on her own, till she chose her victim—and Khalil had a sudden angry premonition. Then someone used a lighter and he saw her on the stairs.

Khalil gripped her by the wrist and yanked her to her feet. She squealed in fright as he took her by the elbows and swung her to the window. "You bitch!" He clamped a hand across her mouth and saw her eyes staring at him in the glimmer. "I told you to fuck him, not her! What are you trying to do to me?"

She gasped for breath when he released her mouth. Then she too spoke in Arabic. "There's time for that. I don't need the charm for that."

"You're right," he said. "Where is it? Where is it?" he repeated, his knuckles against her belly. She took the gold coin from somewhere and put it in his palm. He closed his hand, and she saw his lips twist in a smile. "Go on down," he said in a gentler tone. "Go do your job." He glanced toward the couch. "I'll take care of her."

She was totally loose, like a puppet with its strings cut. Even her lips and eyes seemed deprived of their controlling functions. He removed the underwear that was around her ankles, and pulled off his galabiya. Mary saw the broad-shouldered demon climbing onto her.

There was a faraway response. He sensed it as he penetrated her: something tinkled in the distance. Then nothing. Teeth gritted angrily, he realized that he would lose this race. Just the knowledge of who she was, near-dead as she was, would bring him to orgasm before she even understood what was happening. He felt himself being drawn in.

"You bastard!" she said.

His eyes popped open.

"I'll kill you, Khalil."

Her body jerked. It happened when his fingers moved across her back. She had clicked on. Her brain was there. And by sheer chance, he had discovered the key to her.

She jerked again as he ran his fingers down her back. The sound she made was soft and pleading. His eyes gleamed in the darkness. He maneuvered her, established a slow rhythm, and ran long, tingling fingers down her spine. It was the key!—as she began to throw herself against him.

Girgis Green could not believe his luck. At first he'd almost jumped out of his skin when she touched him on the neck. He'd tried to scream, failed, and she'd clamped a hand across his mouth.

"It's me, you fool. Shush!"

Green had seen her earlier, revealing her lithe body, then disappearing like a sorceress, while men drooled. It was all too much. Her body, this house she owned, all combined to let him know that he could never have this woman. So this could not be true. She could not possibly be doing this, as he lay spread-eagled on his back. But she was doing it. *She* was doing it . . . My God, he was in her!

Eyes closed tight, his mouth stretched wide across his face, Dr. Girgis Green arched upward, and poured his brain into Yvette Montagne.

Chapter 18

WHEN MARY woke, she had no idea for a moment who she was, or what age, or where. The yellow curtains looked familiar, with the sun pouring through, but nothing connected right away. She could have been a child, on holiday somewhere. But there was something missing. A black hole in her memory . . . then she was lying on her bed, in her own apartment in Cairo, staring at the window. At least she was alone.

The headache started the moment she moved. It was like an ax in the middle of her skull. She struggled to rise, fell off the bed, and finally made it to the kitchen. There was no thought as yet. All she wanted was a couple of aspirin. She got them down, felt like throwing up, but didn't. On legs that felt about two feet long, she stumped to the bathroom, where she saw that she had vomited the night before. She had no memory of that. No memory of getting home. Had she been alone when she stripped—or was stripped? She had a bitter laugh at that, as though it mattered, remembering what had happened earlier.

By midday, she had exhausted herself thinking about it. She remembered him sitting cross-legged on the bed, lamplight on his face, discussing mass psychology. She had listened, watching him talk, while his penis began to stick up hard and straight again. She had been fucked. She remembered that. There was nothing for it but to leave Cairo. Later, there had been more confusion. She remembered being downstairs, talking to the cross-eyed servant. Then to Yvette, who seemed totally subdued, sitting curled up on a couch in the now-empty house. She had the vaguest memories of getting home by taxi.

During the afternoon, she got down some tea and toast without throwing up. But nothing cured her headache. She noticed something slapdash and willy-nilly in everything she did. After a while, she realized that she was not hung over—yet. She was still drunk.

Khalil sitting cross-legged over her. The sated satyr, talking to the shadows of his room. It was mass psychology, he told her. Like control of the masses wherever it was practiced. Castle Bianca was an exercise in mind control. It depended on presenting something in the right way, to a group of people in the right mood, so that each one would accept it, because each one thought the next one would. Most people spent their lives just standing by. Not accustomed to authority, they watched others take it. Then came the subtle forces of incumbency. Once a regime was in place, certain types of behavior were rewarded. It didn't matter how absurd the approved behavior was—in this case being sexually humiliated in public—it became the way to get on in life, and people did it for that reason. People would do anything to get on in life. Anything at all. Mary remembered his intensity as he spoke this way, his pale eyes gleaming in the lamplight. Like the eyes of the god Pan, she imagined. Then his weapon had stood up again, the talk ceased, and like any other dumb female waiting for her moment, she had experienced orgasm . . . again.

In the afternoon, the depression hit her like a body blow. It was the worst performance of her life. She couldn't even blame Khalil. He had found her brainless in his bedroom. She had vague memories of Yvette in this context, but did not pursue them. The villain of the piece was Mary Miles-Tudor, in the most shameful and outstandingly disgusting performance of her life.

Summer school was over. She had committed herself to teaching here for the next year, but could back out of that. Then she began to wonder where she'd go. Her parents were not in England at the moment. They were in Greece. She could join them there, but feeling the way she did, she was afraid of ruining their holiday. She had friends in London. Most of whom would laugh like hell—as would her brother—if she told them why she was running out of Egypt. The hell with it! To hell with Ibrahim Khalil! With the feeling that nothing in the world would ever be right again, she poured herself a gin and tonic . . . and that did help, surprisingly.

When Khalil walked into her bedroom, Yvette knew immediately that something had happened to please him. He had a smug look that she knew from childhood, which meant that he had triumphed in some way, usually at someone else's expense. He sat by the open window and lit a cigarette.

"I've just had a call from your friend and mine."

"Mary?"

He nodded. "Or it might have been her little lamb." He grinned cryptically. "She called to thank us for the party. And to ask if it were still going on. She seemed quite disappointed when I reminded her that she was the last one to leave. She's had a terrible day, she says. Very hung over, and very bored, after all the excitement."

"Did you offer to go and cheer her up?" Yvette was tight-lipped. It galled her to think of Mary and her brother—while she was left with Girgis Green. That was what they had been discussing—how to follow up on Green—when the telephone rang, and Khalil had decided to answer it for once. He never answered the telephone when she was there, but this time he had done so. Sometimes she thought he must be psychic. She remembered also that he could be lying through his teeth.

"I might just do that," he said. "She's drinking gin. I think women are sexy when they're drunk, don't you?" He was turning the knife. Sometimes she wanted to leap at him and scratch his face. "So let's finish what we were saying."

Khalil sat forward. She saw the outline of his cheekbone in silhouette against the window. Yvette was draped on one of the couches in the room.

"Next Saturday night," he said. "I want him eating from your hand. I don't care how you do this," he said generously. "But it's got to be complete, because we're going to ask him to violate security, and some men don't do that easily. This is important, Yvette. I must communicate with the outside. Some people are waiting to hear from me."

Yvette reached for her glass of wine. She seemed to spend her evenings drinking wine, her mornings in bed, and her afternoons burning off the calories in lengthy workouts. She had a remarkable physique for a woman, but her life-style was a mystery to him. How could anyone live like that, so aimlessly?

"Ibrahim . . ." He looked up inquiringly. "I know that what you're doing is important, and very dangerous for both of us. I don't mind that—you know I don't. But this time, I can't even guess what you're about. Don't you think I have a right to know?"

"No, I don't!" His brows had gathered angrily. "Nor do I see why you should want to be burdened with

such information." He looked at her narrowly. Did
her question mean that she had guessed something?
After thinking for a moment, he rose abruptly. She
recognized the signs and tensed involuntarily.

"Events are taking place." He looked at his watch.
"Even tonight, there is an event that we've been waiting
for." He glanced at her. Her face was blank. After
thinking for a moment, he went on as though embarking
on a new subject. "I suppose you've read that Sadat has
been meeting with some of the Soviet puppets here in
Cairo. First informally, then formally, he has agreed
with them that the American plan for peace in the
Middle East will be rejected." Khalil laughed. "Sadat
does not make enemies. That's why he will be the next
president of Egypt. Most people don't think so. They
think he will be pushed aside by the pro-Soviets. A lot
of people are wrong about a lot of things."

Yvette's eyes were wide. "Why do you speak about
the next president?" she asked quietly. "Is Nasser so
sick?"

"He is sick in the head. And surrounded by enemies.
He is like a mad dog in the street. They will come
for him."

"They?"

He looked down at her in the darkness. "Next Saturday night," he reminded her. "I want him eating from
your hand."

Back in his own room, Khalil bathed and scented his
body. He was going out, but not to Mary's apartment.
Mary had called asking for Yvette. On hearing his voice,
she had been polite, as though nothing had happened,
but there was certainly no warmth. He had said what
he did just to irritate Yvette. Also to alleviate a strange
urge in himself that he scarcely understood. But Mary
had sounded on an even keel, thank God. He would

never have forgiven himself if his weakness the night before had prejudiced his plans. He had been afraid of that all day. Now he could relax. It was a sign that it was his destiny to succeed in this operation.

When he left the house, Khalil drove across the bridge to Rhoda Island. Baldwin had a package for him, as well as some news he had been promised that was not on the radio. Khalil wondered if the package had been delivered through his wife. Thinking of the mouselike spouse of the giant Baldwin, Khalil suddenly became priapic. He had not satisfied himself the night before, not nearly. Thank God, he had at least managed to restrain himself from that—or was it something in her that had restrained him? If he ever found himself alone with Baldwin's little whore, there would be no need for restraint.

The Ilyshin *U*-62 touched down at Cairo airport and taxied toward the cluster of beige buildings. When it stopped, the first people out were two men in dark suits, who descended and watched carefully as a small fleet of cars drove out from the buildings. They checked the lead car, recognizing the faces of the driver and one passenger, before signaling to other men who stood above. Surrounded by guards, a tall man came down from the aircraft and was quickly escorted into the reinforced car.

President Nasser of Egypt puffed out his cheeks. "Thank God to be back." He gazed out at his convoy. "But why all this?" Normally, Nasser would have walked to the terminal, over the unenclosed tarmac.

The passenger gestured apologetically. "Everybody's nervous. The Palestinians, you know." Nasser frowned. "You're looking well though, Boss." The passenger looked closer. "I say, you really do look well!"

Nasser smiled, eyes closed, and laid his head against the upholstery. "I took the 'cure.' Rejuvenation of the body cells in the cosmonauts Oxygen Room." His eyes blazed open, with a fierce twinkle. "Do you think they're trying to kill me?"

It was a moment before the other man smiled. "You look twenty years younger," he said. "How do you feel?"

"Depressed."

Anwar Sadat said nothing. Nothing seemed to help these days, or improve the matter one iota. Nasser had been in Moscow for nearly a month, and it was clear that nothing had improved.

"No deterrent weapon," Nasser said. "Flat refusal." Sadat said nothing. "I accepted the Rogers Plan."

"What!"

"I accepted it." His eyes turned to his deputy.

"You have done the right thing," Sadat said slowly. "I think the Soviets would only lead us to disaster."

Nasser gazed out at the familiar airport complex. He breathed deeply in and out again before he said, "I tell you, Anwar, the Soviet Union is a hopeless case."

They were close to Manshiat al-Bakri, the army barracks on the outskirts of Cairo where the President lived simply with his wife and family, when Nasser came back to his first question. Instead of the usual couple of guards outside the house, there were soldiers everywhere. "What's going on, Anwar? Has there been some problem?"

Sadat sighed. He hadn't wanted to burden Nasser with this right away, but if he did not, others would. "There's a bit of a scare going on. It may be important, or it may not. There are agents in Cairo and we don't know what they're up to."

"Go on."

Sadat explained the story as he knew it. Nasser was concerned enough that he had the car sit outside his home while Sadat described the outbreaks of terrorism in the Arab world in the wake of Nasser's May Day speech. Sadat could not connect this logically with stories of an operative in Cairo, but he indicated that there had been killings and a lot of talk.

"What are you saying, Anwar?" Nasser asked sharply. "What is it that you're not quite telling me?"

"I wish I knew." Sadat took out his pipe and stuck it in his mouth. "The whole thing is quite a puzzle. But there are those who think we should be extra careful for a while, just in case."

Nasser put his hand on the door lever. "You say this spy seems to be a local man. A fundamentalist?" Sadat gestured, saying, Who knows? and Nasser grunted. "Shall we never be rid of them?" he muttered.

Sadat dropped his eyes. The fundamentalists, the feudalists, the Americans, the Jews. The Arab leaders inflamed by interference in their domestic affairs, fanned by the insistent propaganda of Radio Cairo, the "friends" as well as all the enemies of the self-proclaimed leader of the United Arab Republic. As Nasser walked into his protected house, a tall, athletic figure, certainly looking years younger after his "cure," Sadat spoke quietly to the night, answering the rhetorical question.

"No, Boss, you will never be rid of them. Not in this lifetime."

Chapter 19

MAHROUS DIDN'T know what had wakened him. His alarm clock said three A.M. There was nothing unusual in that, he often wakened in the night. Sometimes he went straight back to sleep, sometimes he didn't. It was one of those times when he lay awake, thinking.

Julia Sa'id was on his mind. Especially since that spontaneous moment when she had kissed him, and then almost died of embarrassment, he had found himself thinking of the girl and her predicament. She was a modern girl. Many Egyptian women, even after years of marriage, would never be alone with a man other than their husband. Even a guest who came to the house would often be left to sit alone, if the husband were not immediately available. Julia was different. Independent, proud, compassionate. Mahrous thought of his own unburdening that night. It was years since he had spoken to anyone that way, and her sympathy was comforting. But that wasn't what had wakened him. There was something else at the back of his mind that had gone on prodding while he slept. He thought suddenly of his first fiancée. Did Julia remind him of another youthful girl, her smile as wide as her face? He lay still, staring at the window. The glow of the city could be seen, reminding him that it was out there, surrounding his capsule. All of a sudden, he thought of Annas Khalil!

Annas! That had been his father's name, and what they always called him. The name that he had seen recently in a file that had stuck in his mind was Ibrahim. Could the name Ibrahim be in the family? The Khalils had always had a house in Cairo. And there was a younger sister. He calculated quickly. Annas Khalil would be thirty-six, ten years younger than himself. The age was right. He remembered sensing something in the report: something in the Detective Sergeant's manner, even in the way he wrote up the interview. That would be understandable if the man he'd been talking to were Annas—or Ibrahim—Khalil.

Mahrous rose and dressed immediately. He didn't have the patience to shower, or shave, or get into his uniform. He threw on a pair of old pants and a corduroy jacket, and went down to the government car that he had taken to signing out.

It would take some time to get together a full report on the younger Khalil, who had no police record. But the father was a famous case. Mahrous set things in motion for a background check on the son, and pulled the file on the father.

During the years of British occupation of Egypt, and especially later, during World War II, a religious group known as the Muslim Brotherhood had emerged as the social conscience of the country. Many people had contributed money to the Brothers, who worked to bring education and medical attention to the poor. As time went on, the Brothers had become increasingly political in outlook. Under the leadership of Sheik el-Banna, of the famous Al-Azhar Mosque, they had become dedicated to changing things from the top down, which brought them into conflict with the British, with King Farouk, and with the corrupt political parties of the time.

After the defeat of the Egyptian military in what had been Palestine in 1948, serious rioting broke out in Cairo. Not only in the Jewish quarter of the city, but in Jewish-, British-, and French-owned businesses, bombs went off killing scores of people. Sheik el-Banna was a careful man, saying nothing in public to implicate his group, but everyone knew that the Brothers had turned militant. In common with those of their sister faith, Christianity, men who loved and worshiped God—like men who didn't—were not averse to violence.

Late in 1948, the chief of Cairo police was assassinated by a group of students. Nothing was proved against the Brothers, but Prime Minister Nukrashi ordered the organization banned, and its property confiscated. According to police reports, huge quantities of guns and other weapons were found in caches around the country, and the public was shocked. The Jihaz el-Sirri was formed, a militant arm of the Brotherhood, dedicated to overthrowing the government by violence.

Three weeks after the death of the police chief, Prime Minister Nukrashi was killed by a Muslim Brother disguised as a policeman. Two months after that, the famous and revered Sheik el-Banna was murdered in public by Farouk's secret police. The war between religious extremism and the forces of government was on, and was here to stay, as it turned out. A climax came in 1952, with the great Cairo fire, mass lootings by the public, and violent demonstrations against the King, whose Cabinets were resigning one after the other. It was during this unrest, inspired by the Brothers, that a secret group of army officers, the "Free Officers" as they called themselves, who had been conspiring for years, saw their opportunity and took over the country.

Reading in his office as the sky turned gray outside, Mahrous sat back and reflected for a moment. In a sense, the Muslim Brothers had projected Nasser into power. Only two years later, they tried to kill him. Attempts to eradicate the Brothers had never done more than drive them underground. They always reappeared. How sophisticated was their organization now, he wondered, in 1970? What resources and connections did they have, in Egypt, in the Arab world, beyond?

After the revolution of 1952, when the army took control, spoke loudly of democracy, and implemented yet another dictatorship, neither the public, nor the Muslim Brothers, were happy for long. The Brothers remained critical of anything that was not strictly from Islam, and felt betrayed by the new regime. During a trip to Alexandria in 1954, Nasser was shot at by a would-be assassin. A simple plumber supplied with a revolver, he'd soon broken down under questioning and implicated the Muslim Brotherhood. Once again, the clash was on between the forces of government and the fundamentalists, and in the severe crackdown against the Brotherhood that followed, one Annas Khalil, a wealthy landowner from a village in the Nile delta, was arrested in Cairo.

Mahrous had been born and raised in that same village. He well remembered Annas Khalil Pasha, and his beautiful wife, a languorous French woman. Khalil senior, like his son after him, had been educated in Paris. He had studied medicine at the University of Paris and was a fully qualified surgeon, though he never practiced. In those days, before the revolution, many landowners had spoken French instead of Arabic, to put themselves above the peasants. Khalil Pasha was not one of those. In spite of having married a foreign

woman, he remained Egyptian, and a devout Muslim.
In later years, Mahrous had inquired gently of the
younger Khalil, the son who was born in 1934, about his
mother's religion. It was strange indeed that a man like
the father would have married a Roman Catholic. He
would never forget the answer of the younger boy—or
rather his expression—as his intent blue eyes went dead
for a moment, staring straight through Mahrous. "She
is not a Roman Catholic," he had said tonelessly. "She
is Muslim." This was hardly the truth. The Pasha's wife
could be as flamboyant and immodest as an American
film star. Her husband, on the other hand, was one of
the founders of the Jihaz el-Sirri.

This had come out in 1954 when the father was
arrested. Directly incriminated, he had been taken
to the dungeons of the Central Prison in Cairo and
interrogated. The son, who was studying overseas at
the time, had flown to Cairo immediately when he
heard the news. He arrived just in time to hear that
his father had "died" in his cell. In addition to this,
the family's land, all but two hundred acres, was to be
confiscated by the state according to new laws, aimed
partly at breaking the power of the wealthy, who were
not noted for their revolutionary zeal.

There was also the psychological fact that the leaders
of the revolution were all from working-class families,
and nothing seemed to give them greater satisfaction
than attacking the wealthy, which they had continued
to do with increasing fervor until the present day.
Mahrous had heard of the son's brief appearance back
in the village at that time. He had heard of his visit to
a local government official in charge of legal arrangements for the land. This man had almost died of fright
when the solid wooden door to his office had suddenly
been splintered from the outside, and a man stepped

in. Khalil had thrown a signed paper on the desk, some money for the demolished door, and left, without a word. He had broken the door down with his hands. People said that the official had never been quite the same after that, that his sleep became disturbed and he took to beating his wife.

From passport records, Mahrous was able to trace subsequent visits of the son to Egypt. He saw that he'd been here in 1956, the time of the brief Suez war, in 1965, and again in 1967, a date of infamous memory. The next known visit had begun a few weeks ago, and yes, it was surely the same man! The name on the passport was Annas Mustapha Ibrahim Khalil—a tall, subliminally frightening man, with abnormal strength and penetrating eyes, who had made his impression that night on the policeman who had interviewed him.

By midday, Mahrous hadn't learned much more. After graduating from the Sorbonne with a Doctorat de l'Université degree, Khalil had traveled in Europe and the United States, and studied politics and philosophy at Harvard. Like his father, he had made no formal use of any of this training. Mahrous looked skeptically at the official history. Khalil was a partner in an import-export firm in Greece. He still traveled frequently for supposed business purposes. It was later in the afternoon when some further information arrived from intelligence sources overseas. In 1966, and again in 1968, Ibrahim Khalil, as he preferred to be known by then, had visited Moscow. The trips were described as a mixture of business and pleasure—like his current trip to Cairo. He had no police record, nothing with INTERPOL, and his name did not appear on any intelligence file to which Mahrous had access. There was, however, one report that caught his brief, bitter interest.

The report came from the archives of the Egyptian Embassy in Paris. It concerned an Egyptian national—Khalil—who had been the center of an ugly incident involving three girls. The girls were students at the Sorbonne. They had shared an apartment in the Orleans district of Paris, and one of them was friendly with Khalil. One night in the apartment, Khalil went berserk. He tied up two of the girls, and raped the third repeatedly till she became inert. In the end, the charges were dropped. Reading between the lines, Mahrous had the impression that money was used. The girl he had picked on was unhurt physically, but was badly shocked and covered in bruises. According to the witnesses, she had been attacked with a ferocity that had seemed endless, one completed act of rape following another without pause. The estimate of how many times she had been raped was probably exaggerated, the report said.

Mahrous read this with a lump of emotion in his throat. From his own experience, he knew of this sexual savagery that could possess Khalil. As a young teenager, he had twice enticed girls from the village and attacked them sexually. The first of these was the girl to whom Mahrous had been engaged—though it was years later before he heard the full story of what had happened to her that night, after she laughingly accepted an offer from the young Khalil Pasha to ride in his car.

None of this was material. Mahrous swallowed hard, feeling the pain in his chest, but it did not affect his thinking. The incident in Paris was the only one of its kind that was recorded. But Mahrous did not assume that Khalil had changed. He had probably just learned to be more careful.

Mahrous spent an hour filling out forms requesting an in-depth search of all military and counterintelligence files in Egypt. He wanted a directed search for possible associates of Ibrahim Khalil, concentrating on the time periods when he was in Egypt. He specified Dr. Hannas Badaway, ex-professor at Cairo University. There was something Badaway had been holding back during their interview, aeons ago. Mahrous thought bleakly of trying to justify all this and getting it cleared through Touhami. "So what exactly have you got against this man?" Touhami would ask. "That he beat you at chess, and stole your sweetheart?" After a moment's thought, Mahrous decided against ordering routine surveillance on Khalil. But he decided to order full-scale "City Eye" surveillance, and selected a couple of photographs and drawings.

Mahrous was keyed up as he did his paperwork. Hope was in abeyance—he had nothing yet. But as he lived and breathed, he was convinced that he had found his man . . . Khalil . . . It was a well-known name and not uncommon. Still, he could not believe that he had not thought of Annas Khalil when he first read the report. Staring at the face on the identikit, drawn from the memories of people who had seen him in disguise, he superimposed, from his own memory, the features of Annas Mustapha Ibrahim Khalil.

They fitted.

Khalil resisted the temptation to spend a day in Alexandria. He could have driven to the beach, had a civilized meal, spent the night in a hotel, and maybe snagged some innocent. Instead he got onto the desert road and headed back for the heat and dust of Cairo.

His mother had looked well. God, she must be sixty now, but she didn't look it. There would be men who would desire that woman. Just back from the Riviera,

she planned to spend a couple of months at home, more
in Alexandria than at the village, before she started
thinking about where she'd spend the winter. She was
a cosmopolitan woman. With no skill in the world,
except that she could play bridge in any company. She
was empty-headed and brilliant, like her daughter. He
wondered what her life would have been like if his father
had lived. What all their lives would have been like.
She had been vaguely pleased to see him, interested
for the first ten minutes, then ready to say good-bye
for another five years. Having accomplished what he
had set out to do, Khalil felt much the same way.

The road was soporific. His tires hummed in the heat.
Seeing a couple of men on camels ride along the edge of
the desert, he sat up straighter in his seat. This was no
time for engine trouble, or for stopping for any reason
on the long, featureless road. Many who had done
so had been found with their throats cut and their
cars ransacked. The desert men were not squeamish.
Another man's life for a wristwatch was an obvious
exchange to them. When he reached Cairo, he ate a
meal of leftover kebabs and rice, then retired early.
Yvette was out, entertaining Girgis Green, he hoped.

The next morning he rose early. He was ready now
to visit a man whose name had been passed to him
through Baldwin. It was one of those days when he felt
optimistic, in spite of the adversities. After breakfast,
he played the piano for a while, read the newspapers,
and left the house at midmorning.

The government buildings in central Cairo were old
and rather beautiful. Marble staircases wide as a street,
polished wooden banisters, and marble floors. Khalil
went to a reception desk in the huge ground-floor area.
He gave his name, stated his business, and asked the
advice of the male secretary. He had the name of a

man he would like to see. But he was rather lost in this grand place, unsure of the correct authority, and would be happy to do whatever he was advised. The secretary was dubious. But he lifted his telephone, and after a while, another man came to the desk. Khalil told his story for the second time, and was taken to an office belonging to the Ministry of Presidential Affairs. He identified himself, filled out forms, and told his story for the third time. Then he was told to wait. It was three o'clock in the afternoon when he was interviewed again, and given an appointment for the next day. Khalil left the building feeling satisfied. His contact might also have to do some checking.

Achmed Ali was a brother to a son-in-law of President Nasser. He was director of the office of Sami Sharaf, the Minister for Presidential Affairs. Nasser had never been shy about advancing members of his family. It was the Egyptian way, Khalil thought, as he entered the palatial office, and Nasser was no exception. He had been waiting for two hours. His written appointment had been read by twenty people, and he had been thoroughly searched twice, once just before he entered the office. The fact was not lost on him that security was tight, even at this level.

Achmed Ali was about Khalil's age, very westernized, with a hairstyle of thirty years ago. He sat behind a desk like the deck of a ship and stared impassively at his visitor. Khalil bowed in the doorway. "Good morning, Your Excellency." Ali's lips moved slightly. He was not the Minister, and did not warrant this address. He was studying Khalil closely.

Khalil told his story yet again. This time he added all the details, including monetary values, and produced documents to support what he was saying. His family had owned large tracts of land in northern Egypt. Their

farms included several villages and were among the most
fertile in the delta region. Most of this had been taken
from them years ago, all except a couple of hundred
acres from each farm, and the land divided up among
the villagers. Now, in response to the latest round of
agrarian reform, it would all be taken except for a
single lot of one hundred acres. But Khalil was not here
to plead poverty and hardship. On the contrary, he was
here to sign over—not only the last hundred acres—
but thousands of pounds worth of farm equipment and
barns for storing cotton and dates. He wanted it known,
he explained, that the Khalil family was not one of those
that resented the reforms being introduced by the revolutionary government. On the contrary, they wanted to
do everything they could to assist the new owners of
some of the finest land in Egypt. Khalil had titles to
the extra land and properties, and to the machinery.
He was ready to sign these over now, for disposal as
the government saw fit, asking nothing in return. He
explained that he'd been overseas, and had made this
decision only recently, after reading an article in *Al
Ahram*.

Achmed Ali heard all this without expression. His
own family had owned land in Upper Egypt, which
was to the south of Cairo. Before the revolution, they
had literally used trucks to transport their money to the
bank. Things were different now. The official studied
the man who had come to see him.

"This is a generous offer, Mr. Khalil. I don't believe
that I have ever heard one like it. May I ask what your
present business is?"

Khalil told him that his company provided an overseas market for Egyptian craftsmen. He displayed his
cuff links, and a ring on his finger, intricately worked in
gold. They also had a big market in leather goods. This

was the true forte of the Egyptian people, Khalil said. Craftsmanship—not high technology. The government man said nothing. He served an administration that was trying to introduce the high technology. "Also farming," Khalil said. "But I am not a farmer. My father was a farmer. But my sister and my mother and myself—we are not farmers."

"Your sister and mother own title to the land?"

"Yes. But I have their signatures."

Achmed Ali thought for a moment. He had been told to expect a visit from this man, but had not been told what else to expect: just that he should follow the man's lead.

"This is a very patriotic gesture, Mr. Khalil." Khalil smiled modestly. But Ali saw the faint wrinkle on his brow, as though he expected more. "You say you read the article in *Al Ahram?*"

"Yes, Your Excellency. But I want to make it clear that I am not doing this for any kind of publicity."

"Ahh . . ."

"I know that there is going to be a ceremony in Cairo. That's why I was anxious to meet with you, instead of going through lengthy channels—like writing to the Ministry of Agriculture, for example. I don't know if the ceremony is public . . . ?" he asked, and paused inquiringly.

"It is not."

"But I'm sure it will be reported. I ask nothing for myself, you understand, or even for my company."

"Of course not."

"But I would be happy, as an Egyptian, if our example were followed by other families."

"You would like to attend the ceremony?"

Khalil gestured elaborately. "Oh, I don't expect that, Your Excellency. Would it be correct? I don't want anyone to think . . ." He trailed off, shrugging.

"Some important people will be there. It's going to be quite an affair."

"Oh, really? I thought it was mostly for the farmers."

"There will be some farmers there for the publicity. But the main purpose is promotional." After a moment, Achmed Ali asked evenly, "So you would like to be there?"

Khalil met his eye. "Put it this way, Your Excellency. If you think it can be arranged, I would certainly be honored."

Ali nodded, thinking. Khalil's smile covered his thoughts. As a relative of Nasser's, this man had influence beyond his rank. In addition, Khalil sensed a man who was dedicated to the cause of the liberation of Egypt. "Make sure you leave your address and telephone number with my secretary," Ali said. "You will hear from us in the next few days."

As he ate supper that night, dining on calamari and Greek salad, Khalil reflected on the indomitable nature of the human spirit. Plagued by setbacks, almost captured in a series of disasters, he was now basking in the afterglow of the one little thing that had gone right. People were like that. Adversity went by, and any little piece of hope was taken to the heart. That was what made the world go round, and allowed dictatorships to flourish, and be destroyed.

The week ended. Khalil spent Saturday morning reading and talking to his sister. As for Dr. Girgis Green, he had enjoyed the most fantastic week of his life.

Chapter 20

KHALIL PARKED his car in a side street near the Khan Khalil in an old part of Cairo. The car was an Austin-Healey that he'd bought during the week. Like most cars in Egypt, it was a few years old, but it was more powerful than Yvette's MG. The street he parked on was a quiet one. It was far enough from regular taxi routes, and doormen accustomed to reporting to the police, but wide enough that his car was not conspicuous.

He walked to the restaurant. Dressed in a green sports jacket and gray slacks, he was noticeable only as a well-setup man, who might have been a tourist. He was in disguise, but subtly. Large glasses and a wig changed his appearance entirely. He was tense, but mentally prepared for what he had to do that night, after a long day of rest and careful thought.

Yvette and Green were already in the restaurant. She had succeeded in getting a table by the window, and he saw her blond head immediately. She was wearing a wig of fine gold hair. With that, a sheer black dress that stopped above the knee, and six-inch heels, she looked more like a woman from Los Angeles than an Egyptian. Her companion, with his large, flat spectacles and green sports jacket, looked like an amateur pilot who'd forgotten to take his goggles off.

Khalil took a walk around the area. He passed one of the famous cafés, which was abuzz with tourists, smoking harmless hookahs. There was music in the streets, a beggar danced, and people carried brass urns here and there. He was unobserved. He returned to a café opposite the restaurant and ate a meal of hummus and pita bread, washed down with water.

It was nine-thirty in the evening when they left the restaurant. It was clear that their mood was high, as their voices floated out of the parking area. "It's only an old building," said Green's voice. "There's nothing to see, really." There was a pause while Yvette whispered in his ear. "Oh, my God," he said in a tone of never-ending wonder. She had conditioned him well. He knew her as a woman of strange fancies, but worth giving in to.

The building certainly didn't look like much from the outside. Nor was it adequately protected, as Khalil knew, because they expected nothing like the bold attack that would take place tonight. It was a two-story building, painted gray. There was an iron fence, so close to the wall that anyone who dropped down there would scarcely be able to move or breathe. The only other protection was a security checkpoint at the front. Girgis Green drove up to this and stepped out of his car. Walking with the spryness of too much alcohol, he strode up to the box and spoke to the guard, a retired military policeman. The guard's white eyebrows rose. He looked past Green at the tall blond woman, who gazed up at the building. "If you say so, Dr. Green." Of the people who came here, Green was the most senior. He was the boss—and there was nothing gets slack like security, Khalil thought, watching from a distance. He willed his sister to glance in his direction, where he stood in the shadows of the street. She did not. But a faint smile crossed her lips, as though they had communicated all the same.

Shortly after they had gone inside, Khalil saw the lighting change in the upstairs part of the building. From being bright all over, it became dim at one end. That would be where the tracking system was, if Yvette had followed her instructions. The main computer room would be at the other end. Khalil saw the shadow on a window as Green checked the blind. He made a mental note to be careful of that. They were on the edge of the old quarter. The street was neither residential nor part of the tourist area, and was deserted at this hour. He stood in the shadows, alert but calm. He could not afford to fail tonight. Failure now would mean the end of the operation. He told himself calmly that any necessary risk would be taken without hesitation. He watched the downstairs windows. The rest room was on the ground floor. There it was! A flicker of light by a small window.

Khalil scaled the fence and dropped down between the iron spikes and the wall. For a claustrophobic moment, his fingers sought the small gap she should have left by opening the window a fraction. She had left it tight. There was scarcely room to insert a fingernail. But he found enough purchase to open the window, fell inside, and closed the window behind him.

The room was an office. It belonged to the station manager, probably, with a metal desk and filing cabinets. The downstairs part of the building was in darkness. He saw what looked like a small machine shop and working bay. There was a staircase leading up. At the top of the stairs, a corridor went two ways. To the left, he heard the voices of Green and Yvette, coming from the darkness at the far end. To the right, a deserted lighted area. Khalil went to the right.

The night operator was a short, curly-haired man, wearing jeans and a white shirt. He sat behind a glass window, punching something into a keyboard. Khalil saw two large disk drives and a variety of terminals around the main computer. It looked as though the station had other functions, besides the tracking system. In spite of what was going on at the other end of the corridor, the lone night man seemed intent on his job, running a program of some sort.

The man looked up when Khalil tapped on the window. The door was locked, with a sign that forbade the entry of unauthorized persons, but the operator must have thought he recognized the face of Dr. Girgis Green. The man saw his mistake as he opened the door, but by then it was too late. Khalil walked in, hit him in the throat, then broke his neck with a chopping blow. He lifted the body out of sight behind a shelf of disks and tapes.

At the other end of the corridor, rooms were divided by movable partitions. He identified the one from which the voices came, walked up silently, and looked over. Yvette was on her back on the floor. Green, who appeared to have finished a brief lecture on the functioning of the machinery, was now getting down to the main reason for the visit, which was making love "in front of the computers." In the whirlwind week during which he'd known Yvette, Green had become accustomed to her eccentricities. He had possessed her in his car, in the grounds of the Gezirah Sporting Club at night, and even in a box at the opera! He knew it couldn't last. Neither he nor his pocketbook could stand it if it did. But for a magic time, this beautiful, crazy socialite was his, and he was having the time of his life. Yvette's legs rose, like the stretching arms of a fantasizing girl, and flexed themselves around the waist of Girgis Green. She saw Khalil's head appear above the partition.

Khalil recognized the dials on the Russian-made equipment. These would be read electronically when the antennae on the roof were activated. He was familiar with the basic software too, but not the details of the operating system. There was one terminal, which Green had activated for display purposes, and a printer. The only light was from the corridor, and the glow of the machinery.

Yvette felt fear when Khalil stepped around the partition. She had obeyed his instructions to the letter, playing on Green's vanity and his liking for letting people know that he did top-secret work with military application. She had known in advance that the only toilet was downstairs. The whole thing had been amazingly simple, as Khalil had said it would be. What she didn't know was what Khalil planned next, and she was afraid.

Khalil pulled Green to his feet with a force that seemed unnatural, and doubled him over with a blow to the side of the stomach. This was followed by a blow to the face that knocked the priapic scientist backward. Shocked and semiconscious, Green offered no resistance while Khalil lashed his wrists and ankles to a chair, leaving his genitals exposed. Yvette rose, got herself in order, and stepped back in the darkness.

Khalil sat down at the terminal. "I am going to ask you some questions," he said. "You will answer promptly, otherwise you'll be extremely sorry." He took a penknife from his pocket and opened the razor-sharp main blade. "Go and get some water," he said to Yvette, to get rid of her as much as anything.

Green's mouth and jaw were trembling badly as he stared at Khalil. "Who the hell are you?"

"That is of no importance. I am interested in the main processing program for determining the direction of a signal. In what directory is it contained?"

Green licked his bloodstained lips. He was still trying to come to terms with this sudden nightmare. "You can't get to it from where you are. I logged on under Operations."

Khalil typed "BYE" and the operating system kicked him out. He hit return, and was promptly asked for user name. He looked inquiringly at Green.

"I don't know what's going on here. I don't know what you want." Green opened his mouth with the intention of yelling for help. Khalil hit him in the mouth, and nothing was heard but a rasp of pain as Green reeled in his chair. Green's hair hung over his brow, his spectacles were gone, and his lower face was a mask of blood. Teeth were broken and his nose was crushed by the punishment from the gloved hand.

"What name do you use?" Khalil asked calmly.

Green began to pant, his eyes wild. He then showed the kind of grit that some men have, and some don't. "Go fuck yourself," he said.

Khalil lifted the knife and took Green's scrotum in his left hand. He cut the skin in a long thin line, and paused inquiringly.

"No!"

It wasn't clear if this were supplication or refusal. Khalil cut this way and that, and one testicle fell to the floor. Green fainted.

Yvette almost vomited when she reappeared around the partition. She staggered, and Khalil took the pan of water she'd brought as she made it to a chair. He threw this in Green's face, and the man stirred and moaned.

"The salts," Khalil said, his open hand extended to Yvette. Her eyes averted from the horror in the chair, she found smelling salts in her purse and handed them to him.

When Green came to, his face was a mask of terror. He stared at Khalil as though his mind had gone. "What name do you use?" Khalil asked again. When Green hesitated, he lifted the knife, and intelligence returned immediately to the man's eyes.

"Girgis."

Khalil typed it in and hit return. "Password?"

"Neptune."

The system took the word, showing nothing on the screen, and responded immediately. Khalil knew that he had logged on. "Am I in the right directory?" Green nodded. He looked ready to pass out again. "What is the name of the main processing program, and how do I call it to the editor?"

Once in the program, Khalil knew exactly what to do. He knew the mathematics of the algorithms used to calculate direction, and soon identified the variable names used by Green. Green watched this with a strange fascination, though he moaned horribly every few seconds. He made no attempt to scream, and answered Khalil's questions.

"How do you compile?"

Green told him.

"And link?"

The sobbing scientist told him that too. There were no compilation errors. After the small changes to the code, Khalil had not expected any. It linked, and he was convinced that he had a good executable version. "One last thing, Dr. Green. How do I replace the production program by this modified version?"

Green told him.

"And the backup?"

After a series of commands, Khalil had replaced every copy of the code with his modified version.

Khalil was signing off and closing down the terminal when there was a sound from downstairs. From the corner of his eye, Khalil saw Yvette stiffen, and there was a jerk of Green's head. As the voice of the security man came from downstairs, Khalil struck Green with a backhand chop that came straight from the keyboard. The man's head flopped forward, with a crack from the neck, and the chair toppled sideways. Khalil caught the chair, lowered it to the floor, and cursed violently under his breath. "I don't want this," he hissed. "I don't want this!" He gripped Yvette's arm, stilling her. "What the hell does he want?"

"Dr. Green? Dr. Green, sir? There's a routine call from headquarters. They call every hour. I had to tell them you were here, and they want a word with you. Lieutenant Colonel Mahrous's orders, sir."

A stream of curses ran through Khalil's mind. A routine check! But the name he'd heard left no room for doubt. If the security guard did not return to the telephone, there would be a procedure in place for storming the station. Khalil had no transport in which to get away other than the car belonging to Girgis Green. If the guard did not return, a description of that car would be circulated on the move to converging police vehicles. Khalil remembered how suddenly and completely he had been surrounded once before, and knew that he could never bluff his way out of a net like that a second time. He felt trapped, saw no way out, and panic set in quickly. He had no answer.

Yvette shook herself free. "Strip," she said, and his eyes flew to her. "Strip!" she repeated as she kicked off her shoes and pulled her dress over her head. Khalil responded immediately. He threw off his jacket, kicked off shoes, and opened his pants. Their clothing hit the floor like autumn leaves, or shells from an automatic weapon.

The security man's steps came along the corridor. His flashlight hit the partitions, walls, ceiling, as he shuffled into the darkened area. "It's only a routine call, sir. I said you were here, and they just asked me to check that everything was okay." They heard him curse under his breath as he stumbled over something.

Their partition was not the first one he came to. They heard him bump against others as he peered over them and shone the flashlight. Then his grunts and breathing came this way. They heard the scrape of metal on metal, and suddenly the blinding light was on them. Yvette was on her back, knees raised. Khalil was hunched over her, one hand raised to shield the light. The light landed on Yvette's breasts, stomach, and the dark bush beneath.

"Oh, my God!" The light wavered like a trembling leaf. Then it slid along Yvette's thigh. "Oh, God, I'm sorry, Dr. Green, sir . . ." The light seemed glued to Yvette's body, playing on her breasts once more before finding a spot to rest just beyond her averted face. "Terribly sorry, sir," he said again. The beam slipped across her shoulders before it finally tore itself away. "I'll tell them everything's okay." The elderly guard retreated wide-eyed to make his report.

Khalil stared down. Yvette's black eyes were twin pools with a trace of a mocking smile in them. He pushed himself violently away from her.

There were no words between them as they dressed quickly. On a kind of automatic pilot, Yvette preceded

him down the corridor and waited by the stairs, while
Khalil worked rapidly and methodically. He wrecked
the machinery connected to the directional antenna
on the roof. Then he walked to the computer room
and did about a million dollars worth of damage in
a few minutes. When they left the building, Yvette on
his arm, the watchman did not challenge "Dr. Girgis
Green" as they drove off in his car.

Chapter 21

YVETTE'S LIPS were white as they drove out of Khan
Khalil. They had changed cars. Khalil saw the fixed
look in her eyes and knew that the strategy now was
to keep her moving. In any case that was what he had
to do.

"Take off the wig," he said.

After a moment she did so, shaking out her black
waves. Her appearance underwent a total change, but
not the expression in her eyes.

"I want you to call Mary. If she's home, I want you
to get her out of the apartment. I need some time in
there."

Her great eyes moved to him. He continued looking
straight ahead.

"You ask me to do that now?"

"Obviously. That is the purpose of what we did
tonight."

"Take me home," she said. "I'm going to bed."

He continued driving west, down Kasr el Nil. Her head went back against the seat, her eyes closed. He gave her a few moments.

"I know that what happened tonight wasn't pleasant," he said. "Unfortunately, one has to do that sort of thing from time to time. Otherwise, we would simply lose the war against people who have no scruples of their own. If we don't resist them, they go on. If we resist, we have to be prepared to fight. It is war."

"He was innocent," she said.

"He was a casualty. I regret it as much as you do."

He drove her to within a block of Maxim's Bar, and pulled up in a side street. She had gone from total exhaustion to a kind of staring resignation. She knew that she had to go on helping him. She had no choice. He told her what he wanted her to do.

"This is the last time, Ibrahim."

He closed his hand on hers. "I do love you, sister."

It was ten P.M. when the telephone rang in Mary's bedroom. She picked it up with premonition and tried to make her voice sound cheerful. Yvette had never returned her call of last week, after the party. Mary hoped that things were all right between them.

It was Yvette's voice. "What are you doing?" she asked.

"Reading on my bed."

"Get your clothes on. I'm in Maxim's."

"Oh, God . . . look, Yvette, I think I'm coming down with something." This was true. Mary had the kind of aching in her bones that spelled the flu. "Why don't we—"

"I want company. They've got quite a mixture here—

Americans, Egyptians, secret police. I haven't seen you
for a while. I want to talk."

"So do I. But what about the morning? Why don't
we meet in—"

"I don't get up in the mornings, you know that. Have
you ever been in Maxim's?"

"No."

"They've got a snake dancer. She's an English girl
from Yorkshire."

"Oh, my God."

"She's quite good, actually. Why don't you come?"
Mary sighed. "All right."

"Make it soon. I am being eyed by a couple of
gorillas at the bar." Two men with Texas accents,
oil engineers in Cairo for the weekend, smiled and
went on listening to her conversation. "Do I have to
pick you up?"

"No, I'll walk. It's no distance."

Khalil watched Mary leave her apartment. Dressed
in whatever she had thrown on, she was still a figure
that took the eye, even from a distance. Khalil watched
her with a mixture of emotions. Why was it that such
women were never for him?

He had no problem entering the apartment. It was a
quiet building, of the Egyptian upper middle class, and
he saw no one in the elevator. Mary's bed was turned
down. Her underwear lay on the floor. She had been
reading a volume of Russian short stories.

He took the briefcase to the spare room and set up
by the window. He tapped out a recognition signal
and requested interactive mode. Having parted with
his equipment, he had no prepared rapid burst transmission. That should not be necessary tonight. The
reply came, and he tapped rapidly. He had a sheet of

notes to help him with the encoding.

THIS IS A SAFE TRANSMISSION   PLEASE ANSWER FREE-
LY   I HAVE DISABLED A TRACKING STATION AND
SHOULD BE ABLE TO TRANSMIT AGAIN TOMORROW
NIGHT BUT NOT AFTER THAT   GOOD NEWS   CONTACT
WITH THE MINISTRY OF PA POSITIVE I HAVE AN OFFICIAL
INVITATION TO THE FUNCTION   CAN YOU NOW CONFIRM
THIS OPERATION AND THE PRESENCE OF NECESSARY
PEOPLE   OVER

This was acknowledged, and the reply came promptly.

WELCOME BACK COMRADE   YOU HAVE BEEN EAGERLY
AWAITED   THE OPERATION IS CONFIRMED   WE ADMIRE
YOUR COURAGE BUT I AM INSTRUCTED TO CONVEY THE
FOLLOWING   THIS IS OMEGA   YOU WILL HAVE COMPLETE
AND UNRESERVED SUPPORT BUT WE MUST BE ASSURED
OF YOUR COMMITMENT TO ALL CONDITIONS   OVER

Khalil's eyes were bright as he tapped back:

AFFIRMATIVE WHY DO YOU ASK SUCH QUESTIONS
WHAT ABOUT THE WEAPON   OVER

Again the reply came promptly, but in the form of
a question.

ARE YOU STILL NEGATIVE ON NERO   OVER

Khalil pursed his lips as he typed back.

NEGATIVE   UNLESS THERE IS NO CHOICE   OVER

The reply came:

UNDERSTOOD   CAN YOU TRANSMIT ONE MORE TIME
FOR DETAILS OF DELIVERY   OVER

Khalil had half expected this. Caution and slowness
were the price of working with a large bureaucracy,
but they were efficient. He sent back:

I SHALL TRANSMIT ONE MORE TIME TOMORROW NIGHT
PLEASE BE READY FOR TIME IS GETTING SHORT
ONE LAST IMPORTANT THING   THE MAN LEADING THIS
INVESTIGATION IS A LIEUTENANT COLONEL MOHAMMED

MAHROUS HE KNOWS MY NAME FROM CHILDHOOD
AND THERE COULD BE PROBLEMS IF HE LEARNS THAT
I AM IN THE COUNTRY WE MUST NOT ALLOW THIS
UNPREDICTABLE MISCHANCE TO BECOME A PROBLEM
OVER

The reply came. Khalil could almost hear the tension
in the tapping of the key.

YOU SAY HE KNOWS YOUR NAME OVER

HE WOULD RECOGNIZE IT IF HE COMES ACROSS IT
OVER

POINT NOTED WE AWAIT YOUR CONTACT TOMORROW
NIGHT OVER AND OUT

In the operations room in Damascus, Andrei Varsanyi logged off the terminal and returned to his office.
The long exchange with the Cairo operative had left him
feeling drained. There was something oppressive about
the man, an intentness that conveyed itself even in the
way he used the key. He established a secure line and
made a local telephone call.

Dr. Mohammed Mohieddin received Varsanyi's call
in the private study of his Damascus home. This was a
room with marble flooring and a vaulted wooden ceiling.
The room was not brightly lit, for the aged man's eyes
were weak and protected by dark glasses at all times.
He listened to the text of the communication with Khalil
and acknowledged approval.

"Have you contacted your principal?" Mohieddin
asked.

"Not yet, sir. He will have only one question."

"And that is?"

"The operative has confirmed his commitment to
Omega. But given the risk, we must be sure that he
will adhere to all conditions, especially the last."

Mohieddin sighed. "I have told you many times."

"I know, sir. But they will ask for my judgment one more time."

"Your neck is safe. We can depend on him. I am more concerned about this policeman."

After hanging up, Dr. Mohieddin sat for several minutes with his eyes closed. He understood Varsanyi's trepidation. The operation was high risk, and exposure would be politically disastrous. But one thing he did not doubt was the commitment of the operative. He had known Ibrahim Khalil from childhood. He was the grandson of his sister.

When he lifted the telephone again, Mohieddin made a call that opened a chain of command that was ready and waiting. He ordered the mobilization of assigned personnel, who would be contacted within hours and briefed on the details of their cellular participation in the operation that was code named "Omega."

Khalil returned the briefcase to its cupboard and left everything as he had found it. He was tense, but unhurried as he moved around her apartment. Tasteful, he thought. Her bric-a-brac was well chosen and attractive. She had been to the bazaars. A complete woman. A perfect mate. If things had been different, and his life different, he reflected . . . but there was no point in that.

Yet thinking of her brought a strange sweat to his brow. He blinked rapidly for a few moments. Lips tightened angrily, he strode to the bathroom, meaning to masturbate quickly. But meeting his eyes in the mirror above the washbasin, he changed his mind. He walked back into the main room and picked up the telephone.

Baldwin answered in his deep rumble. As usual, he sounded on the verge of drunkenness, but that was not the case. Khalil spoke without preamble.

"I have to see you."

"Oh . . . Hallo, old chap."

"Where we first met."

"What? Oh, God, does it have to be there? Why don't you come here?"

"I want it to be there. Things are happening."

"But it's safe here."

"That could change. I'll see you in thirty minutes."

He hung up while Baldwin was still rumbling.

Chapter 22

MAHROUS WAS telling Julia about Ibrahim Khalil when the telephone rang. When he first arrived, he always asked her how she was, and she would tell him her news: how the baby had moved, and she had spoken to some neighbor. She was living proof that life did not have to be packed with incident and excitement for a person to be happy. Then it was his turn. He had brought a basket from the delicatessen and they were about to eat. She was cutting meat into pieces for him on his plate when her newly installed telephone rang and he reached for it. He saw her face fall. This could mean only one thing.

Seconds later, he was on his feet. His face was ashen as he barked into the receiver. "What do you mean, there's no direction? There has to be a direction!"

"Only a line," the harried voice came back. "The old city station's not reporting."

"Not reporting?" Mahrous felt a sickly touch of premonition. He could almost tell what the night would bring. First he asked, "But what about the other two? Two lines must cross somewhere."

"Not if he's on the straight line between the stations," the voice came back. "He must be on the line between them."

Mahrous passed a hand across his brow. He saw Julia's eyes on him, wide and frightened. "Check the eastern station," he said. "Call the guard and send a car there right away—and ambulances. All men armed and on full alert."

He grabbed his tunic and she helped him on with it. In those few seconds, he told her quickly what had happened and what he feared. He'd been telling her about Khalil and the English girl who had been with him on the night of the last transmission. Julia had agreed that he should not approach Khalil meantime. It might be better just to keep an eye on his beautiful accomplice.

She had shown anger over the problems he was having with his boss. How could one man obstruct an important investigation just by being stupid and unresponsive, she had asked, knowing nothing of the government. Mahrous had come here for an hour off. Just an hour to relax and eat: to see how she was, and to talk with someone. Damn! As he clattered down the steps outside, it occurred to him that if Julia were an agent, she was doing a splendid job on him.

By the time Mahrous reached his office, there was a furor going on among the night watch at the tracking station. Two men dead, including Dr. Girgis Green, whose mutilated body had been found beside the wrecked equipment. The entire computer room was wrecked. The security guard told an incoherent tale. Green had shown up with a beautiful blond woman and had made love to her upstairs. The guard had seen this with his own eyes, and there was no doubt, he told them, they were screwing. Then they'd left. The same woman and a man, whom the guard had assumed was Green. "But he was doing her!" the man repeated. "Right there on the floor. I shone my light on them. I saw her bush!"

Mahrous's mind was spinning as he gave orders. He could not believe the cunning and the savagery of this fiend. He ordered a full investigation, all procedures to be followed. He would be there as soon as he could.

He called the Chief of Technical Operations. The man was not at home, but had left a number where he could be reached. He was at a party. Mahrous heard music and voices in the background. The division chief came to the telephone sounding worried, but turned nasty when he realized who was speaking.

Mahrous told him quickly what had happened. The man's response was a barrage of antagonistic questions about what had been done and not been done. Mahrous interrupted.

"I think our first priority is to get the station operational, sir. He's going to transmit again. He did more damage than was needed just to disable the station for tonight. He thinks he's wrecked it so that it's out of action for some time. That's where we catch him." At this point the other man came in angrily about being called in the middle of the night. He switched from this to demanding that Mahrous tell him precisely what damage had been done.

Mahrous was too busy thinking to get angry. "The entire computer system's wrecked, but we don't need all that. All we need is the directional system and enough computing power to support it. The software's a problem. That may have to be keyed in anew. So long as we get finished by tomorrow afternoon."

"Tomorrow afternoon? You are insane!"

"I'd better not be, sir. Any later might be too late to catch him. We need a computer of some sort. Just enough to make the tracking system work. And we have to repair the machinery. Better get a team together. We start immediately, of course. This can't wait till morning."

"Excuse me, Lieutenant Colonel—"

"Sorry, sir, but if you would excuse me a moment longer. I don't care how many men it takes, or what it costs. This must be done by night fall tomorrow night—say in eighteen hours from now. I believe he will transmit again. But this man is so cagey and so shrewd, I don't think he'll take a chance beyond tomorrow. That's why we simply can't afford to wait, or waste time arguing." As he hung up, Mahrous reflected that he had never spoken to anyone like this in his life before, certainly not a superior officer. What it meant was that, however things turned out, his days in this job were probably numbered. You could not make enemies like this. He was history.

Things did not improve when Touhami arrived. Mahrous was on the telephone, trying to check on the whereabouts of Ibrahim Khalil through "City Eye" surveillance, when a detective appeared in his doorway with the message that Touhami wanted to see him. Not liking the sound of it, Mahrous went to his chief's office.

Cadaver like in daytime, Touhami looked as though he had risen from his coffin to be here at midnight. His face was more gray than brown, and the rimless sun-shades were like black holes into his skull. He had a pile of folders in front of him and couldn't wait to start on Mahrous.

"Two men dead! Does that increase the list of widows you'll be comforting from now on?" Mahrous vowed to control himself. He sat down and said nothing.

"And incalculable damage done to valuable equipment . . ." Touhami breathed hard. "This material on Ibrahim Khalil. Why am I only seeing this now?"

"It's brand-new, sir. I only spotted his name the other day."

"How so? I thought he was in one of your routine reports."

"Yes, but he was one of many. And although I knew him in the past, it was under a different name. We're still checking on him."

"Checking!—checking!—how long do you plan to go on checking before you do something? How many more people does he have to kill?"

"Hold on, sir. We have no proof that Khalil is doing any of this. No evidence, even. If we pull him in and can't hold him—"

"Evidence? Where have you been, Lieutenant Colonel? How do you think we get evidence? We pull people in and then we get the—blasted evidence."

Mahrous took a deep breath. That was what he said now. Until Mahrous acted on his own authority. There were several reasons why Mahrous hadn't gone this route, and Touhami was one of them.

In the last two days he had pulled out the stops on Ibrahim Khalil. Working through the Egyptian embassies in Europe, the United States, and Russia, he had traced the man's movements around the world, checking his activities and associations. What he saw was the life-style of an agent. Always legitimately doing this or

that, but always in the right place at the right time—
if you looked at world events in the "right" way—or
within reach of it under a false identity. But none of this
proved anything. True, it was one of the intangibles of
intelligence work that if you could not prove a suspect
innocent by looking at his background, the chances
were that he was guilty. But it was also true that if
a suspect did not break down and confess, you often
found yourself with nothing. In that case, Touhami
would be the first to ask sarcastic questions about the
evidence against this man. Even after what he had just
said, Mahrous did not delude himself, it could still
happen that way. He had been through this scenario
in his mind.

"Maybe it's because I know this man, sir. I know
that he won't intimidate easily, and—he may have
well-placed friends." Mahrous paused. A moment later
he produced a line of thought that he had certainly not
prepared for the occasion. "I remember my baby had
salmonella once. We got very impatient with the doctors
because they didn't want to give him penicillin. Because
if you hit that virus not quite hard enough to kill it, it
can entrench and come back stronger than before. I
don't want that to happen with this man. When I hit
Ibrahim Khalil. I want to have all the evidence I need
to crush him."

Touhami removed his sunglasses. For a moment
Mahrous saw his gray-brown eyes, with an expression
of exasperation in them, before the dark glasses were
replaced. He looked better with them on.

"How legal and correct! In spite of the meaningless
analogy, I suppose you can't be censured for choosing
this time to go by the book. My God, how often can it
happen! A man you've known from childhood! Could
the gods have done more to put this one in your lap?"

It was at this point that Mahrous realized that Touhami was impressed by his work on this case, and was afraid that others would be too. He felt better for realizing it, though it didn't help a bit. "He is under surveillance, of course."

"No, sir."

"What!" Spit flew from Touhami's mouth.

"If Khalil is who I think he is, he would spot surveillance. He would then either go underground, or work around it in some way. But every street informer in the city's on the lookout for him, and not only Khalil. We now know that there's a female accomplice. I'm interested in an English girl who had been seen with him. I'm sure they're going to act again, that they'll transmit again . . . and this time I'm going to catch them."

Touhami used both hands to gesture. He filled his chest and expelled air. He was dealing with an underling of such stupidity that it took all his control to be polite. "We've heard that before," he said. "What we want now is results." Touhami then dropped his bombshell. "I suppose you know that Hassan Badaway killed himself tonight?"

"What?" Mahrous was shocked.

"You ordered him arrested?"

"That's right. But—"

"You told the men to be easy on him? Well, they were. They let him go into his bedroom to change clothes, and he had a revolver." Touhami's voice rose. "While you were tucked away in your back street, with whatever little bit of stuff you have there, another witness blew his brains out!"

Mahrous was stunned. He thought of the mellowed man, who had once been a strong and fiery man, and the five children he had left behind, and felt sick to the stomach.

Touhami had gone still. He was intent now, staring at
Mahrous. "So you want to let him run?" Mahrous came
back to earth and nodded. "That's a grave responsibility." There was a long pause. "But I've been asked to
give you full cooperation in this case, so I am reluctant
to overrule you." Another pause, while he considered
if his back were truly covered. "All right, Mahrous,
do it your way. For now . . . now get going," he said
abruptly. "Get yourself to Khan Khalili and investigate
this new, disastrous incident. I want a full report by
morning."

Mahrous rose and walked to his desk. In a welter of
emotions, he disorganizedly gathered up some things
and left the building.

Chapter 23

KHALIL PARKED a block away from Baldwin's building.
He knew that he had not been followed, and spotted no
surveillance on the building, but preferred to take the
precaution.

Baldwin's wife, Marina, opened the door to him.
When she saw her visitor, she stared at him for a
moment, before one eyebrow lifted. Khalil pushed the
door open and stepped in.

"John isn't home," she said.

"I know that."

"I thought he'd gone to meet you."

"I decided to wait here."

"Why don't you come in?" she said ironically as he gazed across the hallway at the private rooms of the apartment. The bedroom door was open. She had just come from there. Her legs were bare beneath a hip-length purple robe. "Have a drink. Make yourself at home."

"That's a good idea," he said. "Give me a Scotch."

"Well, well, well," she said as they walked into the dining room. "I thought you were one of them teetotallers?"

He said nothing. It occurred to him that he had not prayed this evening. It was a time of impurity.

He watched her rear as she poured the drinks. A Scotch for him and a Stolichnaya vodka for herself. She had the figure of a girl of twelve. He found her looking at him in a mirror in the drinks cabinet and met her eyes.

"Let's go," he said.

She blinked as he snapped down the liquor and took her by the arm.

"So where's my husband, darling?" she asked as he steered her across the hallway. "He might be very angry, you know." He pushed her into the master bedroom, a room with an enormous bed surrounded by mirrors.

Khalil gripped her by the hair and twisted back her head. He took the glass from her hand and forced the vodka down her throat, saying, "Drink!" She coughed as the liquor spilled down her neck.

"Something tells me you're not going to be too gentle," she said calmly.

He kissed her openmouthed, tasting the vodka, and pushed her hard onto the bed. Marina saw her red slash of mouth in a series of mirrors as he bore down on her.

*   *   *

Baldwin knew there was something wrong the moment he entered the apartment. Even as he closed the door behind him, he stiffened and became alert. Cigarette smoke. Marina didn't smoke. Baldwin's hand went to a small gun he always carried as he walked into the dining room.

The dining room was empty. But the drinks cabinet was open, and he spotted an empty glass on the table. He sniffed the glass. Scotch. Marina never touched Scotch. His eyes went to the closed door of her bedroom. There was no sound in the apartment. After standing in the hallway for a full minute, he moved on his toes, with surprising agility, to the open door of his study, which was in darkness.

Khalil was sitting on the balcony. Baldwin recognized the outline of his head, as he gazed out across the desert. Baldwin's jowly face went blank, the eyes turning flat and dead.

"So there you are. I suppose we must have missed each other. Is that what happened, old chap?" Baldwin stepped into the room.

"I got held up. So I came here."

"Well, it's nice to see you finally. But this is terrible. Sitting on your own?"

"Marina gave me a drink."

"Oh, that's nice. I hope she looked after you."

Khalil rose and opened the screen door. For a moment, Baldwin saw his tall figure in silhouette against the stars, before the room went black as he pulled a cord that closed the heavy curtains. Seconds later, a standard lamp came on by the mantelpiece, to which Khalil had moved. Baldwin had also moved. He now stood against the wall, the gun in his hand, pointing at Khalil.

"You're right to be nervous," Khalil said. "Things are happening, or soon will be. We should all be alert."

Baldwin came and sat down. His face was still stony, but Khalil's little bit of theater had cleared his mind. Things were coming to a head.

"I used the radio tonight," Khalil said. "I received some information and there will be more tomorrow. Until then, I'd like you and your wife's lover to stand by, in case of emergency. After that, if all goes well, you can forget that I exist. But stay by the telephone until tomorrow night. Does this seem clear?"

Baldwin nodded. His fat-embedded eyes were like small stones as he stared at Khalil.

"Good." Khalil lit a cigarette and looked around the room. A smile was born, seemed to tempt him as it grew, till finally he laughed. "So how were the baths? Did you fondle any little boys?"

Baldwin opened the drinks cupboard. Not for the first time, he reflected on the remorselessness of Khalil. Khalil would drive you to the brink, then, instead of pulling back, simply push you over, without emotion. Treated in this way, most people would just slither down the other side.

Baldwin smiled, and struck a conversational tone. "So things are winding up. Tell me, old chap. Apart from small fry like myself, and my ' wife's lover,' " he said, drawing out the words, "who else have you got behind you in this business? How far up do they go?"

Khalil said nothing. Behind a causally raised eyebrow, he wondered how inconvenient it would be if he had to kill Baldwin now. There was something in the man's tone that set a danger signal in his brain.

"Apart from your friends overseas," Baldwin said, "of whom I met a representative in Switzerland, I can think of three groups of people in this country who might be sympathetic to . . . shall we call it your 'cause'? There are the politicians, of course, who will do what they're told so long as they expect to benefit. Then there are the fundamentalists, with their religious passion." Baldwin cocked an eyebrow. "Are you a religious man, old chap? The third group is probably the most dangerous. The wealthy, who have been persecuted under this regime, and some of whom now live abroad. That's a risky business, don't you think? Persecuting men with money? Look what happened to poor old Abdel Hakim."

Khalil was in the act of lighting a cigarette. His hand paused momentarily before he lit up and inhaled deeply. "You mean Amer? Who committed suicide?"

"Well, that's the story. Maybe it was suicide."

Abdel Hakim Amer had been commander-in-chief of the Egyptian armed forces in 1967. After a career of incompetence, during which he had nonetheless amassed great power as head of the Council for the Abolition of Feudalism, Amer, who was a rather lovable figure for all that, had, with justification, taken the brunt of the blame for the catastrophic defeat at the hands of Israel. When Nasser, who had always shown great tolerance for Amer, finally imposed house arrest, Amer had taken poison. Khalil looked at Baldwin as though he found it hard to follow his train of thought.

"He had the poison strapped to his thigh," Khalil said. "Isn't that pretty conclusive?"

"Maybe, maybe not. The point is, someone could have got to Hakim. But Nasser?" Baldwin shook his head. "I'm sure you've thought of it from every angle. But I don't see how anyone—especially someone from outside—can possibly hope to get to Nasser . . . unless he has a lot of help, of course?" Khalil said nothing. His smile was fixed as he stared at Baldwin, a strange light in his eyes. "Which brings me back to my question—which you haven't answered yet, old chap. How high up do they go? What does Sadat know, for example?"

The question shocked Khalil. Even after what he had heard so far, the boldness of it stunned him. He wondered if Baldwin had become unhinged.

Baldwin was saying more than he had intended. In a sense, it was premeditated. Thinking of the future, he wanted to assert himself. He wanted to establish his role, if there was advantage to be gained. But he was also stung, by what he sensed had happened in his house tonight, and was going further than he meant to.

"Don't forget, he's been there," Baldwin said. "Old, gentle, smelling-like-a-rose Anwar Sadat. Let me remind you of a little history. Shall we talk a little history?" Baldwin reached for the Benedictine. He splashed some into a glass and sipped a few times before going on.

"In 1946, a man called Amin Osman, who was leader of a political party called the Revival League, was shot dead in Cairo. The Revival League was one of the many political parties in Egypt at the time—to every one of which Anwar Sadat belonged—did you know that, by the way? Osman was a British puppet. He signed his death warrant by declaring that the union between Egypt and the United Kingdom was like a Roman Catholic marriage—it could never be annulled. Sadat was not the trigger man. He has never been that kind of fool—no offense, old chap," Baldwin said, with a sudden smile. "But he did the planning, and as he's admitted since, he was sitting in a nearby café when Osmin was shot coming out of his house. You know all this, of course. Sadat was arrested by the British, who knew damn well that he was guilty. But after a long imprisonment and trial, during which he consistently denied everything, he was finally acquitted. A folk hero. At least in his own eyes. This is the man who everybody thinks is weak, and who claims to be disinterested in power. Who do you think will step up when they finally get to Nasser?"

Khalil had a smile carved on his lips. He had come to a decision regarding Baldwin. But his voice was smooth as he spoke lightly, ignoring the last question.

"Nasser has admitted that he once belonged to a death squad that planned to kill Farouk. Sadat's probably just trying to go one better—to improve his image." He rose, smiling. "Good night, Mr. Baldwin. It is always interesting to talk to you."

As he walked out, Khalil said over his shoulder, "Give my regards to your wife."

Khalil regretted the senseless urge that had driven him to the pointless act with Baldwin's wife. The root cause of it was the damnable effect on him of the other woman. Yet it was fortuitous. It had provoked the fat man, revealed the extent of his ambition, and shown him capable of resentment. That was bad. Backbones were made to be broken.

When he reached home, he was surprised to find Yvette still in the kitchen. Then he surprised her by filling a glass with brandy and joining her at the table. Yvette was shaken. He had anticipated this but had seen no way to shield her from the brutality of killing Green. She would just have to be tough. She was his sister, she would not let him down. Khalil had never told Yvette that there was a time in Russia when he had taken to alcohol and used it heavily. He had never told her about this, or his one brief bout with love, with Myra Petrovina . . . Myra—Mary! As she told him that

Mary was sick tonight, with a severe dose of Cairo flu, he realized with a shock that the names were anagrams of each other. Khalil believed in Destiny. He could not ignore this strange connection with the past. He thought of Myra, his beauty on ice, who had given in to him just once, in the United States, after which he had followed her across the world, in vain. Absurd. It was absurd that he could not forget that one occasion—as he could not forget his time with this other Myra—Mary.

Was it love? Khalil did not think so. He did not consider himself capable of love. As a little child, perhaps. Before things like the sexual urge and other passions like the hatred of injustice had appeared: all the things that separate a man from an enduring love. As a child, he had loved his father, he remembered . . . Mary had almost fainted at the bar, Yvette was saying. Yvette had rushed her home in a taxi. Did Khalil believe in two-day malaria? The question brought him out of his reverie. If Mary were sick and confined to her apartment, how could he transmit from it? Yvette seemed to rally as she spoke to him. That at least was good, for he still needed her. He told her to be strong, to have faith in him at all times, and, whatever happened, to maintain her inner strength and innocence. She was innocent, he told her. In the eyes of God, she had done no more than a soldier in battle. He reminded her that a warrior killed in battle goes straight to paradise.

Chapter 24

MAHROUS GOT home at three A.M. He still had a few ounces of old Scotch and told himself he liked the taste as he kicked a chair and sat down. Memories hit him almost instantly. He saw the little face again, with its baby-teeth grin, and seemed to hear voices in the house. He cursed at life. The only one who seemed serene and happy was Julia, and her world was made of paper. Like a child talking to itself while its parents quarreled. He worried about what would happen when reality crushed down on her.

Light-headed as the Scotch went down, Mahrous turned his mind to the mountain that had grown, like a great cancer on his life, for which he would sacrifice his health, his job, and even his pride, as he concentrated on the single goal of catching the killer of Julia's husband. Other aspects of the case had diminished, almost disappearing in his eyes, but not this one.

The assault on the tracking station was like a strong attacking move in chess. Against such moves, a steady defense often has the advantage—if the defender can think of everything. At first, Mahrous had been overwhelmed by the physical damage to the equipment, and had focused on that. But remembering the cunning of this fiend, he had tried to stay alert, watching for the hidden threat, the change of tack. He assumed that another transmission was planned and had to counter that. But maybe the attack would come from more than one direction. One good thing was that a disk containing backup software had miraculously escaped the carnage. This was fortunate, because there was scarcely time, he had been told, to key in and debug such a long system of programs. His mind moved to the now-known fact of a female accomplice: the blond-haired woman who could watch a man brutally killed and then make love, or whatever they'd been doing. These people seemed to Mahrous like creatures of another species. As he raised his glass, wondering what it would be like to make love to such a woman, something struck Mahrous. It was one of those times when synapses seemed literally to pop inside his head. After staring for a moment, he rose and walked to his study.

On his study wall there was a map of Cairo. On it, he had marked the positions of the now-so-crucial tracking stations, and his eyes went to them as he strode into the room. Seconds later he was grabbing for a meter rule. Shaking with eagerness, he struggled to place this on the map with his one hand and line it up with the two undamaged stations. There was no question. His breath came faster as he stared. The line passed through an apartment building in Midan el Tahrir, and it was her building. Plumb on the corner with Kasr el Nil, it was the apartment building of Mary Miles-Tudor.

There was now no question of sleep. First he picked up the telephone and called the Khan Khalili station. The engineer in charge was obviously tense. He sounded ready to quit when Mahrous asked if there were hard copy of the code that could be checked against the backup version. Of course there were listings, the man said. But before the backup could be printed out, or even seen on a screen, it would have to be set up

on a system that they were still trying desperately
to repair. He laughed when Mahrous asked if there
was anyone who would then be able to read the code
and quickly detect any changes to the mathematical
algorithms. The only way to check these would be to
go over a printed copy line by line and compare it
with the hard-copy records—and had Mahrous ever
seen a program like this? There were endless pages
of Fourier transforms and God-knows-what, and no
one available who understood a word of it. Even a
scientist with the appropriate background would need
days, if not weeks, to get up to speed. If they managed
to mount the backup version and get it running by
nightfall, that would be a sufficient miracle, he said,
never mind all this double checking. Mahrous tried to
remain calm. As soon as a copy could be printed out,
he wanted a team of programmers to start checking the
code symbol by symbol. This could be done while other
tests were being performed. He stressed the importance
of the work.

After that, he slept for about an hour. The predawn
whiskey did its work, and produced fantasies. He
dreamt of a sexual encounter with Julia. In the dream,
she was the one who demanded gratification, and he
was afraid of her, with her distended belly. Shocked
and guilty though he was, when he woke with a start,
he took this as proof of one thing that seemed important:
that any feelings of sensuality he harbored for the girl
were not based on superficial beauty.

As soon as a computer was on line in the Khan
Khalili station, they printed out the backup version of
the code and gave it to a team of programmers. Later
in the day, when the directional equipment had been
patched and cludged together, they tested the whole

system and found that it ran normally—which ought
to be good enough for anyone, the engineer in charge
told himself. How could any intruder have sat down
and made subtle changes to the code?—so subtle that
everything would seem normal under test procedures?
Checking the code was not an easy matter. The programmers had to stop repeatedly, rubbing their eyes
in a room full of tobacco smoke. The general attitude
was that this was all a massive waste of effort.

They found the changes to the code in the late afternoon. A couple of angles had been interchanged in a way
that made it difficult to spot unless you were reading
the sense of the equations. Was it real? the engineer
in charge asked himself. Sometimes little modifications
were made to an active code and not recorded. He
flew to the telephone. This was one for someone else.
Mahrous immediately became emotional. He ordered
the source code changed according to the listing. The
program would then have to be recompiled and linked
before another executable version could be moved up
and tested—everyone within earshot of the telephone
in the tracking station groaned.

And the checking must go on! They could not assume
that only one change had been made until they had
checked the entire code. Exhausted programmers
almost mutinied when they heard this. Who was this
fanatic? Was he never satisfied?

In his Garden City office, Mahrous wrestled with
other aspects of the problem. Khalil was either guilty
or not guilty. If he were guilty, and Mahrous put a tail
on him, there would be no transmission. Same with
surveillance on Mary's apartment. Close surveillance
would either be irrelevant, or would prematurely spring
his only trap. Working hastily, Mahrous had detailed a
few men to stroll around the square outside, keeping an

eye on Mary's building, but for God's sake not to be
noticed. He decided to wait until nightfall. If time passed, and there were no transmission, he would consider
contacting the English girl on the pretext of a routine
follow-up of the raid on the Mentakis restaurant. He
was aware at this time of how totally shot his nerves
were, and how careful he would have to be not to make
an error of judgment.

Yvette Montagne spent most of the day with Mary.
She took some food, and some medication more powerful than the aspirins the girl was swallowing. The Cairo
flu could be a killer. There were tough bugs in the city.
The servant came and did her rounds, after which
Yvette dismissed her. Miss Mary would be fine: she was
going to do some sleeping now. Yvette watched the clock.
Before she left, she would give Mary a strong sleeping
pill, as she had promised her brother she would do.
When the girl passed out, she would call Khalil and
leave. Yvette found it very difficult to act normally as
she spent the afternoon with her light-headed friend.

Khalil spent that day in meditation. He read from the
Koran, played the piano, and repeated every prayer
thirty times. After receiving Yvette's call, he spent an
hour on his knees with his face pressed to the floor. In
doing this, he yearned for the company that he prayed
he would soon have again, when this was all over, of
those who thought as he did and with whom he could
talk freely. Then he rose and exercised for twenty
minutes, toning his body. He bathed, and dressed in
crisp new clothes: a pair of jeans, a white shirt open
at the neck, and leather shoes. In his car there was an
old brown suit, a pair of spectacles, and a fez. When
he donned these, he would resemble, at a superficial

glance, the figure of a man he had seen who lived in
Mary's building. When he left the house, the sun was
going down, and the air was filled with cries from the
minarets of Cairo.

In her part of Cairo, Julia Sa'id was finding it difficult that evening to stop thinking of the policeman
who had befriended her. There was something about
him that made her wish sometimes that he would take
her in his arms—not like a lover, surely, but not quite
like a father either. She was drawn to him. She admired
the character in his face and the sense of masculinity
about him. She had tried to guess his age. Forty-five to
fifty maybe—then she told herself he didn't look it. Her
time was close. When it came, he had promised that she
wouldn't be alone, and she hoped that he would keep
his promise. Julia had by no means finished mourning
for Abdel. She never really would. But there was a
life in her now that would never know Abdel, and
because of that, she had to think of other things. She
was twenty-two years old. She had nothing in the world
except her own life and the baby's, but she knew things
that Mahrous did not know. She knew that what she felt
these days was not wickedness, but natural. Unlike her
grief, it was instinctive, all part of the grand plan that
affected men, women, and little ones.

Not wickedness, but foolishness, maybe . . .

Chapter 25

THERE WAS a certain mustiness to the apartment. The sweating girl, in her bed, had touched the air with her faint scent. She was lying facedown on the sheets, uncovered, wearing only panties and a T-shirt. He took in the smooth curvature of rear and thighs, blinked once, and his lips tightened. She was breathing heavily. But she stirred and moaned when he entered the room, making him freeze. There was rice and cooked chicken by the bedside, and a bottle of quinine water. These had been left by Yvette, with the medication. He waited till she settled. The sweat was on his brow already.

He had a bad moment with the door of the cupboard that contained the radio. It was in the bedroom, and the door was tight. He turned the handle all the way and pulled with a contained force. Even so, it came open with a jerk and creaked loudly. He cursed furiously. Why had he not noticed this before and fixed the door?

After setting up in the spare room, he took out his prepared and coded messages. He also had a small vocabulary of coded words for possible replies. He was tense. He had already removed everything incriminating from Yvette's house, just in case. The air in the apartment was warm, and he was sweating hard as he tapped out the recognition signal, followed by the first part of his message.

I AM UNDER PRESSURE PLEASE SEND DELIVERY
DETAILS BRIEFEST POSSIBLE OVER

While he waited, he fought the urge to light a cigarette. Seconds ticked by, and he wondered what the
hell they could be doing. When the signal came, he
was astonished to see that it was in plain, uncoded
English.

YOU ARE AT RISK IN THIS TRANSMISSION   ADVISE SIGN
OFF IMMEDIATELY   DETAILS IN TRANSIT VIA NERO   OVER

Shaking with nerves, Khalil dove back to the keypad.
He realized that they had sacrificed coding for the sake
of speed at his end, and his sense of urgency rose. All
the same, he judged that he should still be safe as he
transmitted another prepared message:

NERO DANGEROUS REPEAT DANGEROUS   AND THEY
STILL PRESS ME SHARPLY IN THIS INVESTIGATION   I
MUST HAVE PROTECTION   OVER

Again the reply was sent so that he could read it at
a glance.

PROTECTION GUARANTEED   WE HAVE OMEGA   DONT
WORRY ABOUT PERSON NAMED IN LAST TRANSMISSION
HIS WINGS WILL BE CLIPPED   OVER AND OUT

Working quickly, he packed the case. He was confident that the tracking software would malfunction, and
wondered why there was such tension at the other end.
He was tiptoeing across the hallway when the telephone
went off like a fire alarm.

Khalil put the case against the wall and dove for the
instrument in the main public room. He lifted it and put
it to his ear, saying nothing. He heard a male voice at the
other end. "Hallo? Hallo?" This was in English, with an
Egyptian accent. He was about to replace the receiver
and get out when Mary picked up the instrument by
her bedside. It sounded as though she half knocked
the receiver from its cradle as she did so.

"Hallo?" Her voice drawled drunkenly.

"Miss Miles-Tudor?"

"Yes?"

"This is Lieutenant Colonel Mohammed Mahrous of Internal Security. And let me say right away that this is an unofficial call—you are not in any kind of trouble, Miss Miles-Tudor." He had a deep, easy voice. Khalil could almost hear the smile of reassurance in it. "But I would like to talk to you. And it's a little urgent. Would it be possible for you to come by my office this evening?"

Khalil eased gently back from where he sat. Through the open door of the bedroom, on the other side of the hallway, he could see Mary's hand on the telephone, and her blond hair hanging over it.

"Excuse me, Lieutenant Colonel—er—Mahrous? I'm in bed sick. I've got the flu, and I'm doped up. I can scarcely even . . . speak. Can't you tell me what you want?"

"I see. Well, I must say, you don't sound too well. Would it be too much trouble if I came to your apartment?"

Mary started to answer in a rambling way. But while she did so, something happened at the other end. Khalil heard a sharp voice speak to Mahrous. His response was a quick interrogative, followed by a muffled sound as he gave what sounded like an order with his hand half over the receiver. Then he was back and speaking urgently. "I'm sorry you're sick. Please get well. I'll call later." And he hung up without waiting for her reply.

Khalil hung up silently and rose. He moved behind the door of the main room, and looked through the crack. Mary was still holding the receiver, still talking dazedly. Even from the distance, her eyes looked glazed—much as they were that night when he had found her in his room . . . Khalil realized that he must get out immediately. He guessed what had happened at the other end of the line. During his call to Mary, Mahrous had received word that another transmission was on the air. Khalil didn't think they could have tracked his transmission, nor did he plan to stay here and find out. *And why were they calling Mary?* He would worry about that later.

She had managed to return the telephone to the cradle. Then she sat on the edge of the bed, running her fingers through her hair. He calculated the chances of dashing quickly to the door without being seen. Not good, unless she lay down again. She did not. She rose, swayed, touched the doorpost on the way out, and padded to the bathroom.

Khalil heard her urinating. He looked carefully around the door. She was sitting on the toilet, her head down. But the bathroom door was wide open with a clear view of the hallway. If he tried to slip out, she could raise her head and see him. Even in his loose disguise, she might know him. In any case, all hell would break loose.

He did not want this. *God is great.* He did not want this. *There is no god but God . . .*

He stepped back as she rose to wipe herself. Again he watched through the crack in the door as she seemed to feel her way out of the bathroom. Eyes half-closed, she kicked the briefcase in the hallway, and went to her knees. Khalil's face went blank as he heard her exclamation of surprise. After a moment, she levered herself up, butt first. She stared at the briefcase, the wisp of silk around her middle only half in place. Then she turned and swayed back to her room, just making it to the bed, where she fell facedown.

He moved like a shadow across the hallway.

*   *   *

When Mahrous got word that a signal had been tracked, the cars were already on their way. There had been a brief, but manual transmission. Then, on the same frequency, another that they had been lucky enough to lock on to. There was a good fix, and the cars would secure the area almost instantly. He heard this as his own car swept around Midan el Tahrir.

A minute later, he knew that there was something wrong. The cars were concentrated on the main road along the Nile, and a group of officers around a map were staring out. Mahrous experienced a sinking feeling. He felt excitement give way to the knowledge of failure. "Oh, God!" he said as he sagged in the back seat of the car. He could not believe this.

The first two stations gave the same line as before. The line from the Khan Khalil station intersected it— but in the middle of the Nile River. Mahrous climbed out and wearily instructed his men to unblock the road. He felt as though his throat had been cut.

"I don't understand it, sir. The system couldn't be so far out."

"Maybe he's got a submarine," some wag suggested. The smile on the Detective Sergeant's face vanished quickly as Mahrous glared at him.

Mahrous closed his eyes. Was there no end to the ingeniousness of this fiend? "The software," he said exhaustedly. "The bastard must have changed it in more than one place." Then his eyes snapped open. "Let's go get him!" he said harshly.

Chapter 26

MARY WAS in the deepest sleep of her life when the house began to vibrate. She was still deep when she realized that the percussion was in her head. She groaned guiltily, turning on the bed. Hung over? Then she realized that it was coming from her eardrums. Someone was pounding on the door.

She staggered off the bed, and her knees buckled. Damn! What was this? Like a boxer who couldn't believe he'd been knocked down, she stared up at the stuff around the bed. Food, a bottle of something, pills. She was sick. She remembered now. They were still pounding on the door.

Too groggy to wonder about anything, she made it hand-assisted to the hallway. There she stopped, leaned on the wall, and felt her way back into the bedroom for a robe. The robe was an absurd thing, bought in France, that covered her above the waist, not much below. She fumbled around the cupboard till she happened on a raincoat, which she threw over the robe and pulled tight around her waist. By this time, her legs were working better, if not her brain.

"Who is it?"

"Police. Open up."

"Police?"

"Open up, Miss Mary."

She did so and they piled in. A dozen men in suits. Several of them carried guns.

"Where is the radio?"

"I . . . What?"

"The radio . . ." His eyes flicked around the hallway. "Check the east-facing rooms," he said in Arabic. She met a pair of dark eyes.

"I have two radios," she said, pointing. "There's the stereo, and one by my bed." He almost smiled. "What's this all about?"

He walked into the bedroom. His men had opened one of the cupboards, and were examining the belongings of Michael Pappas. He stepped forward with interest. "This suitcase here. What was in it?"

She stared at the suitcase, which was half-open. Who could have opened it? "That isn't mine. It belongs to someone else who left it here. I can explain that."

"Do so."

A man took down details as she told what she knew of Michael Pappas. Then the one in the uniform came back to his original question.

"Now tell me what was in it that has been removed? Something the size of a briefcase?"

"A briefcase?" She stopped short. "There was a briefcase." She stared at the hallway. "That's odd. I fell over something earlier. I think it was a briefcase." It occurred to her then that someone had been there, while she was passed out, and she felt faint for a moment. Then her brain ticked over.

"Yvette. It must have been Yvette."

The policeman stared at her for a moment. Then he spoke in Arabic. Mary didn't know it, but he was giving orders for the suitcase to be carefully fingerprinted. She recognized him now. The dark hair pushed to one side, the mustache, the stocky chest and shoulders. His left

arm was missing, the empty sleeve pinned to his tunic.
She remembered him clearly from the night in the
Mentakis restaurant. She also recognized his voice.

"Did you call me earlier?"

"That's right. At a time when you and your accomplice were actually using the radio. Who is Nero?"

"Nero?"

"Who is your accomplice?"

"I have no accomplice. I don't know what you mean.
But there was a briefcase in the hall. I remember . . .
falling over it." She screwed up her face. "After you
called? When did Yvette leave?" she asked herself.

He watched her closely. His eyes were narrowed as
though puzzled. "I think you have your wits about
you better than you pretend, Miss Mary. It is now ten
o'clock on Sunday evening. Where were you twenty-
four hours ago, at ten o'clock last night?"

"Last night?" She passed a hand across her brow.

"Let's say, between eight P.M. and midnight?"

"I was here . . . hold on, let me think . . . then I
went out." His dark eyes were steady. "I went to Maxim's Bar. I shouldn't have, for I was sick. But a friend
called me."

"Your friend's name?"

"Yvette Montagne. The same one who was here this
evening."

"What is her address?"

He signaled to a man who wrote down what she said.
While this was going on, others came and spoke to him.
Mary swayed.

"May I please sit down?"

"There are signs that a radio transmission was made
from this apartment," he said. "My men have identified
where he set up his equipment and attached his aerial.
Are you a doctor, Miss Mary?"

"No, I'm not."

"Can you explain the presence of smudge marks in your apartment, as from surgical gloves? Some look fresh."

"Please, Lieutenant . . . Colonel . . . Whoever you are . . . I haven't the faintest idea what's going on. It's so confusing . . ."

He stepped in just before she fell. Mary found herself caught deftly, in his one arm, and lowered to a chair. Her head cleared, and he smiled down at her.

"Do you remember a night in the Mentakis restaurant, back in July?"

"I remember it well. That's where I first saw you." Her eyes unfocused. "You were looking for a spy."

"Who were you with that night, Miss Mary."

"Just Mary," she said absently. "I was with Ibrahim Khalil."

"Yvette's brother?"

"That's right."

"Had he recruited you by then?"

"Recruited me?"

"Yes. How did he do that? Sexually?"

He saw her lips quiver. Then—astonishingly—there was the merest beginnings of a smile as she stared at him.

"Who is Nero?"

She shook her head.

"What is Omega?"

"I really haven't the faintest idea what you're talking about."

"We have been intercepting your transmissions, Miss Mary. We know all about it."

"Not my transmissions. But I think you know Khalil." Again she floored him with that flicker of a smile. "He said he used to beat you at chess."

It took Mahrous a moment before he asked, "He recognized me?"

She nodded. "He told me all about you."

"I see." His eyes unfocused for a moment. She saw them, like black olives in his head, totally lost in his reflections. Remembering the story about his fiancée, she felt almost sorry for him for a moment.

Mahrous blinked. He met the blue gaze of the English girl and realized with a plummeting sensation that she was innocent. He felt despair, and an odd kind of relief. Her life was not over.

"I think you're going to have to come with us, Miss Miles-Tudor."

"You mean . . . I'm being arrested?"

"I'm afraid so."

She swayed in her chair. He patted her shoulder as she looked around dazedly.

They allowed her to dress in the bathroom. Watched by two women who had appeared from somewhere, she slipped on a pair of jeans, a blouse, and a pair of pumps. They let her take her handbag and some lipstick, but they searched the bag very carefully. When they stepped out, one of the women spoke briefly to Mahrous. She spoke with a tight smile and he nodded, with an embarrassed glance at Mary. He knew that Mary had understood none of this, but was embarrassed all the same. The woman had said, "It's blond." He had asked her to note the color of Mary's bush. He saw the girl standing there, pushing back the hair that kept falling in her face, thought of Hassan Badaway, and felt the touch of nausea that he seemed to live with these days.

The gravity of things was coming home to Mary. As she was taken down in the elevator, she realized that she was being arrested, not by the ordinary police, but by the dreaded secret police, and on the most dreaded of all charges, spying. Spying against a country that considered itself at war. She remembered tales of horror that her father had told her when advising her against this trip to Egypt. In a situation like this, the rights or wrongs of the matter made little difference, as did innocence or guilt. She was a pawn now in a ghastly game. As for Ibrahim . . . she could make nothing of this. Even little Michael Pappas, hastily leaving Egypt. Maybe she was mixed up in something terrifying. She walked out and saw a cleared street, spectators far away, and dozens of cars.

"My name is Lieutenant Colonel Mahrous."

"I know."

"I'm afraid I have to make you wear this."

She was sitting between two men in the back seat of the car and Mahrous was one of them. The other slipped a blindfold over her eyes.

"Oh, really! What's the point?"

"Intimidation."

She could almost see his trace of smile, though her eyes were covered. There was no bullying, no attempt at real intimidation. Yet something told her that if she were guilty, she would be terrified of this policeman.

"You are being taken to Cairo Central Prison for interrogation. To be frank, I do not believe that you are guilty, but there are lots of questions we must ask. You will be detained for a while. Innocent or not, I think you have information that can help us in a serious investigation. Now please listen to what I say. This is very important, Mary. You must answer everything we ask with complete truthfulness. Tell us the complete truth and hold back nothing. If you are innocent—as I repeat I think you are—you will soon be released. You have my word on that. Do not fear a political detention. Such things are actually rather rare. Those who are publicly accused of spying are usually guilty."

"That's not what my father says."

His soft laugh sounded genuine. "Maybe he believes his own country's propaganda . . . But seriously, Miss—er—Mary. I am arresting you, but not charging you. Don't let us frighten you too much." Beneath the blindfold, her eyes moved instinctively toward his voice, and her fear subsided. She trusted him.

But it was still a nightmare, and it was just beginning.

The car stopped. She heard the clanging of an iron gate and soldiers' voices. The man beside her spoke in Arabic and they drove on through.

"Who else has been arrested?" she asked. "Ibrahim?"

"Not yet."

"Do you think he's a spy?" No answer. "Or some kind of terrorist?"

"That's interesting." She felt him looking at her. "That you should ask that. I am also very interested in this Michael Pappas."

"Oh, he's innocent," she said.

Once out of the car, she was gripped on either side by hands that were less than gentle. She was taken up a flight of stairs, down stairs, along corridors, down more stairs. Voices began to echo in these passages.

When the blindfold came off, she was in a cell. It was eight or nine feet square, painted gray, no windows. Away from the door, there was a raised part. No bed, just raised cement, painted gray. There was a hole in one corner and a tap. Looking up, she saw a narrow chimney that she sensed led to the open air, far above.

Half a dozen men stood in the doorway, their eyes on her. There were also a couple of hard-faced women,

one of whom stepped forward. She pressed Mary back
against a wall, and looked over her shoulder. The one-
armed man was looking fixedly at Mary. He caught the
glance of the woman officer and nodded.

Mary had gone still. Was this woman going to beat
her up? She waited for the blow. Where would it be—
to her stomach? She would close her eyes and bend
her knees, and just sink down against the wall.

The woman reached out abruptly and began to search
her. She searched her brassiere with expert fingers,
and her underwear. Mary closed her eyes. Her purse
was taken, and her wristwatch. She wore no rings or
jewelry. Her shoes were examined carefully, the cloth
of her clothing, all waistbands, cuffs, any thicker place
where small objects might be hidden. Her raincoat was
taken from her, and her mouth was probed. Then she
was alone. The woman stepped out, the door was closed,
and she was alone. The door was solid, with a small
metal window that could be opened from the outside.

Here there were no reassuring words.

Mahrous returned to the makeshift office he was
using in the Central Prison complex, picked up the
telephone, and asked for contact with Military Intelligence Headquarters in Athens. He wanted Michael
Pappas located immediately. Whether or not the
Greeks proved sticky about having the man extra-
dited, Mahrous planned to request that he be pulled
in and questioned without delay. While waiting for a
connection, he asked for any reports from the men who
had been watching Mary's building—there was nothing
significant—and arranged to meet a couple of men and
brief them for an immediate trip to Athens.

Chapter 27

IT WAS after midnight when Baldwin's telephone rang. The familiar voice at the other end was as smooth as ever, but the instructions given were to be carried out immediately. After hanging up, Baldwin walked to the dining room.

Marina was at the table surrounded by books. She was taking a degree in business management at the American University, for what purpose Baldwin didn't know. "I have to go out," he said. She glanced up over her spectacles, regarded him for a moment, and then nodded. The bruises on her arms and throat were still clearly visible from the night of Khalil's visit.

The tall, gray-haired man was at the bar, lingering late with a group of others in the Gezira Sporting Club, when Baldwin lumbered in. He was laughing, and looked very relaxed, as he waved in recognition. Baldwin ordered a Benedictine and went to a table. He gave no sign of noticing when there were snickers from the bar as the Minister dropped his voice, before detaching himself and coming to join Baldwin. It was only when the man was seated opposite that Baldwin saw the tension in his eyes.

Baldwin heard the shocking news that Mary Miles-Tudor had been arrested. This had happened a couple of hours earlier, only minutes after an important operative had made a transmission from her apartment. Part of the emergency was that the operative now needed information that he had not received in the transmission. Once again, Baldwin was to be the channel for that information. He was the only one who had personal contact with the operative. He was given a sealed envelope and told that the man would contact him before morning. There was no reason to panic. He was warned to be on full alert for any sign of surveillance, but was assured that there was no reason to expect this. He was not in jeopardy.

Baldwin knew that he was a link in a chain. The longer the chain, the more links to be followed to the top, which gave time for the chain to be broken, in case of an emergency. A chain was broken by breaking any link. Baldwin reflected on these and other matters as he drove back to his apartment.

He was waiting by the telephone in his study when the doorbell rang. Half awake, half sleeping, he had been recalling the testimony of spies he had known. Many spies were ordinary people who had been recruited because of their access to secret information. After exposure, they often told of how their lives had been completely taken over by what they'd done, leaving them capable of thinking of almost nothing else from that point on. Baldwin was applying this to himself, wondering if he had started something that would never finish, when the doorbell buzzed, startling him. Khalil was dressed like many a denizen of the Cairo streets at night. He wore dark glasses, a seedy suit, and other touches of disguise that made him look like a totally different person. He had no time for Baldwin's feeble attempt at joviality, and did not even glance into the dining room, where Marina still sat with her books.

Marina Baldwin looked up and gazed at the study
door as it closed behind them, her eyes skeptical and
world-weary.

Khalil knew of the arrest. He had practically been
there, he reminded Baldwin, and had stood in the
crowd when Mary was led out blindfolded. Had Baldwin
been contacted? His relief showed momentarily when
Baldwin affirmed this and produced the package. Apart
from that, his manner was as mechanical as ever.

Khalil tore open the envelope. Baldwin lit a cigarette
and poured a glass of sweet liqueur. Khalil read. Then
he grunted and glanced up. "Was nothing added to
this?" Baldwin shook his head. Khalil frowned. "I am
to meet this man in person?"

"If that's what it says." In spite of everything,
Baldwin burned with curiosity. Khalil nodded and
moved on.

Mary's arrest was an unforeseen emergency, Khalil
said. He did not know by what process Mahrous had
stumbled onto her, but he was sure to have Khalil's
name by now, and his slow brain would be working.
This was no cause for panic: the matter was in hand.
Khalil would be protected, and there was no danger to
Baldwin. The man was a machine, Baldwin thought.
Even now there was no real fear, no thought for anything except his mission. Baldwin listened impassively,
his face like marble.

Khalil had one last instruction. From now on, he
would not be at his sister's house. He had seen no sign
of surveillance, but had decided to go underground in
any case. Baldwin was to remain by the telephone.
This line was still safe, and would be their sole means
of contact from now on. Before leaving, he shook the
fat man's hand and looked him in the eye, with one of
his rare smiles.

Baldwin was left thinking about all these reassurances of his own safety.

Michael Pappas had been drinking in a club near Constitution Square. He was with his brother and some friends, and had been drinking into the small hours, after a late meal in the Plaka. That was one of the real pleasures of being home. The spread of Greek food and wine in a noisy, bustling taverna. But he hadn't settled in to his new life yet, or had any constructive ideas for the future. He lacked peace of mind.

Pappas did not know that in the last few hours his name had been mentioned in communications between Greek and Egyptian Military Intelligence. He was unaware of the fact that at this moment, two Egyptian officers were on their way to Athens with the request that Pappas be pulled in for questioning. Sometimes Pappas worried about what he'd done before leaving Egypt. But when the Egyptian secret police told you to do something, you just did it, you did not ask why. As Pappas saw it, he had no choice. And he was safe, he told himself, because he had done as he was told. He just kept wondering what had happened to the English girl.

One of the positive things in life at the moment was his new car. Pappas had bought himself a little Renault, and was as proud of it as if it were a new wife. He'd spent hours polishing the car. Outside his parents' home in Tenedou Street, where he was still staying, it was like a jewel, ruby red in color, a pleasure to the eye, the nose, the ear, as you climbed in, smelled the upholstery, and started the sweet-purring engine. Pappas had never owned a new car. Living in Egypt, he'd been lucky to learn to drive. To be truthful, he wasn't too sure of his skill as yet, as he drove in the

still-heavy downtown traffic, with his rowdy friends,
but he was being careful. He was the one car in the
street that was the proper distance from the car in
front—which was probably why he got rear-ended.

Pappas couldn't believe it when the car was jolted
by a solid hit from behind. With a cry of anguish,
he leapt out and stared at the damage to his fender
and rear light. "You idiot!" he screamed to the man
behind the wheel of the other car. "You blind, idiotic
fool! Look what you've done to my car." Pappas did
not hesitate to express himself. He was with his brother
and three friends, and there were only two men in the
other car, one of whom stepped out.

The man who climbed out and came toward them
with short, solid steps was taller than he looked at
first, being very broad. He wore a hat pulled low to
the eyes, with no sign of hair under it. Pappas paid
little attention to those details as he pointed in anger
at his car. His brother was writing down the number
of the other car.

The man looked unimpressed. He glanced at the
damage and shrugged. "I give you fifty drachmas,"
he said in heavily accented Greek.

Fifty drachmas? He had to be crazy. They rounded
on him. The stranger's eyes moved from one to the
other. Did he have insurance? The man shook his head.
All right, that settled it. They would go right now to a
police station around the corner. They would leave the
cars right here. Right where they were, the evidence
untouched. Let the cars behind them blare their horns.
The police would see the evidence for themselves . . .
Pappas was dead almost before the others noticed that
anything had happened. The knife came up through his
diaphragm and sliced the heart in two. Shock prevented
them from acting as the stocky man stepped back into

his car, which immediately shot out of the traffic and into a side street.

Ivan Torbek cleaned the blade using a box of tissues on the dashboard. "Now get rid of this heap and take me to the airport," he said as the expert driver gunned the car away.

It was shortly after dawn when the Minister of the Interior made a telephone call from his residence in Cairo. In response to pressure that he did not question, which had come in the form of a telephone call that got him out of bed, he called the Director of Internal Security on the subject of the arrest of Mary Miles-Tudor, a matter of which the Director had no knowledge at that time. The arrest was entirely spurious, the Minister said. The Lieutenant Colonel who had ordered it had picked on the girl simply because she was a foreigner who happened to have been in a certain restaurant that he had raided one night. The Lieutenant Colonel had a bee in his bonnet about this, and was simply lashing around in frustration. But it happened to be a serious embarrassment, for two reasons. One: the girl was having an affair with the nephew of someone high up, and the nephew, who was engaged to be married, had been with her that night. Second: the girl's father was a British diplomat who would raise hell if she were harassed without good reason.

The Minister wasn't telling the Director what to do. He was just telling him to be damned careful how he handled this one, unless he had some evidence. The harassed Director then called his Deputy. He wanted to know who the hell was Mohammed Mahrous, and on whose authority was he running around arresting foreigners? Why was a case of this stature in the hands of an obscure lieutenant colonel in the first place?

The Deputy Director said that he would look into this immediately, and would examine the facts of the case personally. The next person down the line was Brigadier Touhami. He had no sooner sat down at his desk that morning when he received the kind of call that fed the ulcers eating their way through his duodenum. He promised action. None of these men knew about Ibrahim Khalil, or his mission in Cairo, or the conditions of the Omega agreement.

Chapter 28

MARY WASN'T sure if she grasped the full significance of all this. Even now, she possibly still believed, deep down, though her brain told her differently, that this was all a terrible mistake that would be cleared up when her innocence became apparent. Either that, or it was the reassurance of the policeman that sustained her. She took things one at a time.

The cell was about nine feet square. Nothing in it but the tap. The door was solid, with a small window that could be opened from the outside. Shortly after being left alone, she rapped on it, and a mustached face appeared. It was the face of an angry-looking jailor, in plainclothes.

She demanded the right to make a telephone call. She wanted to call the British Consulate and explain what had happened. No phone calls, she was told. But

this was her right! she asserted. She was told that she
had no rights. She had been arrested on suspicion of
spying, and they had enough evidence against her to
have her shot. The window was snapped shut.

She paced the cell. There were no real thoughts, and
she felt physically wretched. She rapped on the window
again.

No, they would not give her a mattress. She had no
right to that either. And she could not see a doctor,
she was told angrily. She was a political prisoner.
The man's English began to desert him as she persisted. He gazed at her with the kind of physical interest that was akin to hatred and violence. But during
this another man appeared in the corridor outside
and spoke in a more level tone in Arabic. She heard
the word "nada," which was repeated incredulously
by the guard. Later the word "Mahrous." The guard
slammed the window. But a few minutes later, the
door was opened and they dragged in a filthy mattress. This was thrown on the raised part of the cell
and the door was closed again, the guard pushing
Mary inside when she tried to lean in the doorway
and look along the corridor. Anything was better than
the cell.

She lay on the mattress and pretended to sleep, in
hope of provoking some reaction from her imprison-
ers. The last thing she could ever do was sleep. But if
she pretended to, they might act to keep her awake.
Even if they opened the door, just once, it would be
worth it. She heard the window being opened as they
peered in. She kept her eyes closed, breathing evenly.
The stray thought occurred to her that the tap must
be for Muslims to cleanse themselves for prayer. She
wondered what would happen if she asked to be taken
to a lavatory . . . Very far from sleep.

It worked. The door was opened, and two men came in. Without explanation, she was blindfolded and taken out into the corridor.

More noise. They passed a man who was being dragged along the corridor. His screams of terror filled the air and Mary could smell his fear as they brushed past. She would not be treated in that way. If so, there would be no screaming, she told herself. She knew that there were concentration camps in the desert. They were for political prisoners, and for people accused of "counterrevolutionary activity"—which could mean a word of criticism, or reported criticism, of some high official, or relative of such, especially Nasser himself, who was said to react violently to any whisper of an attack on any member of his family. Mary chose this time to remember all her father's warnings, and the fact that he was always right—except for one thing, maybe. The man who had arrested her had said that when they publicly accused a person of spying, that person usually really was a spy, and Mary knew that she was innocent. She closed her mind to fears of being taken off and raped somewhere.

When the blindfold came off, she was in a larger room, painted green. The walls were bare, but this time there was a table, a chair, manuscript paper, and lots of pencils. She was told to write her statement. She was to explain every detail of how she came to be in Egypt, why she had come here, how she had arranged it, and what she had done during the last few months. In particular, she was to explain how she had met Ibrahim Khalil, and everything that she had done in his company. She must take her time. She could take all day, if necessary. She was offered water, and told that she could visit a lavatory on request.

Mary sat down and composed herself to write. Without her watch, in these windowless dungeons, she had no idea if it was night or day. She hoped that Lieutenant Colonel Mahrous would be present when she was finally interrogated.

Mahrous stood behind the one-way mirror and watched Mary write her statement. A handsome girl. He noted the long brow and straight nose, the blond hair clinging to itself in yellow strands as she pushed it back repeatedly. She hadn't had much chance to make herself pretty. But she didn't look like a girl who had been dragged from her bed and thrown into the dungeons of Central Prison. Sitting with one knee crossed over the other, pencil poised, she looked more like a student who had rushed to a university after a night of cramming to take an exam.

He read the first version of her statement. As he had expected, there was nothing to show a connection between Khalil and the Cairo spy, or even the mysterious briefcase in her apartment. She still claimed to have seen a briefcase. But she was quite confused as to when, and there was the fact that Khalil's sister had been around, which might explain things. The truth was that there was no real evidence that anything untoward had happened in her apartment. He read that Khalil had possessed her sexually: that she had behaved foolishly at some party and ended up being "done," as she put it. Sexual recruitment? Mahrous did not believe it. But after his literally fatal error with Hassan Badaway, he vowed not to make the same mistake again. The girl might be innocent. But he planned to interrogate her all the same, and now that he'd arrested her, maybe it was time to bring in Khalil and his sister. With the horrible feeling that he'd drawn a blank again, he

walked back, sighing, to the temporary office that he
had commandeered, where he met Touhami, who was
waiting for him like a spider.

Touhami was sitting at the desk. He had copies of
Mary's statement in front of him and looked up with
an antagonistic stare when Mahrous walked in. "What
the hell do you think you have been doing?" Mahrous
stopped in his tracks. "What do you mean by arresting
this girl?"

Mahrous was a little stunned. Even for Touhami, this
was a blunt reversal of his previous position. "I thought
I'd mentioned, sir. She was with Ibrahim Khalil in the
restaurant that night."

"Oh, yes. The night of the disappearing radio."

"Then I realized that he might be transmitting from
her apartment." He explained about the straight-line
geometry.

Touhami was not impressed. "Oh, so that's your
'evidence'? She lives on a straight line through Cairo?"
His voice rose. "That's your reason for arresting a
girl—whose father happens to be a member of the
British Shadow Cabinet, by the way. Have you gone
insane?"

Mahrous raised a hand, blinking hard. The gravity
of this sudden quarrel with his boss hadn't hit him
yet, but it would. "I think we can justify it, sir. As
it happens, I believe the girl is innocent. But I still
think she might have been used without her knowing it."

"Used by whom?"

"Khalil and others."

"Oh, I see." Touhami spoke with icy sarcasm. "Without justification, you arrest a totally innocent girl. Now
you're going to tell me you happen to have stumbled on
a hotbed of spies and killers?"

"One moment, sir! She's mixed up with Ibrahim Khalil. The one we were discussing a few days ago."

"Oh, yes, your childhood friend. The one you told me all about—except for the fact that he seduced your first fiancée!" Touhami seemed ready to explode. "For God's sake, man, is there no end to your prejudicial involvement in this case?"

Mahrous felt for a chair. "That's not material," he said. "That's got nothing whatever to do with it."

"I know damned well it's got nothing to do with it! That's exactly what I'm saying."

Mahrous stared at the floor. Touhami had struck a chord that echoed sharply. It echoed the fear he felt deep down that this could be exactly what he'd done: that he had built all this suspicion around Khalil because of personal resentment. Then he looked up. "How did you learn about that? About Khalil and Dalia?"

Touhami hesitated. "Because I've also done some checking. Because I'm taking heat for this, damn it!" He exploded suddenly. "Your handling of this case is leading straight to an international incident. Are you aware of that? Are you aware that Michael Pappas has been killed in Athens?"

"What!"

"Stabbed in the street. After drinking all night in a transvestite club." Touhami gripped his head in both hands. "Is there no end to your genius for invoking the most embarrassing of almost impossible coincidences!"

Mahrous felt faint. He could not believe this. Was it possible for anyone's luck to be so bad? His eyes narrowed. Or for anyone to have acted so quickly. He stared at Touhami.

"Don't suggest it," Touhami said. "Don't even suggest that he was killed by international conspirators. No one's buying. No one's buying anything you've done in this whole damned investigation. So you are relieved of it," he said abruptly. "You are relieved of all responsibility in this investigation. Effective immediately. No more arrests, no more theories, and you will not discuss a word of this with anyone. You will write a report. Try to give some kind of justification for arresting the girl. But no flights of fancy, for God's sake—no one's in the mood. After that, it will depend. I don't know whether you will be terminated or just suspended for a while." Touhami took a breath and his manner softened slightly. "I shall make the case that you have been working night and day and were appalled by all the brutal murders. I don't know whether that will help or not. Now get out of my sight."

Mahrous rose automatically. It was beginning to hit him now, but would get worse. He was out. This was coming not from Touhami but from above. It was final. He was walking aimlessly along the corridor when a female officer ran after him. There was an urgent call for him from North City Hospital, she said.

Chapter 29

THE U.S. expert on Egyptian affairs, Elliot Richardson, looked at some points he'd jotted down while waiting for a connection to the Oval Office in Washington, D.C. The connection was made.

"Mr. President?"

"Go ahead, Richardson."

"There are a couple of things, sir. Nasser has finally admitted that he was in Moscow. No missiles, but get this . . . he has verbally accepted the Rogers Plan."

"Well, I'll be damned."

"Meantime, Sadat and the Supreme Council have recommended rejecting it."

"Who do you believe?"

"Well, there's only one boss. I think it's a case of the left hand not knowing what the right hand's doing. He's pretty mad at the Russians."

"Interesting . . . very interesting."

Richardson agreed. Russia had long handled Egypt's foreign policy, and been her spokesman on international affairs. That could be about to change. He glanced at his notes before going on.

"The other thing may or may not be related. It's a little hard to sort things out at the moment. Excitement here is mounting by the hour. I don't know why, exactly, no one seems to know quite why. They arrested an alleged spy last night."

"They did? Who is he with?"

"It's a girl. And that's not clear. It may be Israel, or it may not. As usual, there is total confusion at the top level. And now that Nasser's back, no one wants to say word one. But I've just heard that a key witness has been killed in Athens. There's something going on."

"Any comment from our friends in Israel?"

"Only that she's not theirs. Some say that there has to be an accomplice. There have been some killings that look like a man's work, unless she's one hell of a gal. Personally, I think they've jumped the gun. But the excitement is coming from the top, and seeping down, not only in Egypt. It is confirmed that Hussein is getting ready to crack down on the Palestinians in Jordan. Nasser wants an Arab summit with Arafat and Qaddafi."

"Those two monkeys?"

"He still wants to be the grand mediator, sir. He'll never give up that dream."

"I know. The devil of it is he might get somewhere this time. What about the Soviets? I mean the local ones, in Egypt."

"Tight as a clam. My impression is they're under orders."

"What kind of orders?"

"God knows. Sadat is also pretty quiet. I just have the strongest feeling that everyone's waiting for something."

There was a brief silence on the line. Then Richard Nixon asked one of his blunt questions. "What do you make of Sadat? If anything happened to Nasser, would he last?"

Richardson answered promptly. "No chance. British Intelligence estimates about six weeks. I'd say that's max."

"One last question. Is there anything we can do?"

The envoy's smile went sideways. "Not a damned thing."

"Keep me updated. Thanks, Richardson."

The Soviet Ambassador to Egypt was not connected to Leonid Brezhnev. He was connected to the head of the KGB.

"Go ahead, Venogradov."

The Ambassador spoke with some tension in his voice. "With reference to our last conversation, sir, there is now no doubt in my mind that our people are acting under orders. No one will say it, but there is a unanimity of action and opinion that seems planned. I believe the source of the orders is Egyptian," the Ambassador said, striving to speak with no inflection in his voice. "If so, it must be a person or persons of unusual influence. Even I am subject to suggestion—very strong suggestion. Are you aware of this, sir?"

"Aware of it?" Yuri Andropov's voice was a blend of smoothness and reproach. "Why don't you make me aware of it, Ambassador?"

Venogradov became crisp. What he said was conveyed in a few sentences. He finished by saying: "Nasser has been resting. But he has agreed to see a group of them this evening to discuss security, among other matters. As I said, I have been subjected to suggestion only. Specifically, I have been asked to agree to something that strikes me as a little odd. But it comes from our people, and they want an answer."

Andropov came to a decision almost instantly. "Then why hesitate? If it makes our Egyptian friends happy—what's wrong with that?"

"Are these your orders, sir?"

"Suggestions," Andropov said smoothly. "This is not an official conversation, after all."

"I see."

"I really don't know what the fuss is all about, do you?"

"No, sir."

"Keep me informed, Ambassador."

The group of visitors arrived at Manshiat el Bakri, the army barracks where President Nasser lived. The officers on duty checked each visitor carefully before Nasser received them in his garden. There were several

members of the Supreme Council of the Arab Socialist
Union, two men from Army Command Headquarters in
Nasr City, and some senior ministers. The group was
politically mixed. Not all were pro-Soviet, though that
group predominated. Nasser sighed inwardly, expecting
more criticism of his recent behavior toward Russia.

But there wasn't much of that. The men were anxious
to compare notes with Nasser after his absence, and
that was the substance of the late meeting. The self-
appointed chairman was one of the Supreme Council
members. He was one of the "old boys" of the revolution, one of those close friends of Nasser's from the
Free Officer days, who now held prominent positions
in his regime, and struggled against each other for his
power. But Nasser sensed an air of urgency in the men
this evening that might supersede their partisanship.
He switched off the pain in his legs that had bothered
him all day, and joined the discussion.

There was concern over Arab reaction to Nasser's
apparent dealings with the United States, and his
acceptance of plans for a truce with Israel. There
was fear of terrorism from the Palestinians, fear of
military action from King Hussein of Jordan against
the Palestinians, and anger that the American-Israeli
alliance, with its policy of keeping the Arab states
divided, had such good cause to be rubbing its
hands with glee at the present time. Nasser joined
in vigorously at first. But he seemed to tire, and
became preoccupied and brooding as the discussion
turned to questions of security, including his personal security. This led to a matter being raised
that had obviously been discussed beforehand, but
which was new to Nasser. His interest revived as
he sensed a subtle difference of opinion among his
councillors.

The spokesman took the lead. He was impartial, but spoke with no great conviction. Nasser became alert and listened closely.

"On the subject of security, Gamal, I am sure you are aware that there has been some excitement while you were gone. There is a spy in Cairo, and no one seems to know what he is up to. The situation is confused. There have been some killings, which might be related or might not. But there are aspects to it that some of us feel you ought to know."

"Good," Nasser said. "I've been hearing whispers about this all week. What do you think I ought to know?"

"You are aware that someone has been using a new technology to send messages out of Egypt?"

"Yes."

"You know that he has sent a number of these messages, and we've no idea what they are about?"

"Right."

"Well, I won't burden you with all the theories. But there's one that is—more imaginative than most." He looked at a man who wore the uniform of lieutenant general. "Do you want to tell us in your own way, Abdel?

Abdel Riyad was Chief of Staff of the Egyptian armed forces. He had held the post since shortly before the suicide of Abdel Hakim in 1967, after the disastrous six-day war with Israel. Nasser turned with some relief to a man who was a competent soldier, not a politician, and who had less of an ax to grind than most of the others in the room.

"I'm sure you remember the fifth day of June, 1967, sir." Nasser nodded grimly. It was a date that was imprinted on his memory. "Before the Israelis struck that Monday, we'd been expecting an attack all weekend and couldn't understand what they were waiting for. Well, here's something I keep thinking about. We don't all think it's important," he said, glancing at the spokesman, "but here it is. During that week-end, there were a number of mysterious transmissions made out of Egypt. These were short, and apparently garbled—of exactly the type that we've been hearing recently." Nasser's eyes were riveted on the speaker. "They made no sense to anyone at the time. But the fact that they happened is recorded. Now add the following facts. When the Israelis struck, the Commander-in-Chief of our armed forces, Abdel Hakim, was in the air. He was on a tour of inspection of our forces, and in accordance with his prearranged schedule, he was flying between one place and another—together with all his chiefs of staff—when they attacked. As a result, there was no one to order the use of our SAM missiles against Israeli jets. They came in scot-free."

Nasser was staring in astonishment. In the dim evening light, his large eyes seemed to burn. "What are you saying, Riyad? Are you saying that Hakim was manipulated?"

"Maybe. Either that, or it was clever spying, sir."

"And you think he's back? This spy?"

"I think someone is using the same technology."

Other voices joined in at this point. Some were intrigued, some skeptical. The pro-Soviet group was conspicuous by its silence.

Dr. Mahmoud Fawzi, the War Minister, cleared his throat. Nasser looked at his sharp-featured face. This was another of the men he trusted, a group that grew smaller every day.

"I don't know if the signs are worse at the moment than they normally are, sir. The American surveillance satellites are taking pictures of our installations. This information is going to Israel, and we're not in good shape for battle at the moment. Hussein is losing patience with the Palestinians. He could start to crack down any day now, and your reaction is predictable."

"Predictable?" Nasser had been frowning. Now a ghost of a smile appeared.

"Would you permit the destruction of the Palestinians?"

"By no means."

Fawzi shrugged eloquently. He did not have to say that once again Nasser was surrounded by enemies, and without a friend. Nor would he improve his popularity by going to the aid of the Palestinians. For that he would get no thanks from anyone, least of all from Yassir Arafat. The Russians would not lift a finger.

Nasser looked at the grim faces ringed around him. "The East, the West, our Arab friends, and Israel. Have I failed to mention any of our enemies?"

"The Brothers are strong again," someone said.

Nasser snapped his lips. "Enough of this! You have me jumping at shadows."

"Sometimes there is danger in the shadows, Boss."

This came from Anwar Sadat, who had been sitting quietly, an unlit pipe in his mouth.

Nasser rose suddenly. It was sheer nervous energy that pushed him from his chair. "Let me tell you about our friends the Russians. There will be no missiles. No fighter planes. We don't even have ammunition for our guns! That's the kind of help we can expect from our friends the Russians." As he paced this way and that, the others braced themselves for an outburst of temper, but this didn't come. He returned to his seat and sat staring at the ground.

One of the men from Military Intelligence raised a finger. "I have to point out, Mr. President, that some of us feel there could be danger at home. We do not rule out the possibility of a terrorist attack in Cairo—or even a direct attempt on your own life. Later this month, when the summit meetings start in Cairo, there will be a huge influx of foreigners. There will be representatives from many states, many of them hostile, and easy cover for all kinds of hostile professionals. Coming back to this spy. If there's one thing we know about him, we know that he's a professional. I would not rule out the possibility that he is here to prepare for some kind of serious attack." He looked across the forum. "Apropos of which, I believe there was an arrest last night. Do we have information on that?"

"An arrest?" Nasser had obviously heard nothing of this. "What kind of arrest?"

The Minister of the Interior took a breath. "Oh, it's nothing, I'm afraid. Some policeman got carried away and arrested a girl who was obviously innocent. She has already been released."

The meeting didn't last much longer. They discussed plans for the Arab Summit later in the month, and it was agreed that a special group be formed to handle the security. Nasser had never heard so much talk of security. They were discussing public appearances when he thought of something that had come to his attention earlier. "Speaking of that, what's this thing in the Semiramis tomorrow night? How did I get roped into that?" he asked his Minister for Presidential Affairs.

The Minister in question looked puzzled for a moment, then his brow cleared. "Oh, yes. The land ceremony. To be honest, Gamal, the first I knew of that was the announcement in the *Al Ahram* today. I suppose Achmed Ali must have put it there."

Nasser had been about to speak, but checked himself when he heard the name of his relative. It was Anwar Sadat who came in.

"You don't have to do it, Boss. I can handle that."

Nasser frowned, still thinking. Then it was the senior member of the Supreme Council who spoke quietly. "It is an important function, Gamal. It is the first night of an international fair, and part of the Agrarian Reform. Venogradov called specially and asked if you were going to be there. I suppose we should have checked with you, but you can always pull out."

"Venogradov?" Nasser's eyebrows rose. Then a smile tugged at his lips. "Do you suppose it would be a slight to our Russian friends if I backed out?"

"Oh, I don't think so," the Supreme Council member said. "If you don't feel up to it, we can tell Achmed Ali to get someone else."

Nasser shook his head. "No, I'll do it. I don't quite have one foot in the grave—not yet. Just check with me next time. Why is it scheduled for the evening?"

"Tomorrow is the start of Ramadan. Had you forgotten?"

Nasser banged his forehead. "My God! Don't let that get into the newspapers, for God's sake."

As the visitors trooped out, Anwar Sadat hung back and spoke privately to Nasser. "I don't know, Boss. It's not only the Russians." He nodded toward two of the most senior of the departing ministers. "They've been opening mail and tapping telephones again. Just the way Hakim used to do—till 1967."

Nasser's eyes snapped onto him. "What are you driving at, Anwar?"

"I don't know. There's just so much going on."

"Not only the Russians, you say. Who else stands to gain if I go?"

"That depends on who follows you."

Nasser laughed and slapped his deputy on the back. It could have been Sadat's seriousness that made him do this. But Nasser was serious a moment later when he said, "This ceremony tomorrow night. Just as a precaution, I want security doubled and redoubled. See to it personally, Anwar. I don't want a hostile mouse in that hotel tomorrow night."

Chapter 30

ZACHARY TOWFICK went off duty at eight P.M. He walked from his place of work, which was the Hospital for Tropical Diseases, to a café where he habitually ate his evening meal. He ordered a sandwich and coffee, and settled down with a newspaper.

The man he was expecting arrived on time. Towfick had been given no description, but noticed the man immediately when he walked in. Tall, aloof, tense. Glancing around, he saw Towfick's thin face and came his way.

"Greetings, friend. Not much of a meal, for the eve of Ramadan—or do you not observe the fast?"

Towfick, who was Jewish, answered quietly, "I observe the fast."

This completed identification, and the man sat down.

Towfick took a small box from his pocket. It was a gift box, and contained a pair of gold cuff links, beautifully worked and inlaid with black onyx. The visitor removed these and weighed them in his hand. He continued to examine the craftsmanship, while Towfick spoke quietly across the tabletop.

"I am instructed to tell you that all is in readiness for what you have to do. The people you expect to see will be there tomorrow night, and so will—certain friends." The visitor's eyes glanced up and down again. "Your emergency is being dealt with. Nothing will be allowed to interfere with you in any way. I am instructed to say that you can rely on this completely." The visitor nodded, indicating that he understood. His strangely sculpted face was flat as he continued to pretend to examine a potential purchase.

"There is only one more thing I have to say." Towfick closed his hands to stop them from trembling. "I am asked to remind you of your commitments." The visitor looked up. "Especially to the third face of Omega." Towfick thought that he had never seen such cold eyes on a man. "That is all. I am asked to say that the prayers of your brothers go with you." This was acknowledged with a nod. To anyone watching, it would seem that an agreement had been reached. Some money was passed across the table, they shook hands, and the visitor rose and left, taking the cuff links with him.

Towfick went to the telephone. He dialed a number and spoke quietly when the ring was answered. The dagger was drawn, he said. Were there any more instructions? He was told no. He should go home now. He had done well and would be rewarded.

The owner of the café was a Greek. It did not offend him to serve Towfick with a glass of brandy after his frugal meal. Towfick had two glasses that evening. His plan then was to return to his room and sleep, before spending the next day with his radio. That was his plan.

As he went outside and stepped from the sidewalk, a car accelerated and was moving fast when it hit him. The experienced driver had no doubt that he had killed his man as he screeched around a couple of corners and away.

Mahrous listened to the heartbeat on the monitor. In the short time that he'd been here, the rate had risen from a hundred fifty to a hundred sixty-five, and was still rising. No one seemed worried. The other vital signs were good, he was told by the ladies who had done the epidural earlier. They had returned to check on their patient, in the small private room.

"Sounds like a girl," the senior woman said.

"Dr. Abo-zena says a boy."

"Oh, he's just guessing."

Mahrous wasn't sure about their casual attitude. Julia had been rushed here after her water had broken prematurely just as she went into labor. Now there was the danger of infection. She had been calling him. Finally, the hospital had tracked him down. He sensed their disapproval and felt guilty as hell.

"Why is she in such pain?" he asked.

"I don't know that, sir." The woman frowned for a moment. "That's a question for the doctor."

Abo-zena was a tall, elegant man, a fashionable gynecologist. Mahrous had engaged him to look after Julia, and was glad that he had done so. It was her first child and it wasn't going smoothly.

"Dr. Abo-zena never said it's going to be a boy," Julia said. She was trying to smile, but looked as though she had been beaten up. "He always said things like . . . 'Sounds like a boy today.' "

"What I don't understand is why everything just seemed to stop," Mahrous said. "You are fully dilated, but the baby doesn't come." She was also in extreme pain. The epidural had alleviated this, but not stopped it. "I'm worried, Julia."

"I know." She was worried too, and very frightened, trying not to show it. A baby might be dying, he thought, and they were afraid to argue with the damn doctor.

"That's a stubborn boy," the nurse said. She nodded knowingly. They were all so calm, just doing their jobs. Mahrous had once been enrolled in Cairo Medical School, before canceling out at the last minute. He often wondered what would have happened if he had pursued that career.

He walked out and asked a receptionist to page Abozena. He felt ready to be aggressive with the doctor. Mahrous was not one of those to whom tragedy was unbelievable. He knew that the very worst and most irreversible could happen: it had happened to him. The nurse followed him outside.

"I'm so glad you came," she told him. "She kept calling you."

He ran his fingers through his hair and nodded, staring bleakly at the floor.

Abo-zena walked up, very smooth and confident. He went into the room and spoke to Julia while he checked the vital signs, then stepped outside again with Mahrous.

"I think we must consider surgery."

Mahrous closed his eyes. "What's the problem?"

"I don't know. The child seems fine, but it isn't coming down."

"Have you told Julia?"

"She'll go along with what you say."

Mahrous heaved a sigh. He wondered if they even knew that he was not the father. "Let's do it then." He looked at his watch, as though that mattered.

"It would help if you were there," Abo-zena said.

Mahrous's head spun around. "You mean—during the operation?"

"Certainly. She'll be wide awake. We use local anesthetic."

"For cutting her belly open?"

"They are preparing the operating room now."

The call came while the doctor was scrubbing up. Someone must have pulled some rank because the receptionist came running down the corridor to find Mahrous. He told the doctor that he'd be right back and went to a telephone.

It was a Lieutenant Izzaz calling from the offices in Garden City. He was an officer who had worked with Mahrous for many years, but had not previously been assigned to this case. "The boss asked me to call you, sir. He said to remind you that there's some important paperwork to be done. He said to tell you that Mary Miles-Tudor was released this afternoon."

Mahrous shook his head. Then something made him ask, "Where is she?"

"As a matter of fact, she's not at her apartment. She packed a bag and went to a friend's house, to the south of Garden City."

"Yvette Montagne's?"

"I think that's right."

"Oh, my God!" Mahrous instantly didn't like this. "Where's Khalil?"

"Khalil?" Izzaz didn't even know the name. "I don't know about all this, sir. Just to tell you that the boss is pretty mad, and wants you back here right away."

"I'll be there as soon as I can." Mahrous hung up.

When they entered the operating theater, he was relieved to see that they had erected a screen between Julia's head and her stomach. He had no wish to witness

her being cut open. Julia was on her back, arms spread
as though for crucifixion. Either due to the anesthetic
or for other reasons, she was trembling violently. They
started work, their shadows on the screen. Abo-zena
and the others joked and kidded, like the characters
in a zany comedy. All in the day's work.

"That's the problem," Abo-zena said. "The umbili-
cal cord's around its foot." A moment later the baby
cried.

"Funny-looking girl," the pediatrician said as he put
the baby in a bath of water. Julia's face lit up in a giant
beam.

"It's a boy," Mahrous told her.

He went with her to the recovery room. She seemed
quite calm, waiting for her baby to be brought to her.
"Why don't you go and get some sleep?" she said. "I'll
be all right now." He shook his head. Anxious to be
gone, and feeling guilty for that too, he mumbled that
he would stay with her for a while. Her hand came out
from between the sheets. "Thank you, Mohammed. I
thank you so much for everything. But I'm all right
now, really."

He kissed her on the cheek. He would be back soon,
he said. And she was the one who patted his hand.

Khalil spotted the tail while driving north on Kasr
el Eini. He was no longer staying at Yvette's house,
but had returned there briefly, to check on his sister's
state of mind. He was not happy with this. Yvette was
under strain. But there was nothing incriminating in
the house—nor in this car, he thought quickly. Now
someone was following him.

If he hadn't used the back streets, he might never
have noticed the small Peugeot. Once he reached the
major road, it tagged along a few cars behind, and was

not conspicuous. He slowed down, and it did too, not coming close enough for him to see the driver.

Khalil did not allow himself to panic. He had been assured that everything was under control, and had faith in his colleagues, which was essential at this time. His eyes showed nothing as he watched the driving mirror.

When he reached Midan el Tahrir, he decided to check if they were a team. As though uncertain of his way, he drove around full circle, passing all the radiating streets. The little Peugeot stayed behind, following unembarrassedly, even when he finally swung back down the way he'd come. What kind of surveillance was this? Telling himself to stay calm, he pulled over and stopped suddenly. The Peugeot was unable to do the same, but it slowed, tooted, and the driver pointed to a café by the roadside. Khalil saw the mustached, grinning face of Mohammed Mahrous.

Khalil walked into the café and ordered coffee. A couple of denizens looked up from their game of backgammon, then ignored him. Mahrous came in, his hand outstretched, and Khalil rose to meet him.

"Annas Khalil! I can't believe it! How long is it since I saw you last?" They pumped hands like long-lost brothers. "Fourteen years? Was that the last time?"

"That sounds about right."

Mahrous sat down and beamed across the table. "I can't believe it. I was reading a report on you the other day, but I didn't recognize the name at first. Then it connected. Ibrahim?"

"My grandfather's name."

"When did you start using that?"

"After my father's death."

"Ah, yes . . ." Mahrous dropped his eyes. "I'm sorry about that, Annas. Or Ibrahim, if you prefer. I might be a policeman now, but I don't approve of everything that happens. As a matter of fact . . ." Mahrous lifted his bottle of Stella beer. It was a liter bottle, with condensation on it, and he poured the beer into a small, straight-sided glass. "I've been reading about that too," he said easily. "Cheers."

Khalil shook his head. "Still the iconoclast, I see."

The cold beer tingled on Mahrous's throat. "I don't have your faith, Ibrahim."

Khalil sipped his coffee. He did not have to wonder why Mahrous had been reading up on him. He assumed that his name had been noticed, and his background checked meticulously. Mahrous was nothing if not meticulous. Hence Mary's arrest, which showed that he'd been thinking. None of these thoughts showed in Khalil's eyes, as he kept up the game. "Fourteen years," he said, harking back. "Before that it was 52. Another year of infamy," he said with forced calmness.

Mahrous smiled. "I see your politics haven't changed," he said tolerantly. He gazed at his boyhood acquaintance as though with nostalgic memories.

"What happened to your arm?" Khalil asked.

"The Yemen. 1962."

"A bullet?"

Mahrous shook his head. "Hand grenade."

"Oh, dear. Were you throwing it, or was it thrown at you?"

Mahrous sipped his beer. Then he chuckled unexpectedly. "You think I'm fool enough to pull the pin and not throw it, don't you?"

Khalil grinned, and his pointed canine teeth appeared.

It was a sniper who had thrown the hand grenade. And the memory still hurt, even now. Khalil saw his old protagonist blink rapidly a few times.

Khalil's mind was working fast. Mahrous had nothing, he told himself. Otherwise there would have been
a warning. This was nothing. A last-ditch bluff. Still,
it was nerve-wracking.

"I saw you from the restaurant that night," Khalil
said. "But you were obviously busy, so I didn't inter-
rupt. Did you ever find who you were looking for? A
spy, was it? That was the rumor we all heard," he
added.

Mahrous nodded. His eyes were somber, gazing at
his old acquaintance. "A spy, and a killer."

Khalil looked back steadily. He acted no part, showed
no reaction whatsoever, and left the ball in Mahrous's
court.

"So you've done some traveling?" Mahrous sat back
and stretched his legs. "The States, Europe. Even
Russia?"

Khalil nodded. After a moment, very unexpectedly
he spoke in a voice that was a little louder than normal,
saying, "I fell in love. With an ice skater. That's why I
went to Moscow."

"In love?" Mahrous's brows were up, lips parted in
a smile. But the funny thing was that he believed it.

After a pause, Khalil had himself in hand. "Ice ska-
ters are usually short," he said, "like gymnasts. But
Myra was quite tall, and very beautiful. She made the
others look as though their feet had been sawed off. But
the American judges killed her. I could have strangled
the fool who made the commentary for their television.
There is nothing more disgusting," he said with feeling,
"than politics in sports. Especially when the victim is an
athlete who has devoted her life to what she does."

Mahrous nodded thoughtfully. He was thinking that
whatever else Khalil had done in Russia, there was

enough emotional noise around here to hide the truth
from any form of questioning. He changed tack.

"And now you are in business?"

"That's right."

"What kind of stuff do you export?" He seemed
interested to hear.

"Soft goods mostly. I made some contacts in the
United States, and hooked up with an old friend in
Greece. Don't scoff," he said. "I can buy a hand-
made leather pouf in Egypt for two dollars, and sell
it in the States for a hundred. A thousand of these
don't even take up space in a container. Do your
arithmetic."

"So you're getting rich?"

Khalil shrugged. As Mahrous well knew, he had never
been poor. "It gives me something to do."

"And it satisfies you?"

Khalil began to feel it now. The gentle pressure on a
soft spot in his cover. Anyone who knew Khalil would
know that this was not his life. There was really only
one thing he could be doing, and that was what he did.
If he'd had any doubts before, he had none now: he
was being interrogated.

"How is Yvette?"

"She's well."

"I was on my way to visit when I saw you leave the
house. Do you think Yvette would mind if I dropped
in on her sometime?"

Khalil's eyes narrowed. The last thing he wanted
was Mahrous talking to Yvette. "You might not be
very welcome," he said easily. "She has one of her little
friends staying with her now—the one you arrested, in
fact. Yvette's like a dog with a bone, when she's got a
little friend."

"A girlfriend? You mean that innocently, of course."

"I mean a little friend. As I would have a little friend. I caught them at it."

Mahrous dropped his eyes. A moment later they came up in baleful disbelief. Khalil laughed inwardly.

"Well, I might drop in on them in any case," Mahrous said. "Just routine, you understand. You don't plan to leave Cairo anytime soon, do you, Ibrahim?"

Khalil decided to bring this to a head. He wanted to be very calm, relaxed, but the fact was that the fool was getting to him. "Look here, Mahrous, is this official? Are you arresting me?"

Mahrous looked quite astonished. "My dear chap! Good heavens, no. I was just—"

"You didn't pass me in the street. You must have staked out the house." And damned cleverly too, he thought. Khalil was sure that he had not been followed earlier, when he had approached Towfick. He had exercised great care. But the proximity made him very nervous, as did the gift box in his pocket. He was suddenly anxious to be out of here, and to have a chance to think.

"Well, it's been nice talking to you, Mohammed. But it's getting late, and I really must be off." He stretched his hand across the table. "Keep well. I'm sure our paths will cross again, one of these years."

Mahrous took the powerful, long-fingered hand. He resisted the childish impulse to apply pressure and try to crush the bones. His smile remained, but dying on his lips, as he watched the tall figure walk out.

"Sweat, you bastard," he said quietly.

Chapter 31

IT WAS the first day of the Islamic festival of Ramadan. For the next month, Muslims would fast throughout the daylight hours, touching no food, no liquids, nor even their beloved tobacco, until the sun went down each day. For that month, the working days would be curtailed. But in the kitchens of the homes of the faithful, the women would work diligently, preparing their best food for the breaking of the fast at nightfall. By then, many a Muslim would be standing with his hookah in one hand and a match in the other, while his children waited to fall upon the food and feast till dawn. If the days were bleak during Ramadan, the nights were a time of celebration.

Ivan Torbek spent the morning relaxing in his room in a hotel near the airport. It was his second day in Cairo. He had booked in the day before, but had not been contacted. Torbek didn't question this. His instructions were to wait. Shortly before noon, he was approached in the lobby of the hotel by a well-spoken Egyptian who addressed him in English. Torbek was not hard to recognize. In a box-cut jacket that barely covered his square frame, he was completely bald, with a neck as thick as the polished head that it supported, and expressionless blue eyes.

The Egyptian who met him was also bald, but slender and bull-necked, with the thickest spectacles Torbek had ever seen. They went to the coffee shop, which was open for the benefit of tourists. It did not occur to Torbek to wonder why his companion didn't even have a sip of water, while he ordered a substantial lunch.

"Why am I here?" Torbek asked.

The answer was: "Because one of your targets is experienced."

"How many targets?"

"That is still to be determined."

He was given two things. A map of Cairo, with the route marked on it to an address on Rhoda Island. And the keys to a hired car, which was now in the hotel parking lot. The car had a telephone. The rest of his instructions were delivered verbally.

When he left the hotel, he drove across the Tahrir Bridge to Rhoda Island. When he reached the address he had been given, he drove around for a while to satisfy himself that there was nothing untoward. It was a routine assignment. But if the man was a professional, he might be alert, and Torbek liked to minimize risk. He settled down to wait.

It was two P.M. when John Baldwin left the apartment building. He had received a telephone call and been invited—or rather summoned—to the Gezira Sporting Club, which was open for its foreign clientele. Torbek noted that there was still some bounce in the walk of the elephantine fat man. Strength. Torbek watched without emotion as Baldwin plopped his body into the almost-demolished driving seat, making the car bounce on its springs.

Fifteen minutes later, Torbek rang the doorbell of the apartment. In an exclusive part of the city, the building was one of the older types, with no security system. The door was opened by a petite woman, with hair that fell across her brow, and a face that was older than it looked at first glance.

"Mrs. Baldwin?"

"Yes?"

"My name is Ivan Torbek. I think your husband is expecting me."

"Oh, really?" She frowned. "He just left."

Torbek looked at his watch. "I am a few minutes early. Do you expect him back momentarily?"

"No, I don't." She made no move to unchain the door.

"I think I know where he might be," Torbek said. "Do you mind if I use your telephone? We may have confused our arrangements."

"He's gone to the Sporting Club," Marina said. "You'll find him there."

"If I could just make a call?"

Torbek smiled inwardly. She was suspicious. But the instinct to avoid being rude was often stronger than the sense of danger, a conditioning that had cost many lives. In this case, it made little difference, one way or the other.

Marina sighed and opened the door. This saved him the trouble of putting his shoulder to it. He wasted no time on the woman. Clamping a hand over her mouth, he dragged her to the bedroom, where he put one hand on her throat and strangled her on the king-size bed.

Marina had a few last thoughts. They were the continuation of thoughts that had been in her mind a lot lately. Born in London, within the sound of the bow bells of St. Clements, she had met John Baldwin in an East End pub. It was a pub with a drag show. She remembered how she'd made her play for Baldwin. Brought up in

a tenement crowded with kids, she'd seen the polished
fat man as her ticket to prosperity. It had worked. She
had never ceased to marvel at that, the fact that Baldwin
had married her. Now she was a fair-skinned whore in
Cairo, with a husband who almost never spoke to her.
That said it all. There was nothing much more to it
than that: a pathetic little life. Yet she struggled like
a bird in a steel trap, till the strength finally went out
of her.

When he saw that she was dead, Torbek tore the
woman's clothing in a manner that suggested rape.
After dealing with the husband when he returned,
he would ransack the apartment. It didn't have to
fool anybody. The official account would be that an
intruder had raped the wife, and been disturbed while
robbing the premises. That was guaranteed: not that it
made much difference to Torbek.

In the dining room, he found a bottle of Stolichnaya
vodka and poured himself a glass. He had no nerves
whatsoever as he settled down to wait. Five feet ten in
height, Torbek had been a world-class weight lifter in
the heavyweight division. Unofficially, he had broken
the world record for the bench press many times, with
lifts of over seven hundred pounds. He was a master
of unarmed combat, though seldom unarmed. On this
occasion he carried a twenty-two caliber revolver, loaded with high-velocity shells, and a knife. He planned to
use the knife.

Baldwin returned to his apartment in the late afternoon. He was nervous. By no means sure why he had
been summoned to the Sporting Club, where he had
learned nothing that justified the special meeting, he
had a sense of something in the air and didn't like
it. He was about to park outside his building when

he spotted the hired car. That was unusual in the residential street. His eyes narrowed as they rose to the windows of his own apartment.

The unfamiliar car was locked. But there was a map of Cairo lying on the passenger seat. Baldwin saw the route marked from the airport to a point on Rhoda Island, to his own apartment building. The physical sensation was like a thick finger of nausea touching his stomach as he turned and walked quickly back to his own car.

He crossed the bridge back to the mainland and ordered cognac in a café. If he had been in doubt, he could have called his apartment. Not being in doubt, he preferred not to do that. He thought of calling the man he had just left in the Sporting Club. But again there was nothing to gain and perhaps a lot to lose. Baldwin's heart was pumping fast when he went to the telephone. Cairo was a big city. But all of a sudden he was on his own, and with nowhere to hide.

The number he called was one of the listed numbers for Cairo Central Prison. Speaking in Arabic, he asked for Lieutenant Colonel Mahrous, and was told to hold. His palms were sweating when a voice answered.

"Hallo?"

"Lieutenant Colonel Mahrous?"

"Go ahead, please."

Baldwin opened his mouth to speak, but checked himself. It was not Mahrous. It came to him suddenly that Mahrous was under wraps and his calls were being screened—but by whom? Baldwin felt the beginnings of panic as he replaced the receiver.

One of the things he had learned this afternoon was that the English girl had been released and was staying with Khalil's sister. It seemed that the two women were holed up together, which meant that their house was

either the safest or the most dangerous place in Cairo.
They were both weak links in Khalil's chain. Baldwin
scrabbled in the telephone directory again. Yes, it was
listed. The address was there, under Yvette Montagne.
She lived to the south of Garden City, on the edge of
old Cairo.

In a more normal frame of mind, Baldwin would not
have failed to notice that he was being followed when
he left the café. The same car that had been outside his
house was now behind him, keeping several cars away.
Torbek had been watching when Baldwin looked into
his parked car. Even as Baldwin was peering through
the window at the map of Cairo, Torbek had been
leaping down the stairs of the apartment building.
Using the handset from the glove compartment of the
car, he described Baldwin's movements to the calm
voice at the other end. He was told to keep in touch
and await instructions.

Chapter 32

MAHROUS WAS surprised by how much at ease he felt.
When he walked into the quiet courtyard, feeling its
coolness, and the fragrance of the air, he could almost
believe that he had left the troubled world behind him.
That, of course, was an illusion. But the girl added to it
as she came to meet him, wearing white slacks, her hair
tied up behind her head. He made it clear that this was

not an official visit. Mary had been released, she was innocent, and he was not here to interrogate her. She smiled, and was graceful enough not to question that. Yvette was in her room, she said. She was tired, and preferred not to join them. Khalil was not at home. They sat outside, at a table by the fountain, and in a way that he could never have expected, the talk just flowed. They didn't talk about the case. He didn't and she didn't. They talked about England, and about being in Egypt as a foreigner. Some of her comments made him smile. For the first time in years, it seemed, he found himself relaxed, just chatting to a pretty girl and enjoying her company. Even when their talk did turn, as though by a kind of gravitational force, to the subject of Khalil, the atmosphere remained light. They went on talking like old friends.

"I could tell you some stories about Khalil," he said. "My goodness, yes." He chuckled.

Mary smiled. She was thinking that it was the first time since she had come to Cairo that she had enjoyed sitting down and just chatting to a man. At first, she had assumed that he was trying to gain her confidence, to draw her out. Now she doubted that, and was interested in the question: Why had he come here? She knew that he was in trouble for having arrested her, and was no longer on the case.

"Did he ever speak about the Muslim Brotherhood?" he asked.

Her smile faltered for a moment. "No, never." He nodded and went on.

"I'm ten years older than Khalil. We were raised in the same village, as I think you know, and I remember them as children, Ibrahim and Yvette. I used to feel sorry for them. The village was a good place for kids. There were always things to do, helping with the animals, or in

the fields, listening to the men talk. At noon each day,
the women would bring lunches to the men and boys,
who were working in the fields. After lunch they'd stay
to work and the families were all together. It wasn't like
the cities, where so often the father and mother hardly
see each other, or their children. There was always
entertainment in the evening. Someone putting on a
play, or getting married. The simple food we ate was
so delicious. Home-baked bread and onions roasted in
their skins—too much cheese to be good for us, but it
tasted so good. It was different for the young Khalils.
They lived in their big house, and never got to do anything. We all went to school together in the village. First
the mosque school, where we learned the Koran, then
the Christian school, where there was more education.
They had tutors. Then Ibrahim was sent to private
school in Cairo. We used to see them in their father's
car, looking out with blank eyes, and we didn't envy
them, I'll tell you. The father wasn't a bad man, for a
pasha. Some of the landowners were pretty abominable,
speaking French and scoffing at Islam. Khalil's father
wasn't like that—though he married a French woman,
paradoxically. He was a devout man too, though he
married out of his faith . . . I suppose that happens
sometimes. When a young man falls in love, and just
knows that he's got the right to defy anybody—everybody—even God—except that he knows that God is on
his side. He died in police custody, by the way. The
father," he confirmed as her blue eyes came up. "He
was accused of being involved in a plot to assassinate
Nasser, and died under questioning in 1954."

Mahrous saw the information hitting home. She
glanced at him, and he saw that there was something
on her mind. He waited. Finally, she asked: "Is it only
young men who fall in love like that?"

"Oh, I think so," he answered easily. "Later on, it's peace and quiet we want, isn't it?"

Shortly after that, he rose to leave. She rose too, and began to walk with him to the gate. She was thinking that she didn't want him to leave when he asked: "Did you ever find out about that briefcase? The one you saw in your apartment?"

"No, I didn't." She stopped and he did too. His black eyes turned in a lazy sweep and seemed to lock on to hers. "I asked Yvette. She knew nothing about it."

"But you did see it?" She nodded. "So I wonder where it went. How is Yvette?" he asked. "Did you say she was under the weather?"

"She seems a bit depressed." The truth was that Yvette was acting strangely. On being pressed about the briefcase, and whether she'd seen anything unusual in Mary's apartment, she had become withdrawn and would now hardly speak at all.

"And Khalil has disappeared?"

"I haven't seen him today. I don't think he was here last night either. Maybe he's gone back to Greece."

Mahrous took a card from his pocket. "Did I tell you that Michael Pappas was killed in Athens?" Her jaw literally dropped. "Apparently he went drinking in the wrong kind of bar. Just when we wanted to question him." He handed her the card. "This is totally unofficial, Mary. I'm not even supposed to be here. But if you have any problem. Or if you learn anything— after talking to Yvette, for example"—his eyes met hers strongly—"call that number. It's my office number. I expect to be there for a while. Call me if you think of anything, or if you get worried for any reason. Oh, one more thing. I took the liberty of bringing a man with me. He's a handpicked man—very good—and I thought I'd leave him with you. He'll stay by the gate. He won't get in your hair. Just a precaution," he said as her mouth opened to protest. "On my own authority. My last act of defiance." His smile went sideways. "Don't you have servants in this house?"

She looked around. "Yes, we do. I suppose Yvette must have told them they could go."

He pointed to the card. "I don't think you'll have a problem. Khalil very possibly has left the country. But just in case." He tapped the card. "Please take care."

The sun was low, and there were shadows in the courtyard. Lamps had come on, and their light turned golden in her hair. Before leaving, Mahrous took her by the elbow, and to his surprise, she pecked him on the lips.

Chapter 33

BALDWIN WAS convinced that there was a far-reaching conspiracy. He knew that there were foreigners involved, and believed that at least one professional had been sent to Cairo. But equally frightening was the scope of local involvement. It apparently went from a high political level all the way down to the control of police switchboards. Marina was dead. He did not doubt that for a moment. His reaction was a recurring twist of fear. Now they were looking for him.

The house was in a kind of no-man's-land between Garden City and old Cairo. In a city where every dwelling was ablaze with light, as Muslims celebrated the breaking of the fast, it was the only dwelling of substance within sight, and was approached by a dirt road. From a distance, Baldwin saw a police car outside the gates, and drove by slowly. Damn, he was nervous! It seemed hardly possible that orders concerning him could reach down to an ordinary policeman, but it *was* possible. But there were risks he had to take. He drove back to the dirt road.

As he approached the iron gate, he waved reassuringly to the guard who watched him. The man was armed with a submachine gun. Baldwin kept his hands in full view as he hurried over.

"Officer, my name is John Baldwin. I would like to speak to Miss Yvette Montagne." He saw a pair of eyes that were steady and intelligent as the man studied him. "It is a matter of importance, Officer. I am anxious to speak to the lady of the house, and to make contact with Lieutenant Colonel Mahrous."

The man responded to the name. Still studying Baldwin, he nodded and touched a button that activated an intercom to the interior. Baldwin saw that for the gate to open, the officer had to undo a heavy bolt, and someone inside had to buzz it electronically.

The voice that answered from the speaker spoke in English.

"What is it, Mustapha?"

The policeman answered in fair English. "There is a gentleman here asking to speak to Miss Montagne. His name is John Baldwin."

"Baldwin?" There was a lengthy silence. Then: "Put him on, please."

The policeman motioned Baldwin to the mouthpiece. Baldwin saw that every move he made was being watched carefully. He spoke urgently in English. "Miss Miles-Tudor?" Baldwin knew that he was talking to Mary. "I don't know if Miss Montagne knows my name. I have recently had dealings with Ibrahim Khalil, but— I am no longer involved with him," he added guardedly. "I have something urgently important to say to you. Please let me in."

Again there was a silence. Baldwin guessed that the two women were conferring. Then Mary's voice again. "Mr. Baldwin, Yvette knows your name, but she says that she has nothing to do with her brother's affairs. She wants nothing to do with you, I'm afraid. So I think you'd better leave, please."

Baldwin's panic rose sharply. She had to let him in. "Mary, for God's sake, listen. I believe that we are all in danger. You, Miss Montagne, and myself. You have been arrested. You know that there is danger. Specifically, I believe that Miss Montagne has information concerning her brother that certain people will not allow her to divulge. I repeat, they will not allow her to divulge it. I've tried to contact Lieutenant Colonel Mahrous. But you can't get him through the public switchboard, and I don't know how to dial him directly. I am convinced that he's the only policeman we can trust."

After a pause, the English girl's voice was a shade less aloof. "Lieutenant Colonel Mahrous was here this afternoon. He gave me a special number."

"Then for God's sake let me in. You have an armed guard. He can take my gun. We'll try to contact Mahrous, and I'll help you make the house secure." While he spoke, Baldwin was watching the policeman. The man was alert. His eyes went to Baldwin's clothing, checking for the presence of the small gun.

There was yet another pause. Whatever was going on up there, they were taking no chances. Then she was back, sounding very calm as she asked the guard if he thought it safe to do as Baldwin said. The policeman looked at Baldwin's size. But he was holding a high-speed automatic weapon, and Baldwin's hands were empty. He nodded and spoke into the speaker.

Baldwin trembled with relief. There was a moment's tension as he took out his gun and passed it through the bars. "It's a twenty-two," he said unnecessarily. The guard palmed the weapon and put it in his pocket.

The door buzzed and the guard secured the electronic lock. Baldwin glanced both ways along the walls, and the guard did the same, using mirrors overhead. The place was set up for security.

"I'm going to open the gate," the guard said in Arabic. "Step in quickly, please, and keep your hands where I can see them. If you make an unexpected move, I'll have to shoot. Those are my orders." Baldwin nodded, tongue flicking on dry lips. The guard shot the bolt, and pushed the door open.

The man came like a cannonball from a corner of the house. Baldwin saw a bullet head gleaming in the starlight, and there was a sharp crack. The guard spun and before Baldwin could brace himself he was hit with a momentum that shocked him. Thrown against the gate, he saw the guard's silent scream as he was stabbed with an upward sweep of a stiletto.

Baldwin was taller than the man. Feet spread for balance, he fixed his eyes on the knife and his brain worked smoothly. The gun had been pocketed. Any neighbor who had heard the first crack and was listening for another could go back to his revelry. The attacker felt he didn't need the gun. He was confident of his abilities with the knife, and that was Baldwin's chance. He had a defense against any such attack.

The knife changed hands. It was quick, and nearly caught him unawares as suddenly the left hand was swooping upward. Baldwin parried the blow, turned with it, and felt fierce triumph as his fingers closed on the wrist of the knife hand. A man's arm was like a straw against his weight and he swung a leg to throw the body in the air. The man's head came up beneath his chin, shattering bone and teeth, and a fist demolished his nose. Baldwin's fingers lost their grip, and his back hit the wall.

He had a moment in which to know it was the end. In that fraction of a second as the knife came up, he knew that life was over. The knife pierced below the ribs and raked through heart and lungs. It was the oddest thing. Baldwin knew that he was dead. Eyes large and wondering, he sank like a stabbed bull, knees and elbows giving way.

In an upstairs room, Mary ran to a window that over-looked the courtyard. Even Yvette, who had emerged from deep lethargy and had just been saying some things that had Mary staring in astonishment, sprang from her chair and they both looked down. They saw the shadow in the passage from the outside gate. A heavy body and a spadelike hand against the tiles.

"That's not Mustapha!"

Yvette shook her head, agreeing. The man down there was not the guard.

"The lights!"

They ran to switch off all lights. Most of the house was in darkness anyway.

The room was bare, unpainted, dingy, old: like the hotel itself, which was a sleeping-only place, with no restaurant. Khalil had chosen it as one of a thousand

like it in Cairo, and for the decrepitude of the owner,
who had scarcely glanced at him when he checked in
the day before. He had observed no surveillance. But
aware of the subtleties of "City Eye," and shaken by
the incident with Mahrous, he had worn a fez and spectacles, and other touches of disguise, when he stepped
out to buy the newspapers that morning. There was no
news. He spent the rest of the day on the lumpy bed,
reading and thinking.

Logic told him that Mahrous had acted on his own,
and was no threat. Against the support that Khalil
had been assured he had, an assurance that he utterly
believed, a lone policeman was of no account, whatever
his suspicions. It was suspicion only. Mahrous had nothing more, and if he came close to finding an official ear,
he would be the one to suffer, not Khalil. At this stage
of the operation, it was absurd to think that anything
so trivial would be allowed to interfere: still, he spent
a restless day.

At sundown, he went to a basin in the corner of the
room and purified himself for prayer. As he prayed,
facing east and touching his face to the floor, he felt
uplifting strength. He dressed carefully. Not in the
shabby clothing he'd worn earlier, but in a dark suit,
quality shoes, and with touches of jewelry. The old
patron noticed nothing different when he checked out.
Nor did the bulky chambermaid, her legs chafing as
she shuffled along a corridor. Khalil walked to his
car, carrying his bag. The car was clean, as was the
room he'd left behind him. His person would be too,
once he'd discarded a few things. He went to a café,
and broke his fast with water. Then he ate a meal of
hummus and pita bread, washed down with water. His
spirit was calm, though he was hyper-alert. Assured of
his own inner strength, he noted carefully that he was

not being followed as he drove through Cairo to his
destiny.

It was Mary who found a suitable lever in Khalil's
room. It was a heavy tool that seemed to be designed
for prying out nails. She forced it under the lid of
the painted chest and applied pressure, gasping with
frustration when nothing gave.

"Let me," Yvette whispered.

They were both barefooted. Mary had discarded the
white slacks and blouse she wore. At the first opportunity, she planned to look for something to cover
her white skin. For the moment, there were other
priorities.

"Sit on it," Yvette said.

Mary hesitated. "If I sit on it, how can you raise
the lid?"

"Sit on it."

Mary straddled the box. Yvette braced her legs, took
the lever in both hands, and jerked. Mary and the box
both bobbed. Yvette put her feet between Mary's legs
and added her weight to the lid of the box. She reached
down for the lever, took a breath, and Mary saw her
muscles stand out as she heaved. Suddenly the wood
gave around the lock.

They listened to the silence. There were no servants
in the house. They had all disappeared before sundown,
to be with their families on this special day. Mary and
Yvette had seen two bodies lying aginst the wall outside.
And there was a man in the house.

Yvette found the gun. It was a forty-five caliber
automatic, and there was a full clip in place. She found
the safety catch, worked the mechanism to put a shell in
the chamber, and they both flitted from the room . . .
Standing stock-still in the courtyard, in a patch of dark

shadow, Ivan Torbek had heard the crack of the box and was staring upward at the window of that room.

"Can you fire this thing?"

"You point it and you pull the trigger," Yvette said. "I don't know if I can hit anything."

"Can you hold on to it?"

Yvette grinned fiercely. She had snapped out of her despair. She had not quite admitted that her brother was guilty of anything, though she had planted seeds of doubt in Mary's mind, but that was not the issue now. The immediate threat was the man downstairs.

"Do we dare use the telephone?" Mary whispered.

"That or the lights? Which first? I can go downstairs and take the fuses out."

Mary thought for a moment. If the house remained in darkness they might be very hard to find. There were several stairways between the levels, and Yvette knew every nook and cranny.

"Let's find out where he is. If we can locate him, we'll know what we can do."

Yvette nodded in agreement.

They chose a position on the gallery close to one of the staircases. This gave them an escape route whichever way he came. Yvette went to her belly and looked over the edge. Mary watched the room behind, straining eyes and ears.

Nothing. After a few minutes, they exchanged looks and shook their heads . . . nothing. Without words, they agreed to stay where they were.

Torbek was on the main staircase. It was made of marble, and there was nothing to creak under his feet. He knew the room they were in. After the splintering sound as they had forced something open, he had sensed their arrival on one of the galleries above. Both together. That was good—and they would probably remain that way. He had the gun in one hand, and the knife ready to slip into the other. He assumed they were now armed.

He reached the doorway of the room. It was not a simple house. Large and complicated. But the silence was complete at this time of night, and he had good ears. He had identified a couple of light switches. But meantime he was satisfied with the faint glow from the courtyard. He had the advantage of knowing where they were, and was sure that they had not moved.

Mary shivered violently. There was a chill to the night air, but it wasn't only that. She took her eyes from the doorway of the room behind them, and gazed around inside. There was a cupboard that might contain clothing. She was about to whisper to Yvette when suddenly all hell broke loose.

From the corner of her eye, she saw a massive shadow flit into the room. Mary screamed, and Yvette snapped from the floor like a jumping insect as a sharp crack came from the room simultaneously with the splintering of wood on the gallery. Yvette's gun roared with a boom that seemed to shake the house as Mary dived for the escape staircase. She reached the ground in a couple of bounds, and yet Yvette was right behind her. Mary was pushed and almost fell as they ran inside, and Yvette was in command at this point. They ended up behind the grand piano in the music room, and that was when Mary realized two things. One, Yvette was hit. And two, they were trapped. Yvette realized this too.

"I fucked up." Yvette's face was white as she leaned her head against the wall. "I don't know why I ran in here."

Mary put a finger on her lips. Yvette had been hit in the left shoulder. The shell had passed right through her flesh, and blood poured from the exit wound to the back. She put her lips to Yvette's ear.

"Did you get him?" Yvette closed her eyes. Her minute head shake was sensed rather than seen. "Then we'll just have to wait for him," Mary whispered.

Chapter 34

THE PRESIDENTIAL convoy was ready to leave Nasser's official residence, the Koubbeh Palace, shortly after the breaking of the fast at sundown. Nasser took a simple meal, drank water, and finished some business, before asking an aide to remind him of the format for the evening's proceedings at the Semiramis Hotel. He was told that there would be a reception and a buffet supper for those who had been invited to the opening night of the Agricultural Fair. These included farmers who had been awarded land, to whom Nasser would present title deeds in a brief ceremony. Then he would be expected to circulate, look at the exhibits, let the journalists take their pictures, and that would be it. Downstairs, his guards were waiting. Tall, rangy men, some of them bearded, they were stationed around the lighted area outside the palace. Nasser noted their alertness. There were five cars in the convoy that would travel through the cleared streets of the city. Sadat had taken him literally: which was one of the nice things about Sadat, he thought, smiling. It would

be good practice for later in the month, when nationals
from many countries would be in the city under the
auspices of the summit meeting. Nasser walked down,
his back straight, and tried to close his mind to the
pain in his body.

When Khalil walked into the Semiramis and pre-
sented his credentials, he was directed to a room where
guests were being screened. He lined up patiently
behind a group of others, and smiled at the guard
who examined his official letter. The guard studied
him in detail. He saw a tall Cairene of the privileged
class, but politely cooperative in manner, and gruffly
moved him on to another room.

Khalil had never seen such security. Even the farmers, who had been bused down from the delta region,
and many of whom were in a city for the first time in
their lives, were being treated as potential terrorists.
The man ahead of Khalil looked so genuine it made
him want to smile. With his papers clutched in one
brown hand, the fingernails hard and roughened, he
was stripped of his galabiya and every fold of cloth
examined before they let him through. Khalil prayed.
In this part of the hotel, the corridors were thick with
security men. Khalil knew that they had examined every
nook and cranny, and would now stand guard until the
President had left. There would be no escape from this
place. Not for Khalil. It was part of his mandate not to
be captured alive.

In the planning of this operation, many scenarios had
been discussed. One of these, which was the most daring
and nerve-wracking to execute, had been kicked around
enough that it had acquired a code name, Omega. The
name Omega implied three things. First, it implied a
weapon that required close physical proximity. This

had been well tested by Khalil, but the proximity, given that the target was the President of the United Arab Republic, was a problem. That was the second feature of Omega. Extensive behind-the-scenes support and protection from interference for the operative. This, however, came with a price. In face-to-face contact with his victim, the key operative would be unprecedentedly exposed and this led to the third condition. It had never been their plan to shoot Nasser down in blood. The preference was to remove him quietly, leaving political events to take their course. Nor did Khalil countenance failure. He believed in his destiny. But if disaster fell, he had sworn a sacred oath that his knowledge would die with him.

Those were the three faces of Omega. Support, Protection, and Death before capture. But as Khalil liked to tell himself, no solid figure can have three plane faces. There was a fourth face, and it was the base. The fourth face of Omega was Destiny.

He stepped forward to be searched.

Torbek crouched at the top of the staircase they had used. He knew to which side of the house they had fled. It was the side immediately below where they had been. He was not concerned about the booming of the gun. There was no other house near this one that was likely to have a telephone. Nor would these people leave their homes to alert the police. He had time. And he knew that he had hit one of them.

He was standing downstairs, still as a statue, when he saw a splash of blood on the floor. It was near the doorway to one of the rooms, and after waiting for a while, he moved carefully till he could see inside the room. There was a grand piano and other pieces of furniture. Torbek's eyes narrowed. On one wall of

the room was a large window, leading to the patio.
But there was no doorway leading out. If they were
in there, they were trapped. He saw another splash of
blood in the middle of the floor.

Torbek stood still for several minutes. There was
not a breath or any kind of sound. The one he had
hit should be breathing harshly. She was either dead,
or a very strong and determined woman, he thought,
remembering how she had leapt up from the floor. He
became convinced that they were in that room. One
might be behind the grand piano. If so, she must be
on the stool, her legs tucked up from the floor. The
only other piece of cover was a couch and armchair
in a corner of the room.

There was something uncanny in the silence. Torbek
began to feel it, and there was sweat under his arms.
He glanced around, realizing suddenly that they might
not both be in the room. He thought of something else
and retreated to the courtyard.

From the courtyard, he could see the doorway of the
music room, and the window that looked into it. There
were trees that gave him cover. He moved, improving his angle to the window. Now he could see into
the room, and that was when he froze in astonishment.

There was a skin rug just beyond the window. He
had seen it earlier, a hide of lama wool, and from the
doorway, it had seemed empty. It wasn't empty now.
A woman lay on it. On her side, head on arm, legs
stretched, naked. Torbek blinked. He raised his gun,
ready to shoot through the window, but stopped, eyes
narrowing. What was this? Was she alive or dead? He
stared at her breast. The soft, firm curves were there
beneath the shoulder, no movement. Puzzled, he took
aim but held it. Where was the other?

He flitted back to the doorway of the room. His rubber-soled shoes made no sound on the enameled brick. There she was! Not a vision to be seen only through the glass, but large as life and seeming closer now. He stared. In the faint light, her pale skinned glowed. A beautiful, blond, possibly dead woman. His lips tightened and he aimed at her chest again. But where was the other? There was nothing close to the woman on the rug. No cover. The closest thing was the piano, and he'd seen behind that a moment ago through the window. The couch and armchairs were quite distant. Was the other woman crouching there, waiting for him to show himself? Torbek's lips moved angrily. He could see no rationale for this. Surely they did not imagine he would rush in, blind to everything except the beauty of the woman on the rug? What then? Was she ready to spring up with a weapon if he rushed the couch? Or was she lying in a pool of blood that he couldn't see while the other lurked elsewhere, maybe not in the room? He stared again, looking for signs of breathing. She was as still as marble. If it was a trap, it was certainly ingenuous.

He decided to rush her. Even if she had the weapon, he would be on her in a moment. If the other lay in wait across the room with the thundering weapon, which she could hardly aim, he would have the piano for cover. Same if she were not in the room. He stared one last time at the woman on the rug. In a moment he would know her mystery.

Yvette was sure that she would never be able to move. Legs doubled under her on the piano stool, her useless arm draped on the closed lid of the keyboard, she crouched with her head down and the huge gun resting on her wrist. She had been able to move when he went outside, when Mary hissed that he was going to look through the window. With the pain in her shoulder almost unbearable, she had moved again when he returned to the doorway. Now it was the strain in her back and limbs, as well as the hot fire of the wound.

Torbek came in bent double and charged Mary. Yvette bobbed up like a figure on a firing range, and the thunder of her weapon drowned the double sharp crack from Torbek's. She spun to the floor as he ran into a foot that kicked him in the face. He cursed and caught Mary's ankle as she kicked at him again. Yvette's shot hit Torbek in the neck and passed through. For a moment, it seemed that nothing had happened, as his tongue flicked across his lips. Her next shot jerked his body like a marionette and he began to fall as she too passed out.

Chapter 35

THE SEMIRAMIS was not the biggest of the hotels along the Nile. But the ballroom was large enough to house the exhibits, and the buffet tables along the walls, and there was a low stage with microphones, where a band played softly. The guests of honor, the farmers, were agog at all this splendor. They stuffed themselves with food, shook hands with representatives of the Department of Agriculture, and gazed at the exhibits, brows furrowed with the weight of their new responsibilities. It was a big night too for the sponsors of the commercial booths. The vice presidents of companies, many of them children of the industrial revolution in Egypt, extolled the virtues of the products they displayed, hoping to catch the attention of a government official. There were visitors from overseas. Khalil saw a group of Saudis, some tough-looking Libyans, and the Soviet Ambassador. There were also local dignitaries. He recognized the Egyptian Minister of Agriculture, and several members of the Supreme Council of the Arab Socialist Union. One of these was the man who was regarded by many as the potential next president of Egypt. As he moved around, Khalil kept his mind at ease, ready to smile, ready to chat. It was remarkable, he thought, that the Soviets were so unaware of the tides of feeling in Egypt. For all their armies of analysts and intelligence-gathering diplomats, they were out of touch with fundamental things, like their own unpopularity. Another thing that all the pundits underestimated, not just the Soviets, was the determination of Anwar Sadat. Sadat was Nasser's official deputy, a post that had been passed around among the "Free Officers," and was considered a "yes-man." But when he saw the chance to assume real power, the gentle Sadat would turn into a tiger. Khalil took note of nodal areas in the room, where things were sure to focus later. He watched a demonstration of an irrigation technique, designed to use waters from the Aswan High Dam, and chatted to an ex-Egyptian, now a professor in the United States, about the new role of that country in the Middle East.

The presidential group arrived without much fanfare. Khalil noted a couple of tall, dark-suited men who walked in and spoke to the official host, the Minister of Agriculture. This gentleman then headed for the podium, as did other dignitaries, following his lead. The band stopped playing and the crowd turned toward the stage as the Minister called for attention.

"Ladies and gentlemen . . ." The Minister waited till
the buzz of talk and movement in the room died away.
"The President of the United Arab Republic . . ."

The main doors opened and Nasser walked in. Tall
and dignified, the magnetic grin in place, he waved
to the crowd as he made his way across the floor,
surrounded by guards. Up on the stage, he pumped
hands with all the dignitaries. A personable man, he
seemed to have a private word for each of them. It was
good theater. Casual, but impressive, as the platform
party reseated themselves on simple chairs, and the
host Minister raised a hand for silence. Nasser wore a
casual suit, as did most of the others. It was the way in
Egypt. Only the security men were dressed in black.

Khalil stood beside a group of visitors from the
Emirates. His smile was fixed as he gazed toward the
stage, studying the charismatic figure in the center.

*Ah, yes, my fine leader. What chance had the other
members of the dowdy group, who met together in their
barracks rooms? There was one leader. Because of
him, and him alone, it had all happened. It would
end as it had begun, with Nasser.*

Mary was not surprised to find that the telephones
were dead. The lines had probably been cut. Ignoring
the horror of the body in the room, slipping on the
blood, she tried to get Yvette on her feet. Yvette had
a fixed, blank grin.

"Get some clothes on, you crazy bitch." She was in
shock, and close to passing out again.

Mary flew upstairs to Yvette's room.She found a
T-shirt and squeezed into a pair of shorts.

"Yvette, we must get to a telephone. I must call
Mahrous."

"I'll be all right," Yvette said. "Leave me here."

"Don't be silly. We must get you to a hospital."

Yvette's wounds were in the shoulder and the chest. There was no way to stem the bleeding except by holding compressed cloth against them. Mary tried to get Yvette to do this with her good hand, but it was pretty hopeless. They had to get to the car.

Yvette's laugh tinkled out, sounding so normal. "You can't do that," she said as Mary squatted down and maneuvered an arm across her shoulder. "You can't lift me." Mary braced her legs and rose slowly, from a full squat, bringing Yvette to her feet. It wasn't only that Yvette might die. It was what she knew after putting together what Yvette had said last night. The trailing feet worked feebly as they staggered out.

The police car had a radio! Mary could not believe she hadn't thought of that. How to work the thing? She forced herself to stay calm, got the power on, found the switches for transmit-receive, and prayed that someone at the other end spoke English. The weight of what she knew was almost as terrifying as Yvette's ghastly injuries. Yvette was in the passenger seat and had passed out.

"This is Mary Miles-Tudor . . ." There was crackling as someone spoke in Arabic at the other end. "Does anybody there speak English? English! Please!"

It seemed an endless time. Voices came and went, asking questions in broken English. She explained that she was calling from Yvette Montagne's house. There had been shooting. A man had come and killed the guard and tried to kill the two of them. Miss Montagne was seriously wounded. Two men were dead. Three! she screamed. Could she possibly speak to Lieutenant Colonel Mahrous?

Where are you calling from, please? What is the

address? Why are you calling from a police vehicle? Mary screamed her plea repeatedly, and began to realize that she would have to drive. She had to get her information to Mahrous, and she had to get Yvette to a hospital. Suddenly a more authoritative voice came on.

"Miss Miles-Tudor?"

"Mohammed?"

"Lieutenant Colonel Mahrous can't come to the telephone at the moment. What is it that you want to say to him?"

She began to speak, but checked herself. "I must speak to him personally. Please get him, this is vitally important."

"What message shall I give him?"

"No message!" She shook her head, matted hair flying. "Just tell him it's me, and that I must speak to him immediately."

"Hold on, please."

After a moment, Mary put the car in gear. She could not hold on. Nor, all of a sudden, did she trust this calm voice. The wheels and steering system squealed as she swung around in the driveway.

When Nasser had seized power in 1952, albeit behind the figurehead of General Naguib, he had dreamed of a democracy in Egypt. That was his dream, and that was why there was nothing that incensed him more these days, now that he knew the practicalities, than talk of democracy. Democracy was not possible in Egypt. The educational and economic level of the country was not sufficient to support it. To attempt democracy at this time, or at any time in the foreseeable future, would be to return to a corrupt, self-serving regime, like the one they had destroyed in 1952. Nasser knew this. The absurd thing was that for all his intelligence, he had imposed instead a form of authoritarian rule that was just as inappropriate in Egypt—Soviet-style communism. Nasser had discovered that what you want isn't always what you get—even when you are the President of the United Arab Republic.

Khalil did not listen to the platform speech, but the false words rippled on his consciousness. The fact that Marxism had destroyed the economy of Egypt was not mentioned. The fact that there was surely nothing to be hoped for from the paganism of the West, where women walk naked—that was not mentioned. Glory and honor. That was mentioned: the glory and honor of Egypt. Then the farmers were lined up and went to the platform one by one. They shook hands with the President and received the deeds to the stolen land, the start of a new phase of agrarian reform. A new phase too of the persecution of men of substance. How they hated men of substance, these peasants who had risen from the ranks, Khalil thought. His smile stayed fixed. He clapped and cheered with those around him, smiling at the simple, rough-skinned men, who thought their lives were going to change because of what was being given to them.

The aide to the Minister for Presidential Affairs, Achmed Ali, was not one of the platform party. He waited near the stage, ready to join the group when it's members stepped down, and he noticed Ibrahim Khalil, far back in the crowd. Khalil looked relaxed. It was impossible to believe that he had assassination on his mind. Ali had studied the matrix of the terrorist, the profiles and the signs. Khalil fitted none of these, and would alert no one. Ali spoke to a man standing next to him, who was the security chief in charge of Nasser's personal bodyguard.

"You are out in force tonight."

"With good reason."

"You mean because of what we've heard? This spy, who has been killing people? Doesn't sound much like your usual spy, does it?" he probed when the man proved slow to be drawn. "Do you think he could be here tonight?"

After a moment, the security man shook his head. All kinds of people had been cleared to attend the function, he admitted. But every one of them had been subjected to a search that totally precluded the possibility of entering with any kind of weapon. Nor was there any possibility of entering with any kind of a weapon being planted beforehand, because the area had been searched by experts. When Achmed Ali pointed out that this man could kill with his hands, the security chief smiled jeeringly. His men were also masters of unarmed combat. If anyone so much as took out a pencil—to take that example—in the vicinity of the President, he would be pounced upon immediately. "I probably shouldn't say this," he added. "But these men are instructed to kill first and ask questions afterward. And if there happens to be an innocent bystander in the way, that's not going to stop them." Any professional would know all this, he asserted. No professional group would even contemplate such an attack, and if a lone fanatic tried it, he would end up dead or maimed—and unsuccessful. They were too much on the alert. No, sir. Short of tanks and bombs and a small army, there was nothing going to happen to this President this night. Not tonight, not anytime.

Achmed Ali stared out at the crowd, and briefly met the eyes of Ibrahim Khalil.

The homes of Cairo were ablaze with light. People were celebrating now, eating lustily and drinking coffee and sweet liquids. Mary stopped at a café. Potbellied men in galabiyas stared at her in astonishment as she rushed in and used the telephone. She called the number Mahrous had given her. It was supposed to reach him at his office, but again the wrong voice answered. Where was she now, the voice asked urgently. What was her location? She sensed anger that she had not stayed at the house, and threw down the receiver. All this might be mindless panic. But Baldwin had said that outside calls were being screened, and it wasn't just that she had a dying woman on her hands. It was the growing conviction of the urgency of what she knew. The café denizens stared after her as she rushed out. American, they said, as they resumed gorging, remembering the tangled yellow hair and wild blue eyes.

Khalil kept to the background when the platform party left the stage. He knew that the most alert moments for security would be the first moments after they stepped down. As time went by, some relaxation was inevitable, especially since they expected nothing. Some senior dignitaries walked with the President as he began to do his rounds. One of the ministers was the Minister for Presidential Affairs, and his chief aide, Achmed Ali. Khalil never looked directly at Nasser's relative. But he noted that the man was with his boss as they walked around, asking questions, chatting, shaking hands. Khalil stepped out of the hall and headed for a toilet.

The toilet had been searched earlier and guarded since. A security man stood inside the door, his arms folded, a heavy automatic in his hand. He gazed unresponsively as Khalil nodded to him before entering a cubicle. There was no complaint when he locked the door.

It was the work of a moment to open the cuff link and fit the device to his finger. Khalil accompanied this with the sounds of relieving himself. The device resembled a thumbtack, with a ring of clear plastic attached to it. The ring was a tight fit around the tip of the middle finger of his left hand. Once it was in place, the head of the tack lay snugly against the ball of the finger, the fine needle extending about a quarter of an inch. The needle was encased in a miniature plastic sheath. Khalil touched this gingerly, but did not remove it yet. When he did, the tiny weapon would be lethal. The merest scratch would be enough to ensure death, and there was no antidote to the poison. Death would not be immediate. The poison was chemically bound in such a way that it would take several hours to act. When it did, death would come abruptly, with the symptoms of a heart attack. He flushed the toilet and stepped out to wash his hands, the device in the curl of the middle finger of his left hand.

"This is a wonderful occasion," he observed to the guard. The guard said nothing. "Will the exhibition be open to the public for the rest of the week? . . . I shall tell my friends," he went on as the guard remained unresponsive. "It is wonderful what has been done in this country for the ordinary people." The man remained impassive. But being addressed, he held the eyes that looked at him, as Khalil dried his hands. He did not see the outer ring of the device, which was all but invisible in any case. Back in the hall, Khalil headed for the model of the Aswan High Dam, which was one of the highlights of the exhibition.

Achmed Ali followed the movements of Khalil. But apart from that brief moment during the speech, there was no eye contact between them. Ali was in the forefront of the party, with his Minister, who walked with

Nasser. It was all that he could do to preserve his equanimity, and he had no concept—none at all—of what must be going on in the mind of the other man. In an action that would scarcely have been noticed, even if observed, Khalil touched his fingers to his waist and brow, and unsheathed the pin.

The guards at the gate of Central Prison had never encountered a situation like it. Here was an official car, with a badly wounded woman in it, and this wild, blond woman, with blood on her hands and face, and on her bare feet, demanding to be connected to Lieutenant Colonel Mahrous—in person, nothing else would do. They had heard that Mahrous had an eye for the ladies. On a couple of occasions recently, they had heard, he had been shacked up with one when needed for important operations. Looking at this crazy girl, with her athlete's legs and staring eyes, they might have thought they hardly blamed him—but what the hell to do? The officer in charge ordered the injured woman taken to the prison hospital, and finally agreed to call Mahrous. Using an internal line, not going through the public switchboard, he dialed an extension that she gave him. The instrument rang at the other end and was answered immediately. The officer nodded, and the anxious girl grabbed for the receiver. Mahrous was at his desk, surrounded by files, nervously trying to put together his report, but distracted.

When she heard his voice, the girl's wildness disappeared. The soldiers all noticed this, though none of them understood the quick words she spoke in English.

"The Semiramis Hotel. Some land ceremony. Nasser's there and Yvette's convinced that Khalil is too. She thinks he's going to kill Nasser."

Mahrous was in full uniform. That fact flashed across

his mind as he grabbed his hat and dashed for the staircase. He spoke to no one. He had no authority, and no time to argue. Nor time to sign out a car, even if they'd give him one. The fact was that he was unprepared. Although a part of him was by no means sure that he had scared off Khalil, he had basically given up wondering what the man intended. With deep depression at his shoulder, Mahrous had given up thinking about just about everything, except the safety of the girl. Now there was no time to stop, no time to think, as he leapt down the stairs to the outside. Thank God, the Semiramis was just around the corner.

Running with one arm was something that you learned. You swung the arm you had across your chest and swung the other in your mind. He fell on the steps leading down from his building. People stared at the man in the uniform of a lieutenant colonel who barreled across a busy street, his one arm raised, and raced for the road along the Nile. By some miracle his hat stayed on and was still in place when he raced up the steps of the Semiramis.

Nasser was telling the story of a pasha who had stopped to harass a peasant praying in the fields. It was an old tale, but those who stood around loved it just the same, especially the farmers. "What are you doing," the pasha had demanded, 'kneeling in the dirt?' 'I am praying, sire,' replied the peasant. Praying? Let me hear you pray. Ask God for a cow.' The poor farmer had no choice but to obey his master. He put his forehead to the earth, and prayed to Allah for a cow. No cow appeared. 'Ask him again,' the pasha demanded. 'Maybe he is hard of hearing.' The poor man did so. Still no cow. 'Now ask me for a cow,' commanded the pasha, and the trembling farmer did so. He had no wish to insult God. But if he offended the pasha, he would not be able to feed his wife and children. "You ask me for a cow?' said the triumphant pasha. 'Here is a cow. Now tell me who is greater. God, or me?"

Everybody laughed, and Nasser beamed. For a man who was supposed to be sick, Khalil thought, he looked remarkably well, after his treatments in Russia. But Nasser always managed to look well in public. Achmed Ali cleared his throat. Eyes turned to the new voice as the aide spoke smoothly.

"But not all ex-pashas are so bad, Mr. President. I see one at this moment who has been extremely generous, even contributing more than was asked of him."

Nasser's eyebrows lifted inquiringly. He followed the pointing hand of his relative and met the eyes of Ibrahim Khalil.

Mahrous was out of breath when he strode into the hotel. He knew that his only chance was calm behavior. God knows how Khalil could have penetrated the shield around Nasser, but Mahrous believed that he had done it, and prayed that he was not too late.

Two men stepped forward, saluting him politely. He had identification ready, but was recognized. "Who is the officer in charge?" he asked. "Is it Ghali?" One man nodded, and Mahrous spoke confidently. "I have a message for him. Is he in the exhibition hall?"

"I believe so, sir."

"Take me to him, please. And I know you have your orders to be careful, but let's make it quick."

They checked that he was unarmed. These were orders, they explained apologetically. Then they escorted him along the corridors, to the guarded main entrance to the exhibition hall. The chief bodyguard

saw him coming, and his face changed negatively.
Mahrous's heart sank as he realized that word had got
around already that he had been terminated. Putting
his best face on, he stepped into the hall, eyes searching
desperately for Nasser.

Achmed Ali reeled off the facts. Here was a man
who had given up his land, and voluntarily contributed
property and farm equipment worth the staggering total
of ten thousand pounds. One of the farmers recognized
Khalil. "Annas Pasha!" he exclaimed, pushing forward.
Khalil's eyes did not leave Nasser's as he took the bony
hand, scarcely glancing at the lit-up face of the old man,
whom he didn't know from Adam. Nasser smiled. A
couple of the guards moved instinctively as he too
stepped forward to shake hands.

*God is great. There is no god but God, and
Mohammed is His prophet . . .*

Now at last, eye to eye. As he had imagined many
times, in dreams, odd moments, and in training. "You
show a fine spirit," Nasser commended. "I hope that
others will follow your example." A camera popped
as he held out his hand. Khalil muttered that he was
deeply honored.

Their right hands gripped. And in the time scale of
such moments, there might have been communication of
a sort between the two. Nasser's eyes were large, intent,
the kind that can burn warmly, or explode with rage.
Khalil's were gray, or blue, the eyes of imperturbable
determination. Yet they were men of similar personality
in many ways: aloof, removed, suspicious of the world,
and proud.

*What happened to you, Gamal Adbelnasser? A
man so honest and dedicated when you first took
power that old-style Egyptians could not understand*

*you. Men like my father. Perhaps he was prophetic.
Perhaps he saw the monster that would burst forth
from your skin. And in a sense, he did not fail. God
be with you, Gamal Abdelnasser.* As their right hands
clasped, Khalil's left rose to grip the President above
the elbow.

Khalil was totally concentrated on his actions. There
would be the rest of his life to savor this moment,
but for now, it was a sequence of trained moves. A
squeeze of the knuckles, a grip on the arm, and the
tiny prick would go unnoticed. From many trials with
a harmless pin, he was confident that it would not
be noticed. Nasser would go home tonight to his wife
and children. But in a matter of hours, he would be
taken ill and die. His body would not be mutilated
by an autopsy. This was frowned on in the Muslim
faith, and in any case, it would not happen. It would
not happen for the same reason that no photograph
of Khalil, or newspaper article, or official document
containing his name would exist to show that he had
been here tonight. Nasser would be buried, and the
world would hear about his "heart attack." Not seeing
the sudden movement to one side of him, Khalil smiled
as he squeezed the solid hand.

Mahrous dived between two guards and threw himself
at Khalil. His bunched fist drove against the knuckles
of Khalil's left hand, and Khalil felt the tiny stab in
his left palm. Shocked for an instant, eyes bulging
unbelievingly, he stared at the awkward body that
went down beneath two guards, struggling lopsidedly
with its one arm threshing. A message left his brain
to turn again and still grip the arm of the President.
But he was knocked back by guards from either side,
and Nasser too was pulled away, as Mahrous's head
was struck hard against the floor. Again a message left

his brain to kill these guards and lunge for Nasser. But the nine-millimeter shells would stop him, and so did training. In an operation that was essentially covert, his mandate now was to walk away and disappear, not launch a wild attack condemned to failure.

Nasser stared down at the one-armed figure on the floor. "Who is this man?"

The head of the security squad was badly shaken. "I'm sorry, sir. He's an officer who's had some problems."

Nasser frowned. "But what was he trying to do?"

"God knows, sir. He just walked in and threw himself this way."

"Maybe a little overzealous," Nasser muttered. As he turned away, he flexed his fingers, still unconsciously feeling the strength of Khalil's grip. Others followed his example, turning away and ignoring the incident, as Mahrous was rushed out, his head lolling from his shoulders.

Khalil headed for the doors. Totally ignored, he left the hall and went to the toilet. In the cubicle, he opened his left hand and stared at the tiny blotch of blood. He licked it clean and spat into the bowl. But that was nothing but an aimless gesture, as his eyes still stared, his face chalk white. There was nothing to be done. Even hacking off the arm would not help now. A weak laugh shivered through him. Even as a one-armed brother to the unsung hero of a "fool" out there, he could not survive the poison. He dropped the device into the bowl and flushed it. There was cold sweat on his face.

Chapter 36

IT WAS quite strange. Khalil had sometimes wondered what he'd think about if the time ever came when he knew that he had only a few minutes left to live. As the plane reached full height, he tilted back his chair and closed his eyes.

It really didn't feel so different. He thought of a number of little things, as one would do, after rushing to the airport. There were a lot of questions. But with the future almost over, nothing seemed to matter very much.

He hoped Yvette would be all right. He knew that she'd been shot. From the airport, he had telephoned the house and heard that she had been taken to the Maadi Hospital. Prior to that, there had been police vehicles in the parking lot of the hotel. It had been confusing. But he had seen Mary rush from a car to the ambulance that had come for Mahrous, and she looked as though she had been wrestling in a slaughterhouse. No one had tried to stop him as he walked away. The talk he'd overheard had all concerned some incident involving Mary after her arrest. Mary, who had not seen him, had seemed concerned about one thing and one thing only—the well-being of Mohammed Mahrous.

Mahrous. The frustrated "fool," who was now a certainty to lose his job, if he survived his beating. A ghost

of a smile touched Khalil's lips. He had almost completely lost the ability to move. It was typical of Mahrous
that his one great victory should go unknown, even to
himself. Whatever he might hear—through Mary, or
Yvette, for example—he would never know for sure,
nor would they. But there was one thing clear. He had
Mary where he wanted her. In all the confusion back
there, that was one thing that stood out clearly—unless
he found a way to lose that too. A cold smile flickered in
the dead man's brain . . . God, she had looked good,
in Yvette's shorts, with a T-shirt clinging to her.

He was sorry that he had not been able to see Yvette.
If he had gone to the Maadi Hospital, where she was
out of danger, he'd been told, he would probably have
died there. As it was, they had noticed him sweating,
and beginning to slow down. He had only just made it
to the plane.

Oh, dear . . . it was sad that he was going to die,
he wasn't such a bad fellow. He thought of how his
life might have gone, getting older, marrying, having
children. Not to be.

He didn't pray. The mental effort was too great. He
just lay back, with little memories that came and went,
and thought that it was his last Ramadan.

When the Alitalia jet touched down at Rome airport,
one of the stewardesses tried to waken the tall man in
the window seat. She had noticed that his seat was back
when they were coming down, but the man had looked so
peaceful, she had gently pushed the seat forward without waking him. Even now, she didn't realize at first.
His color was so natural. Then she touched his hand,
swallowed hard, and walked back toward the cabin.

"We've got a dead one," she said to the chief stew-
ard.

Epilogue

INSTEAD OF the old Comets and Caravels, they now had 707s and DC-10s. She wondered what else she would find different. The airport looked much the same. Still the impression of beige buildings, and the long walk to them from the aircraft.

Yvette looked astoundingly the same. One hand raised to a chic hat, she was still the same dash of style as she ran down a staircase and into Mary's arms.

"My God, you look better than ever!"

"So do you!"

"Liar."

That was true, when you had a closer look. Mary saw the little crow's-feet around the eyes. She was still an eye-catching woman though.

"How's the shoulder?"

"A little stiff sometimes."

Gropi's was still there. Gropi's would always be there, Yvette proclaimed as they hurtled through the streets of Cairo, so long as there were ladies in the city with money and servants. And the ladies were there, Mary noticed. Clearly more westernized and liberated than before. She noticed other things. The city was more modern.

It was a flying visit. Mary was between Greece and England, having spent the summer with her family in

Greece. Her husband had the kids. Two, she said, both boys. Bill was with the Foreign Office, like her father. Not too much of a stuffed shirt. She was at London University. Teaching was fine. It left the summers free for when the kids were out of school. Motherhood was pandemonious. So traumatic. God knows how it had ever become popular. She'd become so straight. Did you talk about a stuffed skirt? She smiled. It was truly amazing how one followed all the patterns, generation after generation. It made you wonder.

"But are you happy?" Yvette had both elbows on the table, gazing at her.

Mary nodded. "I really am."

"No regrets?"

Mary raised an eyebrow. The gesture took them back ten years: she really hadn't changed, Yvette thought. "You mean, Mohammed?"

"Who else?"

Mary selected a small petit four. "I was ready to fall for him, you know?"

"I know. And when you fall, you fall hard, my girl."

Mary gazed across the room, smiling at her thoughts. She was remembering that morning in his place, bed covers everywhere. The poor man was just out of hospital, but exciting and mature as ever. She remembered his astonished face, when she had literally offered herself. She did fall hard, and was not mature at all, in those days. "I don't think I am your father's dream for you," he'd said. So straight. Or wise and kind. "My father doesn't dream," she'd said. "He expects." "You mean he is a little—inflexible?" She saw him so clearly across the years, sitting on his bed, dark eyes smiling as he deftly changed the mood. "He thinks he is." Her lips curved at the memories.

"He married little Julia," Yvette said.

"I know." Mary laughed. "He told me all about her."

"He now has his own little boy, as well as the other."

"Oh, that's wonderful! I'm so glad!"

"You didn't keep in touch?"

"Not really."

Yvette gazed at her thoughtfully. At the age of forty and still single, she often felt that she had missed the boat in life. She could tell that Mary had great mental wealth stored up in her children. "And he's a big cheese now. He was fired from his job, as you know. But when Sadat took power a few weeks later, one of the first things he did was reinstate Mohammed Mahrous and make him head of some division. The police are different now. Not nearly so repressive. Lieutenant General Mahrous is the Director of Internal Security."

"That's wonderful! God, I'm glad I came."

"So little Julia landed on her feet." Yvette laughed at her own cattiness. "God knows what he sees in her. He could have had you!"

"But he loved her," Mary said, smiling.

They both nibbled, sipped their tea, and Yvette signaled for another pot.

"Stay the night!" she said.

"Oh, I can't. But I've still got two hours."

"Tell me about England. How is it these days?"

"A little disappointing."

For a few moments, neither spoke. They were as comfortable in each other's company as if the gap of years did not exist.

"What do people think about what happened here? Nasser? Sadat? Do they believe Nasser had a heart attack?"

Mary shrugged. "Some people might be skeptical."

"It was the most predictable political assassination in history," Yvette declared. "Do you know what Chou Enlai said afterward? He told Sadat that it was the Russians who had killed Nasser. He could have been speaking figuratively, of course." She shrugged. "Have you heard the glass of water story?"

"Vaguely."

"Nasser drank a glass of water intended for Arafat. This was at the Arab Summit, after a series of disgusting scenes with Arafat and Qaddafi, when Nasser was trying to save Arafat's skin in Jordan, and he and Qaddafi were behaving like spoiled children. He succeeded too, and still got no thanks for it. Then he was seeing people off that day, just a few weeks after you left—September twentieth. People said that Nasser was sweating profusely, and could hardly move. He died that evening."

"What are you saying, Yvette? That he took something intended for Arafat?"

Yvette shook her head. "Some people believe that. I don't."

"You think they tried again? Khalil's people?"

"I know they did."

They both remembered. They remembered Mary's efforts, even her father's efforts, to get some official credence to her story. But Yvette had clammed up again, and then Nasser died, and there was nothing. No hint of a public statement, either in Egypt or in Britain.

"I was told to forget about it," Mary said. "I was told not to contact you, or anyone in Egypt, and not to come here. I was told that your police can keep a thing like this on ice for years. I was accused of spying, you know."

"That's true."

Yvette cut a little French pastry, looked at the interior, and sampled it. "I suppose you know Khalil died?"

Mary nodded. "The Whitehall people told me." When Yvette did not go on, she added, "I heard it was a heart attack."

"Oh, yes. Like Nasser. Everyone believes in heart attacks." She looked up, with a sniffing smile, then became herself again.

"When Nasser died," Yvette said, "they took his body to the palace and had it preserved for the funeral. On the morning of the funeral, Sadat had a real heart attack—his second—and when he woke up, the first thing he did was ask if Nasser had been buried. He explained this by saying he was afraid that the crowd might have stolen the body and taken it away somewhere. But one has to wonder if what he really meant was: Has Nasser been buried, or have they decided to examine his body to see how he died?"

"I never heard that," Mary said. "Do you think Sadat knew something?"

Yvette finished chewing, sipped her tea, and shrugged. "They all knew something. They all knew that this was going to happen, and when it did, they knew it had happened." She shrugged again.

"So what he said proves nothing."

Yvette laughed. She was laughing at the fact that Mary was as logical as ever.

"If it were the Russians, they certainly miscalculated," Yvette said. "Because Sadat somehow survived politically and has done everything they didn't want. Do you know that his first act as president was to ban all telephone tapping and lift state custodianship of private property? That's defensible action, of course, but I know people who'd have killed Nasser just for that—and so did Ibrahim." Her eyes unfocused for a moment. "For Ibrahim, it wasn't just political. He had other motives. I never saw his body, you know. They cremated it." Mary took her hand. Yvette had always clung to the belief that Khalil knew nothing of the attempt on her and Mary's lives and would never have condoned it.

"I wouldn't have missed that year for anything."

Yvette drove her back to the airport. She seemed deflated now, with Mary leaving.

"You should come to England," Mary said. "Come and visit us."

"I'll think about it."

Her forlorn figure stood there, recognizable in the distance, in her chic hat, till the plane took off.

Afterword

IN THE year 1970, the festival of Ramadan did not fall in September, the month in which President Nasser died unexpectedly. To the author's knowledge, this is the only historical fact distorted in the story.

Norman Lang was born and educated in Scotland. He has traveled in the Middle East and Africa and studied mathematics at Tulane University, New Orleans. He now lives with his wife and family in the northeastern United States and is currently working on his next novel.

📖 HarperPaperbacks *By Mail*

Craig Thomas, internationally celebrated author, has written these four best selling thrillers you're sure to enjoy. Each has all the intricacy and suspense that are the hallmark of a great thriller. Don't miss any of these exciting novels.

Buy All 4 and $ave.

When you buy all four the postage and handling is *FREE*. You'll get these novels delivered right to door with absolutely no charge for postage, shipping and handling.

EMERALD DECISION

A sizzling serpentine thriller—Thomas at the top of his form.